THE
Passion
COLLECTION

Get your pulse racing and the pages turning with
bestselling Mills & Boon author Miranda Lee
and her classic Blaze novel *Just a Little Sex...*

"Miranda Lee turns on the heat with a sensuous
story, dynamic characters and a wild premise."
— *Romantic Times*

Then enjoy more thrilling encounters in
two **BRAND NEW** novels, each packed
with burning Desire!

Forbidden Passion by Emilie Rose

An unforgettable earth-shaking encounter may
have left more than memories behind for Lynn
and Sawyer, as they realise sometimes even the
forbidden cannot be denied.

Perfectly Saucy by Emily McKay

Jessica Summers has never been one for
passion but this good girl decides to finally go
after what she really wants – bad boy and
secre̶t̶ ̶c̶r̶u̶s̶h̶ ̶A̶l̶e̶x̶ ̶M̶o̶r̶e̶n̶o̶

D1584724

Miranda Lee is Australian, living near Sydney. Born and raised in the bush, she was boarding-school educated and briefly pursued a career in classical music, before moving to Sydney and embracing the world of computers. Happily married, with three daughters, she began writing when family commitments kept her at home. She likes to create stories that are believable, modern, fast-paced and sexy. Her interests include meaty sagas, doing word puzzles, gambling and going to the movies.

Emilie Rose lives in North Carolina with her college sweetheart husband and four sons. Her love for romance novels developed when she was 12 years old and her mother hid them under sofa cushions each time Emilie entered the room. A sucker for any stray, Emilie has been known to bring home orphaned squirrels, bunnies and kittens, much to her sons' delight. She is also a lover of anything cute and fuzzy, which explains the incredible variety of pets her children have had. Letters can be mailed to Emilie at PO Box 20145, Raleigh, NC, 27619, USA or via e-mail to EmilieRoseC@aol.com.

Emily McKay has been reading romance novels since she was 11 years old. In her spare time, she loves to garden and cook…well, bake. Mostly cookies. Naturally, she still loves to read a good romance book. She's been blissfully married for nearly nine years. When they can ditch their five pets for a couple of weeks, she and her husband like to travel to exotic and exciting locations, such as Greece, Costa Rica and Ignorant Flats, Texas. Emily has been writing seriously for four years. In 2001, one of her dreams came true when her manuscript *Love Letters to Tabitha* was a finalist in the Romance Writers of America's Golden Heart contest. Just over a year later she got "the Call".

THE *Passion* COLLECTION

MIRANDA LEE
EMILIE ROSE
EMILY McKAY

DID YOU PURCHASE THIS BOOK WITHOUT A COVER?
If you did, you should be aware it is **stolen property** as it was
reported *unsold and destroyed* by a retailer. Neither the author nor
the publisher has received any payment for this book.

*All the characters in this book have no existence outside the imagination
of the author, and have no relation whatsoever to anyone bearing the
same name or names. They are not even distantly inspired by any
individual known or unknown to the author, and all the incidents are
pure invention.*

*All Rights Reserved including the right of reproduction in whole or in part
in any form. This edition is published by arrangement with Harlequin
Enterprises II B.V. The text of this publication or any part thereof may not
be reproduced or transmitted in any form or by any means, electronic or
mechanical, including photocopying, recording, storage in an
information retrieval system, or otherwise, without the written
permission of the publisher.*

*This book is sold subject to the condition that it shall not, by way of trade
or otherwise, be lent, resold, hired out or otherwise circulated without the
prior consent of the publisher in any form of binding or cover other than
that in which it is published and without a similar condition including this
condition being imposed on the subsequent purchaser.*

*MILLS & BOON and MILLS & BOON with the Rose Device
are registered trademarks of the publisher.*

*First published in Great Britain 2006
Harlequin Mills & Boon Limited,
Eton House, 18-24 Paradise Road, Richmond, Surrey, TW9 1SR*

THE PASSION COLLECTION
© by Harlequin Enterprises II B.V., 2006

Just a Little Sex... © Miranda Lee 2001
Forbidden Passion © Emilie Rose Cunningham 2004
Perfectly Saucy © Emily McKaskle 2005

ISBN 0 373 60391 6

055-0106

*Printed and bound in Spain
by Litografia Rosés S.A., Barcelona*

JUST A LITTLE SEX...
BY
MIRANDA LEE

For Tony
My inspiration

1

ZOE didn't have one hint of premonition as she stepped out of her office building and headed for her lunchtime meeting with Drake. Everything seemed wonderful in her world.

At long last.

Five years it had been since she'd come to Sydney from the country, a plump naive twenty-year-old with so many hopes and dreams. What a learning curve that first year had been! Hard to think about some of the things which had happened to her without wincing. Greg was the worst memory. What a louse he'd turned out to be!

Still, she'd survived, hadn't she? And she'd come through it with even more determination than ever to make a success of her life, to become the woman she'd always wanted to be.

Okay, so it had taken her another four years of driving and depriving herself, of crummy day jobs and endless night schools; of diets and grueling workouts at the gym.

But it had been worth it, hadn't it? she told herself as she strode down George Street in the direction of the harbor. She looked pretty darned good, even if she said so herself. She had a challenging job, a fab place to live, and best of all, she'd finally landed herself one fantastic boyfriend.

Drake was everything she'd ever dreamed about. Not only was he tall, dark and handsome, he was a success at his job and had money to burn. His most wonderful feature, however, was that he was mad about her.

Sometimes, she could hardly believe her luck.

They'd met four months ago when he'd been selling her boss a plush inner-city apartment. That was Drake's job, selling apartments in the high-rise buildings which had been mushrooming up all over Sydney's central business district, capitalizing on the growing number of professionals who wanted to live near the city and didn't care what they paid for the privilege. Drake had literally made a fortune in commissions and had been able to afford to buy one of those same luxury apartments for himself.

He'd asked Zoe out the very first day they'd met, claiming later it was love at first sight. Zoe had been a little wary at first—once bitten, definitely twice shy—but it wasn't long before Drake was the main focus of her life. Gone were the long lonely weekends. Gone, the depressing moments when she wondered what on earth she was doing with her life. Gone, the fear that she would never experience the sort of love and romance every girl dreamed of experiencing.

Gone. Gone. Gone!

Zoe glanced at her watch when the lights at the next intersection turned red. Twenty-three minutes past twelve.

She frowned.

It was normally only a ten-minute walk from her building down to the Rocks area and the restaurant where she regularly met Drake for lunch. The Rockery was his favorite harborside eating place, a trendy little bistro on the upper floor of a converted warehouse. He'd said to meet him there right on twelve-thirty today and not to be late, because he only had an hour.

Drake hated being kept waiting, even for a few minutes. Zoe supposed this impatience came from being a perfectionist. And a planner. She was a bit like that herself.

It seemed ages before the lights turned green again. Zoe hurried across the street, her heart racing for fear of being late. But she made it down to the restaurant with three minutes to spare.

Fortunately, Drake had not yet arrived so she made a dash to the ladies' room for repairs, where her reflection in the mirror showed a perspiration-beaded forehead and wind-ruffled hair.

That was the trouble with walking. Still, it only took a few strokes of her brush and a fluff-up with her fingers to make her hair fall back into its chic auburn-tinted, shoulder-length, multi-layered, face-framing style. She'd had it cut and colored by one of Sydney's top hairdressers, who charged a small fortune. But the end result was well worth the money.

Admittedly, she had to rise almost an hour earlier every morning to get ready for work these days. Blow-drying her willfully wavy hair straight was not a quick process. Neither was applying the sort of makeup which covered every flaw, looked almost natural and didn't require constant touch-ups during the day.

Except when you sprinted down George Street on a warm summer's day.

A swift dabbing of translucent powder over her slightly melted foundation, a refreshing of her lipstick, and she was ready.

Another glance at her watch showed she was now officially one minute late. When she emerged Zoe groaned to find Drake already sitting at their regular table by the window, tapping his fingers on the crisp white tablecloth.

Darn, darn and double darn!

Dredging up a bright smile, Zoe hurried toward him. His head swiveled her way, his dark eyes definitely displeased. Zoe couldn't help some exasperation of her own. Truly, anyone would think he'd been waiting half an hour instead of a couple of minutes at best.

She mouthed an apology as she approached and his scowl metamorphed into a marvelous smile, his eyes full of admiration as they raked over her slender gym-honed body, encased that day in a chic black-and-white silk shift dress.

Zoe's inner tension vanished in an instant. She loved it when he looked at her like that; like she was the most beautiful girl in the world.

Yet she knew she wasn't. She'd simply worked very hard on her body and learned how to make the best of herself.

Drake, she realized with a sudden flash of insight,

was of a similar ilk. Although attractive, he had several physical flaws which he'd learned to hide, or which you didn't notice once he turned his charm on full wattage, as he was doing now. His dazzling smile and dancing black eyes distracted from the fact his nose was too large and his lips a bit on the thin side. The superbly tailored suits he always wore masked his less-than-perfect frame, providing broader shoulders than he actually possessed. Although he did weights in the gym and was very fit and toned, Drake did not have a great natural shape.

Not that Zoe cared. She would have been the last person on earth to judge anyone by their body alone.

''Now that's a sight worth waiting for,'' he complimented warmly, rising to go 'round and pull out her chair for her.

''I really was here on time,'' she said as she sat down. ''But the wind had done dreadful things to my hair.''

''Looks perfect to me. There again,'' he added on his return to his own chair, his gaze still appreciative, ''you always look perfect to me.''

Zoe laughed. ''You should see me first thing in the morning.''

One of his dark brows arched. ''But I have, haven't I? And I can testify you look even more beautiful then.''

Zoe smiled a little sheepishly at this particular compliment. That was because she always crept into the bathroom before he woke up and fixed her face and hair before slipping back into his bed.

Her fear of Drake seeing her at less than her physical best was deep, and probably irrational, given that he truly loved her. But she couldn't help it. Goodness knew what she would do if he ever asked her to have a shower with him!

"They say love is blind," she quipped.

"I don't think so. Not with me, anyway. When I look at you, I know exactly what I see. The perfect woman. You're beautiful. Smart. Sexy. But best of all, you know what you want in life and are prepared to work hard to get it. You've no idea how attractive I find that." He reached over the table and picked up her left hand, stroking its perfectly manicured fingers. "I'm crazy about you, Zoe."

Her heart melted as it always did when he told her things like that. "And I'm crazy about you," she returned softly.

"Then why won't you move in with me?"

Zoe smothered a sigh. This was the second time Drake had brought this subject up.

The offer was flattering, she supposed, but not what she wanted at this time in her life. Zoe had just discovered dating and romance, and she didn't want to give it up just yet. She knew what happened when people started living together. Soon, they were taking each other for granted or arguing about the housework.

Alternatively, the girl did everything then resented her boyfriend like mad. Zoe had been an unpaid, unappreciated housekeeper for her father for several years, and once was enough!

But she could hardly tell Drake that. It would sound...selfish.

"Drake, look, I'm sorry," she said gently. "I love you to death. And I love the time we spend together. But I'd rather leave things as they are for now. I mean...we haven't known each other all that long, have we? And living with each other is a very big step."

His lips pressed tightly together and Zoe felt a moment of panic. Was this it? Was he going to dump her, just because she wouldn't live with him?

Drake eventually cocked his head on one side and smiled a wry smile. "Is this your way of playing hard to get again?"

Zoe blinked. "What do you mean?"

"Well, it took me two months to get you into bed. That's a record, believe me. I was beginning to think you were frigid."

Zoe suspected her refusal to sleep with Drake had only made him keener, but she honestly hadn't been playing a game. The truth was her relationship with the ghastly Greg had left her with a host of insecurities and an appalling self-body image. Despite now having a figure most women would envy, she'd still needed to be endlessly pursued and flattered by Drake before feeling confident enough to expose herself physically to him.

He'd finally succeeded in seducing her, courtesy of two bottles of wine over dinner, two hours of foreplay and umpteen declarations of devoted and undying love for her.

Being frigid hadn't been the issue at all.

Of course, Zoe had to concede she wasn't crash-hot in bed. How could she be when her only other experience had been with a wham-bang-thank-you-ma'am kind of man? Drake's well-practiced technique in bed had been a real eye-opener. When she'd even had an orgasm that first night, she'd been over the moon.

Unfortunately, once she returned to being stone-cold sober, having a climax during sex became as scarce as chocolate éclairs in her diet.

Not Drake's fault of course. He was a wonderful lover. Attentive and tender and romantic, always doing and saying the right things. The blame lay entirely with her. Once naked, she always worried too much about what she looked like. Exercise and dieting might have gotten rid of the fat and the flab, but not those wretched old tapes playing in her head.

Thinking negative thoughts about herself was obviously a killer when it came to coming.

When her not having orgasms began to bother Drake, Zoe did the only thing a sensible girl in love could do. She started faking them. After all, why should Drake have to feel guilty or inadequate when the inadequacies were all hers?

And who knew? Maybe one day, when she felt *really* relaxed and not the result of an alcoholic coma; when all her old doubts and fears had been firmly routed, she would come like clockwork. 'Til then, Zoe wasn't going to stress over one small imperfection in their relationship which had nothing whatsoever to do with Drake and everything to do with her own personal physical hang-ups.

"Have you ordered?" she asked, deftly changing the subject away from moving in with him.

"First thing I did."

The drinks waiter appeared on cue, with a glass of chilled Chardonnay for Zoe and Drake's usual lunchtime liquid of mineral water. He never drank when he had to return to work.

"I've ordered the food, too," he added when Zoe went to pick up the menu.

"Oh." Zoe tried not to feel irritated, because once again, she only had herself to blame. During her first half dozen dinner dates with Drake, she'd always deferred to his greater knowledge of wine and food, and now, he often presumed to order for her.

"I couldn't wait for you to arrive," he said, perhaps seeing her slight annoyance. "I told you. I don't have much time. I have to pick up a client at the Hyatt at one-thirty. Businessman from Hong Kong. Wants a penthouse smack-dab in the middle of Sydney. Money no object."

"Wow. Sounds like a good prospect."

"You can say that again. Sydney's moved up a notch in popularity since the Olympics. And why not? It's the best city in the world. And the most beautiful."

"You don't have to sell me on Sydney," Zoe commented. "I love the place. Just look at that view." From where she was sitting, Zoe could see the Opera House on her right and the bridge on her left. Straight ahead, a sleek white cruiser was slicing through the sparkling blue waters, its decks filled with photo-snapping tourists.

Zoe was sipping her wine and admiring the view

herself when she heard Drake suck in sharply, as though in shock.

Her eyes snapped back to find him staring at something—or someone. She heard him mutter under his breath.

Zoe swiveled 'round in her chair to see firsthand the object of Drake's agitation.

She was blond, and she was heading their way.

Zoe didn't recognize the woman and she would have, if they'd met before. Stunning six-foot blondes with double-D-cup breasts were hard to forget.

"Well, well, well," the blond bombshell said with a saccharine smile as she stopped beside their table. It took a moment for her impressive cleavage to jiggle to a halt. "If it isn't Drake Carson, the man of a thousand lines and even more broken promises. Sorry to interrupt, honey," she directed at Zoe, "but Drake and I have some unfinished business. You did say you'd call, didn't you, lover? I mean, I know it's only been a couple of weeks since the conference, but I was beginning to think you hadn't found me quite so *special* after all. Surely you aren't one of those creeps who lie their teeth out to get a girl into bed, the type who thinks they can do what they like when they go away, without any consequences and without the little woman back home finding out?"

Drake glowered at her but said nothing.

Zoe felt like a big black pit had yawned underneath her chair and she was about to fall in. Drake had gone to a sales and marketing conference in Melbourne just two weeks earlier. He'd rung her every night of the three days he'd been away, saying how much he'd missed her.

She stared at him, wanting to believe this woman was some crazed jealous troublemaker intent on breaking them up for her own devious reasons. But the cornered guilt on Drake's face simply could not be ignored. Or denied.

"Oh, so you *are* one of those creeps?" the blonde taunted. "Well, I never! Aren't you lucky I'm not a vengeful bitch like that blond chick in that movie? What was it? *Fatal Attraction?* I mean, the way I see it, if a guy's a liar and a cheat, I don't really want any more to do with him." She turned back to face Zoe. "Gee, honey, you're looking a little pale. Don't tell me you're the little woman back home. What a shame. And you look real nice, too. Poor you. 'Bye, 'bye, Drake. Have a nice day."

Zoe watched, dry-mouthed, as the blonde stalked back to where a tall, elderly man was waiting for her near reception. He was frowning like he didn't now what was going on. The blonde whispered something to him, took his arm and they both left.

Drake still hadn't said a single word, but his eyes told it all.

Zoe felt sick. And stunned. And shattered.

"You slept with her, didn't you?" she choked out. "At the Melbourne conference."

"It wasn't like she said," he muttered, not meeting her eyes.

"Then how was it?" Zoe heard herself ask in a cold flat voice. She couldn't believe this was happening to her again. She could have sworn that Drake was nothing like Greg; that he truly loved her; that their relationship was not just a cruel joke.

His eyes lifted from the tablecloth. Panicky, pleading eyes. "God, Zoe, don't look at me like that. I love you, darling. Honest."

She winced at the darling. "Then you have a funny way of showing it," she bit out, "making love to another woman."

"But I didn't make love to her. You're the only woman I make love to. It was just sex. It meant nothing. *She* meant nothing."

Zoe despised men who said things like that. "She obviously thought she did," she pointed out tartly, "or she wouldn't have been so hurt."

"Don't bet on it," he countered, his cheeks flushed with anger. "Some women are right bitches. Believe me, she knew the score. She knew it was just a one-night stand right from the start, and now, for her own warped reasons, she's pretending it was something else."

Zoe shook her head which was a bad move. It was already spinning. "How can you possibly be in love with me and go to bed with another woman? *How?*"

Drake began to look belligerent, as he did when someone expressed an opinion different to his own. "I told you. It was just sex. There's a big difference. Love and sex don't always have to go together, Zoe. I thought you'd know that by now. You're not a baby. You're twenty-five years old. Hey, Zoe, *try* to understand." His hands lifted to rake through his thick black hair. They were actually trembling.

For the first time since that blonde dropped her

bombshell, Zoe began to believe that Drake might love her, despite everything.

"I'm sorry," he went on urgently. "More sorry than you can ever imagine. But it wasn't like she said. I'm not some kind of serial sleazebag. I was just weak for a moment. You're the one I love, Zoe. Too much perhaps. I was missing you terribly and wanting you like mad. I couldn't stop thinking about you and it got me so darned horny. It happened on the last night of the conference. We'd all been drinking heavily."

"You never drink at *all* when socializing at work," she reminded him with a rush of anger, not wanting to be soothed by excuses and explanations. Didn't he understand what he'd done? He could call it whatever he liked but he'd still been intimate with another woman. And whispered sweet nothings in her ear while he'd been doing it.

Perhaps that hurt even more than his actual physical betrayal. The things he must have said.

"The conference was virtually over," he continued explaining. "I didn't have to drive anywhere so I let my hair down for once. Look, she threw herself at me. Followed me into the elevator at the end of the night. Practically ravished me then and there. I hated myself afterward, but what can I say? I'm not a saint. I'm just a man. I made a mistake. I'm so terribly sorry, Zoe. I never meant to hurt you. I never thought you'd find out."

"Obviously." She could no longer look at him. All she could think about now was that blonde and him, doing it in an elevator of all places. How tacky!

"Don't be like that, Zoe. *Try* to understand."

"I don't think I can," she said wretchedly. Which meant there was nothing left to do but to split up with Drake. She'd vowed after Greg that she'd never put up with a man treating her badly ever again. Which was why she'd been manless and dateless for almost four long years.

Still, the thought of going back to a single lifestyle made her shudder. She didn't want to be that lonely ever again. She'd thought she never would be. She thought she had Drake. She thought after a couple of years of their being girlfriend and boyfriend, they'd eventually get married and have kids and live happily ever after.

A sob broke from her throat, tears stinging her eyes.

Drake groaned. "Don't cry, darling. Please don't cry. If you forgive me," he urged, reaching over the table and grabbing her hands, "it won't ever happen again. I promise."

A sudden and overwhelming wave of bitterness had Zoe yanking her hands away from his. "And what happens the next time you're at a conference, and some sexy-looking blonde with big boobs throws herself at you?"

"I'll know what I'm risking if I go with her, so I won't."

Zoe stared at him with pained confusion in her eyes. "But you'd still *want* to?"

He groaned again. "For pity's sake, Zoe. I'm only thirty years old. I'm a normal red-blooded male in his sexual prime. Loving you doesn't mean I won't ever be physically attracted to another woman ever again.

That's unrealistic and unnatural. But I give you my word, I will never act on any such attraction ever again.''

Zoe stared at him. She wanted to believe him. She really did.

But then she thought of that blonde and what she had said in parting.

Poor you.

''I think,'' she said tautly, ''that I'll skip lunch and go for a walk. I need some fresh air. And time to think.''

''Please don't do that, Zoe. Stay and talk to me.''

Zoe shook her head then bent to pick up her handbag. Staying and talking to Drake was the last thing she should do. He was too good a talker. Too good a salesman. Perhaps too good a liar.

''We can work this out, Zoe,'' he insisted. ''Truly we can. I don't want to lose you, darling. I love you. And I know you love me.''

She glared at him. ''Yes, but your idea of love and my idea of love are poles apart. I know I would never have done what you did. Never, no matter what the circumstances.''

''Isn't there anything I can say to make you understand?''

''Not right now.''

''What about later?''

''Leave it for today, Drake.''

''I can't. I'll call 'round tonight after you get home from work.''

''If you must.''

''I must. I won't let you go, Zoe. I mean it.''

"I know you do," she said. Which was another reason why she needed to get away from him. Because she feared Drake would talk her into forgiving him without her ever understanding what had happened, and why? Love was a very weakening emotion. In a woman, anyway.

She stood up just as the waiter arrived with their meals. For a split second, Zoe was tempted to stay and shovel every morsel of the delicious-looking food down her throat.

Misery always made her hungry.

But being overweight had made her even more miserable, so she knew there would be no comfort for her there. No comfort in Drake's presence, either. She wanted to strangle him for doing this to her, for spoiling everything, for being a typical male.

She'd thought he was different. Deeper.

But he wasn't.

"I have to go," she said raggedly, and fled.

2

___

ZOE didn't go for a walk. When she felt more tears threatening, she headed straight back for the office, making it to the downstairs lobby of the multi-storyed building in six minutes flat. She kept a tight grip on herself in the ride up in the elevator, since she wasn't alone, but could feel her control slipping by the time the doors whooshed back on the twelfth floor.

Unfortunately, the rooms which housed Phillips & Cox, Attorneys at Law, were right down the end of a corridor along which more people were coming and going. It was lunchtime, after all.

Crying was not an option 'til she had total privacy.

Clenching her jaw to keep her chin from quivering, Zoe launched herself down the gray-carpeted hallway, delivering a plastic smile whenever she passed an acquaintance.

Finally, she made it, only to find that June, their receptionist, was eating lunch at her desk, instead of in the café downstairs, as she usually did.

"What are you doing back so early?" June probed when Zoe walked back in. "Weren't you supposed to be having lunch with the boyfriend down at the Rockery?"

Zoe's teeth clenched even harder in her jaw.

"He was called back to work early," she managed with feigned nonchalance, "so I thought I'd come back and have my coffee here."

"Silly you. I'd have stayed down there. The coffee here is just instant muck. You could have had the real McCoy at the Rockery."

"Oh, well..." Zoe shrugged, smiled an indifferent smile, then sped down to the tearoom, hoping it would be blessedly deserted and she could have a good quiet cry. But as luck would have it, her boss was there, making coffee and muttering away to herself. 'Til she saw Zoe.

"What on earth are you doing back so early?" Fran asked. "I thought you were having lunch with Drake?"

It was too much for Zoe.

Fran literally gaped when Zoe burst into tears. In the six months Zoe had worked for her, the girl had never cried once. Or even seemed flustered. She was so cool and competent that sometimes Fran forgot she was only twenty-five.

Fran was not by nature a soft or sympathetic person, but she'd had considerable experience in handling weeping females. Considerable experience in the cause of such weeping as well. Her part of the practice specialized in divorce cases.

Fran didn't have to be told that a man was behind Zoe's tears. And there was only one man in Zoe's life. The very charming and successful Drake Carson.

Plucking a handful of tissues from the box sitting on the counter, Fran pressed them into her assistant's hands, then led the weeping girl back to her office.

Fortunately, this didn't require going past June, who was the office gossip.

"Sit," she ordered, pushing Zoe down into one of the large comfy chairs facing her desk before returning to her own black office chair. There, she waited patiently 'til the worst of the weeping was over.

Zoe's sobbing eventually subsided to a sniffle.

"Can I get you something?" Fran asked at that point, her tone matter-of-fact. "Coffee? Brandy? A hit man?"

Zoe's head jerked up and she laughed a rueful laugh.

"Want to tell me about it?" Fran said.

Zoe looked at her boss and suddenly saw, not just the smart-as-a-whip lawyer, but the woman. Thirty-eight and still very attractive, with jet-black hair—cut into a short chic bob—piercing gray eyes, a pale un-lined skin and an hourglass figure which looked good in the severe black suits she favoured. Highly respected by her colleagues and clients, she was married to Angus Phillips, the senior partner in the firm.

But what about before that? She must have had other men, a woman like her. Plenty of them. She'd seen so much more of life than Zoe. She might be able to explain what had happened between Drake and that blonde so that Zoe could forgive him and go on as before.

Because that was what she really wanted to do. Now that she'd had time to think about it, breaking up with Drake was just too horrendous to contemplate.

So she told her boss what had happened. Fran listened without interruption, her face not giving away a thing. But Zoe suspected she wasn't shocked. Which shocked Zoe.

"Aren't you surprised?" she said at last.

Fran smiled a dry smile. "Nothing men do ever surprises me, Zoe. The more attractive the man, the less I'm surprised. So no, I'm not surprised. I think it's a shame, however, that you found out about Drake's little indiscretion. If you hadn't, you'd still be perfectly happy with him."

"But...but...it wasn't just a little indiscretion. He was unfaithful. And more than once, I suspect. I don't believe for a moment he only slept with that woman on just the last night."

"Why? Was she so very beautiful?"

"She was stunning, with the biggest boobs I've ever seen outside of one of those magazines."

"Maybe he has a secret boob fetish. Or maybe she gave him something you don't. Forgive me for prying, Zoe, but I can't advise you without knowing all the facts. Are you sure you satisfy Drake in bed?"

Zoe floundered at this point. "I...I thought I did."

"Why? Because you have sex a lot?"

"Well...isn't that the main criterion?" Zoe had always been under the impression that most men complained that they weren't getting enough.

"Not necessarily. Some men are more interested in quality rather than quantity. They like different positions. Different places. You're not one of those silly girls who insist on always doing it in bed with the lights out, do you?"

"Of course not," she denied hotly. And in truth, she didn't.

It was Drake's idea that they always do it in bed. He was big on creating a romantic atmosphere with satin sheets and scented candles and soft dreamy music.

Not that she wasn't happy with the arrangement. Zoe liked comfort. And candlelight was so very flattering. As for different positions... Zoe was more than grateful that Drake didn't want to do it doggie-style on the floor, or up against the wall in the shower or with her on top.

Even *thinking* of the physical exposure such positions would inflict on her made her cringe.

Now she wondered if Drake had secretly craved doing it in just those ways all along, but hadn't wanted to ask. It had taken a brazen blonde in an elevator to fulfil his sexual fantasies.

"What about oral sex?" Fran persisted, and Zoe could feel herself blushing. But it did seem odd having this very frank conversation with her boss when up 'til today, their relationship had been strictly professional.

"It's...er...not my favorite form of foreplay," she confessed. She'd done it once. Sort of. For about twenty seconds. But thankfully, Drake stopped her before the unthinkable happened. He'd never asked for it again, or steered her that way a second time, and she certainly wasn't going to do it off her own bat.

"I don't think it's Drake's, either," she added, a touch defensively.

"Really? That's unusual. Most men are pretty keen. But I guess it takes all types and you'd know your boyfriend best."

"I thought I did," Zoe said wretchedly. "Maybe I don't know him at all. Maybe our whole relationship is a sham. Maybe he's having affairs right, left and center."

"I don't think so, Zoe. If he was, I'd know about it."

"Huh?"

Fran gave her a droll look. "Angus and I have been living in the same building as Drake since the time you started dating him. We share the same garage, the same elevators, the same swimming pool and gym. I've never seen him with another girl except you. Not once. Clearly, he's not in the habit of two-timing you, or I'd have caught him at it by now."

Zoe brightened a bit at this news. "But what does Drake mean when he says it was *just sex* with that blonde, and that she meant nothing to him? I got the impression he didn't even *like* her. I can't seem to get my mind 'round that concept. How can you have sex with someone you don't even like, or really know? Is it just a male thing? Is that why I can't understand it?"

Fran gave her an incredulous look. "Haven't you ever fantasized about having sex with a stranger, or met a man and been struck with instant lust for him? All you want is to get laid, right then and there. No getting-to-know-you stuff. No prelims. No niceties. Just down-and-dirty sex."

"Good Lord, no," Zoe denied, her face hotting up

again. "I can't think of anything worse. I have to at least *like* a man before I can go to bed with him." She'd even liked the ghastly Greg, 'til he'd shown his true colors. "I haven't even looked at another man since going out with Drake, let alone want to get laid by one."

"You've never had a one-night stand?"

"No. Never."

"My, my, you are an original, Zoe. Maybe that's why Drake is so crazy about you, and doesn't want to lose you. Such romantic idealism and tunnel-vision loyalty is rare in this day and age. He could trust you anywhere, anytime. Which brings us back to the point. Can *you* ever trust *him* again? Should you or should you not break up with him? Should you believe him when he says he's sorry, and give him another chance?"

"That's exactly my problem," Zoe said unhappily. "I honestly don't know what to do."

"And I honestly can't tell you what to do. It has to be your decision. All I can say is I'd like a dollar for every woman I've represented who's later regretted breaking up her marriage over a spot of adultery. She ends up miserable and lonely whilst the husband simply moves on to the other woman."

"That's what I'm afraid of," Zoe mumbled. "Being miserable and lonely."

"Then give him another chance. What have you got to lose?"

"My pride and self-respect?"

Fran laughed. "Most of the divorced women I

know don't find pride and self-respect much solace in their beds at night.''

But it wasn't the sex Zoe was going to miss so much. It was the company. And the sense of purpose. The promise of a happy future together.

She sighed. ''I suppose I will take him back. In the end. But I hate the thought of his being forgiven so easily and so quickly. Drake's coming over after work tonight and I just know he'll talk me 'round in no time flat.''

''You'd rather him suffer a while longer, is that it?''

''Yes, I guess so. Then he might understand how much he hurt me by what he did.''

''You know, that's not such a bad idea,'' Fran said, twisting back and forth on her swivel chair, a thoughtful expression on her face. ''Why don't you go away somewhere for the weekend and not tell him? Let him sweat for a while. Let him worry and wonder over where you are, and who you might be with. I guarantee, when you finally get back, he won't take you for granted ever again.''

The idea did appeal.

''Why not go home for the weekend?'' Fran suggested.

''That'd be the first place Drake would think of. He'd ring there for sure.''

''Haven't you heard of little white lies, Zoe? Just don't answer the phone yourself and get whoever does to say they hadn't seen hide nor hair of you.''

''Yes, I could do that, but the trouble is Betty would ask all sorts of awkward questions.''

"Who's Betty? I thought you were an only child and your dad, a widower."

"I am and he is. Betty's his housekeeper. She's a lovely lady, but she's far too intuitive and too darned good at worming things out of me. I honestly don't want to tell her about this. Drake came home with me at Christmas and he wasn't on his best behavior. He never is when he's bored stiff. I don't want to blot his copybook any further, not if I aim to forgive him."

"Okay, so home's out…" Fran started chewing the end of a biro as she did when working out some legal strategy. Finally, she snapped forward on her chair and stood up. "I have it! I'll ask Nigel if you can use his weekender. He's not going up there this weekend, because he's off to the opening of some play tomorrow night, starring his latest love. Wait here."

Fran was gone before Zoe could say yeah or nay.

Nigel was Nigel Cox, the third partner in the firm. Fortyish and openly gay, he represented several highly paid clients in the entertainment and sporting world. Zoe didn't really have much to do with him. He had his own assistant, as did Angus. She'd heard of the weekender, though. From June, who called it Nigel's little love nest.

Apparently, it overlooked a small beach up near Port Stephens, just far enough off the main tourist route for privacy, but close enough to civilization for essential supplies and services, which meant a good selection of five-star restaurants. Nigel's second favorite hobby in life—according to the ever-knowledgeable June—was gourmet food.

Fran swept back in eventually, carrying a set of keys and two hand-drawn maps.

"Mission accomplished," she said, dumping everything in Zoe's lap then perching up on the edge of her desk. She looked very satisfied with herself. "Nigel, the dear, generous boy, never asks any awkward questions. Just handed these over and said he hoped everything would work out for you. Actually, you're not the first female in crisis I've sent up there and they all spoke highly of the place afterward."

"What's it like?" Zoe asked.

"Never been myself. It isn't called Hideaway Beach for nothing, and peace and quiet is not my bag. Neither is the sun, sea and surf. I can't swim, for starters, and I burn like mad. Anyway, Nigel said to tell you the kitchen cupboards, freezer and wine rack are all stocked up and to help yourself. There's also a gas station and general store half a mile down the road which fortunately has a liquor license. It has practically everything you might need. Fresh bread every day, milk, cigarettes, chocolates, condoms."

"Very funny, Fran," Zoe said dryly. "I don't think condoms are going to be high on my shopping list."

"Well, you never know. His only warning is for you to leave before three this afternoon as after that the traffic heading north on a Friday afternoon would give blood pressure to a corpse. And he suggests you get up very very early on the Monday morning rather than try to drive back on the Sunday evening, for the same reason. You do still have your car, don't you?"

"Well, yes, of course I do, but..."

"I know exactly what you're going to say. You

don't finish here 'til six at the earliest on a Friday afternoon, since you have a slave driver of a boss who never knows when to quit. But just this once, I'm going to give you an early mark, starting right now. After all, we females should stick together. Can't have the males of the species thinking they have us taped, can we?''

Zoe didn't know what to say.

''No need to thank me,'' Fran said, laughing at her girl Friday's dumbfoundedness. ''I'll work your butt off next week to make up for it.''

Zoe smiled wryly. She didn't doubt it. Her boss was a workaholic if ever there was one. ''If Drake rings here or contacts you, you won't tell him where I am, will you?''

''I'll just say you asked for the afternoon off, you've gone away for the weekend but I don't know where. Now don't forget to turn your cell phone off as well. Or better yet, don't take it with you.''

''I always take it in the car with me for safety reasons and emergencies. But I'll definitely leave it turned off all weekend.''

''Excellent.''

When Zoe stood up with the map and the keys in hand, she was struck with a moment's doubt. ''Are you sure this is the right thing to do? Maybe Drake will get angry and dump *me*.''

''If he does, then he doesn't really love you, does he?''

''You're right.''

''Off you go now. And have fun.''

Zoe didn't think that was likely. But she smiled. ''Thanks again, Fran.''

Fran smiled back. ''My pleasure.''

3

MELINDA was home when Zoe let herself into the apartment. Not an unusual occurrence, even at two on a Friday afternoon.

Melinda was what was often cattily termed a rich bitch. But that wasn't strictly true. Sure, her father had given her this fully furnished two-bedroom apartment for her twenty-first birthday a couple of years back, but it was no palace, or penthouse.

It was, however, near new, with plush gray carpet, white walls and the sort of sleek modern clean-lined furniture which Zoe loved, so different from the clunky heavy wooden furniture filling the farmhouse back home.

Actually, on the market today, Melinda's place would have sold for close to half a million. No doubt about that. Even the grottiest apartment in Milson's Point was worth a packet.

Melinda was a very lucky girl to have received such an expensive present. Unfortunately, despite her darling daddy being a racehorse-owning billionaire, the day Melinda received the keys to the apartment, her allowance had been cut off.

"I've given you a roof over your head and that's all I'm going to do from now on," her father had bluntly announced at the time. "If you want to feed and clothe yourself in future you'll have to get a job. Your brother had to make good on his own after twenty-one. I see no reason why you shouldn't do the same, just because you're female. You girls wanted equality. Well, now you've got it!"

Despite not having any practice at the art of supporting herself—she had done absolutely nothing since leaving school except socialize and shop—Melinda had risen to the challenge with gusto. First, she'd rented out the other bedroom in the apartment— Zoe was not Melinda's first roommate—then set about finding work as a model. She wasn't really qualified for anything else, and had no intention of serving in a store or working as a waitress. She wasn't tall enough for catwalk modeling at only five-eight, but her long blond hair, sultry face and cup-C breasts gave her plenty of work doing photographic modeling for fashion catalogs, especially those of the lingerie variety.

Modeling, however, was just a stopgap. Her ultimate ambition was to marry someone far richer than her father.

But not for some years yet. At twenty-three, Melinda was concentrating on having fun.

And have fun Melinda did! Although Melinda had a steady boyfriend named Ron, she also went out a lot without him. Parties. Premieres. Gallery openings. The races. You name it, if she was asked, Melinda went. And with her looks and social contacts, she received a lot of invitations.

Zoe found her a delightful roommate. Always

bright and cheery, and not at all lazy around the place. Which was a surprise, since Melinda had obviously been spoiled rotten as a child. But she liked and valued beautiful things and treated her own little home and her possessions with great respect. Open her closet or drawers any day, and all her lovely things would not only be beautifully arranged, but spotlessly clean. As was the apartment. She never dropped her clothes on the floor, or left dirty crockery around.

Best of all, Melinda didn't smoke. A rare breed, Zoe had found after sharing places with various other girls over the last few years. Most of them smoked like chimneys. It was so pleasant to come home to nice-smelling rooms, even when all the windows had been shut all day.

When Zoe walked in, Melinda was perched up on one of the white kitchen stools, carefully painting her fingernails at the black granite breakfast bar. She was dressed in traffic-stopping short-shorts and a cropped top, both blue. Melinda just loved blue in clothes. And why not? The color suited her blond hair and blue eyes.

"Good grief!" she exclaimed when she saw Zoe. "Have I lost track of time? Don't tell me it's gone six. Ron's picking me up at seven and I've only just started getting ready!"

"Don't panic. It's only twenty past two."

"Thank God. But that's silly daylight-saving time for you! You never know what time it is by looking out the window. So what are you doing home? You can't be sick. You never get sick. You're not sick, are you?" she asked, peering more closely at Zoe whilst she flicked her nails dry. "You do look a bit stressed."

"No. I'm not sick. Fran gave me an early mark."

"You're kidding me. Commandante Phillips let you come home early and you're not even sick!"

"Nope." Zoe walked over, dumped her bag on the counter and switched on the electric jug.

Melinda eyed her warily. "This is very strange. So what's up? Was there a bomb scare at the office? Some disgruntled husband whom your boss screwed over in court?"

"Nothing like that."

"Then what? The mind boggles over what earth-shattering catastrophe could have led to such an unlikely occurrence."

"Come now, Mel, Fran's not that bad. She's just a hard worker."

"She works *you* hard. That I know."

"But she appreciates the job I do, and she pays me well."

"Huh."

"You just don't like her, do you? Yet you've only met her once."

"Once was enough. That woman is tough as an old boot. Maybe that's what's needed to be a top divorce lawyer these days, but I sure as heck wouldn't want to be married to her."

Although Zoe thought Melinda was being a bit harsh, her comments brought home the fact that perhaps Fran hadn't been the best person to go to for advice over her dilemma with Drake. Fran was pretty cynical when it came to her views on life, men and sex. She'd accused Zoe of being a romantic idealist, but Zoe didn't think it was unreasonable to expect the man you loved and who said he loved you, to be faithful.

"For pity's sake, are you going to tell me why you're home early," Melinda burst out impatiently, "or are you just going to stand there for the rest of the day, staring into space?"

"I don't have much time," Zoe said, popping two slices of bread into the toaster. "I have to be packed and gone by three and I'm in desperate need of some food first."

"Packed? Gone by three? This is getting curiouser and curiouser."

"If you want to know all the grisly details, then don't interrupt," Zoe warned, already sensing that Melinda wasn't the right person to ask for advice, either. She just didn't take life and love seriously enough.

Melinda's big blue eyes rounded with even more gleeful curiosity. "Grisly details! Oooh. Do tell. Sorry," she said swiftly when Zoe threw her a baleful glance. "I won't say another word."

And she made a zipping gesture across her mouth.

Zoe rolled her eyes at her friend's pitiful attempt at a chastened face. This was going to be a total waste of time, but Melinda wouldn't give her any peace 'til she knew the ins and outs of everything. Just like June at work. And Betty back home.

Zoe supposed most women had a natural affinity for talking and gossiping. But she didn't. She'd always been more of a thinker than a talker. An introvert, as opposed to Melinda's extrovert nature. The good communication and social skills she now possessed hadn't come naturally. They'd been acquired. With a lot of practice and hard work. By nature, she was quite shy. And private. And particularly possessive about her innermost feelings.

Sometimes, Zoe felt that the person she now projected wasn't the real Zoe at all. Occasionally, when she looked in the mirror, she still saw the fat, shy tongue-tied teenager she'd once been.

"Zoe, for pity's sake!"

"Yes, yes, I'm just wondering where to start."

"Anywhere will do. Just *start!*"

Telling Melinda all the gory details took Zoe less time than it had to tell Fran, possibly because she wasn't sobbing hysterically anymore. Frankly, her overriding emotion now was just plain anger.

"I don't believe it," Melinda blurted out when Zoe had finally finished the sordid tale. "Drake cheated on you with some blond piece, just because she had a 'Baywatch' bustline? That doesn't make sense. I mean, not once, in all the times he's come here, has he ever given *me* the eye. And *I'm* a crash-hot-looking blonde with very nice boobs."

Zoe smiled a wry smile. Melinda never let modesty get in the way of self-praise.

"Let's not forget Drake has actually confessed here, Mel," Zoe reminded her ruefully. "But of course, it was only *just sex,*" she added with extra tartness. "And the woman threw herself at him. Practically tore off the poor darling's clothes. He was feeling like a bit of action and he couldn't help himself. She meant nothing to him at all.''

''Well, I could have told you that. Drake's crazy about *you*.''

''So he keeps telling me. But explain it to me, Mel. I mean, have *you* ever met some guy when you were crazy about someone else, but fancied this new guy so much that you just had to go to bed with him right away?''

''But of course! When I met Ron I was going out with Wayne who was a right hunk, I can tell you. But once I met Ron, I dropped Wayne like a shot.''

Zoe rolled her eyes. ''Yes, but you weren't in love with this Wayne, were you?''

Melinda shrugged. ''I guess not. Which is just as well,'' she added with a wicked grin. ''Because Ron's much better in the sack.''

''Oh, you're hopeless. You never take anything seriously.''

''And you, Zoe Simons, take life much too seriously. Look, for what it's worth, I agree with your boss for once. I think you should forgive Drake. Give him another chance. It's not as though he kept on with the blonde after he came back from the conference, did he? And she must live in Sydney to show up at the Rockery.''

Zoe took a bite of her toast, munching it thoughtfully before swallowing. ''No, I don't think she comes from Sydney. Drake was far too shocked at seeing her. I think she might have just been here for a visit. That old chap she was with could have been her father.''

"Okay, dump him then. Whatever makes you happy."

"But that won't make me happy, will it? I'm going to be utterly wretched and lonely without him."

"Rubbish! You're one hot-looking babe. You'll find another guy in no time, especially if you start coming places with me. You'll have so many gorgeous men hitting on you, you won't know which one to date first."

"But I don't want to date some other guy," Zoe said frustratedly. "And I don't care how gorgeous he is! I just want things the way they were. With Drake."

Melinda sighed an exasperated sigh. "Okay, give him another chance, then. But if you're going to do that, then what's the point of going away all by yourself up to some remote beach for the weekend? You might as well stay here, tell Loverboy you forgive him when he shows up tonight, then spend all weekend in the sack making up."

Zoe cringed at the thought. How could she possibly go to bed with Drake with the image of him and that blonde doing it in an elevator still so clear in her head? "I can't do that," she said, shuddering. "Not this soon. Besides, Drake doesn't deserve to be forgiven that quickly. He deserves to suffer."

Melinda frowned at her. "That doesn't sound like you, Zoe. That sounds more like your boss. She'd be right into suffering. Bet she and her lawyer hubbie are into S & M in private. You know, bondage and black leather and stuff. But he'd be the one tied up and she'd have the whip. You could count on that."

Zoe stared at her roommate, shocked. "Don't be silly. Normal people don't do things like that."

"Don't you believe it. Lots of normal-looking people are right into S & M. Or some form of it. Hasn't Drake ever wanted to tie you up?"

"Of course not!" The very idea! She'd had enough trouble just getting naked with him. The prospect of being naked and tied up sent a shudder of revulsion all through her, especially the thought of Drake looking at places she couldn't bear the thought of him looking at without her being able to move or cover herself up.

"Ron's always wanting to tie me up," Melinda confided blithely. "I might let him one day."

"Are you crazy? What if he...you know...did things you didn't want him to do?"

Melinda pulled a face. "Yeah, you're right. You'd have to trust a guy a hell of a lot to let him tie you up. And I'm not sure I trust Ron enough for that yet. I think I'll tie him up instead," she said, grinning. "Now *that* would be almost as much fun."

Zoe shook her head. "You're mad."

"Mad and bad," Melinda joked. "You should take lessons. Now, if it was *me* going away for the weekend after my boyfriend screwed some other female, I wouldn't be going to some lonely old beach shack. I'd be heading for some swinging resort and looking for a bit of action myself. Yep, I'd be giving ole Drakey boy a bit of his own medicine. That's what I'd be doing."

"But I'm not you, am I?" Zoe said, almost wishing

that she was. It must be great not to feel things so deeply for once.

"Which is just as well," Melinda countered, "or I wouldn't like you as much as I do. Look, don't take any notice of me, Zoe," she went on, her smile fading abruptly. "I can be a vicious bitch sometimes. Why do you think I want to marry a man richer than my father? Because I want to show that old tightwad a thing or two. I'll never forgive him for tossing me to the wolves like he did. If he'd wanted me to be a career girl from the word go, then why ever didn't he say so when I was still at school? Then I could have made something of myself while I had the chance. I wouldn't have to make a living being a clotheshorse and putting up with men's preconceptions of me, simply because I'm an underwear model!"

Zoe stared at her friend, amazed by the wealth of very real feeling behind her outburst. She hadn't realized Melinda's father had hurt her so much over what he did.

"Sorry," Melinda muttered. "You have enough problems of your own without my going off."

"I…I didn't realize you felt that way about your job. And I didn't know men treated you badly because you were a model."

Melinda shrugged. "Mostly they don't. But I met this pathetic example of the opposite sex today when I was on a shoot and he ignored me. Treated me like I was a nobody. Yet I was standing in front of him in the sexiest black lace underwear you've ever seen."

"Who was he?"

"Some self-made upstart of a millionaire who's buying the fashion magazine I was doing the shoot for. Brother, did he think he was somebody. But my father could buy him ten times over!"

"Good-looking?"

"Yeah, I guess he was. He has the blackest of eyes and the longest eyelashes. And a great body for someone over thirty. But he was so arrogant."

Zoe smiled. "You were attracted to him."

"I was not!"

"Yes, you were. And your nose was put out of joint because he didn't seem to want you."

"Well...maybe a bit..."

"Will you be seeing him again?"

"I doubt it."

"Will you be doing any more shoots for that magazine in the near future?"

"Next week. My agent rang me about it today. Some other girl was supposed to do it but she rang in sick and the magazine asked for me to replace her."

"What a coincidence."

Melinda frowned at Zoe's tone. "You don't think..."

"It's possible, isn't it?" Zoe said with a shrug. "Let's face it, most men would at least *look* at you, Mel. Especially half-naked. The fact this chap ignored you says one of two things to me. He's either gay, or he does secretly fancy you, but he doesn't want to be obvious."

"Good grief!" Melinda exclaimed. "Do you always think this deviously?"

"I didn't once," Zoe said dryly. "But my experience with men is beginning to make me think outside the envelope. Now I really must get going or I'll hit the traffic. If and when Drake calls, tell him I've gone away for the weekend but you don't know where."

"He's not going to be happy."

"Too bad. I wasn't happy today."

"Oooh. Them's fightin' words."

"I'm in a fightin' mood. Which is why I'm going away. I need time to think. And time to calm down. Maybe by Monday, I'll see things a little clearer."

"Nothing in relationships with men is ever clear, Zoe," Melinda said. "They're a breed unto themselves. Impossible to really understand what makes their peculiar male minds tick. It's a case of can't live with them, can't live without them."

"Oh, I can live without them," Zoe said. "I've done it before and I can do it again. I just have to work out if I want to."

4

Zoe didn't have to consult Nigel's map for the first part of her drive north. She knew the way to Port Stephens. When she'd first bought her much-loved car a year ago, she'd spent every weekend going for long drives and investigating all the seaside towns within a half-day distance of Sydney.

Zoe had a secret passion for trips to the beach, perhaps because she'd rarely gone to the seaside during her growing-up years. The children of dairy farmers learned young that you can never go far from home, or for long. Having to milk the cows morning and afternoon tied you to the place, good and proper.

Unfortunately, Zoe soon found that going away by yourself for the weekend wasn't all that much fun. It was reasonably pleasurable during the day, sightseeing or strolling along a beach, but when the day ended and she returned to her motel room all alone, her mood would change.

Eating alone in restaurants was the worst. And watching other couples, holding hands across candle-lit tables. She discovered there was nothing worse than not having anyone to talk to and share your experiences with. When her solitary excursions began to seriously depress her, she stopped.

Which made her wonder why on earth she'd agreed to this silly idea of going away for the weekend on her own this time. She would have far too much time to think and brood. She would have been better off staying home and sorting things out with Drake, one way or another.

Zoe sighed in disgruntlement. It was too late now. She was almost at Port Stephens. Which meant it was time to pull over to the side of the highway and consult Nigel's map in more detail before she missed the turning to Hideaway Beach.

Five minutes later she was safely on the side road leading to her destination. It was narrow and winding, with nothing on either side but the kind of low trees and rather unattractive scrub one found when you were this close to the sea. The soil was mostly sand and just didn't grow lush green grass or nice tall trees. There were no houses, either, which meant it was probably a state reserve.

Zoe felt she'd been driving for ages by the time the gas station came into view on her left. It was ancient, as was the general store attached, but surprisingly well stocked, with a cheerful old guy behind the counter who liked to chat.

It was just after six by the time Zoe was on her way again with her passenger seat carrying a bag full of fresh bread, milk, eggs, two wickedly fattening bars of chocolate and a couple of her favorite magazines. She hadn't thought to throw in a book to read before leaving home and didn't trust the likes of Nigel Cox to have anything on his bookshelves she might enjoy.

Frankly, she hadn't thought about this trip enough at all, she now conceded. She hadn't even bothered to change clothes before leaving. Just chucked a few items in an overnight bag and got going.

It wasn't like her to act so hastily. The drama with Drake had tipped her world upside down, and her with it.

Zoe rounded a long sweeping curve and there, straight ahead, lay the horizon of the Pacific Ocean, big and vast and blue. Her heart lifted at the sight, and she was suddenly glad she'd come, if for nothing else than this moment.

But the moment was gone all too quickly, cold, hard reality returning to darken her own personal horizon. This weekend escape was not going to solve anything. She was just delaying the difficult decision over what she should do. Forgive and forget? Or dump Drake and try to move on...

The car slowed to a crawl as Zoe's mind drifted once more. It was all very well for Mel to say she'd find someone else in no time. Zoe had never been the sort of girl to pick up men easily, even now, when her looks were no longer a drawback. Men often found her standoffish. Some had even called her stuck-up.

But she wasn't. Not at all. She was just reserved. And naturally wary. She didn't warm to strangers easily. She was slow to give affection and friendship, and even slower to accept it from others. Which made her instant liking of Melinda, for instance, most unusual. She hadn't even really liked Drake at first meeting. He'd impressed her, yes. But liked?

No...not exactly. She'd thought him a little pushy. But she'd found his dogged pursuit of her very flattering, and very seductive. There'd been the flowers twice a week. Phone calls every day. Presents. Poetry, even.

How could she help falling in love with him in the end? Or going to bed with him? Or being devastated by his cheating on her? He'd made her think she was his entire world, and vice versa.

The sound of a horn honking loudly made Zoe jump in her seat, her eyes flying to the rear-vision mirror. A bright yellow truck was right behind her, several surf boards strapped to the roof. The male driver was making an impatient left-handed motion with his hand.

Zoe hadn't realized she'd been stopped, smack-dab in the middle of the road. Embarrassed, she smiled an apology at the driver in the rear-vision mirror. After a moment's hesitation he smiled back, and the oddest little quiver ran through Zoe from top to toe.

It shocked her so much that she stared at his reflection for a few seconds before moving her car over to the left, carrying with her the image of the bronze-skinned, blond-haired, broad-shouldered hunk wearing wrap-around sunglasses and the brightest orange T-shirt she'd ever seen. His sun-streaked hair was short and spiked, and his face had that chiseled structure which you saw a lot on male models, his lantern jawline covered with a few days' stubble. Naturally, in those sunglasses, she couldn't see the color of his eyes, but she guessed they would be blue.

This last train of thought startled Zoe. What on

earth was she doing, speculating over what color eyes he had? But even as she reprimanded herself for such silly nonsense, he was driving by and peering at her through their respective side windows. Her heart began to race and she started wondering if *he* was speculating on the color of *her* eyes, which were similarly masked by sunglasses. Her hand lifted and she almost took them off, wanting him to see that her own were big and brown and long-lashed.

They were her best feature, her eyes.

But she caught herself just in time and the moment of madness passed, as did the truck. Thank goodness.

What had she thought she was doing?

A minute before she'd been agonizing over how devastated she was by Drake's cheating on her. Then the next moment, there *she* was, almost flirting with some stranger.

There was absolutely no excuse for such behavior, no matter how sexy the guy in the truck was.

Sexy?

How could she possibly tell if he was sexy from a couple of brief passing glances? She hadn't even seen all of him. For all she knew, he could have beady little eyes, a big blubbery butt and the personality of a store mannequin.

Oh, yeah, scorned some new inner voice which Zoe had never been tuned into before. *Who do you think you're kidding, honey? He's going to have beautiful blue eyes, tight buns, and the charm of the devil.*

Zoe groaned. This was crazy and so unlike herself. There again, today hadn't exactly been like any other day. She'd been brought face-to-face with her boyfriend's raunchy new friend; quizzed by her boss on intimate sexual matters; then been told by her roommate that she shouldn't be slinking off by herself. She should be throwing herself into a fun fling out of revenge.

Was that what this was? Her subconscious wanting to punish Drake by flirting with another man? Her own shaky self-esteem, perhaps, looking for reassurance that she *was* attractive?

She sincerely hoped so. She didn't want it to be that other sordid scenario Fran had described of being struck by instant lust for some good-looking stranger and wanting nothing from him but down-and-dirty sex.

No, no, it couldn't be that. She didn't want to even consider the possibility. But even as she dismissed the idea, Zoe sincerely hoped she wouldn't run into the man in the truck again.

When she looked up, his yellow vehicle had reached the end of the road and was turning right. Within seconds, it had disappeared from view.

Zoe sat up straight, her stomach crunching down hard.

Right. He'd turned *right.*

She snatched up Nigel's second map and studied its very detailed drawing of Hideaway Beach's layout.

Her heart rate accelerated as her eyes confirmed what she'd remembered from her earlier perusal. The beach was U-shaped, with rugged peninsulas stretching out into the ocean at each end. Sand dunes rose behind the main stretch of beach, on top of which sat a long, face-the-ocean visitors' car lot. The half dozen or so weekenders which Hideaway Beach boasted were grouped together down the southerly end, their fronts facing northeast. A short dead-end road led 'round to the back of them, a road which required a right-hand turn at the end of this road.

If you were a surfer just come for the waves, you would go straight ahead and park in the visitors' car lot, not turn right as the truck had done.

There was only one logical conclusion. The hunk in the truck either lived here, or was staying here on vacation. If that was the case, she was likely to run into him again at some stage this weekend.

Zoe groaned her frustration. She'd come up here to sort out her feelings about men and sex, not have them confused further.

Irritated beyond words, she switched on the engine, checked there was no car coming, then drove down to the end of the road where she stopped for a few seconds and scanned the vehicles in the visitors' car lot.

The yellow truck wasn't among them.

Zoe hadn't expected it to be.

Sighing her resignation to the fact Mr. Orange T-shirt wasn't a visitor, she steered her small silver sedan onto the dirt track on her right and drove slowly along its pot-holed surface, glancing over to her left every now and then.

Hideaway Beach was certainly very beautiful. But very quiet. Only half a dozen people on the sand. A couple more swimming in the almost-flat waters. There wasn't a single board rider out in the water, which was understandable considering the absence of decent waves. There was no sign of Mr. Orange T-shirt anywhere.

Zoe was annoyed with herself for even looking.

Resolving to banish him from her mind once and for all, she swung her eyes back onto the road ahead and concentrated on finding Nigel's place, which, according to his map, was the second house she'd come to on her left, a white weatherboard cottage with a gray colorbond roof.

Actually, from the road, all Zoe could see of the weekenders were the roofs below her. The first one had an unusual-colored roof. Royal-blue. Zoe had never seen a roof that color before, but she rather liked it.

The gray colorbond roof of Nigel's place came into view a short way after the bright blue, and Zoe began looking for the driveway.

There was a small, white-painted mailbox on the side of the road, but no sign of a driveway. Zoe parked on the grass verge just beyond the mailbox then climbed out to check out what was what.

Nigel's weekender looked very cute and cozy down below her, its back steps tucked in to the hillside, with the beach less than fifty feet from the front porch. There *was* a footpath of sorts leading from the mailbox down to the back door, but absolutely no way of getting her car any closer than where she was. The intervening ground was too steep and too rough.

There was nothing for it but to carry everything down that hazardous-looking path. Zoe glanced over at the weekenders on her left and right, telling herself she wasn't looking for a sign of Mr. Orange T-shirt, even though she was.

The place on her right looked deserted, with no vehicle anywhere. The one on her left with the bright-blue roof was lucky enough to have a driveway leading to what looked like a carport on the other side of the house, but she couldn't see enough of it to make out any vehicles parked there.

Still, it would be just like Mr. Orange T-shirt to live in a house with a royal-blue roof, sky-blue walls and wraparound porches painted a dark rich red. And it would be just like her luck today to have him as a neighbor for the whole weekend.

Shaking her head, Zoe returned to the car, collected her various bags and set off down the pathway. She was halfway down the roughly hewn steps when something orange caught the corner of her left eye and her head jerked in that direction.

Big mistake. She should have kept watching where she was going, especially since she was wearing high heels. The second she took her eyes off the uneven steps, she misjudged a distance, one of her high heels caught against something and she lurched forward. In joggers or bare feet Zoe might have been able to regain her balance. As it was, she whirled with the bags in her hands in the air, and for one adrenaline-charged moment, she thought she could save herself.

But her center of gravity could not be righted and all was finally lost, Zoe tipping full front-forward. With a loud yelp she instinctively brought her hands up to save her face, and the bags came with her.

Just as well. For they cushioned her fall and possibly prevented her breaking an arm, or a leg. She still landed heavily, her knees getting the worst of it as she slid down a couple of steps further before coming to an ungainly halt.

She was still sprawled on the ground, totally winded, when a pair of strong arms slid around her waist.

''Are you all right?'' a male voice asked as he hoisted her up onto her feet.

Zoe saw the orange T-shirt first and groaned silently. It would be him, wouldn't it? Fate was being very cruel to her today.

''Yes, I…I think so,'' she said, delaying looking up at him by dusting down her dress. But good manners finally forced her to glance up at her gallant Good Samaritan and say a proper thank-you.

She had to look up a good way, he was so tall. Taller than she'd imagined. And even more handsome, with a strong straight nose, a cute dimple in his squared chin and a perfectly gorgeous mouth.

But it was his eyes which captivated her the most. They *were* blue, as blue and as deep as the ocean. Eyes to drown in.

Eyes to watch your own wide-eyed reflection in while he rocks back and forth above you, his beautiful body buried deep inside yours.

Did she gasp out loud in shocked horror?

She hoped not.

''You've gone very pale,'' he said, frowning. ''Are you sure you're all right? You're not going to faint, are you?''

"No," she choked out. "No, I don't think so."
Though it was possible.

"Perhaps you'd better sit down for a few seconds,
put your head down between your knees."

Another erotic scenario exploded into her mind,
one in which it wasn't *her* head down between her
knees.

Zoe swallowed a couple more times.

"No, no, I'm fine," she said at last in strangled
tones, desperately trying to pull herself together. "But
I've lost my sunglasses. Can you see my sunglasses?
Oh, there they are." She swooped on them, and
jammed them back on, hoping they hid her escalating
panic.

"You've ruined your panty hose," he pointed out.

Her eyes dropped to her legs, then shifted over to
his legs, which were well on display, his colorful
board shorts not covering up much.

They were the best-shaped legs on a man she'd
ever seen. Totally tanned, long and very strong, with
great thighs.

*Well able to support you when he hikes you up onto
his hips and then...*

"Serves me right for being silly enough to be wearing high heels," she blurted out. "It's just that I drove
straight up here from work. Didn't really have time
to change. I just threw a few things together and
jumped in the car. My main concern was missing the
Friday traffic heading north out of Sydney. But not to
worry. I doubt I'll be needing panty hose up here this
weekend anyway."

She was prattling on like a fool. But anything was

better than conjuring up more appalling scenarios involving them both.

"I think your eggs might have seen better days as well," he said dryly, and Zoe looked blank.

"Eggs," he repeated, indicating her groceries which had scattered all over the place. The half-dozen eggs, which had been carefully placed at the top of the bag, had spilled from their carton, all of them broken.

"Oh, dear..." Zoe sighed, suddenly feeling very tired.

"I could go buy you some more, if you like," he offered.

She stared at him. When guys started offering to go out of their way for you, it usually meant they fancied you. The thought that Mr. Orange T-shirt might be as attracted to her as she was to him, produced a mad mixture of guilty pleasure and even more outrageous thoughts.

Yes, go get me some more eggs, you gorgeous darling sexy man. And a dozen condoms whilst you're at it.

Zoe was infinitely relieved she was wearing sunglasses, for surely the wickedness of her thoughts must be reflected in her eyes.

"Thank you but no," she said stiffly. "I can manage without the eggs. But it was very nice of you to offer."

"No sweat." He immediately hunkered down and began putting her groceries back into the bag.

Impossible not to notice in that position that he

didn't have a big blubbery butt. His buns *were* as trim and taut as she'd feared they would be.

Afraid that any further ogling of his perfect butt would conjure up yet another wicked fantasy, Zoe wrenched her eyes away and hurried to pick up her handbag. But when she moved toward where her overnight bag had fallen, her gallant knight to the rescue was there before her, scooping it up first.

"I think I'd better carry these the rest of the way down for you. You're still wearing those very nice but potentially lethal high heels," he added with a wry little smile.

"Please don't bother."

"It's no bother. I presume you're staying at Nigel's place down there?"

"Well...yes. You know Nigel, do you?"

"Pretty well."

"Oh? How well?" She didn't realize 'til the words were out of her mouth how they might sound. The thought that this fellow might be gay hadn't even crossed her mind.

He laughed, his blue eyes sparkling with genuine good humor. "Not *that* well. But we have a drink together sometimes when he's up here. I live over there." And he nodded toward the house with the royal-blue roof. "For the moment, that is," he added. "The owner's letting me stay while I do some renovating work for him."

"It's a very colorful house."

"Yes. He likes bright colors. So what about you? Are you a friend of our esteemed big-city lawyer? Or a client?"

Zoe felt she had to terminate this getting-to-know-you conversation fairly quickly, or risk giving her far too attractive neighbor the wrong idea. She could not even begin to speculate what she might do if he started coming on to her. The thought was far too perversely thrilling for words.

"No, I hardly know Mr. Cox at all, to be honest. But I...uh..." She hesitated over revealing specific details of her life to a virtual stranger. "I know one of his partners," she said, instead of saying she worked for Fran. "She asked Nigel if I could borrow his place for the weekend. I...um...I needed to get away from Sydney for a couple of days."

"Ah...life in the fast lane getting too much for you, was it?"

"Something like that."

He nodded sagely and Zoe realized he was older than she'd first thought. Late twenties, perhaps. Maybe even thirty. "I know exactly how you feel," he said ruefully. "But a weekend away won't be much of a cure. You need longer than that."

"Well, I have to be back at work on Monday, so one weekend is all I've got. Look, I don't mean to be rude, but I'm terribly hot and tired and in desperate need of a shower. If you'd just drop those things next to Nigel's back door, that would be great."

"Okay," he agreed, but Zoe thought he looked a bit disappointed. Maybe he'd been hoping she'd invite him in for a drink, or something.

Or something morphed in her mind to a scene from a recent movie where the leading man and leading lady—within a few minutes of meeting—pounced on each other like wild beasts. Clothes were ripped off in seconds and absolutely nothing was left to the imagination as the hero, for want of a better word, proceeded to ravish the heroine up against a wall.

At the time, Zoe had thought the whole thing quite incredible, as well as supremely tacky.

She still thought such behavior tacky, but not quite so incredible.

She tried to imagine, as she followed her far too sexy neighbor down to the back door, what would happen if she did invite him in. Would he make a pass? And if he did, what would *she* do?

He placed her bags by the step, then turned to face her, his own expression thoughtful.

"The name's Aiden, by the way," he said. "And yours?"

"Zoe."

"Nice name. Well, Zoe, if you need anything over the next two days, just whistle. I'm always hereabouts. When I'm not off surfing somewhere, that is. I presume you know how to whistle?" he added, throwing a provocative little smile over his shoulder as he started to walk away. "Just put your very pretty lips together and blow."

He didn't look back again as his long legs carried him swiftly away. Which was just as well, because what Zoe's sexually charged mind was doing to his parting words made her face go a brighter red than his porch.

5

WITHIN a minute of returning to his place, Aiden was stretched out in a chair on the front porch, drinking a beer and doing his best not to think about the girl in the house next door having a shower.

A futile exercise. He'd been thinking about her nonstop since she'd smiled at him in her rear-vision mirror and charged up every testosterone-based cell he owned.

Playing knight to the rescue just now had only confirmed what he already knew. That she was big trouble, both to his peace of mind *and* body.

Aiden gulped another mouthful of beer, then sighed.

Six months he'd lasted here at Hideaway Beach without so much as a single bad night's sleep. Six months of wonderfully uncomplicated celibacy.

His life was blessedly simple. He surfed first thing in the morning, and again, late in the afternoon, spending the hours in between doing up the once-ramshackle beachhouse he'd bought a few months earlier. After dinner—which he usually cooked himself—his evenings were spent reading, or listening to music. He didn't have a television and never bought newspapers. If he felt the need for human conversation, he chatted to other surfers, or the local fishermen, or to his mom over the phone. Occasionally, when Nigel was up for the weekend, he went over to his place for dinner and a bottle of good wine.

But he rarely stayed long. He didn't want to be contaminated by listening to Nigel's complaints about his clients and his lovers. He certainly *never* wanted to reminisce on the time *he'd* been a client.

Aiden was well aware his sabbatical from real life would come to an end one day, but only when *he* decided and not before. He wanted to keep the world outside at a distance for a while longer. He certainly didn't want to be attracted to some mixed-up, auburn-haired city chick who was obviously in the middle of a personal crisis which had necessitated her coming up here to Hideaway Beach for a break.

He didn't want to speculate on whether she was in the throes of a divorce, or a palimony suit, or a sexual harassment case, or any of the multiple reasons why women hired lawyers like Fran Phillips, who then took the poor husband or boyfriend or boss to court and screwed them over for everything they were worth, both financially and emotionally.

Aiden checked himself with a frown. Brother, that sounded really bitter. And he wasn't bitter anymore. If anything, Marci had done him a favor, suing him. She'd made him see the emptiness of seeking nothing but superficial success and material wealth; forced him to reevaluate what he really wanted in life.

And when he finally found out what that was—he'd been searching for it in his head for six months now—he'd go after it.

Until that happened, the last thing he wanted was to get back on the sexual merry-go-round. Going to bed with the delectable but obviously distressed Zoe was not a good idea, no matter how much he found her attractive.

The trouble was she wanted him, too. He could tell.

But she didn't *want* to want him. That he could tell as well.

Which was the most bewildering aspect of this whole situation.

Aiden had never come across a female before who wanted him, and had resisted him. If anything, they'd always thrown themselves at him, or at least made him aware they were available, if and when he wanted them. Such was the powerful combination of heaven-sent looks and man-made money.

There again, Zoe didn't know he had money, did she?

Clearly, she hadn't recognized him.

Aiden frowned. Maybe she was the sort of girl who only surrendered to a physical attraction if the man was wealthy or famous? Such females did exist, he knew only too well. Yet somehow he didn't think Zoe was of that ilk. She'd been too sweetly flustered by everything just now to be of the cold-blooded, gold-digging variety.

Why, he wondered for the umpteenth time, had she sent him away just now, instead of inviting him in as most women would have done?

There were only a couple of answers which didn't bruise his male ego. Perhaps she'd sworn off all men for a while, as he had women. Or perhaps she'd been badly hurt by some sleazy guy and no longer trusted the opposite sex. He could identify with that as well. Lack of trust was the reason why he'd lied to her about owning this house.

Another futile gesture, since Zoe clearly wasn't going to come across. But at that moment he'd been hoping she might, and he'd egotistically and rather romantically hankered for her to come to his bed because she wanted Aiden the man, not Aiden, one-time world surfing champion, or Aiden the millionaire owner of the Aus-Surf chain.

Thinking of her in his bed brought his mind back to her very beddable body with its pretty breasts, tiny waist and deliciously rounded derriere. He'd had a good look at *that* when she'd been sprawled facedown on the ground, with her skirt flipped up to her waist.

Aiden had always been a butt man.

And a breast man, he conceded with a wry laugh.

And a leg man.

Hell, he liked every bit of a woman. Their shape. Their smell. Their softness.

His groan carried intense frustration. Whatever had possessed him to give them up? If he hadn't, he wouldn't be here now, with a hard-on the size of the Centrepoint Tower. He must have been mad!

Sculling the rest of the beer, Aiden went inside to get another can. Then another. Then yet another. Dinner that evening was a liquid one. As was dessert.

Aiden was to find, however, that getting drunk was a poor substitute for getting laid. His revved-up hormones still had him tossing and turning for most of the night. Sleep finally came around three, but when he woke, nothing had changed, a fact confirmed by the ready-to-fire state of his sexual equipment.

Aiden shook his head irritably and did the only thing a man of his nature could do. He went for a very long, very cold, early-morning swim.

Then started planning a seduction.

THE brass bed was big, and soft. Very soft. So were the silk scarves which bound her to the bedposts. They didn't hurt at all, not even when she writhed and wriggled.

And she writhed and wriggled a lot, gasping and moaning as her dream lover did things to her with his hands and mouth. Exciting things. Delicious things. Wicked things.

She was naked, of course. Naked and exposed and unable to stop him looking at her and touching her at will. Kissing all her intimate places. Sucking at her nipples. Invading her with his tongue.

But there was no embarrassment. Only pleasure. The most mind-bending pleasure. Sweet and dark and decadent.

Yes, yes, lick me there. Suck it. No, bite it.

She moaned when he did, her head twisting from side to side. If only she could see him. If only he'd take off the other scarf which covered her eyes.

"Who are you?" she asked, though she already suspected. Who else did she know who smelled of sea salt?

"No talking," he replied in a very familiar voice. "If you talk, you'll wake up. And you don't want that, do you?"

She shuddered at the thought. No, no. Not yet. Please not yet.

"I...I just want to see you."

"That's not what you want," he murmured as his hands ran lightly up over her body, across her tensely held stomach, her stiffened nipples, her stretched-up arms.

"This is what you want," he said, and suddenly, he was there, between her legs, filling her, thrilling her.

"Yes," she agreed, her body quivering.

Her climax was but a heartbeat away when her eyelids shot upward like a blind on a window, sunlight spearing her pupils.

Zoe sat bolt upright, blinking, gasping.

It took several seconds for her ragged breathing to calm, and cold hard reality to return.

There was no brass bed. No scarves. No Aiden.

A dream. It had all been a dream.

Zoe groaned. She supposed she should have been relieved that she wasn't really tied, naked, to a bed. But all she felt was disappointment. As much as Zoe knew she'd never enjoy such activities in real life—she'd never be that uninhibited, for starters—it was still hard not to wish that the dream might have lasted just a little bit longer.

Sighing, Zoe glanced at her watch on the bedside table. Ten to eight. Not late. But the sun was already streaming into the bedroom, promising another hot day.

Get up, she told herself. Have a shower. Make yourself some breakfast.

Dragging her body out of bed, she padded down the central corridor into the one and only bathroom. Fifteen minutes later, she emerged with her wet hair wrapped up in one of Nigel's plush navy towels, her steam-pinked body snugly encased in the matching navy bathrobe which had been hanging on the back of the bathroom door.

She was making her way back along the corridor to the kitchen to make breakfast when the doorbell rang.

Zoe halted at the sound, then peered down at the front door with its upper panel of frosted glass, through which she could see a tall, undoubtedly male silhouette.

"Oh, no, Drake," she groaned, and bolted back into the bathroom where she stared in horror at her reflection.

No one other than Mel had seen her totally without makeup in years. She needed makeup to cover the smattering of freckles across her nose and cheeks, and to transform the rest of her from a country hick into a city sophisticate. And she *really* needed her hair styled cleverly around her face to hide its round shape. With it bundled up under a towel and no makeup on, she looked about sixteen, a baby-faced sixteen.

Zoe would rather be dead than to let Drake see her this way. And who else could it be, knocking on the front door here at around eight in the morning?

Drake must have found out her whereabouts from Fran. There was no other answer.

And now here he was, on her doorstep.

Zoe didn't know whether to be flattered, or furious.

"Ahoy in there, Zoe," a male voice shouted through the door. "Don't panic now. It's just your friendly next-door neighbor with some eggs. I had a few to spare."

Zoe's mouth dropped open. It was Aiden. Not Drake.

Oh, my God...

"Just...just a moment," she called back, then went into a complete panic. Suddenly, she wished it *was* Drake at the door. Drake didn't make her mind go totally blank and her body begin to tremble uncontrollably.

Think, girl. Think! He hasn't come over here at this hour simply to give you eggs. You're not *that* naive. He's going to make some kind of pass.

Zoe's lack of makeup and grooming suddenly became a desirable asset. Aiden wouldn't think her so attractive this morning, with her freshly scrubbed face and no-hair look. As much as she hated showing herself like this to anyone, this situation called for drastic measures.

Zoe marched resolutely toward the door, resashing the robe around her waist more tightly on the way.

Unfortunately, this action reminded Zoe that she was naked underneath the robe, her tingling flesh still suffering from the after-effects of that incredible dream. Facing her fantasy lover was not going to be easy, but it had to be done.

Taking one last steadying breath, she pulled back the bolt and opened the front door.

The sight of Aiden standing there in nothing but a

tattered pair of denim shorts, shook Zoe considerably. Okay, so the day was hot. Even hotter than yesterday, but did he have to go around half naked?

Zoe did her best not to appear rattled, or to look at him with anything remotely like the disturbing feelings his near-nakedness evoked in her.

It wasn't desire. Desire was too tame a word for what she felt when she looked at this man.

Lust. That was what it was. Lust. The kind of lust Fran had talked about which didn't require niceties. Or even foreplay.

Her craving was strictly sexual. And incredibly basic. When she looked at Aiden's beautiful male body, all she could think of was how it would feel to touch him and kiss him, to have him on top of her, and inside her.

How she kept her expression as bland as she did, she would never know. Pride, she supposed.

"You're up early this morning," she said, trying to sound casual. But it was hard with him looking *her* over in such an open and admiring fashion. He didn't seem at all taken aback by her less than perfect appearance. In fact, if she wasn't mistaken, he seemed to prefer it.

Maybe he liked the casual, just-out-of-the-shower look. He certainly didn't believe in much grooming himself. He still hadn't shaved. And his hair was sticking up all over the place.

Yet for all that, he looked so sexy it was a crime.

"I'm up early every morning," he returned.

"So am I. Usually. But I slept in this morning."

He smiled. "I'm glad. Otherwise you'd have already had your breakfast. Here,'' he said, handing her a carton of half a dozen eggs. ''Enjoy.''

''You must let me pay you for them.''

''Not at all.''

''You're very kind.''

He smiled. ''Not *that* kind. I have an ulterior motive.''

''Oh?'' she said warily. Here it comes...

''I needed an excuse to come over and see you again.''

She stared at him, surprised by his blunt honesty, and terrified of what he was going to say next. Please don't, her eyes pleaded.

''I wondered if you'd like to come out to dinner with me tonight. There are plenty of good restaurants around and I do own some decent clothes. Not that you'd know by looking at me this morning,'' he added, grinning. ''I'll even promise to shave. So what about it?''

Her mouth went dry. Never had the devil tempted her so badly.

''I'm sorry,'' she said. ''But I...I can't.''

His eyes darkened in the way the sky does just before a storm. ''Can't, Zoe? Or won't?''

''Does it matter? The answer's the same.''

''It matters to me.''

''Won't, then.''

''Why?''

''I...I'm not free.''

His eyes dropped to her left hand. ''You're not wearing any rings,'' he stated bluntly.

"I didn't say I was married. I said I wasn't free to go out with you."

"Are you engaged, then?"

"No."

"Living with someone?"

"No."

"Then you're free in my books."

"But I'm not free in mine," she stated firmly. "I'm involved with someone. And I love him very much."

"But does *he* love *you* very much?" he countered.

Oh, why did she hesitate? "He…he says he does."

"Huh. If he loves you so much, then why has he let you come up here all by yourself? If you were my girlfriend, I wouldn't let you out of my sight."

She stiffened. "Well, I'm *not* your girlfriend and Drake doesn't *let* me do anything. Not that it's any of your business."

"I'm making it my business."

"Then that's very presumptuous of you," she snapped.

"Is he married?"

"No, he is not! Look, I think you should leave, if you're going to get personal and offensive."

He stared at her, clearly taken aback by her stand. His eyes searched her face, as though he could not believe what he was hearing.

"Just tell me one thing. Would you go out with me if this boyfriend of yours was out of the picture?"

She didn't say a word, but her eyes must have betrayed her.

"That's what I thought," he said, a little smugly. "You know, Zoe, you don't love this guy as much as you think you do. If you did, you wouldn't have looked at me like you did yesterday.''

A flustered heat started gathering in Zoe's face. ''Please go. And take your eggs with you.''

When she held them out, he shook his head. ''Keep them,'' he growled, and stalked off.

Zoe almost called him back. Almost. But in the end, decency won and the devil was defeated.

''Well done,'' Aiden muttered to himself as he marched back to his house. ''Very subtle. You'd give Casanova a run for his money with a technique like that.''

Clearly, six months' celibacy hadn't done much for his seduction skills. Or was it that he'd never had any in the first place?

The truth was sex had always come easy to Aiden, right from an early age. He'd never had to chase after it. Girls had always chased after him. At school, he'd always had the prettiest girls in class following him around like puppies. During his years on the world surfing circuit, there'd been gorgeous chicks by the bucket-load hanging around the tournaments. Surfing groupies, they were called. There was never a question of having to work too hard to have any one of them he wanted. He'd just have to give her the eye.

He hadn't bothered with a steady girlfriend back then. That kind of relationship wouldn't have fitted in with his lifestyle. For one thing, he'd needed to concentrate on his surfing. And then, there was the constant traveling.

Casual sex and a pocketful of condoms had been the order of the day. And most nights.

Later, however, after injury had forced him to retire from professional surfing, and he'd turned his ambitions elsewhere, Aiden had considered having a real relationship. He'd even started a couple. But they'd never worked out.

He hadn't been really in love, he supposed. Though he thought he was at the time. Not in love enough, however, for him to put his partner first, before his business. Both girls had complained of his lack of true commitment.

So he'd given up the idea of a steady girlfriend and gone back to dating different girls, if and when he felt the need for sex. He had little trouble finding ''dates.'' Rich men rarely suffered the pangs of rejection. Aiden certainly hadn't had no said to him too often.

Zoe had said no to him today, however, and there was absolutely nothing Aiden could think of to do which would sway her mind. Unfortunately, she was a girl of strong character, and rather old-fashioned principle.

For once in his life, he hadn't got what he wanted, woman-wise, and it didn't sit well with him.

So he did the only thing a man of his nature could do.

He went surfing.

6

You did the right thing, Zoe praised herself after Aiden left. If you'd said yes, you'd have been no better than Drake. Now, make yourself some breakfast and stop worrying. Okay, so Aiden *did* seem a bit upset that you wouldn't go out with him. He'll get over it. It's not as though he's in love with you. He only wanted a dinner date, and then you for afters.

Zoe savoured the thought of being Aiden's after-dinner afters while she cooked and ate two of his eggs for breakfast. What would he be like as a real lover? she started wondering. What sort of things would he do?

"Oh, do stop thinking about that infernal man," Zoe muttered, and forcibly turned her mind to what she would actually *do* for the rest of the day.

Despite the heat, swimming was out, as was strolling along the water's edge. She wasn't going to do a single thing which might risk running into Aiden again. As much as Zoe had smugly congratulated herself on turning his invitation down, she wasn't sure if she would do so well on a second occasion.

Which meant outdoor pursuits here at Hideaway Beach were not on the agenda.

Really, there was nothing for it but to get out of

here. But not back to Sydney. Not yet. She was still very angry with Drake, and still not impressed with his "just sex" excuse. Maybe she understood it a bit better, after meeting Aiden, but if *she* could resist temptation, then why couldn't Drake have done the same? After all, on a scale of one to ten, she'd put the bottle blonde at around nine and Aiden at twenty-five! So whose temptation was worse?

All Zoe could think was that Drake's love for her couldn't be as strong as her love for him. Maybe Aiden had been right about that.

Thinking about Drake gave her a sudden thought and she went to check the message bank on her cell phone.

Nothing from Drake. Nothing at all.

Rather odd, came the caustic thought, if he loved her so much.

Zoe punched out her home number and Melinda answered after several rings.

"Hello," she grumped. Zoe's roommate was not a morning person.

"Hi, Mel, it's Zoe here."

"Oh, hi, Zoe," she said, attempting to brighten up. "What's up?"

"Nothing drastic. Did Drake call 'round before you went out last night?"

"Nope."

"Any message from him on the answering machine?"

"Nope."

"He didn't call my cell phone, either," Zoe said, biting her bottom lip.

Mel's sigh wafted down the line. "Look, just dump the two-timing bastard and be done with it. Then you can go out and have the entire surf club up there at... Where is it you're staying?"

"Hideaway Beach. And there's no surf club here. It's a very small beach."

"Pity. Some of those lifesaver types are real hunks. Nothing screwable at all around?"

Zoe stifled a groan. "Can we get off the subject of sex?"

"If you insist. So when are you coming home? I'm lonely here without you."

Zoe was touched. "I'll probably get on the road first thing in the morning. Then I'll miss the Sunday afternoon traffic."

"So what are you going to do today?"

"I thought I'd drive into Nelson Bay and do some window-shopping. Have a bite to eat. Maybe catch a movie."

"Wow. Aren't you the wild one!"

Zoe laughed. "I'm not a party animal like you." *Except in my dreams!*

"Maybe not, but you should learn to loosen up a bit, Zoe. There's more to life than working like a Trojan and always looking like you stepped out of a band box. So I repeat. Dump Drake and live a little."

"Maybe he's already dumped me."

"That might be a good thing. I've been thinking about Drake and something my father once said. You can never trust a salesman."

"Oh, Mel, that's generalizing and not at all fair. You might as well say all models are dumb."

"And we are! Otherwise we'd be doing something else. Nothing worse than being wanted for your outside packaging alone. What I would give for a guy who liked me for the person I am inside and not for what I look like!''

"It's easy to say that, Mel, when you look like you do. When you look like I used to, you never have a chance for a guy to like *any* part of you, the outside *or* the inside.''

"You always say things like that. I don't believe you were ever that ugly.''

"Maybe not ugly, but I was fat.''

"Codswallop. You were probably just pleasantly plump. I'll have you know a lot of men like a bit of meat on a girl. Besides, you would still have been very pretty. You've got the sweetest face with the loveliest of eyes. They don't even need to be made-up to look good. I'd kill for eyes like that. I have to put a truckload of stuff on mine to look half as good as yours do first thing in the morning.''

"Oh, go on with you. You're such a flatterer.''

"No, I'm not. Trust me on this. I never flatter other girls, not even my best friend.''

Zoe's heart squeezed tight. She'd never had a best friend before. It was so much better than being just a roommate.

"Yes, you would, Mel,'' Zoe returned warmly. "You pretend to be tough, but you're not at all. You're as soft as butter.''

"Now who's the flatterer,'' Mel protested. But she sounded pleased.

"I'd better get going, or my phone bill will be bigger than Ben Hur."

"You be kind to yourself now."

"I will. I promise."

"And don't do anything I wouldn't do."

Zoe laughed. "That gives me a pretty broad canvas."

"It does indeed."

"See you tomorrow, Mel."

"'Bye, sweetie. Love you."

She ended the call, leaving Zoe with a warm fuzzy feeling in the pit of her stomach. There was nothing like hearing someone tell you that they loved you, especially when you felt they meant it.

Drake was always telling her that he loved her.

But did he mean it?

Zoe sighed, put her phone back in her handbag and headed for the door. What she needed was distraction from her carousel thoughts about Drake and those other equally perturbing thoughts about another man who never shaved and didn't wear nearly enough clothes!

The heat hit her the moment she stepped outside the door. The temperature had really shot up since her neighbor's early-morning visit. It was going to be scorching. She would have to find an air-conditioned shopping mall, that was for sure.

Unfortunately, Nelson Bay hadn't changed much since her last visit. Although it was the tourist hub of the Port Stephens area with a huge marina where you could take any number of cruises, the shopping center was still relatively small, with no mall to speak of.

After a couple of hours spent browsing in every air-conditioned store she could find, then lingering over brunch in a café down near the water, Zoe hesitated between actually going on a whale-watching cruise or trying out the local movie house, as she'd said to Mel. The movies won, again because of the air-conditioning, and also the choice available. A hard-edge action adventure flick which had an all-male cast. Consequently, no sex.

Zoe thought her poor brain—and body—deserved a rest from the subject.

The theater was small and crowded, with Zoe having to sit far too close to the screen with her head tipped back all the time. The movie wasn't too bad, but far too long, and by the time she emerged, she had serious cramps in her neck.

She was rubbing them and wandering back toward the spot where she'd parked her car when she passed a small store front advertising remedial massages.

The wooden door was closed, but there was an Open For Business sign hanging on it. Zoe had never had a massage before, but her boss was very partial to them.

What the heck, Zoe thought. It was still too early to go back.

Ten minutes later she was lying facedown on a massage table, dressed in nothing but her bra and panties, and feeling just a little bit self-conscious, despite the masseur being a woman. Her name was Glenda, a tall athletic woman in her mid-thirties who looked a bit like Zoe's sports coach at high school.

When she'd asked Zoe to strip down to her underwear, Zoe had been momentarily transported back to the gym dressing room where she'd been forced to change into a skimpy sports gear every Thursday afternoon.

Thinking back to those days, Zoe realized Mel was right. She'd only been pleasantly plump when she'd finally come to Sydney at the age of twenty, but back then, during her teenage years, she'd been fat. Fat as a pig. Her nickname in high school was Miss Piggy.

Yet she hadn't always been fat. In elementary school she'd been a slip of a thing. But when her mother died of cancer a few days after Zoe's thirteen birthday, Zoe had turned to food for comfort. That, along with the sudden onset of puberty, had turned her into a blob.

The teasing she'd endured over her weight had been pretty awful every single school day, but gym days had been unendurable. Maybe she'd been imagining it, but Zoe thought even the female sports coach had enjoyed some kind of perverse pleasure in seeing her struggle into the short pleated skirt and sleeveless top which showed off every appalling inch of her grossly overweight body.

It had taken Zoe years to eradicate the feelings of shame and self-loathing over her body. In truth, she probably still hadn't eradicated those old tapes entirely. Otherwise, she wouldn't be feeling self-conscious right now.

"You work out, don't you?" Glenda said as she bent Zoe's arms up into a comfortable position on top of the table, then unclipped her bra.

"Yes," Zoe admitted, a tad tautly. But she wasn't

used to this kind of thing. "A couple of times a week."

"You can always tell. You're looking good, girl."

"You really think so?"

"I'll say. Just don't overdo it. Nothing worse than women who work out too much. They begin to look sinewy. But you're just right. Now…let's see if we can do something about these knots in your shoulders and neck. Oh, yes…they're tight as a drum. I'll bet you're from Sydney. We get a lot of stressed out Sydney people up here. Just relax, love…"

Zoe did relax. To begin with. She settled her face into the hole in the table, closed her eyes and let all her muscles go, as per Glenda's instructions. But just as she was beginning to appreciate why Fran was addicted to such pampering, Zoe made the mistake of opening her eyes and looking down at the bright orange carpet.

Immediately, she thought of Aiden. Then last night's dream.

"Hey," Glenda said. "Don't tense up again. Relax."

Relax! How could she relax with last night's dream replaying in her brain?

Zoe squeezed her eyes tightly shut again and tried to banish the erotic fantasy from her mind, but it was impossible. Her lying there nearly naked didn't help. Neither did the fact she had to stay perfectly still. It wasn't the same as being bound to a bed, but it didn't take much imagination to once again summon up the deliciously seductive feelings of being a helpless captive. It was also very easy to pretend it wasn't Glenda's hands on her. But Aiden's.

He'd been so good with his hands in that dream. So very very good.

Zoe stifled a moan as Glenda started working up the back of her thighs toward her bottom.

"Do...do you think you could do my shoulders a bit more?" she said.

"Sure. Goodness, you're all tight there again. What on earth have you been doing to yourself lately?"

What, indeed?

"I guess I've been working too hard," Zoe said.

"Ever thought about changing your job?"

"Er...no. I actually quite like my job."

"Well, there's something in your life which you don't like, love. I suggest you find out what it is and change that!"

7

AFTER the massage, Zoe drove to a local restaurant for dinner, not wanting to cook. By the time she finally arrived back at Hideaway Beach it was getting on for nine and the sun had well and truly set. The air outside was not appreciably cooler, however, and the cottage was stifling from being closed up all day.

Zoe opened up the windows and put on the ceiling fans, but they didn't help all that much. She was still hot. No, she was *very* hot.

The idea of a cooling swim beckoned like a siren's voice and it seemed silly to deny herself the pleasure. Silly to keep hiding in this house as well. Aiden was not going to approach her again. Not at this hour. After her experiences during the massage, Zoe well understood why she'd made the decision to distance herself from his corrupting presence today, but enough was enough!

The decision made to have a swim, Zoe hurried to extract her swimsuit from her bag, pulling out the new black one-piece Mel had talked her into buying at the summer sales and which she hadn't dared wear in public yet. It had a low-cut square neckline which just covered her nipples and was perilously high cut at the sides. You really had to keep your bikini line waxed well to wear it, but that was no trouble to Zoe. She kept everything waxed well.

Five minutes later, she was plunging headfirst into the ocean, surfacing with a gasp. After the intense heat of the day the water was wonderfully refreshing. Unfortunately, she was standing right at the spot where the waves broke so she had to jump up and down all the time, which was rather tiring. A few feet farther out it was almost flat, with just a small swell. There, she could lie back and wallow in the more gentle waves, without getting exhausted or being knocked off her feet.

Zoe wasn't a great swimmer, but competent enough. She'd been taught properly at elementary school and back then, before she'd turned into a blob, she'd spent many a hot summer's day swimming in the local creek.

Diving under the breaking waves, she quickly reached her objective where she was able to float quite successfully. With her hands behind her head, she stared up at the star-studded night sky and tried to work out which ones formed the Southern Cross. She thought she'd found it several times.

Time drifted. And so did she. Zoe didn't realize 'til she decided to swim back in just how far out she was. It gave her a fright, as did the current her feet encountered when she tried to tread water. It was strong and pulling her, not toward the beach, but toward the bluff stretching out into the ocean, where rolling waves were crashing against the jagged black rocks.

Zoe struck out for the shore with slightly panicky strokes, but made little headway against the strength of the rip. When she stopped swimming, it dragged her sideward and backward. Toward the rocks.

Searching the ocean, Zoe couldn't see another single soul. Even the moonlit beach looked deserted. Everyone had gone home. Or gone out. There weren't any lights on in any of the weekenders, except Nigel's and Aiden's.

Would he hear her if she cried out? His house seemed so far away. She didn't want to die.

Damn it, she *wasn't* going to die!

Zoe started screaming for help and swimming at the same time, kicking like mad.

AIDEN was sitting up in an armchair by the window, trying to read, when he thought he heard a faint cry.

His head jerked up from the book, his ears instantly on alert. A gull? The wind perhaps?

The cry came again. Then again. And again.

Aiden was on his feet and running.

Not a bird. A woman. And she was in trouble.

He burst out of his front door, leaped down the three front steps and sprinted across the beach, scanning the ocean as he went. He spotted her about fifty feet out, right down the end where the rocks were.

It was Zoe. He just knew it was Zoe.

Aiden didn't stop to speculate on what she was doing out there at this time of night. He whirled and raced back to pick up his board which was thankfully leaning against the front porch. Adrenaline had him covering the sand back to the water's edge in no time. He ran through the shallows, threw the board across the first wave, dived facedown onto it and paddled like crazy.

If he'd been in one of those lifeguard rescue races, he'd have won hands down, so fast did he cover the distance from the water's edge to where Zoe was valiantly swimming and getting nowhere fast. Once drawn alongside her, he sat up, reached over to grip her under the arms then hauled her up across the board in front of him.

Their eyes connected for a second, hers still wide with fear, his appalled at what might have happened if he hadn't heard her cry out.

"What were you doing," he snapped, "swimming so far out at this time of night? You could have got a cramp and drowned, or been taken by a shark, or smashed against the rocks. You have a death wish or something?"

His own eyes widened with this last accusation. "Hey, that wasn't the idea, was it?" he threw at her. "You weren't trying to kill yourself, were you?"

Zoe didn't have the strength to defend herself verbally, but her face must have told him the truth.

"Sorry," he muttered. "I should have known you weren't the suicidal type. Not much of a rescuer, am I, bawling you out like that. I guess you were just hot and went for a swim, then got caught in the tide. I should have thought to warn you about the tide here this morning, but you made me so mad I just didn't think."

"Same here," she choked out.

Suddenly, she began to shiver violently.

Aiden swore, but Zoe knew it wasn't at her.

His hands were gentle as they shifted her 'round 'til she was lying lengthwise on the front of the board, her back leaning up against his chest. His *bare* chest, she noticed, despite everything.

Did he spend his whole life half naked?

Another shiver ran down her spine. A different sort of shiver.

"Don't worry," he said softly, rubbing her goose-bumped arms up and down. "You're in shock. You'll be right once I get you home and into a hot shower."

Zoe tried to protest when they reached the shore and Aiden swept her up off the board into his arms. But he silenced her with a look, and a sharp, "Don't you think you've been silly enough for one night?"

She closed her eyes and sagged against him.

"That's better," he said, satisfaction in his voice.

Zoe groaned silently, any physical exhaustion she'd been feeling swiftly overridden by the much more powerful feelings she'd been trying to fight all week-end.

Lust, hot and strong, flooded every pore of her flesh, heating her from the inside out, bringing with it an exquisitely tortuous awareness of Aiden's body. Her eyes being shut only intensified the experience. She wallowed in the strength of the arms carrying her; the warm wet wall of chest pressing against the side of her breast; his thighs slapping against her bottom as he strode across the sand.

He was taking her to his place, she knew. Into a hot shower, he'd said.

Oh, God...

The sensible part of Zoe's brain warned her not to

let him take her into the setting of one of her wildest fantasies about him. But she was too far gone for common sense, or willpower, or any high moral ground.

She felt weak with desire, driven by cravings so strong they amazed her. She wasn't used to wanting a man this much. She'd never wanted Drake like this. Lust, she decided despairingly, was nothing at all like love.

Lust focused on one thing and one thing only.

The physical.

She tensed when she felt him mounting some steps, keeping her eyes tightly shut whilst he opened his front door then carried her through, angling her body so that her feet didn't hit anything.

Zoe's heart began to pound.

It was warm inside, but not unbearably so.

He crossed a short distance, then lowered her down onto something soft and squishy. A couch by the feel of it. Leather.

She opened her eyes, then wished she hadn't. For he was looming over her in just the way she'd once imagined.

"Glad to see you're still alive," he said. "I was just about to do mouth-to-mouth resuscitation."

The thought of his mouth on hers banished what little was left of her scruples and she looked deep into his eyes, unable to hide her feelings for him any longer.

Not *wanting* to.

"I'd have liked that," she whispered, and a ripple of exquisite excitement ricocheted down her spine.

He was taken aback. No doubt about that.

But only for a second or two.

His eyes darkened with a desire of his own as he stared down at her mouth. He sat down on the edge of the couch and reached to lift some wet strands of hair away off her face. Her lips puffed apart with a soft gasp.

He didn't say a word, for which she was glad. Words would have shattered the dizzying sense of anticipation which was twisting her stomach into knots. His hands curled over her shoulders and his mouth started to descend. Zoe's heart thudded wildly.

But his head didn't come all the way down. His grip tightened on her shoulders and he drew her up toward him...slowly...then swiftly, their mouths colliding.

Zoe's valiantly suppressed passion for him was unleashed with a rush, her arms wrapping tightly 'round his torso, her mouth as hungry as his. He groaned then pushed her back down onto the couch where he kissed her 'til she thought she might die from lack of air.

He finally stopped, his breathing ragged as he sat back up abruptly, his gaze sweeping down over her own rapidly panting chest. "Let's get this off," he said, and swiftly peeled the almost-dry swimsuit from her fired-up flesh, tossing it carelessly aside.

A stunned Zoe watched it land across a black lacquered cabinet which held a big black stereo. With a single wide-eyed glance, she registered the rest of the room, which was almost as colorful as the outside of the house. Lemon walls. White woodwork. Terra-cotta ceiling.

The furniture was eclectic. A mixture of old and new. Glass-topped, wood-based and wrought-iron pieces sat side by side. The soft furnishings were just as varied, the colors bold. The drapes were black silk and the leather couch she was lying on was a deep burnt orange.

''That's better.''

Aiden's speaking again brought her back to the reality of her lying stark naked in front of him, in quite bright light. Yet oddly, she wasn't besieged by concerns over her body shape or grooming, as she was when she was with Drake. It didn't seem to matter that she had no makeup on, or her hair was sticky with saltwater and hanging down in rattails. If the look in Aiden's eyes was anything to go by, he still liked what he saw.

And she liked what she saw. She couldn't wait for Aiden to strip off as well and for her to see if *all* her fantasies about his body were true.

She swallowed at the thought.

But he didn't undress. He pushed her left leg off the couch and sat down where it had been lying, leaning forward over her body, his hands skimming over the surface of her rapidly heating skin, grazing up over the tips of her breasts.

Zoe gasped, then groaned with disappointment when his hands moved on over her collarbones and up her throat to her face. Holding the sides of her head, he bent down 'til their mouths were almost touching, but not quite. His tongue darted out to lick at her parched lips, working its way right around them. It wasn't 'til he stopped that Zoe realized she'd been holding her breath, not knowing what to do, or what to expect.

Drake had never kissed her like this before, if you could call what Aiden had just done, kissing.

"Give me your tongue," he ordered thickly.

She hesitated a fraction before sliding it slowly out between her tingling lips. She quivered when he touched the tip with his own tongue tip, then shuddered when he sucked on it.

He let it go, his head lifting slightly, his eyes frowning down at her.

She blinked up at him, her own head spinning.

"What?" she said, finding it hard to think clearly.

"Don't you like that?"

"I...I'm not sure," she admitted. "But don't stop."

He laughed a low, deliciously sexy laugh. "No fear of that, honey. I've been wanting to make love to you since you smiled at me yesterday. I've thought of nothing else but you all day."

"I...I've been thinking of you, too," she confessed.

"That's gratifying to hear. I was beginning to think I'd lost my touch. But let's not talk. We can talk later. We can talk tomorrow." His head descended again and he kissed her for real, deep, drugging kisses which had the blood pounding in her temples and her body racing like a Formula One Ferrari on the starting blocks.

She moaned when his mouth abandoned her, then

moaned again when he rubbed his stubbly chin over her breasts. Her rock-hard nipples felt like they were on fire. He licked one, then sucked on it as he had in her dream.

An electric charge zigzagged down through her stomach, centering between her thighs. She cried out and her back arched away from the couch, her hands somehow finding his hair. He stopped momentarily to lift her hands up above her head, out of the way, and they flopped back over the wide leather arm of the couch. His lips returned to take possession of her other breast, his right hand squeezing it at the same time, pushing the whole areola and nipple deeper into his mouth. When Zoe's back went to arch again, Aiden's other hand splayed across her tautly held stomach, his large palm pressing her back down against the leather, keeping her spine still, keeping *her* still whilst he continued his erotic feasting on her breasts.

The effect was incredible, her mind as turned on as her body. She writhed against those captive hands, crying out with the heady mixture of pleasure, and yes, pain. For every now and then he would nip at a nipple with his teeth, then tug on it. Zoe would suck in sharply with relief once he released the pained peak, only to perversely want him to do it again almost straight away. She swiftly became addicted to the tortuously erotic experience, never wanting him to stop.

But he did stop, and the hand on her belly moved down into the damp curls which guarded the most intimate parts of her body. His mouth followed, licking at her navel whilst those knowing fingers parted, probed and penetrated. She gasped, then gritted her teeth. He was touching her in even more ways than he had in her dream, knowing exactly where and how to give her the most exquisite yet almost mind-bending pleasure. She couldn't think. She could only feel, and crave more.

''Please,'' she begged, her head thrashing from side to side. ''Oh, please…''

He responded by flipping her right leg over his shoulder and putting his mouth where his hand had been. When she jackknifed, he gripped her bottom, lifting it, and her hips, away from the leather, giving him better access and stopping any further movement from her.

Oh…!

Drake had *never* done this to her. Never. She hadn't wanted him to. The thought had repulsed her. Aiden had done it briefly to her in her dream and she hadn't been repulsed then, but that had been fantasy. This was real!

Yet there was no embarrassment, only the most intense pleasure. And the most urgent need.

Yes, yes, she craved. *There! There!*

His tongue flicked over her swollen clitoris and she almost screamed. Another flick. Then another. She clenched her teeth harder in her jaw. She was going to come. She was sure of it. He only had to touch it with his tongue again.

He didn't touch it with his tongue again. Instead, his lips closed over the burning bursting nub of flesh and he sucked on it. Hard.

She screamed, then splintered apart, coming as she had *never* come before. Her back arched. Her mouth gaped wide. Her head exploded with a thousand stars. Brilliant and blinding. The spasms went on and on and on, wave after wave, 'til at last, it was over.

Aiden's head lifted, his expression both smug and slightly sheepish.

"I'll have to leave you to go to the bathroom for a minute or two. Your...um...enthusiasm...tipped me over the edge as well. Which is not such a tragedy, under the circumstances. Next time, we can enjoy the real thing together, and for much longer than I was anticipating. Don't go away now," he added, giving her bottom an affectionate smack before lifting her leg off his shoulder and placing it gently back down on the couch.

Zoe lay there, dazed, her other leg still dangling over the side of the sofa. She didn't have the strength to drag it up into a more modest position. Her arms were still flopped over her head and she felt...wonderful. She knew she should get up, make some excuse and leave. But she didn't have the will-power, or the desire.

The *next* time, he'd said. Had he meant tomorrow, or later tonight, after he'd rested awhile? Zoe knew that a man needed some time before he could make love again.

She winced at using that expression, for what Aiden had just done to her had nothing to do with love. It was just sex to him, the same kind of *just sex* sex Drake had had with that blonde. Yet despite knowing that, Zoe had enjoyed it far more than any lovemaking of Drake's.

This realization brought a degree of bewilderment. She'd always believed love made sex better. Certainly sex with Drake had been better than sex with Greg. That experience had been gross!

But this…this was something else yet again…

The bathroom door opened and Aiden walked back into the room, scattering all Zoe's attempts to make sense of this situation.

He was naked. And still stunningly erect.

Zoe couldn't help staring at him. Her fantasies had underestimated things a tad. "I thought you'd said that you'd…um…" Her voice trailed off as he approached her.

"I did," he agreed smilingly. "Just shows you what happens when you haven't had sex for a long while. Time to adjourn to my boudoir, I think," he said, and bent to scoop her back up into his arms.

He carried her over to another door, holding her easily with one arm whilst he opened it and flicked on the overhead light. It lit up a roomy bedroom with polished floorboards, royal-blue walls and ceiling, colorful Indian rugs and a huge brass bed that was startlingly similar to the one in her dream.

She stared at the four solid brass posts stationed at each corner and tried not to picture herself spread-eagled on top of the prettily embroidered white bedspread which looked perversely virginal.

Zoe didn't think there'd been too many virgins gracing this bed, no matter what Aiden said about not having sex for a long time. He probably thought a week was a long time.

"Don't say a word about the bedspread," he advised on seeing the expression and direction of her eyes. "My mother made it for me and I like it." With that, he threw back the spread with one hand, revealing blue sheets.

She blinked up at him. "Your mother?"

"Everyone has one," he returned dryly, and lowered her into the middle of the mattress. "But we're not going to chitchat about family tonight. Or boyfriends, or being free, or any other emotional baggage. We're going to just enjoy each other, right?"

"Right," she choked out, trying not to stare at the part of him she was hoping to enjoy most.

He pulled open the bedside drawer and extracted a box of condoms. Stripping off the cellophane wrapping, he flipped open the lid, and tipped it upside down, at least seven or eight small packets spilling out.

"Don't let me forget to use them," he told her as he climbed back onto the bed and drew her into his arms. "You've got me into such a state, it's the sort of stupid thing I might do."

He didn't forget. And neither did Zoe.

But she forgot everything else. Drake. Her conscience. Her common sense. And every inhibition she thought she had.

They were to return later, along with the shock and the shame of it all. She was no better than Drake. Worse, even.

Zoe was infinitely grateful that Aiden was asleep when she crept out of his house just before the dawn.

8

AIDEN woke with a start. And an immediate sense of something not being right.

He rolled over and realized what was wrong.

The other side of the bed was empty.

Zoe wasn't there.

"Zoe?" he called out, hoping against hope she'd just gone to the bathroom. Or the kitchen, maybe. "Zoe, are you there?"

No answer. There was no noise but the sound of gulls and waves slapping against the sand.

Throwing back the quilt, Aiden jumped out of bed and raced over to the window which gave him a view of Nigel's cottage and the road above it.

Her car was gone. Zoe was gone.

He swore.

She'd run away. Back to Sydney. Back to a lover who didn't love her. Back to a life which had obviously been making her miserable.

Aiden swore again.

She hadn't been miserable last night. She'd been in heaven.

He'd been in heaven, too. He'd never known a girl like Zoe before. She'd been so…he couldn't think of a word to describe her. Or to describe what making love with her was like. All he knew was he'd never experienced the like before.

One night simply hadn't been enough.

Yet it would have to be enough, wouldn't it?

Zoe had made the decision to leave what they'd shared at a one-night stand. To chase after her would be ridiculous.

Yet that was what Aiden was tempted to do.

"Don't be such a romantic fool," he muttered, and threw himself back into bed. "You've been given the perfect out from getting further involved, so be grateful for small mercies and forget her."

But forgetting Zoe wasn't all that easy, especially with the sheets still smelling of her female body. In the end, Aiden was forced to get up and try to rid the room of that tormentingly musky scent.

Stripping the bed clean, however, was no cure for what was ailing Aiden. Zoe was still there, in his mind. Finally, he resorted to pacing around the house, haranguing himself with cold hard logic.

"Get this straight, you dumb fool! You're nothing special to Zoe. Sleeping with you was just an impulse. She was feeling lonely and unloved and you were just there, ready, willing and able to give her a little of which she needed most at the time. Okay, a *lot* of what she needed most," he added testily. "That still doesn't mean a thing. Get real, man. Last night was just a one-night stand to her. Face it and forget it. Forget *her.*"

But even as he said those last words, his memory was propelling him back to the night before and all that had transpired between them.

He hadn't made love that many times in one night for donkey's years. He just couldn't seem to get enough of her. He'd never known a girl so responsive, yet at the same time so surprised by her responses. That was what got to him the most. The look in her eyes when he touched her. The sounds she made when he entered her.

They were addictive, those sounds. He wanted to hear them over and over. Those initial gasps of surprise. Then those soft moans of pleasure. But most of all the way she cried out when she came.

Aiden's male ego was fiercely flattered by the intensity—and frequency—of Zoe's orgasms.

Was he deluding himself in thinking she would not have found so much pleasure with any other man? And was he deluding himself in thinking *he* couldn't experience the like with any other woman?

Common sense insisted yes, he *was* deluding himself. To both questions. If Zoe had been seriously blown away by last night, she would have stayed. She would not have upped and scampered back to Sydney.

As for himself....

He'd had some great sex in his life, with a lot of different girls. Probably, the only reason his experience with Zoe stood out was because it came at the end of six months' celibacy. Naturally, he'd enjoyed it to the nth degree. What red-blooded man wouldn't?

He really had to put what had happened between them into context. They'd been ships passing in the night. For whatever reason, Zoe had needed a man and he'd obviously needed a woman. There'd been no special connection. No romantic overtones. It had been a strictly sexual encounter.

Aiden mulled over this last thought. If it had been a strictly sexual encounter on Zoe's side, then why had she run away? Wouldn't she have stayed the rest of the weekend in his bed for more of the same?

He was to think about that question for the rest of the day.

THE drive back to Sydney was a blur, but Zoe made it in good time, owing to the light traffic and excellent weather. It was just on ten as she let herself into her apartment.

Mel immediately emerged from her bedroom, dressed in her favorite blue silk shortie pajamas. "When you said you were getting on the road early this morning," she said, pushing her long blond hair out of her face, "I didn't think you meant *this* early. No, you don't have to worry. Ron's not here. I didn't let him stay the night and he was seriously displeased. But that's another story. Want some coffee?"

Zoe found a smile from somewhere. "That would be lovely."

"You look tired," Mel threw over her shoulder as they both made their way down to the kitchen. "No sleep, or difficult drive?"

"Bit of both." No way was she going to tell Mel about what had happened with Aiden.

Not that Mel would make a big deal out of it. No doubt she'd be very understanding, but she'd also want to know every single sordid detail. Zoe didn't want to relive what had to be the most shameful night of her life. The only positive aspect to come out of her disgusting behavior was that she finally and completely understood what Drake meant about a "just sex" encounter.

"So what have you decided to do about Drake?" Mel asked as she made them both a mug of coffee.

"I'm going to forgive him. If he'll forgive *me,* that is," she added ruefully.

"For what?"

Several images came to mind, and it was a struggle not to blush. "For going away without telling him where, of course," she answered. "He still hasn't rung? Or called here personally?"

"Not a peep out of him."

Zoe frowned. "I wonder if he rang me at work on Friday afternoon. I'll call Fran later and find out. So what's all this about you not letting Ron stay the night?" she asked, deftly changing the subject. "That's not like you."

Mel pulled a face. "Oh, he started getting all jealous and possessive last night. You know how I can't stand that. Frankly, he irritated me all evening and in the end, I simply didn't want to sleep with him. He wasn't impressed, I can tell you."

"Are you sure you weren't just finding fault because you want an excuse to break up with him?"

"Why on earth would I do that?"

"Because of that other fellow," Zoe said dryly. "The rich one you don't feel attracted to."

Mel blinked, then laughed. "You know, you might be right. I've been thinking about that arrogant so-

and-so quite a bit this weekend. I simply hadn't made the connection with my feelings toward Ron.''

"Be honest, Mel. You told me yourself that once you start noticing a new man, the old one is history.''

"Yeah, you're right. Hard to make love with one guy when your mind's on another.''

Zoe's mind flew immediately to Aiden. How long, she agonized, would she continue to think of him? How long before the memories of that incredible night faded to nothingness?

Never, she had to accept. Sex like that was impossible to completely forget.

But it was still only sex. And casual sex at that. The sort of sex Aiden indulged in whenever he felt the need.

Zoe was no man's fool. Not anymore. She knew exactly what kind of man Aiden was. A beach bum. A surfer. He didn't aspire. He had no ambition other than what wave he would catch that day. He made no solid plans for the future, leading a free-and-easy life with no responsibility and no commitment. Clearly, he had no regular girlfriend, either. He probably just picked up a girl whenever he felt horny. It might have been a while since he'd had sex, but he'd been well prepared, hadn't he? All those condoms at the ready!

Which was why, when she woke this morning in his arms and was tempted to stay, Zoe forced herself to get up and get out of there. She doubted he'd be too angry when he finally woke and found her gone. After all, he'd been well satisfied the night before. Frankly, she hadn't known a man could make love that many times in one night, or that he could find so many positions without leaving the bed. She'd especially liked it when he turned her sideward and...

"Excuse me," Mel said. "Snap. Snap. Here's your coffee, dreamy Daniels." And she plonked a steaming mug on the kitchen counter in front of where Zoe was standing.

"Thanks," Zoe managed to say without looking as hot and bothered as she was suddenly feeling. Damn Aiden. Why did he have to be such a fantastic lover? It was just as well he was living up at Hideaway Beach, well out of reach. Goodness knew what she would do if he'd been a Sydneysider.

She lifted the mug and started to sip.

The front doorbell ringing had Zoe's head jerking up from the drink. "Are you expecting anyone?" she asked Mel.

"No. And I'm not dressed, so I can't answer it. If it's Ron, tell him I went home for the day. He's dumb enough to believe anything." And she scuttled off to her room, taking her coffee with her.

Zoe's heart raced as she approached the door. Logic insisted it couldn't be Aiden. For one thing he had no idea where she lived. He didn't even know her second name.

Yet perversely, she wanted it to be him.

She held her breath as she swept open the door.

It wasn't Aiden. It was Drake.

She stared at him for a long moment, thinking he wasn't a patch on Aiden in the looks department, even with his smart clothes and perfect grooming.

When Drake stared right back at her, Zoe suddenly

remembered she had no makeup on and her hair was a mess. She had showered after leaving Aiden's bed, and thrown on some shorts and a T-shirt, but that had been the extent of her efforts.

"So I was right," he snapped, stalking past her into the apartment. "You didn't go off to some secret destination for the weekend at all." He spun 'round to face her. "That wretched Fran insisted you had when I dropped by your office late on Friday, and I actually believed her. But I got to thinking over the weekend and I finally realized it wasn't at all like my Zoe to do something like that."

Any intention Zoe had of being apologetic and forgiving was temporarily sidelined by his pompous and almost patronizing attitude. She swung the door shut and crossed her arms, struggling to keep her irritation under control.

"I *did* go away," she informed him curtly, biting her tongue lest she add she'd done a lot more than go away for the weekend. She'd gotten herself well and truly laid, and by a far better lover than him!

Guilt consumed her the moment this last thought entered her head. For in all honesty, Drake was quite a good lover. It was just that she was different with Aiden than she was with him. More relaxed. And consequently, far more orgasmic. And how!

"I just got back," she said, not wanting to think about that.

He looked her up and down again. "You look a bit travel worn. Back from where, might I ask? Or am I not to be told where you went as part of my punishment?"

Zoe sighed and uncrossed her arms. "I wasn't trying to punish you, Drake. Not really. I just needed
time to think."

"Then tell me where you went."

"Does it matter?"

"It does, if you want us to get back together
again."

Zoe stiffened. "I don't like ultimatums."

"And I don't like being given the runaround. Either you love me or you don't. Either you forgive me
or you don't. Either you want us to have a relationship or you don't. I've apologized for what happened
down in Melbourne. And I've promised you faithfully
not to do it again. I can do no more. Now the rest is
up to you. So I'm asking you again, where did you
go this weekend?"

For a split second, Zoe was tempted to tell him to
go away. But then she remembered how lonely life
would be without him. It wasn't as though she had
any future with the likes of Aiden. No doubt he was
at this very moment very relieved that she'd done a
flit and left last night at a one-night stand. Men like
him ran a mile from commitment, or complications.

"At a little beach near Port Stephens," she confessed. "I…I stayed at a motel." Zoe thought it best
not to mention she'd stayed at Nigel's weekender.
Drake didn't like Nigel one little bit. He was scathing
about all men—and women—who weren't straight.

"I see." His head cocked on one side and he
smiled one of his most charming smiles. "You
know…I rather like your hair like that. I didn't realize
it was naturally curly." He reached out and picked

up a curl, winding it 'round his finger, then looping it behind her ear. "You should wear it like this more often on the weekends. It looks sexy. *You* look sexy. You're not wearing a bra, either, are you?" he said, his right hand sliding up underneath her T-shirt toward her left breast. She gasped when he touched a nipple which was still hard and aching from the night before.

"God, I've missed you, Zoe," he groaned, sliding his other arm around her waist and bending his head to nuzzle at her neck. "There's no one like you. I love it that you haven't slept around, that you're so sweet and nice." His mouth traveled up her throat, and all the while his hand was cupped around her breast, his thumb pad rolling over the sensitized peak.

A moan escaped her mouth. But the feeling was more discomfort than pleasure. Soon she was screaming inside her head. When his lips finally covered hers and his tongue started to push into her mouth, she gagged and wrenched herself away.

"No!" she cried out.

"What?" For a moment he looked stunned, then merely angry. "More punishment, Zoe? Is that what this is?"

"No," she said shakily, shocked by her reaction to Drake's lovemaking. "I...I just don't want to. It's too soon. I...I need a bit more time. I can't stop thinking about you and that blonde." Which might have been the case last Friday, but no longer. What Zoe couldn't stop thinking about this morning was herself and Aiden.

"When do you think it will not be too soon, then?" he bit out.

"I don't know."

"Don't cut off your nose to spite your face, Zoe. You were enjoying what I was doing just then. Your nipple was like a rock."

She didn't have the heart to tell him the truth. That it wasn't him who'd aroused her.

"I love you, Zoe. And I need you. Don't make me wait too long."

"Is that a threat?"

"No. A fact. When a man loves a woman as I love you, he wants to make love to her."

Zoe stared at him. He was right, and vice versa. Why, then, didn't *she* want to make love with *him* anymore? If she loved him, she would.

Maybe it *was* just too soon. Maybe a bad conscience was the culprit here, that's all. Maybe in time, everything would be all right.

Drake looked belligerent before suddenly backing down, his eyes softer. "Look, I do realize I hurt you. A lot. And yes, I can understand you might need some time to completely forgive and forget. How about I leave you in peace this week and give you some space to get over things?"

"I'd appreciate that," she said.

"But come next Saturday night, I'm having one of my parties, and I'd really like you to co-host it, as you have for the last few times. I don't want to have to explain my girlfriend's absence to my clients and colleagues. Would you do that for me?"

Zoe could not think of a reason to refuse. "Of course I will."

"You're a doll. And you'll help get the food and everything ready that day? As you know, I do have to work on Saturdays. It's our busiest day of the week."

"If you want me to."

"If I want you to! I'd be lost without you. You're such a wonderful organizer. And hopefully, by then, you'll feel comfortable about staying the night."

"Maybe..."

"I promise I won't press if it's still too soon."

Zoe suddenly realized Drake was bending over backward to be understanding and accommodating. Guilt consumed her anew.

"I'm sorry for being so difficult."

"That's perfectly all right, darling. I understand. Honest. The fault was all mine."

Zoe wished he wouldn't say things like that. It made her feel rotten. She would just die if Drake ever found out what she'd done.

Thankfully, there was little chance of that. She had no intention of confessing, and the chance of running into Aiden down here in Sydney was minimal. Even if by some incredible coincidence they did, Zoe doubted Aiden would make an embarrassing scene the way that blonde had done. That wouldn't be his style.

Drake pulled out his wallet and counted out five hundred-dollar bills. "Here," he said. "Buy yourself a smashing new dress for the party."

"Oh, no, no, I couldn't," she protested, shaking her head and refusing to take them.

"But why ever not?" He seemed genuinely perplexed. And he had every right to be. It wasn't the first time he'd bought her clothes and she'd never objected before.

"Well, I...I..."

"Don't be silly," he said, and pressed the money into her hands. "Just make sure it's not too revealing. Can't have all those playboys I sell penthouses to lusting after your perfect little body and trying to chat you up. Not that you'd look twice at any other man. That's the thing I value most about you, darling. Your lovely old-fashioned standards. I could trust you with any man in any situation. But I'll get going now and leave you to have a rest. You do look a little tired. I'll be in touch before Saturday by phone. That okay?"

"I guess so," she said weakly.

"Great. Look after yourself and don't work too hard this week." He bent to peck her softly on the cheek. Then left.

Tears filled Zoe's eyes by the time she shut the door behind him.

I could trust you with any man in any situation.

Oh, Drake. If only you knew.

9

AIDEN dialed the only telephone number committed to his memory and waited for his mother to answer. It rang several times before she picked up.

"Kristy Mitchell," came her softly lyrical voice, sounding just a little fuzzy around the edges, as though she'd just got out of bed.

Given it was only eight-fifteen in the evening, Aiden didn't think she'd been asleep. He smiled. Same old Mom. He wondered who her latest lover was and if he knew he had no chance of either moving in with her or marrying her. His mom was not a marrying kind of woman.

Much like he was not a marrying kind of man. Perhaps it was in the genes.

"Hi, there, honey-bunch," he said in greeting. "How's my best girl?"

"Aiden!" she cried. "Oh, how lovely to hear your voice. I was just thinking about you."

"In what way?"

"If you really want to know, I was wondering when you were going to give up all that celibacy nonsense and get back to normal again."

"Well, actually, Mom, I, er…" His voice trailed off rather suggestively.

"You didn't! I don't believe it. At last! Who was she?"

"Just a girl."

"Just a girl my foot! She'd have to be something special to drag you out of your self-imposed monkhood. The last time I talked to you, you were adamant that you still wanted nothing to do with the opposite sex. You said life was much happier without females in it."

"Yeah and I was right," he snapped, giving in to the spleen which had been building all day.

"Oh, dear. You sound upset. What happened, sweetie?"

"I don't want to talk about it," he grumped.

"Of course you do. That's why you called me. Just wait a second 'til I get myself a glass of wine."

Aiden was left dangling for a minute or two whilst his mother collected one of her favorite creature comforts.

He smiled wryly at how little time it had taken for her to find out the reason behind his call. She was a very astute woman, especially when it came to her one and only son. Because of course he *had* rung her to talk about Zoe. He just didn't like to admit it. He was twenty-eight years old. He should know his own mind by now. And know what he wanted out of life. It galled him that he still felt at sea on such matters.

"I'm back," she trilled. "Now don't go being a typical male. I want the whole unvarnished truth, not some edited version to flatter your ego."

Aiden sighed. Maybe this wasn't such a good idea after all. But it was too late now. So he told her the whole unvarnished truth, right down to the bit where Zoe did a bunk whilst he was still asleep.

"Mmm," was her initial highly instructive comment.

"Is that all you've got to say?"

"Give me a moment, sweetie. I'm thinking, and trying to remember how I might have felt and acted when I was Zoe's age. How old did you say she was?"

"I have no idea. When I first met her last Friday I thought she was in her late twenties, but the next morning, without all that makeup on, she looked about eighteen. My guess is early to mid-twenties."

"And she's from Sydney. And she has a boyfriend. Not a married one, I hope."

"Zoe wouldn't have anything to do with a married man."

"You sound quite sure of that."

"I am."

"Mmm."

There was a wealth of underlying meaning in that "Mmm." Aiden wished he knew what it was.

"Whatever the case," his mother continued, "she still has a lover who's creating problems for her. Perhaps the man in question is her boss. What does she do for a living?"

"I have no idea about that either. But judging by the way she looked and dressed on Friday, she's no factory worker. Something in an office is my guess."

"And what does she think *you* do?"

"Er...not much."

"She didn't recognize you?"

"No."

"And you didn't enlighten her," came the dry comment.

"No."

"Oh, Aiden, Aiden. I thought I taught you to be straight with people, especially women."

"I used to be. But where did it get me, Mom? In court, and in all the newspapers."

"Nothing is to be gained by lying," she pronounced firmly.

"That's not true," he countered sharply. "Marcie gained a million-dollar apartment full, a snazzy little sports car and two hundred thousand in cash."

"Material assets count for nothing if you lose your soul, son."

Aiden rolled his eyes. She was always talking like that. About souls and stuff. Yet she wasn't religious in the conventional sense of the word. There was nothing at all conventional about Kristy Mitchell.

"Yeah, well, maybe I've already lost mine." There was a time not so long ago when all he thought about was material assets.

"Don't be ridiculous. You have a wonderful soul. I know. I gave it to you."

Nothing modest about his mother, either.

"But back to Zoe," she said. "Are you thinking she might be your one true love?"

Aiden rolled his eyes again. Not the one-true-love thing!

"Now who's being ridiculous, Mom. I hardly know the girl."

"I only knew your father one short week and he

was my one true love. I fell for him the moment I set eyes on him and there's never been another to touch him since. I couldn't even bear to be with another man for years afterward.''

Aiden smothered a groan. How often had he heard this same story, about the drop-dead gorgeous hunk she'd met at a party when she'd been sixteen. How she'd been immediately smitten. How he'd gotten her pregnant the same night and been tragically killed in a head-on smash with a truck a week later. He'd been riding a motorcycle at the time. And speeding, of course.

What a hero!

What an idiot.

''Yeah right, Mom. But I rather doubt dear old Dad felt the same way about you. It was more likely just sex. You yourself explained to me when I was a teenager that sex and love were two entirely different things, and not to confuse them.''

''So why are you?''

''Why am I what?''

''Confused. If you're so sure it was just sex, then let it go. Let *her* go.''

''I can't,'' he confessed.

''I see.''

''If you really do see, then tell me what to do.''

''You already know what you should do, Aiden. You just want me to give you a push in the right direction.''

''Meaning?''

''Meaning you should go after her and make sure

of both your feelings, one way or the other. Otherwise you'll always wonder."

"I told you, Mom. I'm pretty sure it was just sex. Admittedly, it was the best sex I've ever had, but I reckon that was because I hadn't had any in such a long time. What do you think? That could be the reason, couldn't it?"

"It's possible, but you can't really speak for the girl though, can you?"

"I guess not," he agreed.

"Look, the least you can do is call your lawyer friend and make a few discreet inquiries about this girl. Find out a bit about her background and this boyfriend of hers."

"Yes, I supposed there's no harm in that."

"No harm at all. Keep me posted."

"I'll do that." Having made up his mind, at least about his immediate course of action, Aiden felt infinitely better. "Thanks, Mom. You're the best."

"And don't you forget it!"

Aiden hung up, opened the drawer which contained his red leather address book and looked up Nigel's home phone number, dialing straight away before he changed his mind.

Nigel answered almost before it rang at the other end. "How dare you call me again!" he raged down the line. "I told you not to. There's nothing more to be said. I won't forgive you, Jeremy, not even if you got down on your knees and begged. Not even if you…"

"It's not Jeremy," Aiden broke in before Nigel

could elaborate on what Jeremy might do on his knees to be forgiven. "It's Aiden. Aiden Mitchell."

"Oh. Aiden. Oh. Er. Right." Nigel cleared his throat. "Sorry. Had a bit of a tiff with Jeremy and he keeps ringing."

"So I gathered. Blotted his copybook, did Jeremy?"

"Unfaithful little… Can't keep it zipped up. But he *is* gorgeous," Nigel added, sighing wistfully. "I guess I'll forgive him in the end. So what's up?"

"I need your help with something…"

It took Nigel 'til mid Monday morning to get the last of the information Aiden wanted and call him back.

"You're out of luck," he said. "She's gone back to Drake. Which is a pity. I can't stand that sleazebag."

Aiden felt like he'd been punched in the stomach.

So she'd forgiven her cheating boyfriend. Straight away. Raced right back into his arms the night after she'd spent with *him.*

When Nigel revealed last night the circumstances leading up to his lending Zoe his place, Aiden had been confident she wouldn't go back to someone who'd cheated on her. He'd also started thinking she might have fled his bed because she'd been confused and embarrassed. He'd started hoping that maybe she'd be interested in their getting back together again.

Just to see, of course, if there *was* any special connection between them.

"How do you know, Nigel?" he asked, frowning.

"Did she actually say so? You didn't ask her any of this straight out, did you? I warned you not to mention me at all."

"Would I do that?" He sounded offended and incredulous at the same time. "*Moi?* The soul of tact and discretion? Lawyer to the stars? Never in a million years! Besides, Zoe and I are not on such friendly terms that I could ask her anything of a personal or intimate nature. Anything I know about this, I've found out through Fran, plus a sneaky peek at the card attached to the two dozen red roses sitting on Zoe's desk this morning. It read, 'To the sweetest, most understanding girl in the world. All my love, Drake.'"

Aiden's stomach tightened. Not much doubt about the situation now.

So what had *he* been? came the angry question. Revenge? Payback time?

Maybe *that* was what was behind Zoe's surprise at enjoying herself with him so much. She hadn't expected to. She'd been out for vengeance, not pleasure.

But she *had* found pleasure. A great deal of pleasure. Strange...if she loved this Drake so much.

Another explanation occurred to Aiden. Maybe she *didn't* love the boyfriend. Maybe she'd been lying about that. Maybe she was just with him for the money. Which explained why she'd enjoyed herself so much the other night, but why she'd still gone back to the boyfriend.

Aiden was rocked by this possibility. No way would he get mixed up with another female who wanted nothing from a man but his money.

But no sooner had he thought this than he remembered Zoe had already proven she wanted something from *him* other than his money. She'd wanted his body, over and over. Whatever had been her initial reason for letting him make love to her, true desire had soon taken over. Aiden knew when a girl was enjoying herself in his bed, and Zoe certainly had.

"How wealthy is this Drake?" he asked Nigel, trying to get the full picture here.

"Can't say precisely. I gather he's one hotshot of a real-estate salesman. He's sold oodles of those flash inner-city apartments with harbor views. Fran even bought one, which should tell you something. She's not an easy sell. He lives pretty high. Owns one of the apartments in the same building as Fran's. But I seriously doubt his bank balance would rival yours."

"Mmm."

"I always worry when you start mmming like that."

Aiden laughed. It seemed enigmatic mmming ran in the family. "Did you find out for me what branch our hot-shot salesman works at?"

"North Sydney."

"And the phone number?"

"What exactly are you going to do, Aiden?"

"That depends."

"On what?"

"On how I feel by the end of this week."

10

ZOE walked from room to room, checking that everything was ready for the party. The flowers. The music. The snacks. The drinks.

A superb buffet supper awaited in the kitchen. Nothing hot, just salads and seafood, plus a selection of mouthwatering desserts, all delivered straight from the best city store food hall.

Drake didn't expect her to cook on these occasions, just order what she thought necessary on his credit card, then be there to collect the food and set everything out. But even doing that was a lot of work for upward of fifty guests.

Drake wasn't keen on hiring waiters to walk around with trays at his parties. He preferred having everything laid out on tables placed strategically around the large living areas, as well as out on the terrace. He liked to create a relaxed, informal atmosphere where people had something to do besides stand stiffly around in groups. Drake found there was more mingling if the guests had to get their own food and drinks.

And he was right. His parties were always a huge success. Drake had his successful-host routine honed down. After answering the door personally for the first hour or so, he then continuously circulated, chatting and telling jokes and making people feel special. Zoe was left to welcome any stragglers after that, as well as ensure the snack bowls were kept filled, ice buckets replenished and supper served right on eleven.

Frankly, for all Drake's talk about wanting her by his side at this do, Zoe would not see all that much of him tonight.

She was glancing around, satisfying herself that everything was ready, when she noticed that the arrangement of fresh Australian flowers on the hall stand in the foyer looked a bit lopsided. She hurried over, changed the position of two of the waratahs, then stood back to inspect the result.

"Stop fussing, darling."

Zoe glanced over her shoulder to see that Drake had finally emerged from his bedroom, ready for the night ahead. He'd chosen to wear all black, a perfect foil for his apartment's largely gray-and-white decor. He looked sleek and successful, and yes, sexy, she supposed. Eight days ago, she certainly would have thought so.

So why didn't she now?

Normally, she would have complimented him on the way he looked, but she found the words would not come. She went back to fiddling with the flowers, even though she knew they were fine.

"Don't change another single solitary stem," he advised. "They're perfect. Everything's perfect. Now go and make *yourself* perfect before people start arriving. As much as I quite like you in those shorts, I can't wait to see you in that fantastic little number you bought. I'm so glad you splurged on a designer dress and not something off the peg. It wouldn't do for my image, you know, if some other female turned up tonight wearing the same dress as my girlfriend.''

''Yes, that *would* be a catastrophe, wouldn't it?'' she snapped before she could stop herself. But her nerves were suddenly stretched to breaking point.

This last week had been the longest and most agitating week of her life. Drake giving her time and space hadn't really worked at all. By Friday, her head was even more full of memories of her time up at Hideaway Beach, and her body strung tight with a frustration she'd never known before.

In an effort to find distraction from her never-ending fantasies about Aiden, she'd worked like a demon at the office, staying back late every night, clearing her In tray to perfection, catching up on filing and correspondence, and being so super efficient that even Fran hadn't been able to find fault. Not once. Which was a first. Fran was a very demanding boss.

Then last night after work she'd spent hours looking for the sort of party dress Drake would approve of. Not that she was complaining. The lengthy shopping expedition had kept her busy, and her mind blissfully Aiden-free for a while.

She'd finally settled on a mauve satin slip dress which wasn't too revealing, courtesy of the bodice being overlaid with pink lace.

Unfortunately—or perhaps fortunately at the time—she had no shoes to match, and it had taken a further hour to find strappy pink-and-mauve imitation crocodile skin shoes.

She'd ended up spending more than the five hundred dollars Drake had given her, adding some of her own money. An unusual extravagance for Zoe. But she'd needed a lift, and she'd wanted to really please Drake.

Guilt, she supposed.

Lots of her actions this past week had been inspired by guilt.

This morning, she'd dragged her dream-haunted sleep-deprived body out of bed and driven over to Drake's place extra early where she'd propelled herself into all the preparations for the party with enthusiasm, angrily resolving not to think of Aiden anymore.

And it had worked to a degree. She'd even convinced herself that if she got nicely drunk tonight, she might be able to successfully go to bed with Drake after the party and rid herself of some of this hideous frustration.

But the moment Drake had come home from the office around five, cock-a-hoop about some wealthy world champion sportsman he'd snared as a client this afternoon, Zoe had found him infinitely irritating, especially when he told her he'd asked the wretched man to the party tonight.

As if he hadn't asked enough people already!

She'd been glad to have Drake disappear for the past hour into his room to shower and shave and dress, but the moment he'd reappeared, he'd rubbed her up the wrong way again, hence her sarcastic remark.

Drake glared at her across the room, his black eyes cold and angry.

Zoe shook her head at herself. She was acting exactly as Mel had done with Ron, deliberately finding fault and picking a fight. The difference in Mel's case, however, was that she'd got together with her new man this week, whereas *she* would never see Aiden again.

"I'm sorry," she said with a weary sigh. "That was uncalled for. I'm just tired, and a little nervous. You know I hate making small talk with strangers, especially rich and famous strangers. I know very little about sport. What was it you said this new client of yours was world champion in?"

"*Ex* world champion, actually. And it's surfing."

"Surfing!" she echoed disbelievingly. Of all the sports in the world, Drake's client had to be involved in the one sport she didn't want to *think* about, let alone talk about.

Drake's expression was wry. "I know. You never think of surfers as ever being seriously rich. But believe me, Mitch is."

"Mitch," she repeated. "Sounds American."

"No, he's Australian through and through. Owns the Aus-Surf chain of stores. He started up several years ago with one small shop after injury forced him to retire early. Now Aus-Surf shops are franchised all around Australia. You must have seen them. They're everywhere."

"Yes, yes, I have." They sold surfing equipment

and clothes and accessories. As much as she liked the beach, Aus-Surf gear was not quite Zoe's cup of tea. Too bright and bold.

"They're doing extra well at the moment," Drake rattled on, right in his element. Whenever he landed a wealthy client, he made it his business to find out all about him. "In the beginning, a lot of people thought the clothes were too loud and bright, but the surfing crowd loved them. Now that big colors have become all the rage in fashion, their sales have soared. Not that *I'd* ever be seen dead in that sort of thing. You should have seen what our multi-millionaire was wearing today. Can you imagine me in a lime-green shirt?"

"No," she said truthfully. But she could imagine Aiden. He'd look gorgeous in it. He'd look gorgeous in anything. He looked extra gorgeous in nothing.

Zoe sighed. Would it never stop, these thoughts?

"I know, I know," Drake said sheepishly. "I do rave on. Sorry. Go and get yourself ready. I'll get the ice ready for the drinks."

Zoe trailed off into the guest room where she'd put her things earlier, depression overwhelming her. All she wanted to do was run away, away from Drake, away from this party, and right away from playboy sportsmen who had egos larger than Mount Olympus and always thought they were God's gift to women. If she was strictly honest with herself, she wanted to run right back to Hideaway Beach. And to Aiden. She didn't care if he only wanted sex from her. That was all she seemed to want from him. It was certainly all she could think about.

Sometimes, she regretted running away from his bed last Sunday. She should have stayed, at least for the rest of the weekend. There was so much she hadn't done with him and which she'd since ached to do. Make love to him in a shower. In the ocean. With her on top. With her hands. Her mouth. Her breasts. One persistent fantasy was to tie *him* to that brass bed. To have him at her mercy. To drive him wild!

"Zoe!" Drake called out. "I don't hear that shower running. Get a move on, darling. Time's a wasting."

Zoe squeezed her eyes tightly shut. Oh, dear, what was she doing, wallowing in such thoughts? They were foolish. Futile. And so frustrating!

Yet, oh, the excitement they evoked. And the heat. She could feel it even now, spreading across her skin. A melting burning heat which scorched her face even as it seared between her thighs. She knew, without checking, that she would be wet. She'd been wet down there all week.

Groaning, she stripped off and plunged into a cold shower.

"Wow!" Drake exclaimed, when she emerged from the guest room fifty minutes later, looking cool and pretty in her mauve-and-pink dress. On the surface there was not a hint of the turmoil which was still rampaging beneath her seemingly controlled exterior.

She forced a smile as Drake walked slowly toward her, his dark eyes eating her up.

"I meet with your approval, do I?" she said.

"And how." He slid his arms around her waist and drew her close. "I might have to keep you really close by my side tonight. Can't have you swanning around by yourself looking this delicious, especially not with men like Mitch on the prowl.''

''I don't think you have to worry about me with men like this Mitch,'' she murmured ruefully, at the same time trying not to physically shrink away at the feel of Drake's hands on her. She managed not to look repulsed, but any hope she'd been harboring that she could go to bed with Drake tonight was well and truly dashed. There was just so much faking a girl could do in one lifetime.

''He's considered very handsome,'' Drake said. ''He's also looking for a penthouse to replace the one he had to hand over to his last girlfriend. She took him to court for breach of promise last year when he tried to dump her, and she won.''

''Good for her,'' Zoe said. ''Should be more of it.''

''Oh, I don't know. Men like that are a target for gold diggers. The girl in question said she gave up her career to live with him and look after him like a wife. She said he'd promised marriage but when she tried to set a date for their wedding, he told her he'd changed his mind, then tossed her out. His defense was that she was lying and that she'd only been house-sitting while he was traveling. But under oath he did admit to sleeping with her, though he claimed it was only once. If you saw the female in question, you'd know that stretched credibility. She was a stunner. Surely you must remember the case. It was in all the Sydney papers.''

''No. You know I don't read newspapers much.

And I rarely watch the news. It's always so miserable.''

"True. Still, it was your firm which handled the defense. Or should I say, the lovely Nigel. No wonder they lost.''

"I don't have much to do with Nigel and his clients,'' Zoe said stiffly, hating the way Drake spoke about gay men. "Still, I think that had to be before I joined the firm. I've only been there five months, remember?''

"You're right. I think it was before that. But enough chitchat. God, you look good enough to eat,'' he growled, his head dipping to her neck.

"Drake, please,'' she said, wriggling out of his arms. "It took me ages to get my makeup and hair just right.''

He stepped back and gave her a narrow-eyed look. "You aren't going to knock me back again tonight, are you?''

Panic struck. "You...you said you wouldn't press.''

"Did I?'' he said coldly. "Silly me. Very well, Zoe, I won't press. But I wouldn't play this particular hand for too long, if I were you. I am not a patient man by nature.''

"I didn't say I *wouldn't* sleep with you tonight,'' she said, feeling wretched.

"How generous of you.''

"Drake, please, don't be like that. If you truly loved me, you'd understand.''

"If you truly loved *me,* this wouldn't be an issue.

You'd be only too happy to make up with me in bed.''

"It's not as simple as that for women.''

"It is for some,'' he muttered.

The doorbell ringing was a relief.

"We'll talk about this later,'' Drake said, firmly taking Zoe's arm and propelling her across the marble-floored foyer. "Meanwhile, stop looking so grim and try smiling.''

"Bob!'' he exclaimed expansively on yanking open the front door. "And Tracy! Now this is a surprise. But a pleasant one, I assure you.''

Zoe smiled at Bob whom she'd met before. He worked as a salesman for the same real-estate agency as Drake. About forty, balding, overweight, and divorced, Bob never missed one of Drake's parties.

She had no idea who Tracy was, but she was very attractive in a brassy bottle-blonde fashion. Thirtyish, she was wearing a short tight animal-print leather skirt and a black lace halter top with a deep crossover V neckline. Her hair was done up in that tousled just-got-out-of-bed look and her earlobes sported diamanté drop earrings which dangled down to her shoulders. Her breasts, which were big, were also braless, with large pointy nipples which were difficult to ignore under black lace.

"I don't think I've had the pleasure,'' Zoe directed at the blonde.

"Tracy is our new receptionist,'' Drake informed her a bit brusquely. "My girlfriend, Zoe.''

Zoe smiled at Tracy who smiled sweetly back

whilst giving Zoe the once-over with her heavily made-up eyes.

"Bob, you sly dog, you," Drake went on with a suggestive chuckle. "I had no idea you and Tracy were dating."

"We're not, are we, love? Tracy kindly offered to come with me tonight when I complained I had no one to bring."

"It was my pleasure, Bob, darling," the blonde returned brightly. "And who knows? Maybe we'll do it again sometime. Well, well, so this is how you live, is it, Drake?" She swept past them into the elegant columned foyer, showing everyone a rear view as provocative as her front. The top had no back to speak of, and she had an enviable behind, the shape of which Zoe knew would never be hers. A small tight butt, with narrow hips. Her legs were of enviable quality too, shapely calves and slender ankles, shown to advantage in black four-inch stilettos, complete with sexy ankle straps.

She made Zoe feel just a little girlish in her outfit. She suddenly wished she'd bought something sexier to wear.

The arrival of more guests was a welcome distraction and she was soon concentrating on her hostess role, all silly female jealousies banished from her mind. Drake handed over the doorman duties to her a good deal earlier than usual, which kept her busy. She tried not to worry about the fact he hadn't smiled at her, or spoken to her personally since their earlier altercation. She understood he was angry with her.

She also understood that if she didn't come across tonight, their relationship was over.

It was a dilemma Zoe didn't want to face 'til she had to. Meanwhile, she downed a couple of glasses of Chardonnay and waited for the alcohol to work. With a bit of luck, it might do the trick and she would suddenly find Drake attractive again. At worst, it would at least make her feel less tense and more relaxed.

The party was humming by ten, with Drake's prized new client not yet making an appearance. Clearly he wasn't going to show. Zoe supposed men like that received invitations to parties all the time. They couldn't go to all of them. Still, Drake was going to be disappointed which didn't augur well for his mood later on.

When the doorbell rang again just after ten, Zoe hoped it was this Mitch fellow and hurried to answer it, sipping her third glass of wine as she went. She swept open the door just as she was lifting her glass to her lips once more.

But it wasn't the missing Mitch. It was Aiden standing there, looking even more handsome than she remembered. He was clean shaven for starters and dressed beautifully in fawn chinos and a crisp blue shirt the color of his eyes.

Zoe's eyes rounded at the sight of him. Her mouth gaped. Her hand froze.

All coherent thought fled.

11

AIDEN knew, the moment he saw Zoe again, why he'd finally given in and come to Sydney. Just the sight of her took his breath away.

But the shock on her face brought home to him that she hadn't expected to see him again. She thought he'd been safely consigned to the closet, a spur-of-the-moment indiscretion which she didn't want to think of ever again.

Facing the cold hard reality that he'd meant nothing more to her than a one-night stand pained Aiden more than he could ever have envisaged. But at least he had answers to his questions now. If nothing else, this trip to Sydney had stopped any stupid fantasy that there was something special between them, or—as his romantic-minded mother would have put it—that Zoe might have been his one true love.

To think he'd even begun considering such a silly idea!

The shock on Zoe's face swiftly changed to a panicky confusion. "I…I never imagined for a moment that you'd follow me," she babbled. "I didn't think you'd care. But…how on earth did you know I'd be *here?* I mean…there's no way that…oh…oh, I see…you found out through Nigel, didn't you? He told you about me and Drake.'' Her big brown eyes suddenly widened with alarm. ''You're not going to tell Drake about last Saturday night, are you?''

Fear over having her own unfaithfulness exposed showed Aiden that Zoe's first priority in life was still the boyfriend.

Which again begged the question of why? Love? Or money?

Aiden was finding it harder and harder to believe it was love. Drake might be a super-successful salesman—and reasonably good-looking—but he was also a major sleazebag, as Nigel had accurately judged. Aiden hadn't needed more than an hour with the man himself this afternoon to prove that. The lewd way Drake had flirted with the receptionist at his office had been a real eye-opener. If that blonde at the conference was the first female he'd two-timed Zoe with, Aiden would eat his hat.

But then…maybe Zoe already knew that. Maybe she'd decided to turn a blind eye to Drake's extracurricular activities in exchange for what he could give her.

Not for the first time, Aiden speculated that perhaps when Zoe found out how well heeled *he* was, maybe she'd change her priorities. It was telling that having seen her again, he no longer held the high moral ground that he would not become involved with another materialistic fortune-hunting woman. As his eyes swept over Zoe in that delicious dress and his body lurched into that unable-to-be-ignored-or-subdued hard-on which had tormented him all week, Aiden realized that he would do whatever it took to have sex with her again. He'd make any compromise. Play any role she fancied. Give her anything she wanted.

"No, I'm not going to tell Drake about us," he promised, since doing so would hardly endear him to her. "So there's no need to worry. But the thing is, Zoe, I'm not exactly…"

"Mitch!" Drake interrupted before Aiden could enlighten Zoe of his identity and financial status. "So you came after all. And you're already trying to chat up my girl. Shame on you!"

"This is *Mitch?*" Zoe exclaimed, clearly stunned. "The same Mitch you were telling me about earlier on?"

"The one and only," Drake confirmed, sliding a possessive arm around Zoe's slender waist and pulling her close. "Why, darling? Who did you think he was?"

"He introduced himself as Aiden," she said coldly.

Aiden wondered what on earth Drake had told her about him to produce such contempt in her eyes.

"Mitch is a nickname I had back in my surfing days," he hastened to tell her. "But Aiden is my real name. Aiden Mitchell." He didn't want her thinking he'd lied to her about everything. Only his owning the weekender.

"Mitch suits you better," Drake insisted.

"If you'll excuse me," Zoe said brusquely. "I have food to get out of the refrigerator or it'll be too chilled for supper. I'm sure you two boys have plenty to talk about."

Aiden could have kicked himself as he watched her

walk off. Hell, he'd handled this all wrong. He should never have accepted Drake's invitation and come here tonight. It was a tactical mistake.

Why hadn't he foreseen how annoyed Zoe would be when she found out who he really was? No one liked to be made a fool of. It just showed you what happened when men started thinking with their bodies instead of their brains. Off goes your head and on goes a pumpkin!

"Don't worry about Zoe," Drake said, waving Aiden inside and shutting the door behind them. "She's in a bit of a mood tonight. Been like it all week."

Now *that,* Aiden liked to hear. It meant that maybe Zoe *hadn't* been able to dismiss him, or last Saturday night, so easily from her mind. Maybe she'd been thinking about him, too.

"Come on, Mitch, I'll get you a drink." Drake led Aiden down some steps into the reasonably crowded living room and over to a side table on which stood a wide array of liquor and a selection of clean glasses. "What's your poison? You look like a Scotch on the rocks man." He reached for a decanter.

"A light beer would do fine. I never drink hard liquor. A habit from my surfing days."

Drake's hand lifted from the decanter. "Really? I'm surprised. Come over here to the bar then. I've got all kinds of beer chilling in the bar fridge. Hi, Alex, Babs," he said to a couple in a dimly lit corner who might have been dancing, or indulging in some foreplay. It was hard to tell which. They were certainly kissing. "Having fun? Great. Change the music if you like.'' A sultry blues number was playing in the background.

"We already did," they chorused back, briefly coming up for air.

The bar was a built-into-the-construction corner, with a gray marble top and stainless-steel stools, reflective of all the furniture which was minimalist and cold-looking.

"Take a seat," Drake offered, waving toward the stools.

Aiden decided to stand. Drake extracted a can of light beer, zapped open the top and poured it into a glass. "I thought surfers were supposed to be a pretty wild bunch, especially with the booze and the broads."

"I discovered fairly early on that a hangover wasn't conducive to good form on the board." He accepted the beer and took a small swallow, wondering all the while how he was going to get rid of this creep and go explain things to Zoe.

"What about the women?" Drake persisted. "Don't tell me you were one of those dedicated athletes who abstained from sex before competition for fear it would drain all your energy away!"

"Can't say I ever subscribed to that particular theory," Aiden said dryly, and Drake laughed.

"Same here. I find sex most invigorating activity. Sometimes, with the right girl, the more I have, the more I want."

Aiden felt sick with jealousy at this revelation, 'til he realized Drake might not be talking about Zoe.

"Well, you do have one very pretty girlfriend," he remarked leadingly.

"What? Oh, yeah, Zoe's pretty enough. But to be honest, she's a bit on the prissy side when it comes to sex."

"Oh?" Aiden had considerable difficulty hiding his shock. There'd been nothing prissy about Zoe the other night. Not once she got going.

"You know what it's like. You're a man of the world." Drake dropped his voice to a conspiratorial whisper. "Some women like their sex all sweet and sugar-coated. Others like it any time, any place, any way. I figured out when I was just a lad that the first kind are for marrying, and the others are just for screwing."

"I presume the blonde at your office today is just for screwing then," Aiden said dryly. "What was her name? Tracy something or other?"

"Hey, man. Hush up. We don't want Zoe hearing anything like that. Not only that, would you believe Tracy's here tonight? Turned up unexpectedly with one of my colleagues. I nearly died. Talk about living dangerously. Luckily, I've been able to avoid her all evening."

"I think your luck might have just run out," Aiden said, glancing over Drake's shoulder through the archway which led into the room beyond. "Because your blonde's heading this way. She's all alone and she looks like she's been drinking."

"Oh, no! Do me a favor, will you, Mitch? Go and keep Zoe busy out in the kitchen while I get Tracy out of here."

"Are you quite sure you want me to do that?" Aiden drawled. "Let me warn you right here and now that, unlike your blonde, I find your Zoe extremely attractive."

Drake laughed. "That's all right, mate. I'd trust Zoe with the most handsome man in the world, and much as you scrub up pretty well, I don't think you're in that league. But go do your best, buddy, if it'll amuse you and keep Zoe busy. But you won't even get to first base. Ah...Trace, honey, I've been wanting to talk to you all evening."

Aiden didn't hear what Trace honey had to say in return. He was already heading for the kitchen, wherever the darned kitchen was. This was one large apartment, with the first living room spilling into a second and a third, all of them chock-full of trendily dressed yuppie types with scantily dressed women on their arms, a couple of which gave him the eye as he weaved his way past.

It amazed him that there'd been a time when he found parties like this fun. Now, he thought them boring and pretentious.

He finally found the kitchen, a long galley-style room with a white-tiled floor, gray-marble benchtops and stainless steel appliances. Aiden thought it looked as soulless as its owner.

Zoe was standing at a far counter next to a huge two-door, stainless-steel refrigerator, peeling plastic wrap off some serving plates and muttering away to herself. She stopped briefly to refill her glass with the bottle of Chardonnay in the fridge door, taking a good gulp before going back to her work. She didn't see or hear him enter. Her back was to him. Her very pretty back.

He closed the door softly and walked toward her. She must have finally sensed something because she suddenly whirled 'round, her lovely eyes widening.

"Don't you dare touch me," she choked out. "I...I'll scream if you do."

"I haven't come in here to touch you. I just want to talk to you."

"I have nothing to say to you."

"Well, I have plenty to say to you. I don't know what Drake told you about me. I dare say something about my court case last year, judging by your negative reaction to me tonight. I just want you to hear my version."

"Now why would I want to hear *your* version?" she snapped. "I think I've already heard enough lies from you."

"I never lied to you, except over the ownership of the house up at Hideaway Beach. Everything else I told you was true."

"Which wasn't much, if you recall. You let me think you were some kind of beach bum."

"I would have told you the complete story the next morning, if you'd stayed."

"Oh, come on now, you expect me to believe that?"

"I'm hoping you will."

"Why?"

His eyes locked onto hers. "Because what we shared the other night was remarkable, Zoe. And it wasn't just the sex, though that was great, too. There was something else. Something…special. I think we owe it to each other to explore our relationship further.''

Aiden was sure that he had her there for a moment. Her eyes had gone all dreamy. But then she snapped out of it, and the contempt was back. ''Might I remind you that I'm already in a relationship, with a man I love?''

''That's trash and you know it. Whatever it is you two have together it's not love.''

''You know nothing at all about Drake and me!'' she protested fiercely.

''I know more than you realize. For starters, I know your boyfriend's a two-timing sleazebag.''

''I see,'' she bit out. ''Nigel *has* been talking, hasn't he? Okay, so Drake cheated on me. Once. He said he was sorry and I forgave him.''

''*Once?* Oh, come on now.''

She flushed a little and Aiden could see even she didn't really believe that.

''Who are you to judge another man's morals, anyway?'' she threw at him. ''If anyone's the sleazebag around here it's you.''

''I've never cheated on a girlfriend in my life.''

''No, you don't keep them around long enough. You dump them as soon as you've had enough of them. And when they won't stay dumped, you pay them off. That's the sort of man you are. A prize catch. A prince. Why on earth would I choose you over Drake?''

Aiden was getting angry. And competitive. When Aiden got angry and competitive, he often forgot the rules. Forgot to be nice. It was win at all costs. His eyes narrowed and his blood began to run red-hot.

"You can't have forgotten last Saturday night that quickly," he brought up ruthlessly. "Do I have to remind you how many times you came? How you cried out for me to do it again, even begged me on occasion? You couldn't get enough. You only ran away because you were scared to stay, you liked it that much. You know in your heart of hearts you want more of the same. If for no other reason, you should choose me for the sex. Because let's face it, sweetheart, sex between you and dear old Drake isn't anything to write home about."

She paled. "How...how could you possibly know that?"

"You were too surprised by how it felt with me inside you. It was almost like you were a virgin."

Now she blushed. Like a virgin.

"There's more to a relationship than just sex," she pointed out agitatedly.

"Tell that to the geriatrics!"

"You're not what I want," she cried.

"Don't be ridiculous. I *am* what you want. I can see it in your eyes." Which was true. Her voice was saying one thing but her eyes were telling him a different story. The contempt was gone, replaced by an anguished longing.

Aiden couldn't resist anymore. He had to touch her. Had to kiss her.

"Zoe," he groaned, and pulled her into his arms.

12

FOR a few foolishly mindless moments, Zoe sank against him and let his lips crush hers, let his tongue slide deep, and then deeper, into her mouth.

The excitement was instant, and overpowering, her mind floundering whilst her flesh wallowed in his kiss, and then his touch. Her head whirled when his hands slid down over her behind, squeezing through the silk and pressing her hard against him so that she could feel his erection.

Only someone opening the kitchen door saved her from the humiliation of losing it totally, right then and there.

"Oops. Sorry. Thought this was the little men's room." A male voice. Slightly slurred. "Don't mind me. I'm outa here."

The momentary interruption thankfully jerked Aiden's mouth up from hers and propelled Zoe back to some measure of sanity. When he tried to resume kissing her, she wrenched her mouth to one side. "No," she said, and was impressed at how firm she sounded, considering her body had gone to mush. "Let me go, Aiden."

"You don't mean that."

"Yes, I do. If you don't let me go, I'll scream my head off."

His arms dropped away, his face mirroring utter shock. "But why, for pity's sake? Didn't I just prove to you that's it me you want, not Drake?"

Zoe shook her head at his obvious bewilderment. "Haven't you been listening to me at all? Okay, yes, so you can turn me on. But that's just sex. I want more from a boyfriend than just sex. Drake gives me more."

"More what?" Aiden growled. "More money? More five-star restaurants? More fancy clothes?" His eyes raked over her designer dress and she colored guiltily.

"So that's it," he said, his handsome face hardening. "Why didn't you say so, sweetheart? You want the high life? I can give you the high life. I can give you anything you want. Just name it and it's yours. I'll deck you out in diamonds. Buy you a whole new wardrobe. Take you on a world trip. Believe me, I can afford to give you a lot more than your present boyfriend."

She blinked her own shock at him. He really must want to have sex with her again very badly. "I don't know whether to be flattered or insulted," she said, shaking her head at him. "Either way, the answer's still no. I'm not for sale. Now please go. And don't come back. I'd also appreciate it if you'd buy your penthouse from some other agent. Drake doesn't need to do business with someone as morally deficient as you, Mr. Mitchell."

"Morally deficient! You call *me* morally deficient? I'll have you know that…that…that…"

The phone rang, putting a merciful end to Aiden's blustering. Zoe swept over to answer it, glad to have a legitimate reason not to witness his ridiculous outrage. Anyone would think he was genuinely offended by what she'd just said. Which was crazy. The man must know what he was. A sleazy opportunist. A sexual predator. A man without honor or decency. He had no compunction about trying to seduce another man's girlfriend right under his nose. And then, when that didn't work, thought nothing of trying to corrupt her with offers of money and gifts, like she was some kind of professional mistress for hire to the highest bidder!

She snatched the receiver up from its cradle and deliberately turned her back on him. "Yes?" she said sharply.

"Zoe. I'm so glad you answered."

"Mel! What are doing ringing me here at this hour? Are you in some kind of trouble? Jonathon didn't get out of line, did he?" Mel had gone out with her new boyfriend that night. Considering what had just happened, Zoe's faith in the behavior of millionaire playboy types had plummeted to less than zero.

"No. Nothing like that. He's been a perfect gentleman. Unfortunately," Mel muttered under her breath. "The thing is, Zoe, when we came back to our place for coffee after dinner, the light on the answering machine was blinking, so I ran the tape and it was Betty, wanting you to ring her at home, no matter when you got in. She mentioned some kind of emergency but didn't say what, so I rang her.''

''Oh, no, it's not Dad, is it?'' Zoe's father was in his fifties and not a man who looked after himself, healthwise. Betty had bullied him into going to the doctor last year and his cholesterol reading was sky-high. Too many dairy products in his diet, he was told. Betty had done her best to make sure he ate more sensibly, but Bill was a stubborn man, and didn't take kindly to advice, or change.

''He hasn't had a heart attack, has he?'' Zoe choked out, feeling quite nauseous.

''No, nothing like that,'' Mel said, and Zoe heaved a huge sigh of relief.

''Your dad slipped over while hosing down the milking shed this afternoon and broke his ankle, so won't be able to do the milking in the morning. Betty says that's one job she never learned to do. She says she can probably find someone local to come in and do it by tomorrow afternoon, but it's a bit hard to find anyone at this time on a Saturday night. She knows she's asking a lot but was wondering if you could drive down tonight and do it in the morning. Apparently, your father is quite confident you could do it single-handed and blindfolded.''

Zoe laughed. ''Wow. Do you realize that was almost a compliment? From my dad, no less?'' Zoe's relationship with her father was very strained. He never seemed to approve of anything she did since her decision to leave home and come to Sydney. He was always criticizing her for her choice of job, choice of lifestyle and especially her choice of boyfriend. She'd taken Drake home at Christmas and he hadn't gone down well at all.

"Too full of himself," his father had pronounced the day she was to go back to Sydney.

"I know what you mean," Mel said dryly. "If my father ever gives me a compliment, I'll faint dead away."

"I feel a little faint myself at the moment," Zoe said ruefully. "I'm also well over the limit. I'll have to find someone to drive me home."

"Gee, Zoe, I can't. And neither can Jonathon. We downed two bottles of claret between us over dinner. I was trying to get him tipsy so that I could have my wicked way with him. I'm so sorry. You know I would if I could."

"No sweat. I'll find someone else. I can always ask Drake. He'll be as sober as a judge. He never drinks at these parties 'til everyone goes home."

"He won't mind?"

"He probably will, but I'm sure he'll still do it, if I ask nicely. Anyway, thanks for calling, Mel. I'll ring Betty straight away, and tell her I'll be on my way shortly." She glanced up at the wall clock. It was half past ten. Home was almost a three-hour drive from here. Even if she got away at eleven, it would be nearly two by the time she arrived. Then she'd have to be up at dawn for the milking. It was going to be a long day tomorrow. Still, when family called on you in a crisis, you went. That was what family was all about, even if your father was a picky, persnickety pain.

"Ring me tomorrow and let me know what happened," Mel said.

"I'll do that. 'Bye."

Zoe called her home number straight away.

Betty was over the moon at her coming to the rescue, but when she started raving on about what a wonderful girl Zoe was and how much they'd both missed her, Zoe cut the conversation short.

"Must go, Betty. I'll see you hopefully around two." She hung up, and just stood there, gnawing at her bottom lip. Drake was not going to be pleased. Pity she hadn't been nicer to him earlier.

"I'll drive you."

Zoe whirled at Aiden's voice. She'd almost forgotten he was there. But only almost. She'd been doing her best to ignore him, and to pretend that her body wasn't still zinging with his kisses.

Naturally, she was tempted to say yes to his offer. Aiden Mitchell was just one big bag of temptation. And he knew it.

It was time, Zoe decided tartly, for another female to dent his massive male ego.

"Are you *still* here?" she flung at him. "I would have thought you'd have been well gone by now."

"I'm not going anywhere, unless it's with you."

"Oh, for heaven's sake, get a life!" She stalked out of the kitchen and went looking for Drake. Her frustration level soared when she couldn't find him anywhere. No one seemed to have seen him for a while. Bob said he'd spotted him by the bar talking to Tracy about fifteen minutes earlier.

"Maybe he's gone to the bathroom," someone else

suggested, and she hurried down the corridor which led to the master bedroom. Drake always used his en suite bathroom on these occasions. His room was one area of the apartment he kept off-limits during his parties.

. The bedroom door was shut and Zoe reached for the knob.

''Are you sure you want to go in there without knocking first?''

Zoe's head whipped 'round to find Aiden standing a few feet down the corridor, watching her.

''Will you mind your own business?'' she snapped.

''I am. *You're* my business. You're why I came to Sydney and why I came to this party. Look, I apologize for the things I said to you in the kitchen. I never did really think you were the kind of girl who could be bought. I guess I was just hoping you were,'' he added ruefully.

''Sorry I couldn't oblige. But we're not far from the Cross here. You'll find plenty of what you're looking for up there.''

''I don't want just sex, Zoe. I just want sex with you.''

She rolled her eyes in exasperation. ''Oh, please, *spare* me.'' And she started to turn the doorknob.

''I'm trying to. Don't go in there, Zoe,'' he warned.

Her hand stopped momentarily. ''Why?''

''A workmate of Drake's named Bob just told me he hasn't been able to find his date, either. She's the receptionist at their office, name of Tracy. Blond. Big boobs.''

Zoe's frustration with him finally exploded into

fury. "If I were a man, I'd flatten you for what you just implied."

"You're welcome to, after I'm proven wrong."

Zoe glared at him, then flung the door open without knocking.

The room was empty.

"He's not in here," she informed Aiden tartly. "Neither is Tracy. Come and see for yourself."

He did, glancing around the room with those beautiful blue eyes of his. They landed on the en suite door which was also shut.

"I think it's time *you* saw for *yourself,*" he ground out, and began to stride across the room.

"No, don't," Zoe croaked, and ran after him, fear suddenly filling her at what was behind that closed door.

But Aiden was too quick for her. He didn't knock. He didn't give anyone inside any warning. He brought up his foot and kicked the door open.

Drake squawked, his head jerking up to stare with horrified eyes at his unwanted intruders. Tracy's blond head didn't lift at first. She kept on doing what she was doing for several ghastly seconds, testament either to her drunkenness, or her dedication to finishing what she had started. But even when she did stop, she didn't seem at all embarrassed at what she'd been doing, or the fact that she was on her knees and stark naked to the waist.

She stood up and ever so slowly pulled her black lacy top back up over her large dark-tipped breasts, smiling a smug little smile as she tied it around her neck. "Oops," she said mockingly.

Zoe felt like she was in the middle of a farce as she watched Drake frantically stuffing himself back into his pants.

If nothing else, the whole sordid scenario proved one thing to her.

She didn't love Drake anymore. She didn't even *like* him anymore. If she had, she'd have been more surprised. And more hurt.

Frankly, her main feeling was humiliation that Aiden was standing right next to her. And that he'd been right. Drake *was* a two-timing sleazebag.

The cynical thought came to her that it probably took one to know one.

Zoe felt such a fool.

"Zoe," Drake groaned pleadingly, his face red as a beetroot.

"Yes, I know," she returned coldly. "It was just sex." She turned to face Aiden. "Your offer still open? As a driver only, that is," she added curtly.

"Of course."

"Then let's go." Whirling, she headed for the bedroom door.

Aiden stared after Zoe for a second, not sure he liked the sudden change which had come over her. The icy toughness. The steely glint in her eye. The bitter decisiveness.

The Zoe he'd met last week was not like that.

There again, the girl he'd met last week hadn't just personally witnessed her boyfriend being pleasured by another woman.

"I don't have a car," he said, catching up with her

in the hallway. "I came in a taxi." He'd left his truck at the city hotel he'd booked into earlier that day.

"No problem. We'll take my car. It's here in the underground car-lot. I just have to get my things out of the guest room."

"The guest room? But I thought…"

"Don't think!" she snapped. "All you have to do is drive." She turned into a bedroom farther along the corridor, and started shoving some clothes and toiletries in an overnight bag.

Aiden wisely kept his mouth shut after that. He didn't want to delay her leaving in case Drake reappeared and tried to stop her. Though goodness knew what that lowlife could say to excuse his behavior this time. He could hardly use the old it-was-only-the-once line again. Maybe he'd try some new male line, like Zoe hadn't been giving him enough and he was desperate.

Aiden raised his eyebrows at this last thought. Maybe she hadn't been giving him *any!* It was certainly curious that her things were in the guest room. The possibility that Zoe might not have returned to Drake's bed this week pleased Aiden no end. But he wasn't going to ask. He might be a fool where she was concerned but he wasn't that much of a fool. Clearly, Zoe wasn't in the mood for chitchat. Or confidences. Or anything else for that matter.

But give her time…

Time, Aiden had. He had all the time in the world.

13

ZOE sat, slumped in the passenger seat, her head turned toward the side window, her eyes shut. She was pretending to be asleep. She'd been pretending to be asleep since shortly after she'd explained to Aiden about the emergency, then given him directions to the farm.

She hadn't wanted to talk. All she'd wanted to do was think, something she couldn't do properly if Aiden started on at her with all that stuff about finding her special and how he'd come to Sydney just to be with her again, et cetera, et cetera, et cetera. So she kept her eyes firmly shut while she replayed the events of the evening over and over in her head, trying to make sense of them all, trying to see the truth.

At least, the truth as she saw it. She couldn't speak for anyone else. More and more Zoe realized that the only person's feelings she could ever be truly sure of in this world were her own.

Perversely, in the end, she had to concede that instead of feeling shattered, or depressed, by Drake's abominable behavior, she actually felt relieved. His doing what he did had forced *her* to do what she should have done in the beginning. Split up with him. She'd hung on to their relationship like some desperado, as though it was better to have any man, even one who cheated on her, than no man at all.

Which had been foolish of her. And rather sad.

She'd honestly thought, after Greg, that she'd stopped being foolish when it came to men.

But she hadn't at all.

Drake had made an even bigger fool of her than Greg had.

Still, Drake had fooled more people than her. Fran. Mel. Betty, even. Betty had thought him charming.

But he hadn't fooled other men. Her dad hadn't liked him one little bit, and of course, neither had Aiden.

Aiden…

Zoe scooped in a deep breath and let it out slowly.

What on earth was she going to do about Aiden?

The realization that he wasn't driving her all the way home to Moss Vale in the dead of night strictly out of the goodness of his heart did not escape Zoe. His kindness had an ulterior motive, just as his kindnesses toward her had always had an ulterior motive. His helping her when she'd fallen over, his bringing her over those eggs, and then his saving her from the ocean. Not because he was one of the good guys. All because he'd wanted to get into her pants.

When his current knight-to-the-rescue act was over, he'd expect to be rewarded as men had been expecting rewards from damsels in distress since the Dark Ages.

Oh, yes. Everything came at a price with men like Aiden Mitchell.

What annoyed Zoe most was his blatant hypocrisy.

If only he would come out and just state the bare truth without trying to dress it up with romantic frills. Why not call a spade a spade? He didn't want to explore a real relationship with her. He just wanted some more sex. That was the bottom line.

And what of your own truth, Zoe? came that taunting and devilish voice which never left her alone once Aiden entered her head. *Are you willing to embrace brutal honesty yourself? Admit it. You* want *him to demand his reward. You want him to forcibly pull you back into his arms like he did in Drake's kitchen. You want him to finish what he started before you were interrupted.*

It came to her suddenly that if that man hadn't come into the kitchen when he did, she would have ended up no better than Drake, having sex with Aiden right there where she stood, mindless of who might come in and find them actually doing it.

A shudder ricocheted down Zoe's spine and sent her sitting bolt upright, her eyes flinging open.

Aiden slanted her a concerned glance. "Bad dream?"

"Yes," she said agitatedly, shaken by this thought. "Very bad."

"Want to tell me about it?"

"No!" she choked out, and shuddered anew.

"Fair enough. Most bad dreams are best forgotten."

If only they could be, she thought despairingly.

"The turn off for Bowral and Moss Vale is coming up," he went on. "You woke up just in time. I wanted to ask you a few things before we get to your place. I don't want to put my foot in my mouth with your folks. Firstly, who's Mel? Your sister?''

"No, my roommate," Zoe returned crisply, happy to talk practicalities with him. "I don't have any sisters. Or any brothers for that matter."

"And Betty? Who's Betty?"

"My dad's housekeeper. He's a widower."

"She lives in, does she?"

"No. She has her own house in Moss Vale. She does stay over sometimes when she ropes Dad into playing Scrabble with her. She's mad about games and never knows when to stop. Scrabble is her latest obsession."

"She sounds a character."

"Oh, she is. She's very kind, too. I love her dearly." If it hadn't been for Betty...

"Any chance of marriage between her and your dad?"

"Lord, no. Betty's only about forty. And quite attractive. Dad's over fifty, overweight and very boring. My dad's not interested in marrying again, anyway. Mom was the only woman for him. He's been miserable and broken-hearted ever since she died."

"What a shame. Still, marriage isn't the be-all and end-all. You weren't thinking of marrying Drake before tonight, were you?"

"The last person I want to talk about in any shape or form," Zoe snapped, "is Drake."

His eyes softened on her before turning back to the road. "I can appreciate that. What happened back in Sydney couldn't have been pleasant for you. But at least you now know that he didn't love you."

"No kidding." She certainly didn't need him to tell her that.

"You don't still think you love him, do you?"

Zoe sighed. "I'm not going to get into one of these conversations, Aiden. I'm far too tired and far too fed up."

"Fair enough. I'll put it on the back burner for now. But don't go thinking I won't come back to it tomorrow. I want to know all about you, Zoe. What you think. What you feel. What you want. I haven't come all this way to be fobbed off. We have unfinished business, you and I. I aim to finish it, one way or another."

Zoe was rattled by such tunnel-vision focus. She speculated for a minute or two if he could possibly be sincere. But then her recently hard-earned cynicism kicked in and she remembered that such flattering talk was only a ploy. He didn't really want to know everything about her. Talking was just a means to an end. And the end was more sex.

But she did wonder what it was about sex with her he found so compelling and addictive that he would work this hard for it. It wasn't as though he hadn't had oodles of sex before, unlike herself.

Perhaps a clue lay in his comment that she'd been like a virgin with him, constantly surprised by her feelings and responses, not to mention all those mind-blowing orgasms.

Maybe he'd really liked that. Maybe, over the years, he'd had so much sex with so many wildly experienced and uninhibited women that he found her relative innocence and inexperience refreshing.

Maybe that was what he meant by special. Maybe what appealed to him was the idea of surprising her a lot more, of introducing her to all those erotic delights she'd not yet tasted. Things such as she'd seen tonight in Drake's en suite.

Zoe wasn't sure if that prospect appalled, or enthralled her. The image popped into her mind of herself on her knees in front of Aiden, not just half naked but totally in the nude. In her mind's eye, he was nude too, his hands in her hair, his eyes downcast as he watched her, watched her doing that to him, watched her take him right to the edge. And beyond.

Zoe swallowed convulsively at the thought, a wave of heat washing through her.

"Zoe?"

"Yes," she choked out.

"We're coming into Moss Vale. Where do we go from here?"

Where indeed? she thought frantically, then gave him directions.

The farm was only a few miles the other side of Moss Vale, a hundred hectares of prime dairy country. The land was mostly river flats surrounding one large hill on which perched the old farmhouse. It was wooden and once was white, with a high-pitched, rust-red iron roof and a wide porch all the way around. A peeling picket fence enclosed the garden and kept out the cows, but the backyard was nothing like when Zoe's mom had been alive.

Zoe sometimes found it hard to look at the now-bland shrub-filled beds which lined the front fence and which had once held glorious displays of Iceland poppies and primulas and snapdragons.

Aiden pulled up outside that same front fence just as the clock on the dash clicked over to two. Before he'd even turned off the engine, Betty burst through the screen door, her short coppery hair glowing under the porch light, her smile warm and welcoming as she hurried down the path and out through the gate.

Zoe opened the passenger door and smiled up at the woman who'd saved her when she'd really needed saving. Dear Betty. Zoe loved her almost as much as she'd loved her mom.

"Hi," she said, climbing out of the car and reaching up on tiptoe to kiss Betty who was very tall. Just on six feet. Betty had once explained that the reason she'd never married was her height, saying with an amused twinkle in her fine gray eyes that she'd never found a boyfriend she could look up to. Zoe reckoned it was because she was far too strong-minded and independent to fancy marriage.

"You needn't have stayed up, you know," Zoe added. "I could have managed."

"Oh, as if I could go to bed. I was too excited at seeing you again. Hey, look at you!" Betty exclaimed, taking Zoe's hands and holding them out wide so that she could better see her dress. "Don't you look pretty in pink. But I do feel terrible at having to drag you and Drake away from your party." She bent down to peer into the car where Aiden was still sitting. "Drake, I..."

She stopped on seeing it wasn't Drake behind the wheel, blinking her confusion at Zoe.

"Betty, this is Aiden," Zoe introduced with an almost weary resignation in her voice. "Aiden, this is Betty."

Aiden climbed out of the car as well. "Hi, Betty," he said cheerily across the hood. "Pleased to meet you. And before you jump to any conclusions. Zoe and I are just good friends."

Betty laughed. "With your looks? I find that hard to believe, and so will Zoe's dad. What happened to Drake?"

"Drake who?" Zoe said with a poker face.

Betty's eyebrows lifted. "Oh, I see. Like that, is it? What did he do? Refuse to drive you down here?"

"I didn't ask him. We're finished."

"Ah, well, no loss, love. If it's any consolation, I never liked him any more than your father did."

Zoe was taken aback. "But...but you said he was charming?"

"And so he was. But it was all surface charm. He had no depth."

"You can say that again," came Aiden's rueful remark.

Zoe whirled on him. "Excuse me, but I think that's the pot calling the kettle black, don't you?" She turned back to Betty. "Sorry, Betty. You know how it is with friends sometimes. Down deep, they love each other, but they fight a lot."

"I know what you mean. Your father and I don't see eye to eye on many an occasion."

"How is Dad, by the way?" Zoe asked. "How long will he be out of action?"

"Weeks. But he'll live. After you called and I gave

him the good news, he finally agreed to take the pain-killers the doctor prescribed and he's fast asleep. But come tomorrow, I want you to try and talk some sense to him. You and I both know, Zoe, that this dairy farm is no longer a going concern. Your father can only afford to keep running it because he inherited some money a few years back. But it's time he sold. He's no longer enjoying it and he's had a good offer from one of those multi-national agricultural companies. I have a feeling he might not want to sell because he thinks you're attached to the place.''

"Me?" She'd always hated the farm. "I can't see why he'd think that.''

"I'm not sure. Perhaps because of your mom. He says the backyard holds precious memories of her for you.''

"Oh. Oh, I see…'' Zoe had never told her dad, but her mom had never liked the farm. Or the house. Never. She'd just put up with it because she loved her husband. The backyard had been her only pleasure. But without her mother in it, the backyard held no precious memories for Zoe.

"I'll see what I can do,'' she said.

Betty smiled. "I knew I could count on you. Sensible girl, our Zoe, isn't she?'' she directed at Aiden.

"Mmm,'' he said, and Zoe heard sarcasm in there somewhere.

"But where would Dad live?'' Zoe asked, suddenly terrified that he might want to come to Sydney and live with her.

Betty shrugged. "I dare say in Moss Vale. He

wouldn't want to move away from the area, and all his friends.''

''Friends! Dad doesn't have *any* friends other than you.''

Betty gave her a reproving look. ''You'd be surprised, missy. Your dad has become quite a popular man down at the bowling club lately.''

''Dad? Popular? At a club? I don't believe it. He never goes to clubs.''

''Maybe he didn't once, but he does now. I got fed up with his moping around the place after you left at Christmas and dragged him down there myself. He had such a great time, he's joined up. Done him the world of good. Found a personality he didn't know he had. Pity about his ankle, though. I was going to take him to a decent hairdresser this week, then on to the menswear store to buy some new clothes. I guess that'll have to wait now.''

Zoe had to smile. Betty had this compulsion, it seemed, for making over ugly ducklings into swans. She might have achieved amazing things with one very fat teenage girl a few years back, but bringing an old fogey like her dad up to date would take a minor miracle. Trendy, he would never be. Still, fancy his agreeing to go to a club. And making new friends, no less. Wonders of the world would never cease!

''But enough of that,'' Betty said. ''I'm sure you two could do with a cup of tea and something to eat after your long drive. I have some fresh blueberry muffins just out of the oven.''

''Fantastic!'' Aiden exclaimed, rubbing his hands together in pleasurable anticipation. ''I'm starving.''

"You shouldn't have, Betty," Zoe chided.

"Had to do something to keep awake. Hard to play Scrabble with myself. You wouldn't happen to play Scrabble, would you, Aiden?"

"Do I play Scrabble! I happen to be the resident Shelley Bay champion. But I'm even more famous for the number of hot muffins I can devour in one sitting. So lead me to the kitchen immediately, Betty. But come tomorrow, look out. I show no mercy when it comes to games."

Zoe had a feeling he showed no mercy in lots of things. He was a winner through and through, which was possibly another reason why he'd chased after her to Sydney. Because he didn't like the fact *she'd* made the decision last weekend to leave things at a one-night stand. Clearly, he liked calling the shots where his sex life was concerned. *He* decided when enough was enough.

"Coming, Zoe?" he said, taking her arm. Betty was already on her way up the front path.

Zoe stared down at his long strong fingers then up into his far too handsome face.

"I need my bag," she said stiffly and extracted her arm from his, turning away to collect her things from the back seat of the car.

"Let me carry it," he offered.

"No, thanks," she said crisply. "Letting you carry my things is what got me into trouble in the first place."

He frowned. "You think I'm trouble?"

"I *know* you're trouble."

"Mmm. And what do you think you are to me?"

"A challenge."

He frowned, then nodded. "I never thought of you in that light before, but you could be right. I do like a challenge."

"Either that, or a titillation for your jaded sexual palate."

His eyebrows shot up. "A titillation!"

"Yes. You think you can teach me a thing or two."

His surprised expression slowly changed to intrigued. "And can I?"

"Undoubtedly," came her droll remark.

"But will you let me?"

She stared straight at him. "Not if I can help it."

"Why not?"

"Because I don't want to get hurt."

"Are you two coming inside?" Betty called from where she was holding open the screen door.

"We're on our way," Aiden returned.

"I won't hurt you," he claimed as he took her arm and propelled her through the gate. "I promise. I won't do a single thing you don't want me to do."

She laughed. Because that was the problem. There wasn't *anything* she didn't want him to do.

14

"HERE," Zoe said, handing Aiden a hose. "You can help with the cleaning up. All the concrete areas in the milking shed have to be hosed down."

Aiden gave her a look of mock surprise. "You mean you actually trust me to *do* something, instead of just stand around like a useless lump while you do everything?"

Zoe shrugged, determined not to bite. "Sometimes it's quicker to do everything yourself than to explain things to someone else. It's not as though you're ever going to be milking cows again, are you?"

"I guess not."

"I did tell you I didn't need your assistance," she reminded him tartly. "But you wouldn't listen. You had to play Mr. Macho Helping Hand. You could have still been in bed, sleeping."

"And miss watching you work in that highly original but incredibly sexy little outfit?"

Zoe winced. She'd been forced to wear the short shorts and top she'd been wearing the previous day before the party, since that was all she'd brought down with her and all her old clothes were miles too large. No way was she ever going to let Aiden see how fat she'd once been, by donning any of those awful baggy things she'd once worn.

The shorts did look a bit risky, however, when combined with knee-high black rubber boots.

Zoe had been fiercely aware of Aiden ogling her backside every time she had to bend over to attach or detach the cups from the cows' udders. She'd pretended not to notice, and also pretended to herself that the beads of perspiration on her forehead were courtesy of the summer sun, and not her traitorous body being revved up by Aiden's presence once more.

"I had nothing else to wear," she snapped. "You're lucky that some of Dad's old things fitted you. Now stop trying to get a rise out of me and start hosing everything down."

"If you insist." Without any warning, he turned on the nozzle and directed the spray straight at her. She squealed, her hands flying up to protect herself, waving frantically from side to side.

Thankfully, the water wasn't cold. It was actually very warm from where the hose had been lying in the sun. But it was still wet, the hot stream quickly soaking her minimal clothes.

"Stop that!" she screamed.

When he didn't stop, she spun away and ran into the first milking stall, but that didn't help at all. The spray easily found its way through the widely spaced wooden slats. She whirled back but found herself cornered, Aiden having moved to block her path, still spraying her with water, and grinning his head off. By this time her hair hung soggily around her face and her top was plastered to her skin.

"Stop it, Aiden," she choked out, spitting one long strand of lank hair out of her mouth.

He laughed. "Never. Not 'til you beg for mercy."

One part of her wanted to laugh back, to play physical games with him as was natural for men and women when in the grip of a fierce sexual attraction.

But she couldn't find the courage to let herself relax with him in such a fashion. If she did, she knew she was lost. Instead, she lunged for the end of the hose and tried to wrestle it away from him.

"Wait 'til I get that away from you. I'll…I'll…"

"You'll what?" he said, calling her bluff by dropping the hose on the concrete where it weaved and danced like some water-spitting cobra.

His action took her by surprise and she just stood there, panting with exertion, her chest rising and falling. He just stood there too, staring at her, his eyes hot on her explicitly outlined breasts and shockingly erect nipples.

"Zoe," he said thickly, and her stomach curled over.

"No…"

"Yes," he insisted, his face and voice vibrating with the most seductive desire. She felt her nipples harden even further, puckering up for him in the most blatant way.

"No, I said," she croaked out again when his hand reached out to touch where his smouldering gaze was riveted. But it was a futile protest, and she didn't really mean it, not once he made skin contact.

She sucked in, her shoulders stiffening, not daring to move a muscle as his fingertips traced the various shapes and outline of her breasts through the wet top. Shivers ran up and down her spine, but not with cold. When she moaned and swayed on her feet, he grabbed her upper arms and spun her 'round, yanking her back against the hard warmth of his own relatively dry body. Once there, his hands were soon busy on her body once more, smoothing down over her ribs and stomach, then sliding up under her top.

She gasped when he reached her bare breasts, the sensations sharper now that there wasn't any material between him and her. She closed her eyes and tried to keep her head. But this was one of the things she'd thought about endlessly. One of the things she craved. His hands on her naked flesh once more.

"Say you'll come away with me," he whispered in her ear, one hand cupping her left breast whilst his right slid down over her stomach and dipped under the elastic waistband of her shorts.

"Take a few days off work," he urged, that knowing hand zeroing in on exactly the right spot.

Everything inside her crunched down hard.

"Tell them you want stress leave," he went on even as she began to spin out of control. "Tell them anything. Only come away with me, Zoe. This week. Back to Hideaway Beach. Promise me."

At that moment, she would have promised him anything.

"All right," she groaned. "Anything. Anything. Just don't stop."

He didn't stop, but his fingers moved on, sliding down into those parts which had been hot and wet for him all week. When his hand began to penetrate her body, her flesh contracted fiercely, gripping his fingers as she would have gripped his penis, showing him how much she wanted just that.

He muttered something but she didn't catch what. She could not concentrate on anything but her own feverish feelings and those devastating fingers. She whimpered when they began a rhythmic stroking, her legs moving restlessly apart as the pressure built and the craving grew even more intense. Desperate with desire, she began rubbing her bottom against Aiden's erection, oblivious of the reckless nature of such an action. Her brain was simply not connected with her body. She wasn't thinking of risk, or danger, just release. Her body was working on autopilot, blindly going after what it wanted and needed.

"Please," she started begging. "Oh, please..."

Aiden muttered a four-letter word, and then something—his thumb pad, she guessed later—rubbed over her exquisitely sensitized clitoris.

Her climactic cries sounded liked the cries of a wounded animal. Her body stiffened then arched as spasm followed electric spasm. Finally, they ended and Zoe sagged at the knees, only Aiden's arms around her waist preventing her from sinking to the ground.

It took a while before reality returned and it was a deeply shaken Zoe who gradually began to appreciate that Aiden could have taken brutal advantage of her just then, if he'd been so inclined.

But he hadn't. Thank God.

Despite feeling mortified at her own lack of control, Zoe could not help but admire him for his. Not many men would have exercised that much control and consideration in the face of such temptation.

Or had he been looking at the bigger picture, ruthlessly exchanging one passing pleasure for the promise of many? A whole week's worth. He'd said he was merciless when it came to games.

But surely a merciless man would have demanded more from her just then. He could have made her do anything he wanted.

"You won't go back on your promise, will you?" he asked as he turned her back to face him.

She looked up into his beautiful blue eyes and saw an unexpected vulnerability. Amazing! Didn't he know how much she wanted him? Couldn't he *tell?*

As blinding as it had been, that one orgasm hadn't satisfied her cravings one bit. If anything, they were stronger than before, like an uncontrollable fire, unable to be doused, still raging and racing out of control. She couldn't look at him without wanting to strip him naked and touch him all over.

Only pride stopped her from doing just that. Pride and the desperate need to take control of her life once more. If she was going to do this—and she was—then she had to do it on *her* terms, not his.

"I won't go back on my promise," she said firmly, and he looked taken aback.

"You won't?"

"No, because it's what I want too," she said boldly. "What I need. A week of sex with you. But just sex, Aiden. Nothing else. So please...don't feel you have to fancy things up with romantic frills. I want no five-star restaurants. No sweet little gestures or gifts. Certainly no poetry or perfume or flowers,'' she scorned, thinking of Drake's tried-and-true tactics. ''But above all, none of that getting-to-know-you garbage. No deep and meaningful conversations. No confiding everything about each other since the year dot. Just sex.''

Talking, Zoe suspected, was the way to a woman's heart, not sex. Because talking led to true intimacy and emotional bonding. It was how Greg had got to her. And Drake as well. The sex hadn't done the trick at all. If she couldn't learn from her previous mistakes then she didn't deserve to be happy.

And Zoe aimed to be happy one day. She just had to get Aiden out of her system first.

''Just sex?'' he repeated, as though he'd never heard of the concept.

''Yes.'' Her chin tipped up. ''That's the deal. Take it or leave it. It's up to you.'' Now that she understood the basic nature of the male beast, Zoe had no doubts he'd take it.

''Mmm.''

''Is that a yes or a no?'' Surely he wasn't going to say no!

''This isn't some kind of revenge or rebound thing, is it? You're not just trying to go one better than Drake, or get back at him for what he did?''

''Don't be ridiculous. If I wanted anything like that I'd have told Drake about you and me when I had the chance. Believe me when I say Drake means absolutely nothing to me anymore. Tracy's welcome to him.''

"Just checking. A man does have his pride, you know."

"Does he?" she scoffed. "I didn't think a man ever let his pride get in the way of a good lay."

"Mmm."

She did so hate those cryptic mmms.

His head cocked on one side. "Is that what you think you are to me, Zoe? A good lay?"

"*You* must think so. Or you wouldn't be so keen."

He laughed. "You could be right there. And you could be wrong. But since we won't be chatting much, you'll never find out."

"I can live with that." She had to. To find out more about him might be the kiss of death. He was already proving himself to be more than she'd imagined. But he was still not a man to be trusted with her heart. Zoe wasn't going to be a silly female fool a *third* time!

"Mmm."

"Must you say mmm like that every second?"

"Does it bother you?"

"Yes!"

"Then I'll try to curtail it, but it's a family trait."

"I don't want to hear about your family. Or your family's traits."

"Oh. Sorry. I forgot. Silly me. So when do you think you might be ready to leave for Hideaway Beach?"

"That depends on whether Betty can get someone to do the milking this afternoon."

"What are you going to tell them at work?"

"Don't you worry about that. That's my problem."

"I think we should still stay down here today and tonight, regardless, Zoe. We might be needed. Besides," he added with a wicked grin. "I promised to play Scrabble with Betty, and like you, I always keep my promises."

Zoe pulled a face at him. "Yeah, right." Like he'd kept his promise to marry that girl. "We could still leave after tea," she suggested.

"And drive up the coast road at night? I don't think so. Too dangerous. We can make tracks first thing in the morning."

"Fine," she agreed offhandedly. But inside, she felt piqued by his plans. Okay, so he obviously wasn't as desperate as she was to be together. He'd already won her cooperation, hadn't he? He already had his precious week of uninterrupted sex to look forward to.

A shudder ran through her at the thought.

"Why don't you go back up to the house?" she suggested sharply. "Betty will have a lavish country-style breakfast ready for you by now. I'll stay here for a while to finish up and dry off."

He gave her one of his thoughtful looks, which were just as irritating as his cryptic mmms.

"I'd rather wait for you."

"And I'd rather you didn't."

When her hands found her hips, he shrugged. "All right. See you soon, then."

By the time Zoe started walking back up to the house almost an hour later, it was way past breakfast time. The angle of the sun in the sky suggested it was at least ten, or later. But she didn't care. She had no appetite for food. She'd lost it when Aiden came into her life, replaced by another more ravenous hunger.

Zoe still could not believe what had happened down at that milking shed. She also couldn't believe she'd rashly promised to get this week off work. She was going to have to spin a good yarn to wangle that. Maybe she could exaggerate her father's need for her. Family emergencies were often looked upon more kindly than just asking for time off out of the blue. She'd also have to give Mel a ring and give her an update. Maybe she'd use the same white lie on her, too.

It was difficult once you started having dirty little secrets in your life.

"Ho, ho, ho."

Zoe's head snapped up at the sound of her father's deep Santa-like belly laugh. She'd just come through the back gate and was only a few steps from the open back door. Surprise understated Zoe's reaction. Frankly, she hadn't heard her father laugh like that in years.

She hurried in through the screen door to find him sitting at the old kitchen table, showing an equally amused-looking Aiden an old photograph album.

Her heart sank when she immediately recognized it as one which contained all her class photos, right from her first year at school, including the dreaded ones taken after her mother had died and she'd become so fat. They were the only photographs of her taken during those awful years, and then only because the school forced her to be in them. Because she wasn't tall, she was always put in the front row, all her grossness there on open display. Not just her fat face but her fat stomach and fat legs. She'd even had fat ankles back then.

A fierce wave of humiliation seared her soul as Aiden looked up, a wide smile on his face.

"You sure were a cute little..."

"How dare you show those photos of me without my permission!" she raged at her father, racing over and snatching the offending album out of his startled hands. Tears welled up in her eyes. "Isn't it enough that you've always put me down? Must you hold me up to ridicule in front of..."

She broke off when she realized the album she was holding wasn't the one with her school photos in. It was the one which contained her baby photos, along with the photos of her parents, when they were young and happy together. That other awful album, Zoe recalled too late, had been long consigned to a dark hiding place which only she knew about. It was just that the album covers were the same...

Everyone was staring at her with shocked eyes. Betty, standing at the sink. Her pale-faced father sitting at the table, his broken ankle propped up on a chair. Aiden, seated to the left of him.

"Oh," she cried, shattered at having made a complete idiot of herself and embarrassing everyone for nothing.

"I'm sorry," she said, and bursting into tears, she ran headlong from the room, clutching the album to her chest.

She was lying facedown on her bed, her weeping having subsided to the odd sniffle when she heard her bedroom door open. She knew without looking 'round, that it would be Betty. Dear, kind, understanding, sympathetic Betty.

"I know," she croaked into her pillow. "I behaved like an idiot."

"Not at all," a male voice answered. "I'm the one who's been behaving like an idiot all these years."

Zoe rolled over at the sound of his voice.

"Dad!"

"Yes, it's me. Not that I've been much of a dad since your mother died. And I'm sorry, Zoe. I've been abominably selfish, too caught up in my own pain to begin with to see yours. When I finally did, I didn't know how to handle you or your weight problem. Thank goodness for Betty, that's all I can say. What a godsend that woman's been."

Zoe watched, too startled to speak, as her father struggled into the room on his crutches and closed the door behind him. When she went to get up and help him, he waved her back and leaned against the dressing table for support.

"Betty just gave me a good talking to in the kitchen and made me see how critical and negative I've been toward all you've achieved. She made me see it wasn't easy for you losing weight, then getting a job and going off to the city to live all by yourself. At the time I took it as a personal rejection of me and our life here as a family. I hated the fact that you hated the farm. Much like your mom did."

Zoe's heart lurched. "I...I didn't know you knew that..."

His eyes carried admission, and true remorse.

"Once again, I pretended I didn't notice. Men are good at that. Pretending not to notice the things they don't want to face. But I knew she was unhappy, just as I knew you were unhappy."

"She still loved you, Dad. And so do I."

"I know that, daughter. And that's what makes me feel even lousier. But hopefully, it's never too late to turn things around. So I just want to say that I *am* proud of you for the success you've made of your life. I wish I had your courage. And your willpower. And your selflessness. What you did, dropping everything and driving down here in the middle of the night, puts me to shame. Not once, in the five years you've lived in Sydney have I driven up and visited you. Not once. All I've done is complain and criticize. I don't know why you still bother with me at all."

Tears welled up in Zoe's eyes again. "Oh, Dad... Thank you so much for saying that, but I'm not such a great success. Not with men, anyway. Did Betty tell you Drake did the dirty on me and I had to dump him?"

"Yes. And good riddance to bad rubbish. You've got yourself a much nicer bloke sitting out there in the kitchen, my girl. He makes ten of that Drake."

"You like Aiden?" Zoe shouldn't have been surprised. *She* liked him, didn't she?

"I sure do. He's a real nice lad. So easy to talk to. And no airs and graces about him, either, despite all his successes. He really likes you too, Zoe. And not because you're done up like a dog's dinner all the time, either. I know you told Betty you were just good friends, but you mark my words. No man would drive you all the way down here because he just wants to be good friends with you."

"Really," she said, trying not to smile. But it was kind of funny.

"Yes, really, I'm a man. I know. I can see the signs."

"Speaking of signs, Dad, I've been seeing a few signs myself between you and Betty. Am I right or am I wrong or are you two more than just good friends these days?"

He blushed. He actually blushed.

"No need to feel embarrassed, Dad," Zoe raced on. "I'm not shocked," she lied. "You're a grown man just as she's a grown woman. You can do exactly as you please behind closed doors. But if you want my daughterly advice I think you should sell the farm, move into Moss Vale and marry Betty."

"You think she'd actually *marry* me?" It was rather touching that he looked so unsure.

Zoe looked her dad over and tried to see him through Betty's older eyes. He'd once been a handsome man and would still be, if he lost some weight, bought himself some new clothes and had his hair cut. There was nothing worse than a man who was going bald who grew what was left of his hair longer, thinking that made up for it.

"I think she might," Zoe said. "But she's a very attractive woman, Dad. Now don't get me wrong, you're still a fine figure of a man but you have let yourself go a bit. If I were you, I'd try to lose a few pounds, get your hair cut in one of those shorter more modern styles and invest in some new clothes, especially for when you take Betty down to the club. You have been taking her down to the club, haven't you?''

He nodded. "And you think that would work?" he asked, looking as eager as a schoolboy trying to wangle a date with the beauty of the class.

"It can't hurt. Go for it, Dad. You only have the one life to live."

He drew himself up taller with her encouraging words. "You're right. But none of this to Betty now. I want to do this all by myself."

15

AIDEN sat with arms folded in the passenger seat, irritated that Zoe had insisted on driving. Like most men, he hated not being the driver.

"For pity's sake, stop sulking," she threw over at him as they wound their way down through cow-dotted fields toward the main road. "It *is* my car. Which reminds me. Where is that chick-pulling yellow truck you usually drive? Or is that just part of the beach-bum role you adopt at Hideaway Beach? You leave it behind when you head for Sydney and put on your millionaire's hat again."

Aiden slanted a thoughtful glance over at her. She really had it all wrong about him. Understandable, of course, given what she'd been told and what she'd been through with Drake this last week. Lies and betrayals always affected a person deeply. You automatically turned cynical and, yes, bitter.

Aiden had been there, done that, and he knew what Zoe was going through. All he could do was be patient and play for time, time for her to discover the real him.

"It's at the hotel I booked into in Sydney. But no sweat, it can stay there for this week. I'll give them a call and explain the situation."

"Oh, really? You'll tell them that you're off for some serious sex with a chick with her own wheels so you won't be needing your own?"

Aiden smiled at her sarcasm. When women got sarcastic, it was often because underneath, they cared. Zoe might think she only wanted sex from him, but he was bargaining she actually wanted more, but was afraid of being hurt. She'd said as much.

For his part, he was sure now that he wanted more from Zoe than just sex. The incident yesterday morning in the milking shed had proved that. If it had been just lust driving him, he would have undoubtedly done something they'd both have regretted afterward.

But he hadn't. He'd stayed in control, wanting to give rather than take.

Okay, so he'd been a bit naughty, using her wildly turned-on state to coerce that promise from her. But as they say, all's fair in love and war.

Aiden was beginning to suspect this could develop into a bit of both.

Whatever, he knew he'd never felt this strongly about any girl before, and he wasn't about to be fobbed off with one week of sex. He aimed to have a real relationship with Zoe. She was going to become his girlfriend, come hell or high water.

In the meantime, he would give her what she wanted, or *thought* she wanted.

"My, aren't we in a touchy mood this morning?" he said lightly. "What's up?"

"You know very well what's up! Last night, over dinner, you let Betty and Dad think you were already my new boyfriend."

"Is that a crime?"

"It's a lie. You are not, and are never going to be, my new boyfriend. You're going to be my sexual partner. For one week and one week only. That was the deal. If you think you can change my mind on that, then think again, lover."

"Fine. Don't get uptight."

"I have every reason to get uptight. As it is, I'll be fielding off questions from Betty and Dad for ages after this is over. They *liked* you. Though of course I can understand why. You went out of your way to be so darned nice to them. Sitting there all yesterday afternoon, watching the football with Dad and drinking that awful beer he likes! Then playing Scrabble with Betty 'til all hours of the night! *And* letting her win!"

"I didn't let her win," Aiden said truthfully. "She beat me fair and square. I guess I'm a bit rusty. I haven't been my hometown Scrabble champion for some few years."

"And that's another thing. You are such a blabbermouth, telling everyone everything all about yourself. I told you I didn't want to know any of that stuff and now I do. Not that it makes any difference. Betty and Dad might have been impressed at what a success you've made of your life after starting out as the poor underprivileged son of a single mom, but you didn't fool me with your sob stories. Amongst other things, what sensible woman would refuse to take welfare, then scratch out some wretched existence selling painted scarves and sarongs to tourists?"

"My mom would," he said ruefully. "Wait 'til you meet her. You'll believe me, then."

"I have no intention of meeting your mother," she said stiffly. "I told you. I don't want to get to know you or your family. All I want is for you to…to… You know what I want you to do!" she finished, flushing prettily.

He never said a word. But he started planning a lot. She thought she knew what she was doing keeping their relationship strictly sexual, but she didn't. She was being naive again.

"Look, I don't mean to be rude," she went on, perhaps reading offense into his silence. "I like you. I really do. You're a very likable person. But we had a deal. We were not supposed to have any getting-to-know-you conversations."

"You started it, complaining about my talking to your folks back at the farm."

"Which reminds me. Exactly what *did* you and Betty talk about after I went to bed last night? You didn't go asking her personal questions about me, did you?"

"Absolutely not," Aiden denied, and it wasn't a lie. He'd asked all those questions earlier in the day, after she'd run off crying to her room and her father had finally followed her.

And what an enlightenment that conversation had proved to be!

He'd already discovered for himself at Drake's party that Zoe was not some kind of cold-blooded gold digger, that she was as sweet and sincere as she'd seemed the previous weekend. But it was good to hear some solid details about Zoe's earlier life, and to work out just what had made her so susceptible to the likes of Drake Carson. Betty hadn't needed much prodding to tell Aiden everything he wanted to know about this girl who'd turned his life upside down.

He'd been saddened to hear of her mother's premature death of uterine cancer when Zoe had only been thirteen, then sympathetic when Betty explained that Zoe had spent the rest of her teenage years being ''mother'' around the house because her father couldn't afford help. She did all the cooking and cleaning whilst still at school, then after leaving school as well. He understood a great deal when he heard about her comfort eating which resulted in her weight ballooning out, thereby undermining her self-esteem. More pennies dropped for Aiden when Betty told him Zoe had retreated from reality into the world of women's magazines where all successful women were slim and perfectly groomed, had interesting careers and handsome boyfriends.

Two events eventually stopped the rot. Zoe contracted mononucleosis, just after her father inherited a wad of cash from an uncle who died. With it, he was able to employ Betty to look after the house and a slowly recovering Zoe.

Aiden didn't have to read between the lines to realize that Betty had brought new life into that once-depressed household. Betty had a vibrant and optimistic personality, and was so full of the joy of living, with a passion for lots of things besides Scrabble. With her encouragement, Zoe had watched her diet, started exercising, taken a secretarial course and finally applied for some jobs, not locally, but in Sydney. Successful women didn't work in the country. They had glamorous jobs in the city.

She'd taken a while but she'd finally landed a position as a clerk in an insurance company where unfortunately, some pig of a man—Betty didn't know the sordid details—hurt her rather badly. Zoe had still been a bit plump at the time so who knew what emotional scars had been inflicted on her still-vulnerable self-esteem. Quite a lot apparently, because after that, she'd steered clear of men for a good few years, choosing instead to work her way up in the world by going to more night schools and trimming off every excess pound from her figure with many more hours spent in gyms, 'til she landed her present job last year.

It had been shortly after she started her job as assistant to Fran Phillips that Drake Carson had come into her life with all his false charm and self-centered ambition.

Aiden knew exactly why Drake had targeted Zoe.

Because he saw in her the perfect wife for a man like him. She was attractive, well-groomed, hardworking. But more importantly, slightly naive, lonely and needy. Not yet life smart, despite all she'd achieved. She stood no chance against him, once he went to work with all those age-old romantic ploys designed to fool women.

Zoe herself had revealed exactly what Drake had used to suck her in when she'd told Aiden what she *didn't* want from him. Flowers. Five-star restaurants. Perfume. Poetry. Gifts of any kind.

No doubt dear old Drake had lavished all these on her at every opportunity.

There was one thing, however, which Drake had never been able to give Zoe, because it couldn't be bought, or fabricated. And that was the sort of sexual pleasure she'd experienced with *him.*

Aiden aimed to take full advantage of that. He aimed to bind Zoe to him through sex, to take her to places she'd never been before, to use physical intimacy to draw her into an emotional intimacy. There would be no taboos this coming week. No nos of any kind. He was going to make her his. Totally.

Zoe's head abruptly whipped 'round to glare over at him. "You're being very quiet, all of a sudden," she said accusingly.

"Isn't that what you want?" he returned, doing his best not to look like a man making a mental list of various wicked activities. "No talking?"

"Huh. Don't play the innocent with me."

He laughed. "I wouldn't dream of it. Hey, watch the road, would you? Or let me drive."

Zoe jerked the car back from where it had drifted toward the center line.

"Speaking of driving," she said. "I think it best you take your own vehicle back up to Hideaway Beach, so I'll drop you off at your hotel in Sydney on the way through."

"Oh, no, no, no," he said, sitting up straight. "That's not on. I'm not letting you out of my sight."

"But I have to go to my place and pick up some things."

"Then I'll come with you."

"But I don't want you to. Mel might be there."

"So?"

"I don't want her to know about you."

His eyes narrowed and his fists clenched. "Then I'll sit outside in your car and wait."

"No," she said stubbornly. "We'll do this my way. You'll just have to trust me. I promised to come and I will."

Aiden gritted his teeth. He supposed he had no other alternative. But this was the last time she'd treat him this shabbily. Come the end of the week, he aimed to have her eating out his hand.

"I guess I'll just have to take your word for it," he said grudgingly.

"I guess you will."

Aiden didn't like the smug tone in her voice. Maybe he'd miscalculated a little here. Maybe her earlier sarcasm hadn't been a sign of secret caring. Maybe all she *did* want from him was just sex.

The thought rattled him. Then turned him on.

He'd thought he'd worked her out there. He'd thought he'd worked *himself* out, too.

Now he didn't know where he was going or what he was doing, except for one thing. He was going to screw that girl's brains out this week. And she was going to love every single second!

16

ZOE was smiling to herself as she slipped her key into her front door. She hadn't realized the satisfaction which came from taking control of one's life, in making your own decisions and then not making any excuses for them.

She'd always been so accommodating with Drake, pandering to his ego and doing everything to please him. Even when she'd refused to move in with him, she'd been apologetic about it.

Did he respect her for that? Heck, no! He'd still thought her a pushover. And a fool. She was never going to be like that again. She was going to be more like a man in future, doing exactly what she wanted to do without saying sorry all the time.

Aiden hadn't been happy with her decision about the cars. But when she'd stood firm, he'd accepted it. She vowed to remember that in all her dealings with him. To stay firm.

"You home, Mel?" she called out, hoping her roommate wasn't in. "It's Zoe!"

"I'm in the bathroom!" Mel shouted back, putting paid to that hope. "Won't be long. Can't talk. I'm cleaning my teeth. I'll be out soon."

At which point she would no doubt ask some sticky

questions. Like, what was she doing here? Where was she going? And why?

Zoe would have to be very inventive with her answers.

Sighing, she hurried into her room and stripped off the track suit Betty had found for her to wear that morning and which had only been bearable because of her car's air-conditioning. The weather was remaining hot and dry, despite the fact that March—and the Australian Fall—had arrived. It looked like they were in for an Indian summer.

She pulled on some loose lemon crinkle slacks which traveled well, and matched them with a white short-sleeved shirt, not tucked in. She popped her feet into strappy white sandals, and bundled her hair up into a tiny ponytail, leaving a few tendrils to soften the rounded outline of her face. Her makeup was nothing but a dash of coral lipstick.

It was not a bad look. Not one she'd wear to work but it would do for today. And for the rest of the week. Aiden was attracted to her, as her dad had noticed, whether she was dolled up or not. So why bother? It would be silly to spend hours every morning doing a full face makeup and blow-dry when she'd wasn't intending to go outside the door. For the same reason, she didn't intend to take up many clothes. She would have no call for them.

Zoe's mouth went dry as she thought of not wearing any clothes at all. All week. Of walking around in the nude all the time. Of always being accessible to him.

A violently erotic shiver ran down her spine.

''So what are you doing home?'' Mel demanded to know as soon as she walked into the room. ''I thought after your phone call last night you were going to be spending the whole week down at the farm.''

Zoe did her best to look calm and carefree, whilst every nerve ending she owned felt electrified. ''I thought so, too,'' she said, not looking at Mel as she went about collecting underwear from her drawers. ''But Betty came up with a local chap who was happy to come in and do the milking 'til Dad's on his feet again. Provided he was paid, of course. So I wasn't needed anymore.''

''I would have thought you'd still have stayed home for a while after what happened with Drake. Moral support and all that. You must have been very upset. What a creep! You did right to dump him. One slip could be forgiven, but twice? No way. So why are you dressed like that?'' she asked, flopping down on the side of Zoe's bed. ''You're obviously not going back to work.''

''Nope. I thought, since I already had the week off work, that I'd go away for a few days.''

''I'm surprised your boss agreed to you having a whole week off.''

''I was too, to be honest. Fortunately, I'd worked like a dog last week so I was more than up to date with everything. Besides, it's not as though I asked for any special favor. I took a week of the two weeks' holidays I'd already accrued.''

''You shouldn't have had to do that.''

''Maybe, but I felt better that way.'' Less guilty.

"And just as well," she added. "Now I'm free to go wherever I like."

"Well, you look beachy, so I presume you're off somewhere coastal?"

"Yes. Back to Hideaway Beach."

"Really? I didn't think you liked it up there that much."

"I always like the beach," she said, keeping busy with her packing. "It was the timing which was wrong."

"I dare say. Er...are you quite sure Nigel's gay?"

"What?" Zoe glanced 'round at her friend and roommate, confused by the question. "What do you mean?"

"I mean he's being very generous, lending you his beach house all the time. Unless it's not Nigel's place you're staying at?" There was a hint of suspicion in that last question.

Zoe wished she was a better actor at this point. Or a better fibber.

With Mel looking straight at her, she just couldn't bring herself to lie.

"No," she admitted, flushing guiltily. "No, I'm not staying at Nigel's."

Mel's blue eyes rounded in surprise, before twinkling with salacious delight. "You've been a naughty girl, haven't you? You did go with some lifesaver up there last week, didn't you? Go on, tell the truth and shame the devil."

"Well...almost."

"*Almost?* How can you *almost* go with someone?"

"No, I slept with him, all right. But he wasn't a lifesaver. He was a surfer."

"A surfer!"

"A very famous surfer, actually. His name's Aiden Mitchell and he owns the weekender next to Nigel's."

"Aiden Mitchell! Oh, my goodness, that's some surfer. I mean he was just the best! He was also on Australia's ten most eligible bachelors list a couple of years ago. I know because I cut it out and did my best to meet every one of them. But I never did come across him. He's not all that social a guy. He keeps a pretty low profile. Or he did 'til last year. You do know about his being sued by that actress, don't you?"

An actress? She hadn't known the girl involved was an actress. Zoe wasn't sure if that was in Aiden's favor or against it. An actress would make an excellent liar, unlike herself.

"I didn't when I first met him," Zoe admitted on a sigh. "I didn't recognize him at all. I thought he was just some gorgeous beach bum, living in the house next door to Nigel's while he was doing some renovation work on it. And he let me think so too, the rat. Still, what can you expect from a man like that?"

"Not an engagement ring, that's for sure. So watch your step."

"I'm not planning on marrying him, Mel. I just want to sleep with him."

"I gather you already did."

"Okay, I just want to sleep with him some more."

"That good, eh?"

"Brilliant."

"Ooh, I'm jealous. Do you know Jonathon won't go to bed with me?"

"Goodness me, why not?"

"He says he loves me too much and I'm far too cynical. He says he wants to wait so that I'll know just how *much* he loves me, that it's not just lust he feels for me."

"Well, I certainly don't have that trouble with Aiden. That's all he wants from me. Sex. And frankly, that's all I want from him."

Mel gave Zoe a worried look. "Are you sure? I mean...that doesn't sound like you."

"I know. But meeting Aiden has opened my eyes to a side of me I didn't know existed. From the moment I set eyes on him, I could think of nothing else but sex. I don't want him to love me, Mel. I just want him to..."

"Make love to you," Mel finished for her on a dry note.

Zoe laughed. "I wasn't going to put it quite like that."

"I know. And that's not like you, either. You're not that kind of girl, Zoe. I don't like the sound of this. Aiden Mitchell! Who would have believed it? Talk about going from the frying pan into the fire. That is one seriously hot-looking hunk of male flesh. And rich, to boot. Are you sure you haven't fallen for him and you just won't admit it?"

"No," Zoe said firmly. "I haven't. And I don't intend to. I'm not the same person post-Drake as I was before, Mel. I won't be giving my heart so easily in future, or so stupidly. No, it's just sex.''

''Not *just* sex,'' Mel corrected. ''*Fantastic* sex, by the sounds of things.''

''True. I've never had anything like it before. And I want a whole lot more. But come next Sunday I'll be back here, I'll be alone and I'll be fine.''

''Wow! I'm impressed. This is pussy power at its best. I love it.''

''I rather like it, too. Now, I just have to get my toilet bag out of the bathroom and I'll be ready.''

''Want me to make you a cup of coffee before you go?''

''Oh, yes, that would be nice.''

Five minutes later both girls were sipping coffee in the kitchen when suddenly, Zoe's courage began to fade.

''You...you don't think I'm being reckless, do you, Mel?''

Mel gave her an exasperated look. ''Now don't go spoiling the new you. I always said you took men and sex far too seriously, Zoe. Time to lighten up and enjoy yourself for a bit. Far from being foolish, I think you've chosen just the right type of man to have a fling with. He's drop-dead gorgeous to look at and he knows all the right moves. Best of all, you have no illusions about him.''

''Yes, that's true. It's just that...'' She sighed. ''Oh, I don't know... Ever since I met Aiden, I haven't been myself. In a way it's good, but in another, it worries me.''

''I think you're addicted to worry sometimes.

Look, you've already decided to have this fling. Then do so, without qualms, without doubts. And stop worrying. For pity's sake, you deserve some pleasure after Drake.''

''I do, don't I?''

''Yes.''

''Wish me luck.''

''What's luck got to do with it?''

Zoe thought about that. ''Nothing. Which reminds me, I'll have to buy some condoms on my way up there. It wouldn't be in keeping with the new me to rely on the man to provide protection. I should have my own.''

''I bought a new box the other day, and it doesn't even look like I'll be opening it. Do you want it?''

''How many?''

''Half a dozen.''

''Nah. Not enough. I'll buy some on the way.''

''Not enough? Now I *am* impressed. You won't be able to walk by the end of the week. Is he built?''

''You have to see it to believe it!''

Mel groaned. ''Lucky you. I'd like to see Jonathon's. I've felt it, mind you, pressed up against me, and it feels formidable.''

''You could get him into the sack if you put your mind to it, Mel.''

''Yeah, I know. But maybe I don't want to. Maybe underneath, I like it when he says he wants to wait awhile. Maybe I like hearing him say how much he loves me all the time.''

Mel's words stabbed at Zoe's heart, but she valiantly ignored the pain. She was sure love was wonderful if it was true, but she could do without the false hope of it.

"I must get going," Zoe said, putting her mug down. "It's gone noon. Now I won't promise to call. If anyone wants to desperately get in touch with me, give them my cell phone number. I won't leave it on, but I'll check my message bank every day."

"Aren't you going to eat something before you go?"

"No. I don't feel hungry." Not for food, anyway.

"Wow, that's a first!"

"I might stop off and have something on the way."

She didn't. But she did drive past the turnoff to Hideaway Beach and went on into Nelson Bay where she bought packets of condoms at three different shops, too embarrassed to buy them all at one. So much for her pussy power!

And then she sat over a sandwich and cappuccino for another hour, trying to get her head around what she was about to do.

It was all very well for Mel to tell her not to worry. Mel had been having sex since puberty. And all kinds of sex, from the stories she told. She was an old hand at "just sex" relationships, whereas Zoe was a novice. What if she couldn't help getting emotionally involved with Aiden? What if she *did* fall in love with him?

What if, what if, a darkly impatient voice piped up inside her head. *Your whole life could go by if you keep sitting here, saying what if? Stop being so wishy-washy. Get up and get your butt over to his place. And when you get there, don't go all mushy and over the moon. Be strong. Be assertive. Be the woman you want to be.*

The stern self-lecture worked, propelling her to her feet and out to where she'd parked her car. She didn't waiver in her resolve during the relatively short drive back to Hideaway Beach, but when she arrived at Aiden's house and saw his yellow truck parked in the carport, fireworks started exploding in her stomach.

Shaking her head, she edged slowly down the steep driveway and slid into the space next to Aiden's van, swallowing as she turned off the ignition.

She didn't get out straight away. She sat for a while and tried to calm her madly racing heartbeat, not sure if she was afraid or excited. Possibly a bit of both.

She was still sitting there when Aiden materialized in front of the car and just stood there, glaring at her through the windshield. He was wearing those raggedy old denim board shorts and nothing else. His hair was sticking up all over the place, indicating a recent swim, and his chin was beginning to sprout some blond stubble. He looked pretty much as he had when she'd first met him. Roughly handsome and sinfully sexy.

Seeing him like that again made Zoe go all squishy inside.

Be strong, be assertive, she reminded herself as she climbed out from behind the wheel and looked him up and down.

"Been for a swim already, have you?"

"You're late," he snapped.

"Am I?" She turned and swung the car door shut before facing him again. "I didn't realize I had to be here at a certain time. Besides, I had things to do. I had to pack. And to change.''

''So I see. You do realize you're wearing far too many clothes,'' he growled.

''I didn't think it would be this hot up here.''

''It's even hotter inside.''

''I'll be fine after I have a cool shower.''

''I'll show you the way.''

''I'll just get my things.''

''Leave them,'' he said sharply, and she glared at him.

''Leave them,'' he repeated more quietly. A request this time, not a command.

Zoe shrugged, struggling now to remain strong and independent. Suddenly, she wanted to run to him, surrender to him, be a slave to him.

She could not understand it. After all she'd vowed!

He reached out his hand and she found herself placing hers in it, letting him draw her with him up onto the front verandah then into the house.

It was hot inside, as he'd said it would be. But not as hot as *she* was inside. He led her down the hallway and into the bathroom, closing the door behind them, closing the world out. With a darkly frustrated groan, he took her face captive in his hands and kissed her harshly, hungrily.

There was no stopping him then. He was like some starving beast who'd unexpectedly come across food. Zoe felt like she was being eaten alive, but, oh, how she loved it. Loved the feel of his mouth devouring hers. Loved his hands ripping off her clothes, then his own. Suddenly, there were no doubts or qualms. This was why she'd come. This was what she wanted.

Barely sixty seconds after his lips had first crashed down onto hers, Aiden was pulling her, panting and naked, into the shower.

The spray hit her breasts first. And then her face. Not cold. Hot. Hot as they were. She gasped and spun 'round in his arms, putting her back to the wetness and the heat. His hands encircled her throat, his thumbs tipping up her chin before rubbing roughly over her bruised mouth.

"Five minutes ago, I wanted to kill you," he muttered, his eyes never leaving hers. "Where have you been all this time?"

"I stopped off on the way to have something to eat," she confessed breathlessly. "And to buy some condoms."

He laughed. "Obviously not at Tom's store. I emptied his supply. The poor old guy thought I was going to an orgy. See?" And he pointed to the pile of plastic squares sitting on the shelf built into the shower wall. "I stashed some in every available nook and cranny in the house. I wanted them to be on hand, no matter where we were. The trouble was, while I was doing that, I started thinking of how I was going to do it to you in that particular place, or room. By the time I finished I had to go for a swim to cool down."

Her head spun with his words. "And how are you going to do it to me in here?" she choked out.

"That depends."

"On what?"

"Have you ever made love in a shower before?" he murmured as he licked at her bottom lip.

"No," she admitted with a quiver.

"How about anywhere other than a bed?"

"Only with you."

"Oh, Zoe," he groaned. "You do things to me which shouldn't be allowed. Here. Feel this," he said, and taking her hand, pressed it against his erection.

She not only felt it, she began caressing it. So velvety soft. Yet so hard. And all because of her.

Her hand curled 'round to grip him tightly before sliding seductively up and down. Up and down. He gasped and leaned back against the tiles, staring down at what she was doing as though he couldn't believe it.

It was an empowering sight, and gradually, Zoe began to feel as she wanted to feel. Not like some submissive love slave. But a love goddess. No, a sex goddess. A wickedly seductive sex goddess.

So what if she hadn't done a lot of things before! She knew about them. And she wanted to do them now. She wanted to do *all* of them.

He moaned shakily when she sank down onto her knees.

She glanced up at him through the shower spray which was now beating against his chest, the water running down his body, the rivulets parting to stream down on either side of his straining erection. He sucked in sharply when she grasped it firmly at the root, directing its straining length away from his stomach and into her mouth, her head dipping as she took him in inch by inch.

When she'd gone as far as she could go, she lifted her head slowly once more, sucking him tightly as she withdrew. He stiffened, trembled, groaned. She kept on doing it, her head rising and falling. When she stopped once to run her tongue around the tip, he jackknifed away from the tiles, gasping.

Her head lifted in a panic. "Did I hurt you?"

"Hardly," he muttered. "But if you do too much of that, I'll come."

"So?" She didn't care if he came, which was amazing. If Drake had suggested such a thing, she'd have been sick on the spot.

He stared down at her for several seconds, then sank back against the tiles, his eyes squeezing shut. "Heaven help me."

Zoe gathered that was the signal to go on. She did, her confidence soaring, her own pleasure immense. She'd heard of power trips but this was the ultimate. She could not get enough of the noises he made, or the feelings they evoked within her. The elation. The excitement. She learned to draw him in deeper and deeper, to suck him just long enough without tipping him over the edge. To stroke and fondle him with wickedly intimate hands at the same time.

"Zoe, stop," he pronounced suddenly, and snapped off the shower. "You have to stop."

She stopped, her eyes glazed as she glanced up. Hadn't he liked what she'd been doing?

He reached down and pulled her up onto unsteady feet, steam rising all around them. "You can do that another time. But not now. Not this first time. I just want you, Zoe. Nothing else. You, in my arms, and your eyes where I can see them.''

He reached for a condom and ripped it open with his teeth, his eyes never leaving hers. Their gazes remained locked while he protected them both, then pushed her legs apart. She swayed and had to brace herself against his chest.

''Keep looking at me,'' he ordered.

She did, her eyes growing round when she felt him rubbing the tip of his penis between her lips down there, grazing over her swollen clitoris with each stroke.

''Don't keep doing that,'' she gasped at last. ''I can't stand it. Just put it in. Please, Aiden...''

He put it in, his swift upward surge lifting her up onto her toes. His hands gripped her behind and he hoisted her up onto his hips, the position allowing him to slide home to the hilt, filling her totally.

It was better than she'd dreamed about.

Better.

Bigger.

''Oh,'' she panted, grabbing at his shoulders for support.

''Brace your feet against the wall behind me,'' he urged. ''I'll hold you in position. Bend then straighten your knees.''

''I...I can't.''

''Yes, you can. Squeeze me tight at the same time.''

She managed it, her mouth gaping open as sensation followed sensation. Oh, it felt so good. So unbelievably good.

His groan echoed her own sentiments. And her rapture.

"That's just incredible," he rasped. "Keep doing it... Don't stop... Faster... Yes, that's the way... darlin'....''

His words excited her unbearably. They were wild and primitive, as their mating was wild and primitive.

Zoe came first, and then Aiden, their cries mingling, their bodies shuddering as their passion exploded from within.

It was some time before their spasms subsided, but they still clung to each other, Zoe sobbing with aftershock, and Aiden rubbing her back, trying to comfort her, his own thoughts confused.

Was she really upset? he began to worry when the weeping continued. If so, why?

It was what she wanted, wasn't it? It was why she'd come here, or so she insisted.

So why was she crying?

When her sobbing quietened to the odd hiccup, he carefully eased himself out of her and lowered her feet onto the floor. Her legs went to jelly and he had to hold her upright. "Are you all right?" he asked gently.

She looked up at him through soggy lashes. "What a silly question," she choked out, then shivered.

"You're cold." He reached out to snap a large fluffy orange towel off the rack, wrapping it around her shoulders.

Her yawn startled her. "I think I'm more tired than cold."

"Want me to carry you to bed?"

She nodded, and he swept her up into his arms, the towel still around her.

She sighed an exhausted sigh and snuggled into him, her cheek resting against his chest, right over his heart. It fluttered, then filled with the most overwhelming emotion. Aiden's arms tightened around her and he knew, without a shadow of a doubt, that he loved this girl. Loved her as he had never loved before. Loved her passionately. Possessively, and rather painfully.

It hadn't been sexual frustration which had racked his insides by the time she'd arrived today. He'd been worrying his guts out that she might have had a car accident.

Now that he'd made love to her properly again, he could not bear to think of her ever being with another man. He wanted her to be his woman, forever. He wanted to live with her, have children with her, grow old with her. Hey, he even wanted to marry her.

And that was not something Aiden considered lightly.

Marriage, he'd always thought, was not for him.

There again, he hadn't met his true love at that stage.

He smiled at what his mother was going to say when he told her. Not that he intended to make such a confession just yet. He had things to do first...like get Zoe to fall in love with him in return.

Aiden carried her down the hallway toward his bedroom, his mind whirling with plans and possibilities. Could he get her to fall in love with him in a week?

Probably not.

Zoe wasn't in the mood for love.

But she was in the mood for sex. Oh, yes. She surely was that.

His stomach contracted as he thought of her going down on him in the shower. She'd been good, for a beginner. More than good. She'd been downright amazing.

Aiden glanced down at her lovely face as he angled her through the bedroom doorway. Her hair was plastered back from it but there was one stray curl stuck to her forehead. He smiled, thinking of that naughty version of the verse about the little girl with the curl in the middle of her forehead. When she was good she was very very good, but when she was bad, she was fucking fantastic!

Aiden understood that Zoe wanted to be bad for a while. Bad in her eyes, that is. Personally, he didn't believe that sex between consenting adults was ever bad, provided you didn't hurt anyone. And who were they hurting? No one.

But Zoe hadn't been brought up like him. She'd been raised with more old-fashioned ideas where it wasn't nice for girls to have sex without love.

Aiden didn't subscribe to that theory at all. Girls had just as much right to enjoy sex for sex's sake as guys did. To have fun for the moment, without always thinking of tomorrow.

So what if she wanted to be treated strictly as a sex object for a week? To try positions she'd never tried before. To explore her sexuality to the outer limits.

He could handle that, provided it was *him* she was

doing the exploring with. Aiden's smile turned wry. Amazing how, when you loved a woman, you weren't quite as liberal-minded about their sexual activities.

Holding her with one arm, he threw back the quilt, eased the towel away then lowered her nicely naked body into his nice big bed.

She immediately rolled over, curling her legs up into the fetal position. He stared at her deliciously curved bottom for a few seconds, before sighing and rather reluctantly covering her up.

"You'll keep," he muttered under his breath.

"Aiden," she mumbled.

He bent down and kissed the top of her head. "What, darlin'?"

"Aren't you coming to bed with me?" she asked dreamily.

"In a little while."

"Oh…all right. 'Night."

He didn't like to tell her it was still afternoon. "'Night. Sleep tight."

She didn't hear him. She was already asleep.

17

ZOE half woke to the feel of someone sliding into bed with her. She automatically rolled over onto her left side, facing the wall, before her memory clicked in and her eyes snapped open into the darkened bedroom. Night had fallen, but there was some moonlight filtering through the open window.

"Aiden?" she choked out.

"Who else?" he said, his arms snaking 'round her waist and scooping her back against him. "All rested now?" he murmured, his head right behind hers, his lips nibbling at her shoulder.

"What…what time is it?"

"Around nine. Why? Does it matter?"

"No. I guess not."

She shivered when his mouth blew warm puffs in her right ear. When he dipped his tongue in and swirled it around, she stiffened, her legs shooting straight out, her behind discovering he was as naked as she was.

His hands started to travel over the front of her body, playing with her breasts, her stomach, then lower. Despite her own insistence that their time together would be focused on sex, her mind initially recoiled at being used in this way. Her body, however, seemed to like it, and in no time she was panting and wriggling her bottom against his erection.

"You're an impatient little thing, aren't you?" he muttered. "Just as well I wore one of my trusty condoms to bed."

Zoe moaned softly when he eased into her from behind.

She wasn't surprised at the position, or the pleasure. He'd done it this way to her on the first night they spent together, and she'd loved it. They were like two spoons, curved around each other.

"You really like it this way, don't you?" he murmured as he rocked gently into her, his hands caressing her nipples at the same time.

"Yes," she gasped.

It felt fantastic. *Too* fantastic. She was going to come and she didn't want to come. Not that soon. She wanted it to go on and on. She wanted...

He slid out of her and she cried out in dismay. His arms squeezed tightly around her, his own breathing ragged. "Patience, my love. Talk to me for a while. It doesn't have to be anything deep and meaningful. I just need a breather and so do you. Try to relax."

Relax! Was he insane? How could she relax when she was screaming inside and when he was still hugging her to him like this, his erection stabbing at her bottom?

"What books do you like to read?" he asked.

"What? Oh...er...um...anything which doesn't bore me."

"You must like thrillers, then."

"Thrillers? Well…some of them. It depends on the author."

"Which author do you like most?"

"I can't think."

"Try."

"Um…Stephen King, I suppose."

"No kidding. I'm mad about Stephen King. I only discovered reading for pleasure this past year and he's the one I have to credit for doing it. My mom gave me *The Running Man* and I haven't had my nose out of one of his books ever since. Have you read *The Green Mile?*"

"Yes."

"It's great, isn't it?"

"Yes, but I liked *The Stand* even more."

"I haven't read that one."

"Oh, you should. It…"

Zoe was to wonder later how it came about that they started talking about Stephen King's books and she forgot all about sex. Until, that is, Aiden reminded her by lifting her right leg up onto his hip and slipping inside her once more.

"I think we might try something slightly different," he said, and rolled over onto his back. Naturally, she went with him, since his arms were wrapped tightly around her waist at the time. She ended up lying on top of him, her back stretched out along his front. He remained inside her, but not quite as deeply.

He let go of her waist and spread her arm and legs wide on the bed on either side of him. She looked and felt like a primitive virgin sacrifice stretched out on the altar of his naked body. No longer a virgin, however, in any sense of the word. She'd never felt so decadent. Or so turned on.

"Tell me what you're thinking?" he asked, his hands skimming up and down the length of her body, grazing over her rigid nipples.

"I...I can't..."

"Yes, you can. You can tell me anything."

"But I can't even *think!*"

He laughed then took her right hand in his and carried it down, down to that excruciatingly sensitive bud of swollen flesh which was at that moment wickedly exposed to the warm night air.

"Touch yourself there," he whispered, pressing her fingers against it.

Her mind once again recoiled but her body had a will of its own.

"Don't come," he advised softly. "Be gentle. Tease yourself. Work out what gives you pleasure without sending you over the edge."

Zoe could not believe she was doing this. Touching herself while he watched and instructed. But once she got over the initial stabs of embarrassment, it was an incredible turn-on. Soon, she was writhing on top of him, her behind clenching and unclenching. A climax was only seconds away.

When he abruptly grabbed her hips and lifted her right off him, she swore at him in mindless frustration.

"Tch, tch," he said, dumping her on the bed beside him and looming over her, his hands pinning her shoulders to the bed. "What would your father say if he heard you using words like that?"

"He'd probably agree with me if he knew what you were up to," she ground out. "He thinks you're a great guy. Genuine and sincere. He doesn't know that you're a sexual sadist."

He grinned down at her. "Think of me more as your erotic educator rather than the Marquis de Sade. I'm teaching you to wait. It will be well worth it in the end. Trust me. I'm also giving poor old Percy here a short rest. He almost lost it again a second ago which will never do. Obviously, he's in sorry need of some serious practice. That six months' spell I inflicted on him hasn't done him any good at all. Hopefully, with a bit of patience and help, he'll be right back in tip-top form in no time."

Zoe didn't think poor old Percy, who was pressing into her stomach at that precise moment, felt at all poor, or old. "Do you seriously expect me to believe that before I came along you'd gone six months without sex?"

"Do you seriously expect me to believe you haven't gone down on a guy before me?" he countered just as cynically.

She opened her mouth, then closed it again.

"Think about it, Zoe. Things aren't always what they appear to be. On top of that, why would I lie? What reason could I possibly have?"

She considered a few possibilities. To impress her somehow? To get under her guard? To make her think he wasn't anything like Drake who obviously couldn't go a week without his regular dose of slut?

None of those answers seemed to gel, which meant he hadn't lied to her. He'd been telling the truth about going six months without sex. Which led to another question. *Why?*

The concept that he might have been seriously hurt by that woman who took him to court was an explanation Zoe didn't want to think about. Because if she did, it meant she was starting to get involved. To care.

She couldn't do that to herself again. Not again. Not this soon, anyway.

"I have no idea," she said. "And I don't really want to know. I'm sorry I asked."

"Don't be," he returned just as nonchalantly. "It served a purpose. You've stopped swearing at me for not letting you come. So, are you hungry? For food, I mean."

Now that he mentioned it, she *was* hungry. It seemed her appetite had returned. And her desperate need for a climax had lessened somewhat.

"You mean you're not going to torture me again?"

"Not for a while."

Was she relieved, or disappointed?

"What have you got to eat?"

"Let's see now...I have a wide selection of frozen food in my freezer, and a trusty microwave to heat them in, but I also make a mean omelette. And I have some excellent white wine chilling in the fridge. I saw you drinking some Chardonnay the other night so I picked up a few good bottles on the way."

"You don't need to get me drunk, you know," she said ruefully. "I'm already a sure thing."

He grinned. "I know."

She couldn't help it. She grinned back. He really was delightfully wicked.

And delightfully wicked she could cope with. Delightfully wicked was far removed from anything deep and meaningful.

"An omelette sounds great. And the wine, too."

"Fantastic." He let her go and leaped out of the bed, turning to hold out his hand toward her.

She couldn't help but stare. "You're not going to walk around like *that,* are you?"

He glanced downward, then up again. "The condom bothers you?"

"No, but what's in it does," she said dryly. He was still fiercely erect.

Aiden shrugged. "At least this way I'm fully armed and ready if the heat of the moment overtakes us. But perhaps you're right. It might be dangerous cooking like this. I'll go to the bathroom and retrieve my shorts. But if you think you're going to put on those clothes *you* wore up here, Miss Pretend Prissy, then you can think again. Here…"

He marched over to the pine tallboy near the doorway and wrenched open the top drawer, pulling out a yellow T-shirt and tossing it to her. "Put that on. That's your uniform while you're here. No bra. And definitely no knickers. Just a T-shirt."

Zoe suppressed a laugh. "Yes, Sarge. Whatever you say, Sarge." Little did he know that wearing a man's T-shirt was overdressed compared to the scenario she'd fantasized over. But once she'd dragged it on, she could see that it was a surprisingly provocative garment. Her lack of underwear was patently obvious with her permanently hard nipples jutting through the thin material and her naked bottom was barely covered. She'd be a right sight if she stretched up or bent over.

"Wait for me," she said, and hurried down the hallway after Aiden.

ZOE found the next hour incredibly enjoyable. Aiden was an excellent cook and an entertaining companion. The wine was superb and so was the ambience of the front porch where they ate their omelettes and bread rolls, warm from the oven. They didn't sit at a table but perched on the porch steps, their plates balanced on their laps, their glasses of wine sitting beside them.

The night air was like warm velvet, the star-studded sky and half moon quite romantic. All was quiet at Hideaway Beach except for some distant music and the lap-lapping of the waves on the sand.

Zoe swallowed the last mouthful, then licked her fingers with a voluptuous sigh. "That was wonderful, Aiden. Thank you."

"My pleasure. Here, let me do that."

Before she could stop him, he took her right hand and sucked each finger in turn, a slow sensuous sucking which curled her stomach and brought her right back to where he'd had her an hour earlier.

"Do you provide this kind of personal after-dinner service for all your women?" she asked in an attempt to keep her cool.

He smiled wryly as he withdrew her little finger from his mouth. "Naughty, naughty," he said, shaking his head. "None of that getting-to-know-you stuff, you said. What I have or haven't done with previous women is on the no-no list of subjects for discussion.''

Zoe was a bit put out. She'd thought he *wanted* to get to know her. ''You asked me about my reading habits and I didn't object,'' she pointed out. ''And we've just spent the last hour chatting about food and wine.''

''Well, we do have to talk about something occasionally, don't we? And chatting about our tastes in books and food and wine is a far cry from revealing details of earlier relationships. Just sex, you said. And just sex you're going to get. So put your plate down, lover, and let's adjourn to the lounge room. I fancy a change of venue and some music. But bring your glass with you and I'll get the bottle. Your education is about to continue…''

18

AIDEN lay stretched out on top of his bed, his hands
and feet secured to the four corners of his bed with
various pieces of Zoe's underwear. She'd laughingly
said they might as well be put to *some* use.

He still could not believe he'd agreed to this. Yet
he had no one else to blame but himself. He'd created
a monster!

"Having fun?" Zoe asked as she sashayed back
into the room, wearing his favorite orange T-shirt and
looking very pleased with herself. And why not?
She'd already had two orgasms to his none.

He regretted now having shown her how to stop
him coming with one simple squeeze in just the right
spot. He hadn't realized at the time how ruthlessly
she would use that knowledge, once she had the
chance.

Zoe's behavior this morning put paid to any ego-
tistical idea she might be falling in love with him.

Over the last three days, he'd stupidly started hoping her feelings might be more than lust, because she
was just so hot for him all the time. She never said
no. He could have her anytime, anyplace, anywhere.

When she'd confided in bed this morning that she
had a persistent fantasy about his tying her up, he'd

been thrilled. Only a seriously besotted girl let a guy tie her up! So he'd been all for it. At that point she'd said she didn't really trust him enough for that, but she also fancied the idea of tying *him* up, if he didn't mind.

Naturally, at the time, he didn't mind one bit. He'd been so turned on he'd have agreed to being tied naked to a spit and roasted over hot coals!

And now here he was, spreadeagled and helpless. A lamb to her slaughter. The perfect victim for her increasingly insatiable appetite.

She wasn't in love with him at all, he finally had to accept. She'd just become sex mad!

He closed his eyes and groaned when she climbed onto the bed and straddled him once more.

"Poor Percy," she crooned as she pressed his rock-hard shaft painfully flat against his stomach. "And poor Aiden. You just have to learn to wait, don't you?" she said, smiling as she bent down to kiss him long and lasciviously, her tongue a worse temptation than the snake in the garden of Eden.

He moaned when she stopped.

"Beg for mercy," she murmured against his lips.

"Never," he bit back.

She smiled. "So be it."

She climbed off the bed and left the room.

Aiden would have screamed and shaken the bed if his pride had let him. But that was what she wanted. She wanted him to become frantic, and to beg.

Be blowed if he would ever do that!

She didn't come back for at least twenty minutes by which time things had thankfully subsided somewhat. But when Aiden saw she was carrying a tray of ice cubes, Percy snapped to attention once more.

"Don't," he croaked before he could stop himself.

"Don't what?" she asked in mock innocence. "You don't know what I'm going to do."

Yes, he did, because he'd done it to her yesterday. Used ice cubes on her nipples. And other places.

She smiled, popped an ice cube into her mouth and climbed up onto the bed.

Aiden gritted his teeth and tried not to cry out. But the sensations threatened to overwhelm him. Talk about fire and ice!

Fellatio on the rocks was a first for him and quite an experience. After the initial shock, the ice made his blood cool and his erection retreat, but that didn't last long. Eventually the cube melted and she didn't stop to get more. She kept on doing what she knew he liked best, taking him closer and closer to a climax. His hips began to lift from the bed and his mind and body strained toward the finishing line.

He couldn't believe it when she abandoned him again, right on the brink. When she got two more ice cubes out of the tray, it took every ounce of his control not to beg.

"Don't worry," she said with wildly glittering eyes. "This won't hurt a bit." And she rubbed them over his male nipples.

His body jerked, his mouth gasping open, his arms snapping his bonds tight as he fought to break free.

He swore. A lot.

She gave him a stunned look. "You don't like it?

But *I* did when you did it to me. I thought it was incredible.''

''I can't stand it,'' he bit out, terrified that if she kept on, he'd be doing worse than begging. He'd be embarrassing himself, totally.

''Well, you only had to say so,'' she said, looking unsure of herself for the first time that day. ''I wouldn't do anything I didn't think you were enjoying. Do you want me to untie you, too?''

Did he?

''No,'' he had to admit. He hadn't been this excited, or this hard, ever before. ''Not yet. But please, Zoe. Stop all that other stuff and make love to me. Properly.''

MAKE *love* to him?

Zoe was taken aback. He hadn't used that particular phrase all week. He'd called what they'd been doing everything else but.

A traitorous warmth curled through her stomach 'til she reminded herself they were still just words, especially in the mouths of men. Did any of them know what making love meant? Or what love meant? Did *she* anymore, for that matter?

She'd thought she loved Greg. She'd really thought she loved Drake. But both had been an illusion and neither had been able to make her feel what Aiden could make her feel. He only had to look at her and she wanted him. He only had to touch her and the craving would return.

It would be so easy to think of those feelings as love.

But they weren't. That was the hard lesson she'd learned this week. It was just sex. What they'd been doing for the last three days had been just sex. What she was about to do to him was still just sex.

But what the heck? If he wanted to call it making love then she wasn't about to object. He could call it whatever he darned well liked. She wasn't going to go all gooey over a silly phrase.

"My pleasure," she murmured, and moved to get one of the condoms which were always at the ready on the bedside table. She had it on him in seconds, having become an expert at the task. He liked her doing it. He said he found it a turn-on.

Not that he needed turning on at that moment. His erection was huge. At least he wanted her. That she *was* sure of.

"Take off the T-shirt," he said thickly when she straddled him once more. "I want to see all of you."

She shouldn't have done what he wanted. She should have smiled and told him that he was hardly in the position to give orders. This was *her* game. She was the one with the whip hand.

But there was something in his voice and in his eyes which she couldn't resist. So she crossed her arms and took the hem of the T-shirt and slowly lifted it up over her head before tossing it away. Staying up on her knees, she watched his eyes while she ran her hands over her breasts.

He groaned. "God, don't do that. Not without me inside you. Put it in, Zoe. For pity's sake."

For pity's sake?

She had no pity for him. But she still did what he wanted.

He sighed with pleasure and closed his eyes. Just in time, too. Because as she took him deep into her body, something happened to Zoe, something perturbing. A great wave of emotion flooded her chest, and tears pricked at her eyes.

That stupid phrase, she thought despairingly. That stupid, stupid phrase!

If only he hadn't said it. If only he'd used one of those other four-letter words they'd both bandied around all week. Why did he have to mention love?

Angrily, she began to move on top of him in the way he'd shown her, desperately trying to focus on nothing but the sex. Physically, it was even better than it had ever been. He was so big. But emotionally, she felt distraught and empty. Suddenly, she didn't want him tied up and she didn't want to be on top. She wanted to be beneath him, with their arms around each other and their mouths locked. She wanted tenderness, not kinkiness. She wanted his whole body, wrapped warmly and securely around her.

In short, she wanted Aiden to make love to *her* properly, not just have sex with her.

Zoe groaned her dismay at what this meant. She had fallen in love with the man. Against all common sense, and all her best resolves. It was irrational to love him, but it was no less real. Awfully painfully real.

"Zoe?" he choked out, his eyes opening. "Why have you stopped, darling?"

She wished he hadn't called her darling. It was like

a dagger into her heart because it was so patently false. But it gave her focus. And courage. And some return to common sense.

"Just giving poor old Percy a rest," she said matter-of-factly.

"He doesn't need a rest," Aiden groaned. "He needs you."

"Really. Well, come next week, he'll have to find someone else, won't he?"

He stared at her and she knew all of a sudden that he wouldn't let her go quite that easily. She'd been more than a good lay over the last few days. She'd been his very own love slave, ready and willing to accommodate him twenty-four hours a day.

Her silly female heart fluttered wildly before she took hold of it once more. At least he doesn't know you love him, she reminded herself. He knows nothing except what you tell him.

Be strong. Be firm. Be assertive. There'll never be a better moment to show him what you're made of, with him flat on his back and unable to move.

"Don't look so down in the mouth," she said blithely, and returned to her rising and falling rhythm. "A man like you won't take long to find a replacement."

"And what if I don't want a replacement?" he grated out.

"You can't always have what you want in life, Aiden," she said as she continued her ruthless rhythm. "I've certainly learned that. I'm surprised you haven't. Money doesn't buy everything, you know."

"I know that, but I… Oh…" He gasped, then grimaced.

Understandable. She'd begun squeezing him tightly with her insides. She had to do something to shut him up and change the subject.

"Do stop talking, lover," she advised dryly. "We both know that men can't do two things at once, unlike us clever little females." I can even do this and break my heart at the same time! "Close your eyes again and just let it go."

And let *me* go, she willed fiercely.

He closed his eyes and came with a rush.

Depressingly, so did she.

Zoe had never hated a climax more.

19

"I'M GOING surfing," Aiden said, and waited for Zoe to say something.

She was lying on her stomach on the bed, her arms curved up under the pillow, her face turned away from him. She'd flopped down there after she'd untied him, saying she was exhausted and needed a nap.

"Fine," she said without moving an inch. "Have fun."

He glowered down at her naked back, then whirled and marched out, wondering what in heaven's name he'd ever seen in her.

Okay, so she'd been a real honey when he'd first met her, but she wasn't anymore. She'd become a tough, cynical, sex-driven bitch!

"You can't have everything in life you want," he sneered as he stomped out onto the front porch. "No kidding!"

A strong gust of wind startled Aiden out of his mutterings. It was another hot day, but by the look of the darkening sky and the storm clouds gathering on the horizon, a southerly change was on the way.

Hideaway Beach was not a good surf in these conditions. The waves would get bigger, but dumping.

And the tide would become stronger and more dangerous.

But he was going surfing, come hell or high water. He'd drive over to Fisherman's Beach which was much more open. The waves there would still be big, but rolling, and less risky.

No, he'd *walk* over to Fisherman's Beach. It was a long walk, but he didn't care. He needed a couple of hours away from Zoe.

Leaving his lighter board leaning against the verandah, he collected a trusty old favorite from the roof of his van, tucked it under his arm and set off across the sand. He briefly thought of going back and telling Zoe where he was going, but that seemed so pathetic. And needy.

She'd still be there when he got back. After all, she hadn't had her daily quota of orgasms!

And if she wasn't?

Aiden decided testily that might be for the best.

ZOE wept quietly into the pillow for a long time after Aiden left.

How could she have been so stupid as to fall in love with him? Mel would be so disappointed in her, but not as disappointed as she was with herself.

Thinking of Mel, however, reminded Zoe that she hadn't checked the message bank on her cell phone since she arrived. Understandable, considering her mind had been elsewhere. She hoped no one had been trying to get into contact with her urgently.

Zoe sighed and sat up, swinging her feet over the

side of the bed. Now where was that T-shirt? And where was her handbag?

She finally found it hanging on a chair in the kitchen.

Zoe winced as she ran through the messages. Betty had tried to ring her yesterday. Fran, too. Both had left a message for her to ring them back. But Fran had added as soon as possible.

Which one first?

Zoe dialed her work number.

"Phillips & Cox," June answered.

"Fran Phillips, please," Zoe said, using a brisk, business-like voice and hoping June didn't recognize her. The last thing she wanted to do was answer the office gossip's questions.

Thankfully, she was put straight through to Fran.

"It's Zoe, Fran. I got your message to call."

"Zoe. I'm so glad you rang back. Sorry to bother you when you're on holidays."

"What's up? Something to do with work?"

"No. Not at all. But, this is harder than I thought it would be. No one likes to be the bearer of bad tidings but I thought you should know exactly what's been going on behind your back."

"Ah," Zoe said, the penny dropping. "You've seen Drake and Tracy together. She's blond. Big boobs. Mouth to match."

"You know about her?" Fran sounded shocked.

"I caught Drake with her in flagrante delicto last Saturday night at his party. I dumped him then and there, so don't worry, Fran. I know exactly what's been going on behind my back. I dare say it's been going on for quite some time.''

''I *knew* there was something more to your wanting time off than just your father breaking his ankle. I just couldn't work out what 'til I saw that disgusting piece of work with Drake at the pool together. She was all over him like a rash. And he was so drunk. I was appalled and I told him so. I can't tell you the language he used back. And in full hearing of lots of people. Goodness knows what's got into him. He'll ruin himself both socially and professionally if he keeps on behaving like that.''

''Good,'' Zoe pronounced. But it wasn't good. It was rather sad, really. Zoe had an awful feeling Drake had loved her, in his own peculiar way. But he'd been addicted to a certain type of sex, the kind he didn't think he could get from her.

''Are you sure you're all right?'' Fran asked.

''I'm fine,'' Zoe lied.

''But you're not still down at your father's farm, are you?''

''N...no,'' she said carefully. ''Why?''

''This is awkward, too. Look, I'll just come right out and say it. The thing is, Zoe, I was so shocked by what happened with Drake that I couldn't help talking about it. Anyway, I was telling Nigel and saying how upset you must be, and this weird little smile came over his face. When I asked what was going on, he said not to worry about you too much, that you'd met someone a lot better than Drake and if he knew anything about life and love, you'd be coming back to work next week all rosy-cheeked and dewy-eyed. When I pressed him for the name of this white knight he said it was Aiden Mitchell, at which point I nearly had a hernia.''

''You don't think Aiden's a white knight?'' Zoe said ruefully.

''So, it's true! You're having a *thing* with Aiden Mitchell!''

''A fling, Fran. Not a thing. It's nothing serious.'' Except that her heart was breaking.

''Are you sure? Nigel seemed to think Aiden sounded pretty serious about *you*.''

Zoe's heart leaped. But only for a second. ''Nigel's a romantic.''

''And you're not?''

''Not anymore.''

''Oh. What a shame.''

Zoe was taken aback. ''What do you mean what a shame? I thought you thought I was a fool for being a romantic.''

Fran sighed. ''I guess I did, when it came to Drake. But Aiden Mitchell! Now he's worth being a bit romantic over. He's one seriously sexy guy. And not quite as callous as the newspapers painted him last year.''

''Not *quite?*'' Zoe queried, surprised that Fran would have anything good to say about him at all. ''What do you mean by that?''

''Look, I have to admit I don't know Aiden all that well. He was Nigel's client. But I recognize a right royal bitch when I meet one and that female who sued him tried to hire me first as her lawyer and I wouldn't touch her with a bargepole. She was an incredibly nasty piece of work. A clever liar, though. And Aiden, unfortunately, has this perversely honest streak. He refused to lie on the stand and that did him in, because when questioned, he admitted to sleeping with her. Then he foolishly added it had only been the once. No one in that courtroom believed him, other than Nigel.''

''Nigel believed he was telling the truth?''

''Yes, he did. And Nigel is a darned good judge of character, except when the guy concerned is gorgeous *and* gay. Which Aiden isn't.''

''No, he certainly isn't,'' Zoe agreed.

''I gathered that. I won't ask you what he's like in bed. I don't want to be jealous. Whatever, I'm glad to hear you're not devastated over Drake. But perhaps it's just as well this isn't serious between you and Aiden. It's a bit soon and you're only young, Zoe. You have all the time in the world. So have your fling. And have some fun. Now…you'll be back at work next Monday?''

''You can count on it,'' Zoe said firmly.

''I knew I could. 'Bye, Zoe. Take care.''

Zoe hung up, shaking her head and frowning. Hard to keep anything a secret in this world. She should have known Fran would find out, especially with Aiden having contacted Nigel in his pursuit of her.

Zoe didn't know what to make of Fran's revelations about Aiden's character. Considering her boss's cynicism about the male sex, Zoe had to take what she'd said at face value. Aiden must have been the injured party in that court case, which certainly would explain why he'd been reluctant to tell her the truth about himself when they'd first met.

Zoe's stomach churned at the thought that maybe Aiden was serious about her. He'd said he was, of course. In the beginning. But serious about what? Getting her into bed again?

Once he'd secured her promise to go away with him and she'd insisted on a strictly sexual affair, he'd quickly dropped all that I-want-a-real-relationship rubbish. Not once, over the last few days, had he tried to change the status quo. In fact, every time *she'd* asked him a personal question, he'd been quick to fob her off and get back to just sex.

Okay, so perhaps he wasn't the liar Drake had been. Maybe he did have some feelings for her other than sexual. He still wasn't a marrying kind of guy. Being his girlfriend was not going to be a permanent position.

No. She wasn't about to give Nigel's view of Aiden's so-called seriousness too much credence.

Neither did she want to get maudlin over the fact she'd fallen in love with the wrong man. Again.

She'd known what she was getting herself into here. She'd gone into it with her eyes well and truly open. Zoe had no one to blame but herself.

She rang Betty next.

Betty answered on the second ring.

"Betty, it's Zoe. I'm sorry I haven't called back sooner. I had my cell phone turned off and I've only just looked at my messages. What's up? Dad okay?"

"Is your dad okay, she says," Betty replied with a

happy lilt in her voice. "I'll say he is. You're never going to believe this."

"He's sold the farm?"

"What? Oh, yes, he's going to do that, too. But that'll take time. That's not why I've rung."

"So what else has Dad done?" As if she didn't know. He must have told Betty he loved her.

"Well, on Monday he made me take him into Moss Vale, crutches and all, and have his hair cut. And then he dragged me into the trendiest menswear shop in town and asked me to choose some new clothes for him. And then…oh, you're not going to believe this! *Then,* over lunch, he asked me to marry him."

"*What?*" Zoe was shocked. She'd thought he was going to wait awhile before he proposed. "So what did *you* say?"

"I said yes, of course. I've been in love with your dad for ages."

"You *have?*"

"There's no need to sound so surprised, missy. Your dad's a good-looking man for his age. You could have knocked me over with a feather when he said he'd been in love with *me* for ages."

"Now, there's no need for *you* to sound so surprised, Betty. You're a *very* good-looking woman. For any age."

"Oh, go on with you. I'm too tall, and too skinny and I have the most awful-colored hair."

"I'll have you know that my dad thinks you're so beautiful and so special that he didn't *dare* ask you to marry him before. He was sure you'd say no."

"He said that?"

"He did, indeed."

"Oh..." For the first time in her life, Zoe reckoned, Betty was speechless. But now Zoe knew the truth over why Betty had never married. Because of low physical self-esteem. All the time she'd been helping Zoe to look better, Betty had probably believed her own looks were a lost cause.

"That is the best news I've had in simply ages," Zoe said. "I'm so happy for you both. Tell Dad I'm proud of him."

"Tell him yourself. *Bill?*" she called out. "Bill, it's Zoe on the phone. She wants to talk to you."

"Zoe."

"Hi there, Dad."

"I did it."

"You certainly did. I'm very proud of you."

"I'm pretty proud of myself. I was going to wait 'til I lost some weight but I decided not to. Life's too short. But I've started watching my diet already, and I'll get right into some proper exercise once I get this plaster off my ankle. Meanwhile, I'm selling the farm and organizing a wedding."

"And when do you think the wedding will be?"

"As soon as we can arrange it. Betty's never been married and I thought she'd like a nice church wedding. What do you think?"

"I think that's sweet." Suddenly, tears filled Zoe's eyes.

There'd be no nice church wedding for her with the man she loved. No wedding of any kind.

"You'll tell Aiden?" her father said.

"Tell who what?" Her thoughts had left her distracted.

"Did I get it wrong? I thought you'd gone away for a few days with Aiden. He'd said you were."

Any tears quickly dried up, replaced by annoyance. "Did he now? Well, he had no right to do that."

"Why not? Anyone could see you're crazy about each other. I don't know why you thought you had to pretend you weren't. I'm no fool, Zoe. I know you and Aiden are more than just good friends. I just want you to know that I heartily approve."

"You approve of my sleeping with Aiden?" Zoe blurted out, astonished. He certainly hadn't approved of her sharing her room with Drake at Christmas.

"No. Of your loving him. He's the real McCoy. So don't let this one get away."

"And what if he wants to get away?"

Her dad chuckled. "Aiden? Want to get away from you? Why would he want to do that? He loves you!"

Zoe's heartbeat bolted. "Did he say that to you?"

"Of course not. I could just tell."

Her heart skittered to a halt, her sigh weary. What a fool she was to get her hopes up like that. Her father had about as much insight into matters of the heart as one of his cows. He'd practically been living with Betty all these years and hadn't gleaned *her* true feelings.

"Whatever you say, Dad."

"You don't believe me!" He sounded truly shocked.

"Let's just say I'll wait for the proposal of marriage."

"Proposal of marriage? He's not going to propose marriage! He's only just met you."

"I thought you said he loved me."

"Men don't propose marriage that quickly. Or that rashly. For one thing, they're afraid of being rejected. If you haven't told him you love him yet, he'll be worried you might not."

"I don't."

"Oh, yes, you do, daughter."

Zoe sighed again. "All right, I do. But I don't want to."

"Why not?"

"Because even if he does love me—and I don't think he does—he's on record as saying he's not a marrying man."

"He hadn't met you at that stage."

Zoe gave up. "Can we just leave this argument for now, Dad?"

"Promise me you'll tell him you love him."

"I can't do that."

"You mean you won't."

"All right, I won't."

"You made me tell Betty I loved her, and you were right. You said life was too short not to, and you were right again. Now take some of your own advice and tell him you love him. Just because one man hurt you, doesn't mean the next one will. I wasted over ten years of my life, thinking no woman would want me because I couldn't make your mother happy."

"Oh, Dad. Mom wasn't *that* unhappy."

"Yes, she was. But I see now we were just mismatched. It wasn't all my fault."

Zoe nodded. He was right. Her mom was not the sort of woman to cope with the lonely life as a farmer's wife. She was not strong enough, or independent enough. Her only outside interest had been her garden, and it hadn't been enough.

"Give Aiden a fair go," her father said. "Don't let past experiences blind you to the present. Promise me that, at least."

"All right," she agreed. "I promise. And, Dad…"

"Yes?"

"I've enjoyed talking to you. Now you take care of yourself and give my love to Betty."

She hung up, frowning over the promise her father had extracted from her. Perhaps she *had* been letting the past blind her to the present. Perhaps she hadn't *really* given Aiden a fair go.

Okay, so she might get hurt again if she took a chance and told him she loved him. But wasn't it worth the risk of further pain, even if there was the slightest possibility Aiden might truly care about her?

There was going to be heartache for her, anyway.

A rumble of thunder interrupted her thoughts. Frowning, Zoe hurried out onto the porch and was shocked that the weather could have changed so radically without her having noticed. Ominous-looking gray clouds covered the sky, blocking out the sun. A brisk wind was whipping up the ocean into high foam-topped waves which curled over and crashed down angrily onto the beach.

Scanning the water, Zoe couldn't see Aiden. She knew the spot he favored when he went board riding but he wasn't there. No one was there. No one was on the beach at all.

It started to rain, large pelting drops which would soak anyone in seconds.

Zoe walked down the end of the covered porch and peered 'round the side of the house to where her car and Aiden's truck were parked side by side. The yellow truck was still there, so Aiden hadn't driven off anywhere else. Which meant he must have gone surfing here.

It was then that she saw his surfboard, still leaning up against the post beside the front steps.

Zoe's stomach contracted into a tight knot of instant fear. Aiden must have gone body surfing, not board riding.

Oh, dear heaven...

Zoe's hands gripped the red porch railing with white-knuckled intensity, her now-frantic gaze searching the ocean once more. She still couldn't see anyone swimming, or body surfing. Not a single bobbing head anywhere.

Suddenly, the waves didn't just look large but lethal as well. Zoe remembered that treacherous tide which had carried her toward the rocks that night. Her eyes swung over toward those rocks and she was amazed to see a couple of fishermen standing on them, still fishing. They had to be insane, she decided. But maybe they could tell her if they'd seen Aiden.

Running back inside, she dragged on some shorts then raced back through the front door, hurtling down the front steps and launching herself across the sand, unmindful of the rain. She was quick across the sand but slow once she came to the rocks, where she had to pick her way carefully over their slippery surfaces toward where the two fishermen were recklessly standing with their rods.

''Hey, there!'' she shouted when she didn't dare get any closer. As it was, every third wave washed over her lower legs, threatening her balance. ''Have you seen anyone swimming in the surf this afternoon?''

''What?'' one of them called back, whilst the other didn't even turn his head her way. He probably hadn't heard her with the wind and the rain and the waves.

She cupped her mouth with her hands and repeated her question. The fisherman shook his head and Zoe's heart sank. She doubted they would have noticed, anyway. Their focus was all on what they were doing.

For the next half an hour she walked up and down along the water's edge, getting soaked to the bone, but unable to go back to the house. If there'd been anyone else to ask for help, she would have, but Hideaway Beach was deserted. There wasn't a single vehicle in the visitors' car lot. Finally, in desperation, she went along and knocked on all the other doors of the weekenders, hoping that Aiden might have gone visiting.

But no one answered. They were weekenders, after all. And it was only a Thursday.

Zoe tried to cling to the hope that Aiden might have gone for a walk, but if that was so, surely he'd have come home once it started to rain. And it had been raining steadily for ages. The persistent thought that something dreadful had happened to him in the surf would not go away, bringing with it a sick churning to her stomach and an even sicker churning in her heart.

What if she never had the chance to tell him she loved him? What if it was all over between them in the most terrible and final way?

She couldn't bear it.

Despairingly, she returned to the house and in desperation picked up her phone. But who to call? If something disastrous had happened to Aiden in the surf it was already too late. She decided to call the triple-O emergency number, anyway, and was punching out the numbers when she heard the sound of a vehicle coming down the driveway. Dropping the phone, she dashed out onto the porch and raced 'round the side of the house.

A battered truck crunched to a halt behind the carport and Aiden jumped out of the passenger seat.

"Thanks for the ride, buddy," he called out as he retrieved a surfboard from the back.

"No sweat," the driver returned. "See you, Aiden." And he reversed up the driveway.

"What happened to you?" Aiden asked when he spotted Zoe standing there, soaked to her skin. "Go for a swim with your clothes on, did you?"

Zoe just stared at him, her emotions utterly mangled. She didn't know whether she wanted to kill him, or kiss him.

"No, you inconsiderate pig!" she threw at him. "I've been looking for your body!"

And she promptly burst into tears.

20

SHOCK held Aiden stock-still for a few moments, 'til suddenly, he saw the truth behind Zoe's tears.

She'd been worried sick about him. She thought she'd lost him. She truly cared about him.

He needed no other encouragement.

Dropping his board, he covered the distance between them in two strides and gathered her into his arms.

"You're right, I am inconsiderate. I walked over to Fisherman's Beach. I should have told you where I'd gone. I was angry with you because I didn't think you cared about me. I thought all you wanted from me was sex. But you do care, don't you, darling? Tell me I'm not wrong about that. Tell me you care."

He tipped up her chin so that he could see her eyes.

They were so beautiful, her eyes. And so expressive. He could see the fear in their glistening depths. But he could also see the love.

Or what he hoped was love.

"Don't be afraid to admit it," he said gently. "I won't hurt you like Drake hurt you. I love you, Zoe. With all my heart. I've never said that to any other girl in my life. I know you think I'm some kind of cheat with women because of that court case last year, but I'm not. I was the victim there, not her.''

''Tell me what really happened,'' Zoe asked.

''I met Marci at a party and we got talking. When she said she'd lost her job that week and had nowhere to live, I stupidly offered her the use of one of my spare rooms for a while. I didn't think anything of it, as I was hardly ever there. Admittedly, I began to feel she was overstaying her welcome after a few weeks went by and she didn't leave. But she always had some excuse why she couldn't move out and I had no real reason to throw her out. It wasn't as though I had a steady girlfriend at the time who was objecting. Then one night, when I came home after being away all week on business, she obviously set out to seduce me. And she succeeded. The next morning, when I explained to her that the night before was a mistake, she showed her true colors and said it was a mistake all right. Mine. She got herself a lawyer who made Attila the Hun look sweet and the rest is history. She was never my girlfriend, Zoe. And I never promised to marry her. My only crime was being a mug, for want of a better word.''

Zoe's eyes searched his face, obviously wanting to believe him, but still hesitant.

''I swear to you that that's the truth. On my mother's life,'' he added solemnly. ''And if you ever get to know me as well I would like, you'll know I would not say that lightly. Because I simply adore my mother.''

Zoe's defenses melted away at this declaration.

"Tell me you love me," he persisted. "Right now. Tell me."

"I love you," she choked out.

The blinding joy which spread across his handsome face soothed any lingering doubts Zoe was still harboring about the sincerity of Aiden's feelings.

"About time, too," he said thickly, and held her close, cradling her head against his chest.

"I tried not to," she confessed. "I tried to keep things to just sex. I told myself I didn't want to get to know you at all, except in the biblical sense. But in my heart of hearts, I always wanted more from you than just sex. I thought I was being sensible and strong in keeping our relationship to a brief affair, when really, I was just being a coward."

He held her away from him, his eyes soft and sympathetic. "You? A coward? Oh, no, Zoe. You're no coward. You're very brave, and I love that in you. You have character and spirit and standards."

"How can you say that? I've been wicked this week. You know I've been wicked."

"Not at all. How can anything we do together be wicked when we love each other so much?"

"Oh, Aiden, I do so love you. What I felt for Drake wasn't real love. I can see that now. As for Greg..."

Zoe bit her bottom lip, but it was too late. She'd already blurted out Greg's name.

"Greg?"

Zoe saw the speculation in Aiden's eyes and decided she wanted no ghosts from the past to spoil what she might have with this man. "A creep I met when I first came to Sydney," she explained. "He was my immediate boss in the section of the insurance company I worked in. At the time I was on the plump side and very shy where the opposite sex was concerned. Apparently, he made a bet with his male colleagues that he could get me into bed within a fortnight. He did, by telling me lies about how attractive he found me and how much he desired me. I was a naive fool to believe him, but then, that's what I was at the time. A naive fool. The day after I lost my virginity to him, I overheard him at work laughingly relating how pathetic I was in bed. He told his buddies that they should pay him double the agreed wager because naked, my body was so gross.''

"Oh, Zoe…how awful for you. It makes me ashamed of my sex when I hear things like that. But not all men are as bad as Greg. Or Drake. Take me for instance,'' he added, suddenly smiling the cheekiest smile. "I'm a prince.''

She laughed. "You're an arrogant devil, that's what you are. You knew I'd fall in love with you if I came away with you.''

"I was hopeful.''

"Even when I said I only wanted sex?''

"That didn't worry me to begin with. I thought sex between us would be a very emotionally bonding experience. But I have to admit I started to worry this morning after I let you tie me to the bed.''

"I can imagine. I was a bad girl, wasn't I?''

"Mmm.''

"But as soon as you asked me to make love to you properly, I realized I didn't want that kind of sex anymore. I wanted to untie you and have you make love to me properly right then and there.''

His beautiful blue eyes danced with a wry amusement. ''Really. You gave a pretty good imitation of a girl only interested in her own pleasure.''

''I didn't want you to know I loved you.''

He laughed. ''That's your story and you're going to stick to it, aren't you? Still, I see it's going to take me a while to convince you that I'm one of the good guys. I think, come tomorrow, I'm going to take you home to meet my mom. But first, I'm going to make love to the woman I love. Properly.'' And he swept her up into his arms.

''Tell me again that you love me,'' he said as he carried her back into the house.

''I love you, Aiden.''

''I want to hear that a lot tonight.''

''Yes, darling.''

''And I want to hear *that* a lot, too!''

''I DIDN'T bring my hair-dryer with me,'' Zoe wailed as she inspected herself in the bathroom mirror the next morning. ''And not much makeup, either. What will your mother think of me?''

Aiden smiled. ''She'll think you're gorgeous. Just like I do.''

''Really?''

Her insecurity over her appearance both irritated and touched him. ''Your hair looks lovely as it is,'' he insisted, ''and your skin has a wonderfully natural glow this morning.''

Zoe had to admit that she *was* looking good. Being truly in love suited her. Or was it being truly loved?

"You don't have to be anything other than your beautiful self around me, Zoe. I do understand that clothes and grooming play an important part in the professional scene around Sydney, but let's leave it there, shall we?"

"I just want to make a good impression on your mom."

Aiden smiled and drew her to him. "You've already made a good impression by falling in love with me. You should have heard her on the phone last night. She was ecstatic. But there's no need to doll yourself up for my mom. She's not into that kind of thing."

"I'm still not going to wear shorts," Zoe told Aiden firmly. "I want to wear my lemon slacks and white shirt."

He pulled a face. "If you must."

"I must." She reached up on tiptoe and kissed him lightly on the lips. "I'll tie the shirt above my waist and I won't wear a bra," she whispered.

He grinned. "That's my girl."

And wasn't that the truth. She was Aiden's girl. For better or worse. For richer or poorer. But would it ever be 'til death do them part?

Hopefully. Zoe knew her dad was right when he said that men didn't propose marriage this quickly. But she felt confident Aiden was already committed to a real and lasting relationship between them. They'd talked a lot last night in between the tenderest of lovemakings, and Zoe had woken this morning feeling happy and optimistic.

There were no guarantees in life, of course. There were no guarantees in anything. But she wasn't going to spoil what she could have with him by indulging in negative thoughts. For once, she was going to enjoy each day as it came and not worry too much, as Mel had advised.

"Just give me another fifteen minutes," Zoe told Aiden, "and I'll be ready to leave."

"I'm going to hold you to that," he said. And did.

The drive north was pleasant, with the southerly change the day before bringing milder fall weather. Just as well, Zoe thought, since they were driving in Aiden's yellow truck and it didn't have air-conditioning. She didn't want to arrive at his mother's place with limp hair and perspiration stains all over her shirt.

Zoe and Aiden chatted companionably the whole way, and it wasn't till Aiden took the turn-off to Shelley Bay, that she began feeling nervous.

"I hope your mom really likes me," she couldn't help saying.

"Don't worry. She will."

Shelley Bay turned out to be a delightful little seaside spot which had no high-rise buildings to mar its semi-tropical beauty. The tall Norfolk pines which lined the white-sanded beachfront made it look like a hundred other coastal towns which dotted the Australian coastline.

"Never changes, Shelley Bay," Aiden remarked happily as he drove down the main street then took a road which wound its way into the hills behind the town. "Which is exactly the way I like it."

"Give it another ten years," Zoe warned, glancing at the magnificent view in the side mirror. "I'll bet some big developer will move in and build a huge resort up on this very hill, and then you'll see some changes."

"I doubt it. I happen to own this hill and I ain't selling."

Zoe was astonished. "You're that rich, Aiden?"

"Filthy rich, actually. But you don't have to worry, darlin'. I won't go buying you all sorts of expensive gifts or taking you to five-star restaurants or doing any of those wickedly corrupting things you once told me not to. But it's going to be very difficult when it comes to birthdays and Christmas if I can't even buy you flowers and perfume."

"Aiden Mitchell, stop teasing me. You know that was before."

He grinned. "Before what?"

"Before I believed you loved me."

"You mean I can spoil and corrupt you with my money now?"

She laughed. "I think you've already corrupted me. But heck yes, spoil me all you like."

"Great. Oops. Almost missed mom's place. Too much talking."

Aiden braked sharply and zapped the yellow truck up a steep and rather rocky driveway, which then flattened out and swung 'round in a circle in front of one of those delightful old wooden houses called Queenslanders. Given this one belonged to Aiden's mother,

Zoe should not have been surprised that it was painted a bright yellow, with white latticework and a deep terra-cotta roof.

Not that the color scheme didn't brilliantly suit its leafy-green setting. Huge gum trees on either side cast shade onto the roof whilst large tree palms and various exotic-looking ferns flanked the white-painted steps which led up onto the wide cool-looking porch.

Zoe was admiring it all when a woman emerged from the house and started walking down those steps, a woman who took Zoe's breath away.

She was tall and slender, with straight honey-blond hair which fell down to her waist. She was wearing an ankle-length, sarong-style skirt in turquoise silk, topped with a vivid scarlet singlet. Her feet were bare and her toenails were painted scarlet. As she drew closer Zoe saw she wore no makeup on her honey-colored skin. But she certainly wore jewelry.

Long multicolored hoops swung from her lobes. She had a gold stud in her right nostril and a snakelike silver bangle wrapped high around her left arm.

She looked exotic and sexy and not like anyone's mother Zoe had ever known.

"Oh, my, Aiden," Zoe gasped. "She's so beautiful."

"Who, Mom?" He seemed startled by the compliment. Then thoughtful. "Yeah, you're right. She is. But her soul is even more beautiful. Come on, come and meet her."

Kristy Mitchell's lovely face was even lovelier when she smiled. And she smiled at her son as he whisked her off her feet and whirled her 'round in greeting, kissing and hugging her at the same time.

Zoe watched, in a type of awe. Clearly, this was how this beautiful-looking woman had brought him up, with a lot of physical expressions of love. No wonder he was such a warm generous person and a simply wonderful lover.

"Aiden, put me down," his mom ordered at long last. "I'm very pleased to see you, too, darling, but don't you think it's time you introduced me to Zoe? That is why you've come, isn't it? So that I can see this very special girl who's revived your spirit and restored your soul."

Zoe's eyes widened at these amazingly flattering words. Was that what he'd told his mom she'd done for him?

She stared at Aiden who shrugged and smiled a little sheepishly at her.

"Trust my mom to embarrass me. But yes," he confirmed. "You did all that. And more." He took her hand and drew her to his side. "So what do you think of my Zoe, Mom? Isn't she lovely?"

Zoe colored a little as those beautiful blue eyes—so like her son's—gave her a long assessing look.

"I think," Aiden's mother said slowly, "that if she is that—*your* Zoe—then don't play games with her, son. Tell her what you told me last night. Tell her now."

Aiden groaned. He should have anticipated this. His mother would not let him make the same mistake she believed his father had once made.

"Aiden?" Zoe asked worriedly. "What does your mom mean? What is it you have to tell me?"

He closed his eyes and suddenly he felt as he'd felt once when he was out on his board and he saw this huge wave coming and he thought, I'm gone. He'd no option then but to gather all his courage and ride that rogue wave, because not to could have been the kiss of death to him as a professional surfer. He might have lost his nerve.

The situation was pretty much the same. He had to go for it. Had to. Because if he didn't, all might be lost. And losing Zoe would be a lot worse than losing his nerve.

He opened his eyes and looked straight at her. "I told my mother I was going to ask you to marry me one day in the near future. She seems to think that that one day should be today. And you know what? She's right. You are my one true love, Zoe. Why wait? Will you marry me?"

Zoe was overwhelmed. His one true love. He'd called her his one true love! On top of that, he'd proposed marriage!

"You don't have to give him an answer straight away," Aiden's mom said gently. "I just wanted him to be straight with you. After all you've been through with that other fellow, I thought you needed to hear up front just how much my boy loves you."

Aiden rolled his eyes. "Mom, will you shut up? And she *does* have to answer straight away. If I've had the guts to ask her, then she has to have the guts to answer me. So what's it to be, Zoe?"

Zoe wondered dazedly what all her friends and

family would say if they were standing here at this moment. Fran. Mel. Betty. Her dad.

Especially her dad.

What would he say to her?

A small smile played around Zoe's lips as she realized exactly what her dad would say.

Go for it, girl. Go for it.

And the others would probably say the same. But still...weren't they going to be surprised when she told them?

Her smile widened as she looked up into the eyes of the man she loved.

"Yes!" Aiden shouted, and punched the air in victory. "She said yes!"

FORBIDDEN PASSION
BY
EMILIE ROSE

Virginia and Angie,
thanks for your help and patience.

One

___

Her husband. She'd loved him. She'd hated him. And now he was gone. Guilt and pain seeped through Lynn Riggan, chilling her to the bone. She'd wanted to end her marriage, but not this way. Never this way.

Eager to shed her painful four-inch heels and a dress so tight she hadn't been able to sit down all day, she closed the front door behind the last of the mourners and sagged against it. God, she hated this dress, but it was the only black one she owned that wasn't cut to reveal more cleavage than she felt comfortable display-ing at a funeral, and Brett had liked it. She took comfort in the fact that today was the last time she'd have to dress to impress someone else.

"Are you all right?" Her brother-in-law's quiet bari-tone scraped over her raw nerves.

She clenched her teeth, swallowed hard and opened her eyes. Straightening, she folded her hands at her waist and forced a smile she did not feel. Her lips quivered, and she knew she hadn't fooled Sawyer when his dark brows dipped with concern.

He crossed the cool marble foyer and stopped in front of her. "Lynn?"

"I thought you'd left." She wished he had because she hated for him to see her this way. Weak. Needy. Her world was falling apart, and she didn't have the strength to pretend everything would be all right—not even for Sawyer's sake.

"I stepped out back for a minute." Losing his beloved baby brother had been hard on him. Grief filled his cobalt-blue eyes and deepened the laugh lines fanning from the corners. A muscle ticked in the tense line of his chiseled jaw. His ruggedly handsome features were drawn and pale, and his shiny dark hair looked as if the late-spring breeze or restless fingers had tumbled it. The rigid set of his broad shoulders beneath his black suit revealed how tightly he held his emotions in check.

"You should go home and rest, Sawyer." Please leave before I crumble.

"Yeah. Probably. But I feel so damned...empty." He shoved a hand through his inky hair, mussing it even more. A lock curled over his forehead, making him look more like a college boy than the thirty-two-year-old CEO of a privately owned computer software company. "I keep waiting for Brett to come through that door laughing and shouting, 'Gotcha.'"

Yes, Brett had liked cruel jokes. She'd been the butt of several. His worst joke yet was the financial mess he'd left for her to unravel. But even he couldn't have faked the fiery car accident that had taken his life.

Sawyer's eyes lasered in on hers. "Will you be all right here alone?"

Alone. Already the walls of this mausoleum of a house closed in on her. Right now she needed a hug more than anything, but she'd learned how to survive without that simple comfort a long time ago. She chewed her lip, wrapped her arms around her middle and avoided his probing gaze. "I'll be fine."

Her eyes burned from lack of sleep, and her muscles ached from pacing the floor all night. She wished she'd never found that key in the plastic bag of personal effects the hospital personnel had given her. If she hadn't found the key, she wouldn't have opened the safe. And if she hadn't opened the safe... She took one shaky breath and then another trying to ward off panic.

What was she going to do?

She'd been searching for a life insurance policy to cover the funeral costs, and instead she'd discovered statements from empty bank accounts and a private journal in which her husband had written that he'd never loved her, that he found her such a dud in bed that he'd turned to another woman for pleasure. He'd catalogued her faults in excruciating detail.

"Lynn?" Sawyer lifted her chin with the warm tip of his finger. "Do you want me to stay tonight? I could bunk in the guest room."

No, he couldn't. She'd moved to the guest room months ago, and if he saw her personal belongings in the room he'd know that all wasn't right in the Riggan household. She didn't want to tell Sawyer that she and Brett had been having trouble for months, and she'd suspected her husband might be having an affair. She'd even consulted a lawyer about a divorce, but Brett had blamed their problems on his workload and charmed her into giving him one more chance. Against her better judgment, she'd allowed him to convince her that a baby would bring them closer, and they'd slept together one last time—just moments before she'd found proof of his infidelity, lost her temper and kicked him out of the house. Minutes later he'd died in the car crash.

"No, I'm okay." Her voice cracked over the last word and a tremor worked through her. She had no money, no job, and no way to pay for this extravagant house Brett had insisted they buy. The house and car payments were due, and she had no idea how she'd make them. As if that weren't enough…

Her nerves stretched to the breaking point. She pressed a hand to her belly and prayed that the intimacy with her husband three nights ago wouldn't result in a child. She loved children, and she'd always wanted a large family, but she didn't know how she'd take care of herself right now, let alone a baby.

Sawyer pulled her into his arms, breaking her train of self-pity. After a stiff moment, she laid her head on his shoulder and selfishly allowed herself to savor the comforting warmth of the strong arms enfolding her and the softness of his suit against her cheek. A sob hiccuped past the knot in her throat. She mashed her lips together, clenched her teeth and stiffened her spine. She was not a quitter. She would survive this.

"Shhh," he murmured against her temple. The whisper of his breath swept her skin, and his hands chafed her spine. The spicy scent of his cologne invaded her senses. A shiver of another kind worked over her. Appalled, she tried to pull free, but his arms held fast. His chest shuddered against hers, and a warm, wet trail burned down her neck. Sawyer's tears.

Her throat clogged and her heart squeezed in sympathy. Sawyer had stood beside her through identifying Brett's body and every step of the funeral arrangements.

The fact that he'd hidden his grief and been strong for her up to this point made his loss of control more heart-wrenching. She focused on his pain rather than her own. It was safer that way, because hers was tied up with so many other emotions. Disappointment. Failure. Anger. Betrayal. Guilt.

"It'll be okay." She parroted the meaningless words she'd heard a dozen times in the past three days. "We'll get through this, Sawyer, one day at a time."

Wanting to offer him the comfort she sorely needed herself, she wrapped her arms around his middle, held him close and patted his back. She whispered soothing nonsense into his ear, but nothing she could say or do would change the past. She couldn't bring Brett back.

Sawyer's arms tightened around her and his chest pressed against her breasts in a warm, solid wall. He lowered his head and tucked his face into the side of her neck. His breath heated her skin. A spark flared in her midsection. She tried to ignore it, but it had been years since she'd been held tenderly, and she'd been frozen inside for so long by her husband's callous treatment. It wasn't Sawyer's fault that her needy body misinterpreted his consoling gesture.

His breath shuddered in and out as if he struggled for control. He loosened his arms, straightened and drew back an inch. Swiping a hand over his face, he grimaced. "I'm sorry. I just needed a minute."

"It's okay." Seeing this strong man break nearly undid her. She rose on her tiptoes to kiss his cheek, but he turned his head unexpectedly. Their cheeks and noses brushed and her pulse skittered. Drawing a sharp breath, she eased back on her heels. The lapels of his suit coat scraped across the thin fabric of her snug dress, and the resulting tingle in her breasts and belly alarmed

her. Shamed her. How could her body respond to Sawyer's, but not to her own husband's?

Brett's last damning words, *Frigid bitch*, echoed in
her ears. She hadn't been frigid until he'd hurt her, selfishly taking what he wanted without concern for her
pleasure. After that something had curled up inside her
each time he'd touched her. She'd dreaded the intimate
side of their marriage because it represented her failure
as wife and a woman.

"I want to forget." Sawyer's anguished whisper
shredded her heart and weakened the emotional dam
she'd built around her fragile emotions.

"I know. Me, too." She traced the deep groove grief
had etched in his cheek with an unsteady hand. His
afternoon beard stubble abraded her fingertips. The
raspy sensation traveled up her arm like a mild electric
current. She yanked her hand away and wiped her tingling palm against her hip.

Scant inches separated their lips, and their breaths
mingled. The pain in Sawyer's eyes slowly changed into
surprise and then into something else—something that
warmed her, scared her, made her heart race and her
muscles tense, but she couldn't look away. She wet her
lips and searched in vain for the words to end this awkward, forbidden moment.

Sawyer's dark lashes swept down to conceal his expression. Before she could step back, his hands cupped
her elbows and his mouth crushed hers in a desperate
kiss. Shock held her rigid, but what stunned her more
than the unexpected kiss was her reaction to it. A heady
rush of desire transported her back to the night of her
last date with Sawyer when she'd thought he might be
"the one." Back to the time before her heart had been
broken and Brett had come into her life, when she'd felt

beautiful and desirable instead of ugly and unresponsive, and she'd still held hope for her future instead of despair.

Sawyer withdrew and their gazes locked for one paralyzing moment. He lifted an unsteady hand to gently stroke her face and cup her jaw in the warmth of his palm. His thumb skated over her damp bottom lip and her breath hitched. Moving slowly, as if giving her the option to object, he bent over her again, peppering kisses over her forehead and cheeks.

Stop this insanity, she thought. But her body had been numb for so long, and Sawyer's touch awakened her as if he'd pushed the stone away from the entrance to the cave where her soul had been entombed for the past four years. Heat seeped through her, thawing the parts of her that her husband had numbed with his caustic comments.

Sawyer's lips touched hers again, this time gentling and clinging before withdrawing a scant inch. His breath hissed in and out, once, twice, sweeping over her skin like a dense seductive fog, before he took her mouth hungrily.

Lynn's blood swept through her veins like a hot desert wind, warming her, stirring her, and her lips parted in a stunned gasp. His tongue found hers. During her marriage she'd become accustomed to Brett's gagging, conquering kisses, but she had no clue how to handle Sawyer's gentle persuasion. Her skin grew damp and tingly instead of crawling with revulsion. She tentatively touched her tongue to the slick heat of his, and his grip on her arms tightened, though his embrace wasn't painful. She wouldn't bear bruises once this lunacy ended. And it should end. *Now.* But she didn't have the will or the strength to break away.

His hands skimmed gently over the sides of her breasts and the curve of her waist before settling on her hips. Her senses rioted and her head spun.

"Tell me to stop," he whispered against her lips, but even though his words urged her away, the hands splaying over her bottom pulled her closer.

The heat of his body permeated the fabric of her dress from her knees to her shoulders. His hard planes fused to her soft curves, and the thick ridge of his arousal pressed against her belly, shocking her. *Arousing* her. She couldn't have pushed him away if her life depended on it, and without his supporting arms, her weak knees would have folded. Curling her fingers into the lapels of his jacket, she held fast and tipped her head back to gasp for air.

She barely had time to draw a breath before Sawyer devoured her mouth with an unleashed hunger that should have frightened her. Instead it made her yearn for more. His hands kindled a fire within her, stroking her waist and then the sensitive skin beneath her breasts. A moan bubbled in her throat when he gently cupped her flesh and teased her taut nipples with his thumbs. His thigh nudged hers apart as much as her snug dress would allow, and hard, hot muscle pressed against her core.

Her belly ached with need—a need she hadn't felt in years. Her knees shook. What was she doing? Was she crazy? She couldn't bring herself to answer the questions. Brushing aside his jacket, she flattened her hands over the thin cotton of his shirt. His heart pounded against her palm, and hers raced just as fast.

He shrugged out of his suit coat with abrupt, jerky movements, tossed it aside and reached for her again. His cobalt gaze locked with hers. She couldn't look away. The fiery passion in his eyes made her tremble. Inside. Outside. All over.

His fingers tunneled through her upswept hair, sending pins pinging onto the marble floor seconds before the long, cool strands of her hair tumbled against her neck and shoulders. Sawyer took one audible breath and then another.

"Lynn." His rough voice pleaded, but for what she didn't know, and it didn't matter because her voice—along with her sanity, evidently—had left her. She couldn't think beyond the fact that Sawyer wanted her.

She touched a finger to the muscle ticking in his jaw. He angled his head, pressing his lips to her wrist, and then his lips parted and his tongue swirled an intoxicating pattern over her skin. Liquid fire surged through her.

His hands skated over her hips and then tunneled beneath the hem of her dress. Her breath lodged in her throat. His fingers burned against the back of her thighs and then through the thin silk of her panties. He kneaded her bottom once, twice. Cool air swept her thighs and then her buttocks as he hiked up her skirt and eased her panties down. His hot, long-fingered hands cupped and caressed bare skin with a gentleness that made her melt. Her entire body flushed and her head fell back. A hollow ache formed in her belly and a moan rose from her chest.

Sawyer nibbled her neck, her jaw, her earlobe. He nudged her backward until the first stair riser pressed her heels. When he urged her to sit she let her weak knees fold. The roughness of carpeted stair runner abraded her tender skin. Sawyer whisked her panties over her ankles, knelt between her knees and reached for his belt buckle. Her insides combusted and her heart jumped to her throat. She dug her nails into the carpet and struggled for sanity.

A fragment of her mind acknowledged what was going to happen if she didn't put an end to this madness. She *should* stop him, but her body tingled with awareness, and her pulse and the juncture of her thighs throbbed with life for the first time in years. She felt like a woman instead of a block of wood. She remained mute.

Rather than shove Sawyer away, she reached for him, helping him push his trousers over his lean hips, and then she burrowed her fingers beneath the hem of his shirt and clasped the supple skin at his waist. His body heat scorched her palms. Her pulse raced faster, and she gulped one lungful of air after another.

His breath whistled through clenched teeth, and his hands tightened on her thighs, easing them farther apart. He urged her back against the carpeted stairs and consumed her mouth with hot, intoxicating, sanity-robbing thoroughness. The thick head of his erection parted her folds, finding her wetness, and then he thrust deep. Air gushed from her lungs at the feeling of fullness.

It didn't hurt, a surprised voice echoed in her head before the brush of his thumb at the juncture of their bodies chased all rational thought from her mind. He thrust deep and stroked her, suckled her neck and caressed her bottom, pushing and chasing her on an uphill climb until she reached the top and tumbled over in a freefall of unfamiliar sensation.

Surprised, she dug her nails into the firm muscles of his buttocks as her body clenched around his in involuntary spasms. His teeth scraped against her collarbone, and then he groaned her name against her pounding pulse point.

Sawyer lunged and withdrew again and again. Twining her arms around him, Lynn held him tight and let the tide of sensation sweep her away. Her loosened muscles gave way and her thighs spread wider, allowing Sawyer to rock deeper inside her—deep enough to reach the portions of her soul that she'd hidden away. Cradling her face in his hands, he slammed his lips against hers, devouring her mouth and tangling tongues like a starving man. A responding hunger rekindled within her. He shifted the angle of his hips, creating a new friction against the sensitive flesh he'd plied so skillfully, and Lynn found herself climbing again. She arched to meet his thrusts. Sawyer shuddered and shivered, pulsing deep inside her core, and she tumbled over the precipice again.

He collapsed against her, sandwiching her body between the scorching heat of his and the hardness of the staircase. Their labored breaths echoed in the two-story foyer. Floating on a haze of satiation, she pressed her lips to his throat and tasted the salty tang of his skin. His chest hair tickled her lips, tantalized her cheek.

She laid a hand over Sawyer's pounding heart and struggled for comprehension. What had just happened? And why now with Sawyer? Every cell in her body pulsed with life. Her heart thundered, and the numbness she'd known for years had vanished. Brett's lovemaking—if you could call it that—had never moved her the way Sawyer's desperate coupling had. Even in the midst of madness, Sawyer had ensured her pleasure, but even before her body cooled, regrets forced themselves forward.

Dear heavens, what had she done?

* * *

Sweat dampened Sawyer's skin, adhering his shirt to his back. His heart hammered and he panted for breath.

Lynn shoved at his chest. The combination of panic and regret in her sky-blue eyes knotted his stomach, and then she looked at her wedding band, tightly closed her eyes and tucked her softly rounded chin to her chest.

What had he done? Regret hit him like a dagger in the heart. How could he have taken advantage of his brother's grieving widow? Stone-cold sober, he staggered to his feet, but his legs quivered beneath him as unsteady as a newborn colt's. Ashamed of his loss of control, he yanked up his pants and shoved in his shirttails. In his haste he nearly maimed himself with his zipper. He swore, and she flinched, biting her plump bottom lip until he expected to see blood. Her posture grew tenser by the second.

"I'm sorry, Lynn. That shouldn't have happened." He sounded as if he'd swallowed a bucket of rocks, but it was a miracle he got any words past the knot in his throat.

Looking everywhere but at him, she struggled to her feet and batted the hem of her dress over her long legs. She finger combed the tangles from her mussed golden hair with trembling hands.

He fisted his hands on the urge to help tame her silky tresses, and followed her horrified gaze to the black panties on the white marble floor by the front door. Self-disgust crawled over his skin. He'd lost control, yanked her skirt above her waist and taken her like some damned frat boy. Hell, they were both fully dressed except for her panties.

Ass. Idiot. What were you thinking?

"It's okay, Sawyer. We were both hurting and

wanted—*needed*—to forget for a moment. It won't happen again.'' The tightness of her voice and the pallor of her creamy skin belied her casual words.

"You want to forget what just happened?" Impossible. How could he forget the silkiness of her skin beneath his palms, the sweet taste of her mouth or the satiny, wet folds that had surrounded him?

"Yes, please.'' Her whispered plea destroyed him.

"Unless you're on the pill, forgetting might not be an option. I didn't use protection. I'm sorry. If it's any consolation, I've never been careless before.''

She closed her eyes and swallowed visibly. Her thin black dress molded every tantalizing curve of her body, making the rise and fall of her breasts on shaky breaths hard to miss.

Get with the program, Riggan. She's your brother's wife. "Lynn, are you taking contraceptives?''

She mashed the bow of her lips into a flat line. Her chin quivered. "I'm tired. Would you excuse me?''

His gut knotted, and sweat beaded on his upper lip. "Lynn?''

Her finely arched brows dipped, and her eyes clouded. "I can't tell you what you want to hear. I'm not taking contraceptives and the timing…the timing isn't the best.''

Hell. He caught her by her upper arms. "What are you saying? You could get pregnant now? How can you be sure?''

Every vestige of color faded from her delicate features, accentuating the dark circles under her eyes. A fine tremor worked its way through her body. The urge to pull her closer made him tighten his fingers before common sense rallied. Comforting her, taking comfort in her, had already gotten him into a world of trouble.

He'd crossed the line. Releasing her, he shoved his fists into his pockets and stepped back.

She lifted a trembling hand to cover the pulse leaping at the base of her throat. Her other hand spread over her flat belly, where even now their cells could be merging to create a new life. He couldn't even begin to put a name to the emotions the knowledge stirred inside him, and fighting the need to lay his hand over hers took everything he had.

"Brett and I were trying to start a family and we…" She ducked her chin. A rush of pink swept her high cheekbones before the curtain of her hair swept forward to conceal her features. "The day he died was the beginning of my fertile cycle."

His belly bottomed out. Could this day get any worse? He'd buried his baby brother, made love to his brother's wife and may have impregnated a woman he should be protecting, not hurting. And then her words sank in. She and Brett had been trying to make a baby. Brett had been the only family he had left, and his brother's seed might already be growing inside Lynn's womb. Sawyer clutched the link to Brett like a lifeline.

He might be an uncle.

Or a father. He swallowed the lump in his throat and struggled to breathe despite the constriction of his chest muscles. The first would be a blessing, the second a curse on his soul for taking what wasn't his and yet, *he liked the idea of Lynn having his baby.* The possibility tied his insides into knots—knots he couldn't unravel when his thoughts were as convoluted as this. He shoved the issue aside to deal with later, when he'd recovered a shred of reason.

He should leave, get the hell out of here before he made things worse, but he couldn't until he knew Brett had provided for Lynn. "I stayed behind because I need to know if Brett's life insurance will be enough to support you—" he swallowed again, but the tightness in his throat persisted "—and a child."

The silence stretched so long that he didn't think she'd answer, and then her gaze met his. She looked so damned fragile. He sucked a sharp breath at the worry in her eyes and battled the urge to pull her close.

"Brett let the policy lapse."

Great. His brother had never been one for what he considered trivial details. "What will you do?"

She shifted on her feet, reminding him that she was bare *and wet* beneath the skirt of her dress. Hell. He yanked his thoughts back on track.

Her jaw set. "I'd rather not discuss this now, Sawyer."

He fisted his hands in frustration. "I'm not trying to be callous. I know you're tired and it's been a rough day, and I've added to that, but I won't leave until I know you have enough money to cover immediate expenses."

"That's not your problem. If I have to I'll get a job."

"Doing what?"

"I don't know. I can always go back to waitressing."

Lynn had been a waitress in a downtown Chapel Hill coffee shop when he'd met her four and a half years ago. She'd lured him with her sunny smile, sky-blue eyes and sun-streaked blond hair, and then she'd hooked him with her contradictions. Her work uniform had consisted of a starched white shirt, pure schoolmarm, and a short black skirt, one hundred percent siren when combined with her long, lithe legs and a no-nonsense hip-swinging gait. She'd been shy until he'd gotten to know her, and then her gutsy and ambitious side had

peeked through and reeled him in. Lynn dreamed big—
something they had in common.

He'd debated for months before asking her out because she was too young for him, but in the end he
couldn't resist. They'd dated a few times, and then he'd
made the second biggest mistake of his life. He'd introduced her to his brother. An extended business trip had
called him out of town, and he'd returned to find Brett
and Lynn married.

Move on, Riggan. You can't change the past. She
chose Brett. "You'd only make minimum wage. You
deserve better."

"Sawyer, I have a high school diploma and one semester of college. I'm not qualified for anything better."

"You should have finished school."

Lynn looked away, revealing beard burn on the delicate skin of her neck. He'd marked her in his passion.
The unexpected urge to soothe her chafed skin with his
mouth hit him hard. "Brett wanted me here."

That wasn't the way Brett told the story. "Have you
gone over the finances with your accountant yet?"

"Brett kept our books."

His belly sank even lower. Brett was a marketing
genius, but numbers had never been his strong suit.
"When will you meet with the lawyer to go over the
will? You need to know if you have enough money to
hold on to the house and your car."

She pressed a hand to her temple and bowed her
head. He wanted to smooth her tangled hair as badly as
he wanted his next breath. He shoved his hands deeper
into his pockets. "I'll meet with the lawyer in a few
days, but I've looked over the accounts. Money is going
to be tight until I sell the house."

Her words didn't make sense. Brett had earned a generous salary as marketing director of Riggan Cyber-Quest. "You're selling the house?"

She lifted her chin and met his gaze. The wariness and fear in her eyes knotted his gut. "It's too big for just me."

He cursed his brother. If Brett had kept up the life insurance policy then Lynn wouldn't be forced to sell the house where she and Brett had lived—he swallowed hard—and loved. "What can I do to help?"

"Nothing, thanks. I've already contacted a real estate agent. He's coming out to give me an appraisal." She seemed determined to tough it out alone.

He was just as determined to help her. Lynn was his responsibility now—especially if she carried a Riggan baby in her belly. "You can move in with me until you find a new place."

Her eyes rounded. "I...no, thank you."

He couldn't blame her, since he'd violated her trust today. He shoved a hand through his hair. "What happened today... I can't tell you how much I regret it. I won't lose control again. You have my word, Lynn."

Why did the words feel like a lie? And why did Lynn flinch as if he'd slapped her? He wanted to kick himself. Instead, he pulled out his wallet and extracted the cash inside. "This is all I have with me, but I can get more—as much as you need."

She recoiled, and her skin flushed. "Are you trying to make me feel like a hooker?"

He winced and his skin heated. "No." *Dammit.* "I thought you might need money for food or...whatever."

She made no move to take the cash. "The neighbors brought enough food to last a week. I don't need anything else."

"I want to help—"

"I know you're used to taking care of Brett, but I'm twenty-three years old, Sawyer. I can take care of myself. Now I'm exhausted, so I hope you'll excuse me." She opened the front door. Her invitation to leave couldn't have been clearer.

"Lynn—"

"*Please,* Sawyer, I just can't do this right now. Go home."

She looked ready to collapse, so he didn't argue. "We're not finished."

Two

"**Y**ou're saying the situation is worse than I thought?" Lynn perched on the edge of her chair across from Mr. Allen, the estate lawyer. Her nails dug into her palms, and her stomach clenched into a tight knot. An hour's worth of legal terminology spun in a confusing mass in her head.

The older gentleman regarded her somberly through his wire-rimmed bifocals from across his wide cherry desk. The richly furnished office smelled like money. Ironically, he'd just told her she had none.

"Your husband's estate is heavily burdened with debt, Mrs. Riggan. You'll have to liquidate your assets to cover those debts. As far as I can ascertain the thirty-percent share of Riggan CyberQuest you've inherited is your only debt-free asset."

Lynn gulped her rising panic and stiffened her spine. "So I should sell Brett's share of the company?"

"Yes, if you hope to have anything to live off, but your brother-in-law has right of first refusal should you choose to sell."

"That shouldn't be a problem. Sawyer will want to buy Brett's share."

Mr. Allen shuffled the papers in front of him until she thought her nerves would snap. "You have rights of survivorship on your home which means you can sell it without waiting for the estate to be settled, and I would highly recommend you do so before the bank takes action, since your payments are past due. I'll have my secretary give you the names of several reputable estate appraisers. You can have your household items assessed and then choose one of the estate men to help you divest yourself of anything of value."

She clenched her hands to stop their trembling and nodded. The tasks ahead seemed insurmountable, but Brett's share of the company should give her enough to start over and to get an education so she could support herself.

The attorney continued, "You've provided receipts showing you've paid for the funeral services, and yet the money wasn't withdrawn from any of your bank accounts."

Lynn twisted her plain gold wedding band around her finger. "No, I returned a gift my husband had recently bought…for me and used that money."

If second thoughts about their reconciliation hadn't driven her from the bed after their intimate encounter would she have ever known about Brett's mistress?

She'd picked up her husband's suit from the floor the way she'd done dozens of times before, but this time a jewelry box had fallen from his coat pocket and sprung open to reveal a huge diamond ring. She'd been touched—not because she'd liked the gaudy ring, but because she'd believed the gift signified a new start to their troubled marriage. The inscription inside the platinum band had crushed her hopes. "To Nina with love, Brett." At that moment her worst fears had been proven. Her husband had been unfaithful.

Stunned, she'd looked at Brett, and he'd concocted a story—he always had a story—about buying the ring for her and then deciding it wasn't her style. He'd claimed he planned to return it the next day and had even produced the receipt to prove his point. The worst part was that she probably would have swallowed his lies *again* if she hadn't read the inscription. He claimed the jeweler had made a mistake, but she knew better. Finally, the rose-colored glasses had shattered, and she could see the lie in his eyes.

If she hadn't been so angered by her own gullibility and lashed out at him verbally, egged on by years of broken dreams, would he still be alive? She'd screamed at him to get out of the house, vowing to file the divorce papers the next day. He'd stormed out, and less than an hour later the police had knocked on her door to tell her Brett was dead.

When it had become clear that there wasn't any money to pay for the funeral, she'd returned the ring to the jeweler's. His mistress's ring had cost more than ten thousand dollars. Her own ring, a plain gold band, had cost one hundred, which only went to show how much he valued her.

How had she been so blind? So stupid?

"Mrs. Riggan?" Mr. Allen's quiet voice interrupted her self-castigation.

She jerked to attention. "Yes?"

"I have one more suggestion. Seek employment as soon as possible."

Lynn had ducked him for the last time. He would see her today, dammit.

Sawyer ground his teeth and navigated through the congestion in Lynn and Brett's normally quiet neighborhood on Saturday morning. During the past week he'd left enough messages on Lynn's answering machine to fill a book. Sure, she'd returned his calls, but she'd left brief messages on his home answering machine when she knew he'd be at work, rather than call him at the office and speak to him directly.

How could he take care of her if he couldn't even talk to her and find out what she needed?

He'd given her time because the memory of her taste, of the slick heat of her body clenching his and her gasps of passion still haunted his dreams, but he wasn't going to let her get away with avoiding him any longer.

He turned onto her street, and traffic slowed to a crawl. The For Sale sign by the curb jolted him, but the Yard Sale sign sent his heart slamming against his ribs.

His brother's belongings lay scattered across the lawn and driveway. Scavengers hunted through the entrails of Brett's life. Rage boiled in Sawyer's chest. Brett had only been gone ten days, and Lynn seemed determined to erase his existence.

Pulling into a spot by the curb, Sawyer threw open his car door and stalked toward Lynn. Her pale-yellow shorts and sleeveless sweater skimmed her curves in a way guaranteed to make any red-blooded male stand up and take notice. Her bare arms and legs were sleek, tanned and toned, and the V-neck of her sweater revealed a mouthwatering hint of cleavage. Her hair cascaded down her back like polished gold, and she'd outlined her mouth in deep pink—the same shade he'd kissed off her lips. His libido stirred, but right now his anger edged out his primeval response by a slim margin.

She glanced up from her cash box and their gazes met. Wariness filled her eyes.

"What are you doing?" He managed not to shout, but fury vibrated in his voice.

Her white teeth dug into her bottom lip. "I'm selling items I won't have room for when I move to a smaller place."

"Those are Brett's books, his golf clubs, *his clothes.*"

"Sawyer, I'm sorry. I should have warned you about the yard sale."

"Hell, you have everything he owned out here." He fought the urge to sweep it all up and carry it back into the house.

Lynn winced and glanced over her shoulder, making him aware that several shoppers had stopped to eavesdrop shamelessly. Catching her elbow, he ushered her to the side of the lawn.

She focused soft, sympathetic eyes on him. "I separated out the items I thought you might want, but if you see anything out here that you'd like, then please, take it."

"That's not the point. It's as if you're trying to erase Brett from your memory." He wasn't ready to let go yet, and she shouldn't be, either. She pulled her arm free, and her silky skin slid against his fingertips, marginally deflating his anger. He shoved his hands in the pockets of his shorts and clenched his teeth on the persistent bite of desire.

"My memories are here, Sawyer." She tapped her

temple and then gestured toward the bounty in her yard. "These are just *things.*"

He paced to the hedge and back. Was Lynn trying to purge Brett from her life? And what if there were a child? He might have a legal hold on his child, but not on Brett's. The big aching void where his heart used to be threatened to suck him into a black hole. "Why are you trying so hard to forget him?"

"I'm not," she fired back defensively and then chewed her lip. She glanced away and then back at him. Resignation settled over her features. "We have a few debts I need to pay."

He zeroed in on the tension in her voice. "What kinds of debts?"

She stepped from one foot to the other and fingered the lock on the cash box. "It's nothing I can't handle."

"Lynn, I can't help if I don't know what I'm up against."

"And I told you I don't need your help." She fidgeted when he stared her down and then sighed. "Credit cards, mostly, but as administrator of the estate, *I* can settle our debts by selling a few items."

Hadn't Brett learned anything from the tightly budgeted years after their parents' deaths? Or was Lynn the one who'd insisted on flashy cars and a luxurious house? Since marrying his brother she'd certainly developed a high-maintenance lifestyle with her flirty body-hugging dresses, long, manicured nails and hair color that changed as frequently as the seasons.

His gut knotted and a sour taste filled his mouth. Brett had bragged that every time Lynn dyed her hair it had been like making love with a different woman, a sexy redhead, a sultry brunette, a tawny-headed temptress. Cheating, but not cheating, he'd said with a wink and a smirk that lit a firestorm in Sawyer every time. He'd once thought he and Lynn had a future together, but that was before she'd ignored his letter and chosen his brother.

Sawyer preferred Lynn's hair blond—which he now knew was her natural shade, dammit—and he'd liked her back when she'd been a waitress who traded her contradictory uniform for jeans after work. Sure, he appreciated the curvy shape her clothes revealed—what man wouldn't?—but he preferred a woman to leave a little to the imagination.

She tucked a lock of hair behind her ear with a long fuchsia fingernail, and in the blink of an eye his mind shifted gears again and his blood ignited. The crescent marks on his butt where she'd clutched him and pulled him deeper had barely faded. He cleared his throat and shifted, trying to ease the discomfort behind his zipper. "How much do you owe?"

Her pink lips pressed in a determined line, and she lifted her chin. "I'm busy now. Can we have this discussion later?"

Several couples hovered as if waiting to make purchases, and Lynn's closed expression made it clear she wasn't going to talk now. He didn't have the right to stop the yard sale, but he couldn't stand around and watch the vultures cart off his brother's possessions without acid eating a hole through his stomach. "What time will you finish here?"

"The neighbors' teenage sons will come back at three to help me pack up what I don't sell."

"I'll be back this evening."

Pretend it didn't happen. Pretend the man striding up your driveway didn't give you more physical pleasure in five desperate minutes than your husband did in four years.

Lynn hovered on her side porch with her cheeks on fire and her insides a jumble. Coward that she was, she'd anxiously watched for Sawyer through the windows and then raced out the kitchen door before he could head up the brick walk to her front entrance. She couldn't face him in the foyer.

Sawyer's navy-blue polo shirt delineated his muscles to mouthwatering perfection. The short sleeves revealed thick biceps and tanned forearms lightly sprinkled with dark hair—hair that matched the denser whorls at the base of his throat. Her lips tingled with the memory of tasting him there, and a shiver slipped down her spine. His khaki shorts displayed rock-hard thighs and calves. Dark stubble shadowed his jaw. She clenched her fingers as she relived the rasp of his chin against her palm.

She'd just lost her husband, and even if she'd quit loving Brett long ago, she shouldn't be having womb-tightening thoughts about Sawyer or his athletic body. Ashamed, she ducked her chin, thumbed her wedding band and hoped the warmth beneath her skin wasn't visible.

"You've been avoiding me," he stated without preamble.

Her heart jumped. Guilty as charged. "I've been busy for the past week with the estate paperwork, the real estate agent and appraisers."

His cobalt gaze raked over her from head to toe, stirring up feelings best left undisturbed and leaving a trail of goose bumps in its wake, but then concern softened his eyes and the hard planes of his handsome face. "How are you holding up?"

His quiet question put a lump in her throat. "I'm okay. You?"

He shrugged and she nearly rolled her eyes. Typical man, refusing to admit to emotion. Her father, the tough cop, had been the same—especially after her mother died.

"Come in." She led the way through the garage and into the kitchen. Even though she kept her back to the curved archway leading to the foyer her heart thumped harder, and the sensitive areas of her body tingled with awareness for the man hovering a few feet away.

She concentrated on keeping her hand steady so she wouldn't scatter the coffee grounds across the granite countertop and then poured water into the coffeemaker and turned it on. Pressing her palm against her nervous stomach, she tried to ignore the tremor running through her. "The coffee should be ready in a few minutes."

"How much do you owe?" Sawyer's tone sounded level, almost impersonal, but the way he looked at her wasn't. His eyes stroked over her, and her skin reacted as if he'd touched her. Intimacy stood between them like a living, breathing being, connecting them in a way they hadn't been linked before.

Don't fool yourself, Lynn. The encounter in the foyer ten days ago had nothing to do with making love and everything to do with forgetting. The regret on both sides proved it shouldn't and wouldn't be repeated. So why couldn't she get it out of her mind? And why, when he looked at her in that slow, thorough way did her awakened body hum with the memory of the way he'd caressed her and with the deep-seated need for him to do so again?

My God, what must he think of her? Had she become the clichéd merry widow? Embarrassment scorched her cheeks. She staggered back a step and retreated to the sunny bay window overlooking her tiny backyard in an effort to clear the unsuitable thoughts from her mind. She fussed with her multitude of plants, polishing dust off this one and plucking a dead bud from another, but Sawyer's spicy scent pursued her relentlessly.

"How much, Lynn?" he repeated.

"Settling the estate really isn't your problem, Sawyer."

He leaned forward, bracing his arms on the table. His biceps bulged and a muscle jerked in the tense line of his jaw. "It's my problem if you have to sell part of the company to cover your debts."

"Actually, I want to sell Brett's share back to you."

He frowned and shoved a hand through his hair. "I can't raise the capital to buy Brett's share right now. The company's having a few difficulties."

A chill chased down her spine. Those shares were all she had. If the company folded they'd be worthless. "But I need the money to start over once the house sells."

"And I need you to be patient. Give me a chance to turn the company around. You'd only get a fraction of the value if you sold now. Where do you plan to move?"

Lynn pressed her fingers against the steady throb building behind her left temple. "My aunt said I could stay with her until I get back on my feet."

"In Florida? If you're looking for a rent-free place to stay, then move in with me. I have the space."

His offer tempted and repelled her simultaneously. She loved this small college town with its steep hills, curvy roads and friendly atmosphere, and Sawyer's spacious home in the historic section had a character and grace that her newer one lacked. When he finished the renovations his house would be gorgeous. She loved the high-ceilinged rooms and tall windows which overlooked a huge yard.

But Sawyer had made her lose control, and she'd just spent four years of her life in a relationship that rendered her powerless. If she lived with him she ran the risk of repeating her mistakes. "Thanks, but let's hope it doesn't come to that."

"Are you looking for a job?"

"Yes." She'd been job hunting for the past three days, but the university students had left town for the summer, and the business owners had cut staff to accommodate reduced trade.

"Come to work for me."

With her stomach churning, she gazed out the window. The last thing she wanted to do was face Sawyer every day and be reminded that she'd thrown herself at him like a woman starved for affection. "I don't know anything about computer software development."

Sawyer moved closer until he stood directly behind her, his reflection showing in the glass. He put a hand on her shoulder and turned her to face him. The heat of his touch permeated her thin sweater, warming her skin. She swallowed hard and lifted her gaze to his. In his eyes she saw sympathy, frustration and heat. He hadn't forgotten what happened any more than she had. There beneath the civilized veneer lay the awareness of what they'd done. Tension spiraled in her belly.

"Lynn, I can give you enough money to cover your immediate expenses, or I can offer you a job. Your choice. But I don't want you to leave Chapel Hill until I'm certain you're not carrying Brett's child…or mine."

Sawyer's baby. Her pulse skipped a beat. She took a

calming breath. It would be one thing to move to Florida alone or with Brett's baby. It would be another to take Sawyer's baby away from him. She could never be responsible for denying a child its father's love.

Don't panic about things that haven't happened yet. You may not be pregnant. The odds for conceiving the first month after getting off the Pill are slim.

"Thank you, but I'd rather earn the money legitimately." She forced herself to look into his eyes and stretched her lips into a smile that felt more like a grimace, but she couldn't do any better with the worry building inside her. Stepping away, she put enough distance between them that she couldn't feel his body heat and wouldn't be close enough to give in to the temptation to lean on him and draw from his strength. It was time she stood on her own feet again.

"I want to help." His voice hardened.

She took a deep breath and faced him. "And I want a *real* job, not one fabricated out of pity."

"This is a real job. Opal, my administrative assistant, needs help. Brett's assistant quit months ago, and Opal's been juggling her workload and Nina's, too."

Lynn's breath caught and nausea rose in her throat. *Nina.* Brett's lover. Her husband went through assistants like most men went through socks. Because he'd instructed her not to call him at work unless there was an emergency, she hadn't even known his latest assistant's name. Did Sawyer know about the affair? Would he lie to protect his brother?

With her heart and head reeling she tried to come up with a logical response. "I have no training."

"You'll learn." The set of Sawyer's jaw promised an argument if she refused his offer—an argument she couldn't contemplate right now.

"I'll think about it. Now, please have a seat at the table. I have something to show you. I have to get it from the bedroom upstairs."

His gaze locked with hers and then shifted to the archway beyond her shoulder—the one leading to the foyer and the stairs. Heat flashed in his eyes.

Her breath caught and her heart pounded. Warmth flushed her skin. She turned away, but not before regret tightened Sawyer's features. "I'll get the box."

After bracing himself, Sawyer lifted the lid of the cheap wooden box on the table in front of him. Gold, silver and other precious metals lay jumbled together without regard for the scratches the heirlooms might receive.

"Did you pack these?"

Lynn hovered near the coffeepot. Her gaze danced to his and then away again, never holding for more than a split second. Pink climbed from her neck to spread across her cheeks. Her nipples peaked, proving she remembered what happened on the other side of that archway, the same way he did. His pulse leaped. Her quick glances told him she wanted to ignore the passion between them, and if he were half as smart as the business magazines said he was, he'd let her.

"I didn't even know Brett had this treasure chest until I searched for the will. I found the box buried in the back of the closet, but I saw your name on a couple of items and thought you might be interested. I'd hate to sell something that holds sentimental value for you."

She flitted from one side of the blinding-white kitchen to the other and back again—probably afraid he'd jump her if she remained stationary. She fiddled with her plants and straightened the already straight row of canisters. He cursed himself. His loss of control had made her a nervous wreck.

"You never found a will?"

"No. The attorney checked the courthouse, the bank and every other logical place where a will could be stored, just in case Brett had done one of those home kits. He found nothing, and I've already searched the house twice."

Another detail his brother had neglected. It infuriated Sawyer that Brett had been so careless with Lynn. If a man loved a woman, he looked out for her, provided for her...and any children they might have.

Shutting down the disturbing thought, he carefully withdrew a gold watch and chain from the tangled mess in the box and traced his finger over the name engraved in the metal. Warm memories swamped him—memories of looking at this watch with his own father and anticipating the day when he would be entrusted with the heirloom. "This pocket watch belonged to my great-grandfather, the first Sawyer Riggan."

She set a mug of steaming coffee in front of him and darted back to the other side of the room. "Why did Brett have it?"

"He asked for it." And God help him, he'd tried to give Brett everything he wanted after their parents' deaths.

"But why give it to him if it was intended for you?"

"I owed him." Owed him a debt he could never repay.

"Owed him what?"

Hadn't Brett told her? "I killed our parents."

Her brow pleated. "Your parents died in a car accident."

"With me at the wheel."

Sympathy softened her eyes. "I thought a drunk driver ran a stop light."

"He did, but if I hadn't shot off as soon as the light turned green, if I'd looked twice before accelerating into the intersection instead of being the lead-foot my dad always accused me of being—"

She returned to the table, slid into the chair at a right angle to his and laid her soft hand over his clenched fist. His words dried up. "Sawyer, the accident wasn't your fault. Brett showed me the newspaper article. The other driver didn't have on his headlights. You couldn't possibly have seen him."

Her touch burned his skin. He sucked in a deep breath. She snatched her hand back and tucked it into her lap as if she regretted the gesture, but the imprint of her fingers lingered.

Since Brett's death Lynn had quit wearing her heavy perfume, and God help him, he could smell *her*. Her light honeysuckle scent was ten times more potent than perfume anyday. She'd also quit teasing her hair into that just-out-of-bed, sex-kitten style. Today she'd brushed it in a satiny wave over her shoulders. His hands itched to tumble her hair into the same disarray it had been when he'd made love to her on the stairs. Not made love, he corrected, had sex. Making love implied he had lingering feelings for Lynn from their earlier relationship, and he didn't.

Clearing his throat, he refocused on the jewelry box, digging around until he uncovered his mother and father's wedding bands. He closed his fingers around them, feeling the loss of his parents as if it had been yesterday instead of ten years ago, and then his mother's last words rang in his ears. *Take care of Brett. Whatever you do, don't let them separate our family.*

He opened his hand to study the intricately carved bands and traced the pattern on his mother's ring.

Lynn leaned closer. "They're lovely. The engraving is quite unusual."

"Brett said you refused to wear Mom's wedding band."

Lynn's brows arched in surprise. "I never saw the rings before this week."

He lifted the smaller band. "He didn't offer this to you?"

Pain clouded her sky-blue eyes and she looked away. "No. Maybe he wanted to keep the set together. You know Brett chose not to wear a wedding band."

It didn't make sense. Brett had begged for the pocket watch and the rings, and yet it would seem his brother had never used any of the pieces.

A delicate silver locket caught Sawyer's attention. He set the rings back in the box and picked up the locket, flicking it open to reveal two tiny pictures, one of him as an infant and the other of Brett as a three-year-old. "This belonged to my mother. She always planned to give it to her granddaughter, if there was one someday."

His gaze met hers and then traveled slowly over her breasts to her flat belly. His child—his daughter—could be growing inside Lynn. His chest tightened, and he lifted his gaze to hers once more. She worried her bottom lip with her teeth. Her lipstick was long gone. The need to lean across the distance and touch his mouth to the softness of hers blindsided him. He sucked in a slow breath and sat back in his chair.

Neither of them spoke of the baby she might be carrying, but the knowledge and the tension stretched between them. He couldn't explain the mixture of emotions clogging his throat. Fear? Excitement? Dread? Anticipation?

Lynn's fingers curled on the edge of the tabletop until her knuckles turned white, and then she stood and carried her cup to the sink. "If you ever have a daughter, I'm sure she'd be proud to wear the locket. It's lovely."

The other items in the box held less value, but Sawyer found a favorite pocket knife he thought he'd lost in high school and the ID bracelet his ex-fiancée had given him. Why did Brett have these? And why had he tossed each piece in a cheap box like yard-sale junk?

Lynn paused behind his shoulder. "These are your memories, Sawyer. They should stay in your family."

"The Riggan family will end with me—unless you're carrying the next generation. When will you know if you're pregnant?"

Eyes wide, she stared at him and then her gaze darted away. Her face paled as quickly as it had flushed. "In a week or so, but let's not borrow trouble."

"You'll tell me as soon as you know." It wasn't a question.

She hesitated and his heart stuttered. "Yes."

"Do you want a baby?"

Worry clouded her eyes. She took a deep breath. "I've always wanted children, but the timing couldn't be worse. And not knowing who—" She bit her lip and tucked her chin.

"I'll stand by you, Lynn—no matter whose child it is."

"Um…thank you." She didn't look reassured.

The doorbell rang. She frowned and turned.

"That should be dinner. I called the Chinese place while you were upstairs." Sawyer rose and strode past her to the front door. She remained in the kitchen while he paid and tipped the delivery man and returned. He set the bag on the counter and opened it. Tantalizing aromas filled the room.

"You didn't have to buy dinner." Lynn inhaled deeply and then licked her lips.

Hunger for Lynn replaced his need for food. He gritted his teeth and reminded himself why he'd called the restaurant. "You need to eat. You've lost weight."

Her spine stiffened. "That's not your concern."

"I'm making it mine."

Three

A polished woman in her fifties guarded the closed door with Sawyer Riggan, CEO, engraved on the nameplate.

Lynn swallowed her nervousness and crossed the threshold of the office. "Excuse me. I'm Lynn Riggan. I'd like to see Sawyer."

The woman's frank appraisal made Lynn want to fidget. She clutched her purse tighter when what she really wanted to do was smooth her French twist and straighten the skirt of her fitted emerald-green dress. She shifted her weight in her three-inch heels, hating the clothes Brett had chosen for her, but until she could afford to replace them she was stuck.

The woman rose. "I'm Opal Pugh, Sawyer's assistant. I'm sorry for your loss, Mrs. Riggan."

"Thank you. It's nice to meet you, Opal." This was

the woman Brett had referred to as Sawyer's drag-
on lady.

"I'll see if Sawyer's free." Opal tapped on Sawyer's
door before disappearing inside.

Lynn hated depending on Sawyer for a job, but everywhere she'd gone the answers had been the same.
Not hiring. Twisting the strap of her purse, she examined the tastefully decorated office. Thick steel-gray car-
peting covered the floor. An oak coffee table gleamed
in front of a burgundy-damask-covered loveseat and
chairs, and the landscapes on the wall looked like orig-
inals.

Before she could step nearer to read the artists' sig-
natures, the door opened and her stomach dropped. Opal
motioned her forward. "He'll see you now."

Lynn's legs trembled as she closed the distance. She
wished she could blame her fluttery nerves and agitated
stomach solely on her dismal financial situation, but the
man rising from behind the wide oak desk in front of
her contributed more than a little. Sawyer seemed larger
than life here on his own turf—every inch a mastermind
who'd taken an idea and turned it into an internationally
renowned company. He'd shed his suit coat and rolled
up the sleeves of his white dress shirt. The loosened
knot of his tie and opened top two buttons of his shirt
revealed a glimpse of his dark chest hair.

"Good morning, Lynn." His baritone voice sounded
deeper than usual. It skipped down her spine like a caress. His intense blue eyes glided over her slowly, thoroughly assessing her.

"Good morning." Her dry mouth made it difficult to
form the words. She cursed the heat flaring in her face
and other places she'd rather not acknowledge and
tugged at her dress. She'd always tried to ignore her

clingy clothing, but after her steamy dreams last night—
dreams featuring Sawyer—her skin was hypersensitive
to the brush of the fabric against her breasts, hips and
thighs.

With a subtle lift of his square chin, he motioned for
Opal to leave them. The door closed and the room suddenly seemed smaller, more intimate. Airless. She
cleared her throat. "I've decided to take you up on the
job offer...if it's still open."

"Certainly. Welcome aboard." Leaning across the
desk, he offered his hand.

If she could have thought of a polite way to avoid
the handshake, she would have. Instead, his long fingers
closed around hers. She tried to focus on something
besides the memory of how those warm, long-fingered
hands had cradled her bottom while he thrust deep inside her, first in her foyer and then again in her dreams
last night.

A hint of his spicy aftershave teased her senses, and
an image of his passion-glazed eyes flashed in her brain.
Her heart jolted into a faster rhythm, and her cheeks
weren't the only parts of her that were growing warm.
Brett had accused her of being a prude, but her thoughts
certainly weren't prudish now.

She pulled her hand free and blurted, "I need to make
it clear that I'm only looking for a job...not anything
else."

He reared back. The nostrils of his straight nose
flared, and she cringed with embarrassment. "I'm sorry.
That was—"

"We agreed that what happened was a mistake." He
gestured for her to take a seat in one of the leather chairs
in front of his desk.

Feeling utterly foolish, she collapsed into the visitor's seat. Of course he didn't want more of her. No man did.

"And your job here will never be based on...fringe benefits, but you're a co-owner of the business, so we will be working closely together. Will that be a problem for you?"

Would it be a problem to work beside him every single day? Yes. "No."

Sawyer settled in his chair behind the wide desk and laced his fingers on the polished surface. "When would you like to start?"

She swallowed to ease the dryness in her mouth. "Today? Tomorrow? But first, I'd like a little time in Brett's office...if that's okay?"

Sympathy filled his eyes, and she felt like a fraud. She wasn't a brokenhearted widow. She'd done her share of grieving over her marriage months ago. Now she just felt foolish for having wasted more than four years of her life on what had obviously been a losing proposition.

"You know where it is?"

"I think so." Brett had rarely brought her to the office and never during regular business hours.

She walked down the short hall on shaky legs and into her husband's office. She didn't have to turn to know that Sawyer had followed. Her personal radar was keenly attuned to his presence just one stride behind.

He reached around her to lift a crystal picture frame from the desktop and his shoulder brushed hers. Her breath hitched and her skin prickled at the point of contact. "I've asked Opal to bring in some boxes. You'll want to take Brett's personal items home—including this."

She took the picture from him and stared at the

blond-haired and blue-eyed couple as if they were
strangers instead of Brett and herself. Her eyes glowed
and she smiled as if someone had just handed her the
world on a platter. How long had it been since she'd
felt even a fraction of that hope and happiness? But
she'd believed in her marriage vows, and she'd tried to
make the relationship work.

Why hadn't she noticed before that the emotion captured in her husband's eyes wasn't love, but possessiveness? How stupid of her not to realize sooner that
she'd been nothing but an accessory to Brett. He'd expected her to dress to suit his tastes, to maintain the
perfect house and image, to be seen and not heard. But
why her? His journal made it clear he hadn't been mo-
tivated by love.

The warmth of Sawyer's hand on her shoulder jerked
her attention back to the concern and sadness in his
eyes. Not for the first time she noted the difference between the two men. Brett's eyes were pale blue and his
hair sandy blond. Sawyer's eyes were intensely deep
blue, shades darker than Brett's, and his hair was
raven's-wing black.

Right now he was frowning at her. "Are you all
right? Would you like for me to have someone else
handle the packing?"

"I can do it. I'm okay," she lied, and stepped away,
but her skin tingled where he'd touched, and the urge
to lean on his broad shoulders nearly overpowered her.

Looking back on it now, she realized she hadn't been
okay since the second year of her marriage when her
husband had started systematically eroding her self-
confidence. He'd begun with suggesting she dye her
hair a more attractive color and then he'd progressed to
urging her to get breast implants and collagen in her

lips. She'd refused the medical procedures but she'd experimented with hair colors. None had satisfied him, and she'd recently returned to her natural blond.

She'd wanted so desperately to have the family Brett had promised her before they married, wanted so very much to please him and to turn him back into the man who'd charmed her right out of her disappointment over the end of her relationship with Sawyer. She'd failed on all counts.

She shook off her depressing thoughts. "Could I have a few minutes alone?"

"Of course. I've spent some time in here myself." The pain in Sawyer's voice made her heart ache. She wanted to reach for him but didn't. With obvious reluctance he backed toward the door. "My extension's marked on the phone. Ring if you need anything."

As soon as the door closed, Lynn lay the photo face-down on the desktop and stepped behind the polished surface. She rifled through the drawers, but she didn't know what she was looking for. Additional bank accounts? Signs of Brett's infidelity? A tap on the door made her jump guiltily. She closed the drawer. "Yes?"

Opal stepped inside with an armload of boxes, which she set in the visitor's chair. "Would you like some help packing?"

"No, thank you."

"Sawyer says you want a job. What can you do?" The woman's cool tone and expression implied she wasn't overly thrilled to have Lynn's assistance foisted upon her. Lynn's heart sank. What could she do besides wait tables and plan elaborate dinner parties?

"I helped Brett whenever he brought work home. I can type. And I—" She bit her lip, hesitant to admit she'd baby-sat for the neighbors' children on the sly for spending money, and then she'd sneaked out to take classes at the local technical college without Brett's knowledge. But Brett was gone. Her secrets couldn't hurt her anymore. "I've also taken a few computer classes at Orange Tech."

Opal's eyes narrowed speculatively and then she moved around the desk and booted up the computer. "That's a start. Let's see how many of the computer programs you recognize."

Familiar icons appeared on the screen and the tension eased from Lynn's shoulders. She could do this. "I've used most of these before."

"Honey, it would be my lucky day if you knew anything about designing promotional brochures. That's what Brett was working on before the accident." Opal shoved her glasses into her graying hair. "I don't know much about graphics, but the project has landed on my desk. I have to finish it or farm it out."

Lynn smiled at the dread in Opal's voice. "Brett worked on the flyer at home on his laptop. He struggled with the software when Sawyer bought it last year. I read the instruction manual while Brett was at work and did the tutorial exercises so that I could demonstrate the program to him." She hesitated and then confessed. "I took a class in the software program last fall."

Opal's penciled brows rose. "Are you willing to take a stab at laying out the brochure? It would save us the expense of hiring an outside company."

What did she have to lose? "I can try."

"Great. Do what you can and then we'll run it by Sawyer. Would it be too difficult for you to work in here? The files are already on this computer."

"This is fine." If she worked hard at it she could probably forget Sawyer was only two doors down.

* * *

"I don't want the Feds in on this, Carter." Sawyer faced his former college roommate across the table in the basement restaurant that had once been their college hangout. "I want to know who's been robbing my company, and I want to keep it quiet."

"No problem. You're privately owned. It's not like you're screwing stockholders by withholding information."

"My sister-in-law and I are the only owners, but I'd rather Lynn not catch wind of the investigation. She has enough on her plate without having to worry about the business going under."

"Yeah, man, sorry about Brett." Carter fingered the paper coaster under his beer. "Do you think it's an inside job?"

Sawyer tried to ignore the ache in his chest that cropped up every time someone mentioned his brother's name. He rubbed the back of his neck and shook his head. "Everything I've found points in that direction, but there are only fifteen of us, and we get along. I can't picture anybody being disgruntled enough to sell company secrets. I've messed up somewhere in my tracking, or someone's laid a false trail."

"Mess up? You? I doubt it. Statistics support the theory of an insider being your leak. Internal theft is number one in the industry."

Bile burned Sawyer's throat at the thought of someone close stealing from him. He ate at his team members' houses, went boating with them on the lake and attended their weddings. They played in a company softball league together. "I trust my team."

Skepticism tightened Carter's features. "Well, it's my job to find out if that trust is misplaced. Do you want me working on the inside or hacking in from outside?''

"Are you kidding? You have quite a reputation for your cybersleuthing. The alarm would sound if you turned up in our offices. I'll grant you access.''

"Won't your team pick up another player in the field?''

"My number-one intrusion detector is on paternity leave for the next month. I'm covering for him while he's out. The rest are neck deep in a custom-designed program for a pharmaceutical company, but I'll give you my password and log-in just in case.''

"You trust me that much, huh?''

"Like a brother.''

"Back atcha.'' Carter sipped his beer. "So how much did this cost you?''

"A bundle. We were weeks away from launching a new program, but somebody beat us to it. Worse, I suspect this wasn't the first leak. We had another incident a couple of years back. I passed it off as bad luck, but now I'm not so sure. I added the past dates to the file.''

"Will the company survive?''

Sawyer wadded his paper napkin and shoved his lasagna aside. "It will if we can stop the leak and prevent it from happening again.''

"Like you said, I'm good at what I do. We'll get your man. In the meantime, I need the names of all your employees, and I want to know who has access to what.''

Sawyer finished his beer. "I'll go back to the office and e-mail that to you from my private account. The place should be deserted on a Friday night.''

Carter tapped the folder on the table. "The information in here is enough to get me started.''

"Thanks, Carter. I'll owe you."

His buddy chuckled. "Nah, man, but we might be even."

She wasn't useless, and she'd prove it. Three days was too long to struggle with this blasted brochure, and Lynn was determined to conquer it rather than have it hanging over her head all weekend.

She swallowed to alleviate the nasty taste in her mouth and resized the image on her screen for the umpteenth time. Her stomach must have finally realized that she wasn't going to break for lunch or dinner. It had quit growling hours ago, and now churned like an agitating washing machine. She should call it a night, but she was so close to finishing.

Her stomach churned harder. A trip to the water fountain might help. She rose. A wave of dizziness swept over her and a cold sweat beaded her upper lip. She had to clutch the edge of the desk for support. Oh, Lord, she couldn't afford to get sick now—not when she had to prove her worth and she hadn't yet built up any paid sick time.

Stumbling around her desk, she headed for the hall. Her stomach lurched, and she thanked her stars the offices were empty and no one would witness her undignified sprint for the ladies' room. She slammed through the door, dropped to her knees in the closest stall and retched.

The door glided open behind her. Alarm pricked the hairs on the back of her neck because the offices should be empty, but she couldn't get up.

"Lynn, are you okay? I saw you run in here."

Sawyer. She cringed and heaved. Why did the man

always find her at her worst? "Fine," she mumbled and promptly made a liar of herself.

Water splashed in the sink. A long-fingered hand entered her peripheral vision a split-second before a cold paper towel touched her forehead.

Grateful, she took the towel and waved him away. He stepped back but didn't leave the room. After what seemed like an eon, her nausea finally abated. The ridges of the cold floor tiles dug into her knees, and a draft of air from the overhead air-conditioning chilled her skin. Flushing the toilet, she slowly rose.

Her knees quivered and her head spun. She braced herself on the cool metal stall. Sawyer stepped forward, hooked an arm around her waist and guided her to the sink. She splashed water on her face, rinsed her mouth and used the paper towels he offered to dry off.

Catching her reflection in the vanity mirror, she grimaced. Not attractive. Dark mascara half-moons shadowed her eyes, and the remnants of her blush looked overly bright on her pale skin. Her blue dress accentuated the shadows under her eyes. *Charming.* She scrubbed away what she could of her ruined makeup before turning to lean her hips against the marble countertop for support.

Sawyer's laser-sharp gaze traveled from her face to her toes and back again, making her aware of how rumpled she must look. "Are you pregnant?"

His words stole her breath and tripped her heart. She did a quick mental calculation and her knees wobbled. Oh, Lord. With the stress of settling the estate and starting this job she hadn't realized she was late. Or maybe she'd subconsciously blocked it out. "I don't know."

"I'll drive you home. We'll stop and pick up a pregnancy test kit on the way."

Alarm prickled her skin. If she was pregnant she wanted time *alone* to digest the fact and to figure out what she was going to do. "That isn't necessary."

"Yes, it is. You could be carrying my child."

The wind sailed out of her. With alarm or excitement? She didn't know. "Maybe this is just the stomach flu."

He didn't look like he bought her flu story. The worst part was, she didn't either. With her recent run of bad luck, it was probably Brett's baby—now when she could least afford the family she'd always wanted. Or Sawyer's baby. Her stomach pitched again. She pressed a hand to her middle and mentally measured the distance back to the stall.

Sawyer yanked open the rest room door, and the gust of fresh air revived her. "Grab your stuff and shut down your computer. When did you last eat?"

She winced and preceded him into the hall. "Breakfast."

His brows dipped. "I'll get some juice and crackers from the break room for you to eat in the car. Meet me outside in three minutes." He issued the order as if expecting unquestioning compliance and her hackles rose.

"Sawyer—"

"Just do it, Lynn." His implacable tone warned her not to waste time arguing and sent an invigorating surge of adrenaline through her system. Brett had been big on issuing commands.

She did as Sawyer asked, however, building her arguments as she closed up her office, but by the time she met him in the parking lot, the jolt of angry energy had subsided, and she was too tired to insist on driving her own vehicle. She climbed into his SUV and nibbled on crackers during the short drive to the pharmacy. He instructed her to sit tight and went into the store without her to purchase the test kit. All too soon he returned.

Twenty minutes later he pulled into her driveway, killed the engine and handed her the brown paper bag. "I'll have your car delivered first thing in the morning."

"Thanks." Lethargy weighted her limbs. She did not have the energy to deal with the test tonight. All she wanted was to crawl into bed and sleep around the clock. "I'll um...see you tomorrow."

Sawyer came around and opened her door. The tension in his face mirrored the knot in her stomach. "I'm coming in."

Her fingers tightened on the bag. The crinkle of the paper seemed unusually loud. With the garage door closed, she had no option but to use the front entrance. Her hands shook as she unlocked the door. It took several tries to line the key up with the lock, but then she did and the knob turned. Sawyer followed her into the foyer. A flash of heat shot through her at the memory of that night. She couldn't look at him, couldn't bear to see the regret in his eyes. She gestured toward the living room. "Make yourself comfortable. Excuse me."

Her heels clicked across the marble floor. The bag weighed her down like lead ballast as she climbed the stairs. Sawyer's tread behind her stopped her in her tracks. She spun around and found her eyes level with his. "What are you doing?"

"I'll wait upstairs while you do the test." The determined set of his jaw and the turmoil in his eyes stifled her protest.

She turned and trudged up the remaining steps. The tension inside her coiled tighter with each riser she climbed. She entered the guest room. Not even for Sawyer's sake, could she bear being in the room she'd shared with Brett—the room where she'd been such a failure as a wife and as a woman—when she discovered whether or not she would soon be a mother.

"You've moved out of the master bedroom."

She cringed at the shock in his voice. He'd obviously noticed her personal belongings scattered about the room and her clothing through the open closet door.

"This was my parents' bedroom furniture. My grandmother made that quilt for their wedding present. I needed to be…" Unwilling to explain and be laughed at, she rolled a shoulder.

"Close to them." Sympathy and understanding shone in his eyes. Brett had never accepted her need for a link to her past. He'd wanted to throw out what he'd called her "old junk."

Her last glimpse as she closed the bathroom door was of Sawyer settling on the edge of her creaky brass bed. Stoic and determined to do the right thing, he couldn't be more unlike his brother, who'd chosen the easiest route more often than not.

The bag rattled noisily when she opened it, and she imagined Sawyer knowing every move she made by the sounds slipping through the closed door. She read the instructions once, twice, and then she unpacked the components and read the directions a third time.

Her hands shook and her queasiness returned. The pieces seemed minuscule and slippery, and her fingers had turned to thumbs. Three minutes. Two lines yes. One line no.

She followed the instructions and then washed her hands and face, brushed her teeth to fill the time and looked at her watch. Two minutes left. Keeping her eyes averted from the test stick, she combed her hair and straightened the items on her bathroom countertop. No sound came from the other side of the door. Was Sawyer as nervous about this as she?

She checked her watch. One minute left. Did she want to be pregnant?

Yes.

No.

She couldn't decide. Reason warred with emotion. She wanted a baby, but she couldn't afford one and Brett's debts, too.

Her heart pounded and perspiration dampened her skin. With her back to the test stick, she focused on the second hand of her watch and counted backward from thirty. Three. Two. One. She closed her eyes. Her feet seemed glued to the floor, and her heart lodged in her throat. Unlocking her muscles, she turned inch-by-painful inch and forced her lids open.

Two lines. Her skin flushed with joy, but then reality settled like a cold, wet blanket on her shoulders.

She was expecting a baby, but *whose?*

Four

The bathroom door opened, and Sawyer turned away from the window. He took in Lynn's shocked expression. His stomach dropped. His heart slammed against his ribs with the force and speed of a jackhammer.

"You're pregnant."

"Apparently so," she whispered.

"We'll get married," he announced without preamble. He'd run the possible scenarios over in his mind, and marriage was the best way to establish a legal connection with the child.

Her eyes widened and she clutched the door frame. Her horrified expression shredded his ego. "But the baby might not be yours."

He ground his teeth against the unexpected burn in his chest. Did it matter who'd fathered her child? This baby was the only family he had left and, dammit, he would keep his family together. "I want to be a father to this child."

"Sawyer, that's not necessary, and if I'm living in Florida—"

Panic clawed his throat. "Families belong together."

She looked trapped. A shaky breath lifted her breasts beneath the bodice of the pale blue dress the exact shade of her eyes—eyes now rounded with horror and shock. "Well yes, but we don't have to get married. If this is your child then I'll find an apartment here in town, and you can visit as much as you like."

"And if it's not?"

"Then I'll move in with my aunt."

He couldn't let that happen. He'd lost Brett, but he would not lose Brett's child. "How will you know whose baby it is before it's born without DNA testing?"

"I won't. I don't know much about prenatal DNA testing, but I think there's some risk to the baby involved. I'm not willing to jeopardize my baby when waiting a few months will give us the answer."

At least they agreed on something. "I want to be the second parent either way. You know one parent isn't as good as two. When we were dating you told me your life changed dramatically after your mother died."

She didn't look convinced. "Sawyer, you're still grieving over Brett and you're not thinking straight. One of these days you're going to want to get married and start your own family."

"Brett would have wanted me to take care of you and the baby."

"I don't think—"

He sliced a hand toward the pile of bills on the dresser and her protest died. "Lynn, you're up to your eyeballs in debt. Admit it, you can't make it alone."

"If you'd buy my share of the company, then that wouldn't be a problem."

"I told you I can't do that now, and the agreement Brett signed grants me twelve months to raise the capital."

She wrung her hands. "Can't you get a loan?"

"For a million dollars? Not without putting CyberQuest up as collateral. I won't do that."

Her mouth dropped open. She probably hadn't realized the value of Brett's share. "I don't want to get married again."

The ache in his chest that had been present since his brother's death expanded until it hurt to breathe. Losing Brett had obviously hurt her as much as it had him. He closed the distance between them, but shoved his hands in his pockets before the urge to reach for her and hold her close overwhelmed his common sense.

"I'm asking for twelve months. By that time I should be able to buy your share of the company, and we'll know who fathered this baby. Regardless of the parentage, I'll establish a trust fund for the baby when we divorce. It'll take at least a year to settle Brett's estate. In the meantime, you'd have the best health care money can buy and a roof over your head."

"You don't know what you're asking," she whispered with her anguished gaze fixed on his face.

The pressure in his chest increased. "I understand that you still love Brett. I'm not trying to replace him. I want to remember him as much as you do."

She hugged her arms around her waist and turned away. Her stiff spine and hunched shoulders clearly shouted refusal.

He wanted to pretend his ego wasn't wounded, but only a fool fooled himself. He closed the door on his emotions and focused on the facts. "North Carolina doesn't require blood tests or waiting periods, but we'll have to apply for a license. It will take about a week to get the paperwork in order. I'll need your birth certificate."

She flashed a deer-in-the-headlights stare over her shoulder.

"I've almost finished renovating another suite of rooms—a bedroom with a full bath and an adjoining sitting room. We'll make it your room and a nursery."

"A marriage without love is a miserable one."

The haunted look in her eyes and the torment in her voice made the muscles between his shoulder blades tense. He'd known her mother died when Lynn was eleven and that afterward her father had buried himself in his work and left Lynn in her maiden aunt's care, but he hadn't realized that her parents had been unhappy together.

He shrugged off his sympathy and lifted the top letter from the stack of bills. "The bank has started foreclosure proceedings against you. The house payment is sixty days past due. Brett's death might buy you a little extra time, but not much. Where will you go?"

He barely heard her gasp, but the pallor of her skin was hard to miss. "You had no business snooping though my mail."

He hadn't intended to look through her personal mail, but she'd been locked in that bathroom for the longest thirteen minutes and twenty seconds of his life, and red past-due notices were hard to miss even from across the room—especially when he was trying not to stare a hole through the bathroom door.

How could Brett let two months pass without making payments? Had Lynn run up so much credit card debt that they couldn't afford the house payment? Questions rolled through his brain, but he didn't voice them. Attacking her now would be like kicking a kitten.

He cupped her shoulders and waited until she met his gaze. "Would you rather I didn't care? Do you want me to walk out of here tonight and let the bank turn you and your baby out on the street?"

He couldn't do it, but she probably didn't know that.

The tension seeped from her shoulders until she looked tired, fragile and on the verge of tears. He wanted to hold her and promise her everything would be all right, but he couldn't, because he couldn't guarantee that he could find the slime ball who was stealing from him.

"No. I just…I don't think I can marry you."

Cripes, was marrying him a fate worse than death? Even without his promise to his mother, he wanted to take care of Lynn and the child growing inside her. He had the strangest urge to see her belly swell as the Riggan baby—whosever it was—thrived. A surge of possessiveness like he'd never before experienced shot through his veins.

"You've seen my backyard, Lynn. It's huge. We'll build a swing set and a sandbox, and you'll still have room for that vegetable garden you always wanted." He despised himself for using against her the dreams she'd told him back when they were dating, but he'd do whatever it took to hold on to this child.

He kicked his common sense to the curb and pulled her close. Though her muscles remained tense, he savored her softness and warmth against his chest, her honeysuckle scent filling his nostrils and the silken touch of her hair against his chin, his cheek. She felt right in his arms, but she shouldn't.

One taste of forbidden passion is all you're going to get, Riggan, so put a lid on it.

He put a few inches between them and waited for his heart to settle and for her to lift her gaze to his. "Marry me and let me make a home for you and your baby."

The yearning in her eyes put a lump in his throat, but it was home and family she craved, not him, and he'd better not forget it. There wasn't any love between them. Nevertheless, his heart slammed against his ribs and the urge to kiss her burned through his veins like a lit fuse. He ground his teeth against the heat in his groin and released her before he crossed the line. Again.

Lynn's knees went weak at the magnitude of what Sawyer asked. She sank down on the edge of her bed and buried her face in her hands. How could she trust another man? And not just any man, but one who would hate her if he knew she'd driven his baby brother from the house that night? No, she hadn't caused Brett's death, but she might have contributed to his reckless mood.

But how could she deny her child a father?

Did she dare risk living with Sawyer? She'd been well on the way to falling in love with him four and a half years ago when he'd taken off on a business trip. She hadn't needed a college education to recognize what it meant when a man left town without saying goodbye and didn't call or write. He hadn't wanted her. He'd found her lacking...just as Brett and her father had.

Sawyer dropped to his knees in front of her and co-cooned her icy hands in his warm grasp. His steady, cobalt gaze held hers. "Lynn, I will love this child as if it were my own, no matter who the father is."

Her heart thundered so hard she could barely think.

She wanted to believe in the honest expression in his eyes, but Brett had fooled her with his false sincerity so many times that she didn't trust her own judgment anymore. Tearing her gaze away from his, she looked from the wedding band on her hand to the stack of bills on her dresser, and felt overwhelmed.

Until she'd posted the notice of Brett's death in the paper she'd had no idea how many creditors she'd inherited. Each day's mail brought a fresh stack of bills. She could only hope the money she'd raised from the yard sale and the proceeds generated by selling everything of value in the house would clear her debts. Brett's own credit card balances would eat up her salary. Living rent free appealed, but the trust fund Sawyer promised for her baby was the clincher.

Money issues aside, what if something happened to her the way it had to her mother? A simple cold had turned into fatal pneumonia. One day her mother had been full of love and life and the next, gone. Her father, while never demonstrative, had completely shut down his emotions. He'd started putting in overtime on the job, leaving Lynn hungry for any sign that her father loved her and didn't blame her for bringing home the virus that had killed her mother. Her unmarried aunt had helped out, but when the scandal broke after her father's death, her aunt made plans to move away the day Lynn turned eighteen. Lynn had felt discarded. Unloved. Unwanted.

She was determined that her child would never experience those debilitating emotions. If something happened to her, Sawyer would never neglect her baby. But could she live with another man she didn't love for the sake of her child? She bit her lip and met Sawyer's gaze. Twelve months. Surely two adults could be room-mates for such a short time?

"What about sex?" Heat flared under her skin, and she wished she'd broached the subject more diplomatically.

Sawyer stilled, his gaze never straying from hers. "What about it?"

"If we're not…intimate, then how will you—" Embarrassment choked off her words. She cleared her throat and tried again. "Where will you…?"

He shot to his feet with a stunned expression on his face. "Are you asking if I'm going to cheat on you?"

Why wouldn't he? Brett had. Besides, this wouldn't be a normal marriage. She wet her lips and tried not to reveal how difficult this conversation was for her. "Would it be cheating if we're not—"

"Yes," he interjected, and then wiped a hand over his jaw and examined her suspiciously. "Are you asking permission to take lovers?"

"No!"

"Good, because I'd have a damned hard time granting it."

"But—"

"Lynn, I've never lived like a monk, and I can't claim I'm looking forward to it now, but wedding vows are sacred even if this is only for the baby, and I won't ask the preacher to drop the 'keep only unto you' part."

Ducking her head, she bit her lip. She'd believed in the sacredness of her vows once, too, but life had taught her that not everyone shared her views.

He paced to the door and back. "I can keep my pants zipped for a year. I expect you to do the same."

The hard look he shot her made her squirm, and then he dropped to one knee and recaptured her hands.

"Lynn, this is the best decision for all of us. I swear on Brett's grave that you won't regret marrying me."

Her stomach clenched. For her baby's sake she couldn't afford not to take a chance on this marriage. Wetting her lips, she said a silent prayer that she wasn't making another mistake. "I hope you're right."

He briefly closed his eyes and then stood, pulling her to her feet. "Come on. You need more than crackers for dinner."

What she needed was time alone to come to terms with her condition and to consider the ramifications of her decision, but Sawyer didn't seem willing to grant it. "I don't want to go out."

"No need. I'll cook." His fingers tangled with hers, and their palms pressed together. The intimacy stirred her already agitated nerves even more. He towed her toward the door and into the hall without releasing her hand.

"You can cook?" Brett had never helped in the kitchen.

He glanced over his shoulder as he descended the stairs and arched a dark brow. "Who do you think fed us after Mom died?"

"It would have been easier for you to let him go into foster care. You were only twenty-two."

He turned, leaving her on the step where she'd sat with him buried inside her. Her thighs trembled and her lungs felt tight. "Sometimes the easy way isn't the right one."

"And sometimes the right one isn't easy. You're rushing me, Sawyer. I need space."

"And our baby needs food. From now on, it's my job to take care of both of you."

* * *

Sawyer was back from his meeting. Lynn parked her car in the space next to his and made her way into the Riggan CyberQuest offices on Monday afternoon. She pressed a hand to her nervous stomach and prayed her lunch would stay put.

Surprise brought her to a halt inside her office door. Someone had placed a tiny refrigerator in the corner of her office during her lunch break. She opened it and found the inside had been stocked with yogurt, juices and bottled water. A colorful bowl on top of the unit held a variety of crackers plus a selection of fresh fruit.

She continued behind her desk, sat in the stiff leather chair and stored her purse in the bottom drawer. Sawyer's bold handwriting on her blotter caught her eye. "Don't skip meals." Her hackles rose at the command. Sawyer was taking his guardian job to the limit, but he had the baby's best interest in mind, and a caring father was exactly what she wanted for her child.

She'd spent most of the weekend trying without luck to devise an alternative to marriage. Sawyer didn't want a wife any more than she wanted a husband. He only wanted access to the child, and the legalities of that should be easy enough to arrange. But this was an open-minded university town. They could share the baby and a home without getting married, couldn't they?

Opal tapped on the door and entered. "Congratulations on your engagement and your pregnancy. I have three children and two grandchildren. Feel free to ask me any questions you have about the pregnancy."

Dumbfounded at the abrupt statement and feeling somewhat trapped, Lynn blinked, inhaled a shaky breath and sank bonelessly back into her chair. How could she break the engagement if Sawyer had already announced both it and her condition to his staff? And if she refused to marry him, would she still have a job? Sawyer couldn't fire a partial owner of the company, could he? But he could make her life a living hell, and she refused to put herself through that again. She'd had enough of feeling unwanted, inadequate and in the way.

"Lynn, Sawyer will take good care of you and the baby. He's a wonderful man, and I'm sure he'll make a wonderful father. I've never known anyone more loyal to his family, friends and staff—even when he shouldn't be." Opal bent her head and busied herself with filing papers in the wooden file cabinet.

The hair on Lynn's nape prickled. Did Opal know about Brett's affair? Did everyone in the office know? Embarrassment scorched her cheeks.

Opal closed the drawer. "Sawyer wants to see you as soon as you get settled."

The butterflies in Lynn's stomach took flight. She rose and wiped her palms over her hips. "Tell him I'll be right there."

"Certainly. By the way, I like your dress. That classic style is flattering."

"Thank you." She loved the way her nearly new navy-blue dress skimmed her curves instead of clinging. If only she could get rid of the stiletto heels as easily, but the shop hadn't had any shoes in her size.

Opal left and Lynn followed her into the hall. What would Sawyer think of the new Lynn, the one who'd traded in her provocative clothing at the local consignment shop for a less revealing wardrobe? Why did she care? She'd wasted four years of her life trying to please a man. The only approval she needed to earn from Sawyer was for her work.

Opal motioned for her to go ahead into Sawyer's office. Lynn paused on the threshold, heart in her throat. The man was stable, successful and gorgeous. He could have any woman he wanted. Why—other than the child she carried—would he settle for her?

Sawyer's attention didn't waver from his computer screen. She took the opportunity to study him. A dark lock of hair tumbled over his forehead. He'd shed his suit coat and rolled up his sleeves. His big hands moved over the keyboard with the same surety that they'd moved over her body. Her stomach tightened. She tried to suppress the unwanted thought.

"You wanted to see me?"

He jerked to face her, abruptly shut off the monitor and stood. Curiosity sparked in his eyes and then his intense gaze swept over her as thoroughly as a caress before returning to her face. "Have a seat."

Her knees trembled as she crossed the carpet to perch on a visitor's chair. "Thank you for the refrigerator and snacks, but if it's to help the morning sickness, then I didn't have any today. And, Sawyer, I'm perfectly capable of feeding myself."

"I'm sure you are. I'm just making it easier. From what staff members and friends have told me about pregnancy, morning sickness doesn't limit itself to mornings. It's supposed to help if you snack frequently." A frown puckered his forehead. "New dress?"

"Yes."

He massaged the back of his neck with one hand and paced toward the window. At the end of the room he turned and faced her. "Why don't you let me hold on to your credit cards for a while? If you find something you really need, we'll discuss it."

She gaped at him. Alarm made the fine hairs on her

skin rise. Brett had scrutinized every purchase she made. "No."

"I know you're upset over losing Brett and that shopping is supposed to be a real panacea for some women, but it would be a good idea if you didn't buy anything else until the estate's settled and you have a handle on your credit card debt."

Stunned, she continued to stare. He thought *she* was the one with the spending problem? She'd been pinching pennies her entire life. "That's an incredibly sexist comment."

He had the grace to flush, but gestured to her dress with the sweep of his hand. "You deny that you went shopping over the weekend?"

"I traded some of my old clothes for gently used ones at the consignment shop downtown. I haven't spent a dime. And for your information, I've already cut up all the credit cards."

"I'm sorry." In three long strides he stood in front of her chair. Their gazes locked. "But, Lynn, you don't have to dress...differently. I gave my word. I won't force myself on you again."

Her cheeks burned, and she looked at the door, longing for escape. Start as you mean to go on. Face the issue and move past it. No more doormat. She stiffened her spine and held her ground. "Sawyer, you didn't force me. We both got a little crazy and lost control. We were hurting and needed comfort."

The muscle along his jaw twitched. "A woman doesn't go from calendar girl to corporate career woman overnight without a damn good reason."

Calendar girl? Her? She nearly laughed out loud. Did that mean he found her attractive? Her breath caught. "For your information, I'm dressing this way because I want to, not because of…not because of what happened between us.''

His disbelieving gaze traveled over her again. ''You're certain that this makeover has nothing to do with the intimacy between us?''

She wet her suddenly dry lips and tired to ignore the sizzle in her veins. ''Yes.''

His eyes narrowed. ''Brett's only been gone three weeks. You're making a lot of drastic changes that you're going to regret later.''

''I don't think I'll have regrets.''

Shoving his hands in his pockets, he leaned against the polished desktop and crossed his ankles. His pant leg brushed against her shin. Her pulse jumped erratically. She didn't think he intentionally crowded her. Sawyer just took up so much…space in the room, in her mind, in her dreams. Inside her body. *Stop it, Lynn. Don't think about it.* Her skin prickled, and warmth gathered between her thighs. She shifted her legs to the side and leaned back in the chair.

He twisted to reach for something on his desk. The fabric of his trousers stretched to outline thickly muscled thighs and his maleness.

She quickly averted her eyes, but heat scorched her cheeks and a few other places. The memory of his taut muscles flexing between her legs and the tickle of his wiry hairs against the sensitive skin of her inner thighs made her stomach flutter and her lower abdomen ache. She bit her lip and pressed her knees together. It was one thing to still dream about that night under the cover of darkness, but she shouldn't have thoughts like that here in the office in broad daylight. Before she could tamp down her body's unexpected and unwelcome tightening, he faced her again.

His gaze met and searched hers. She thought she saw a corresponding fire ignite in his blue eyes, but then he blinked, frowned and directed his attention to the file folder containing her flyer material.

"Lynn, this is good." His voice had a rough edge. "I've made a few suggestions. Incorporate those and then save the file on a disk, and we'll drop it by the printer's this afternoon."

She braced herself, waiting for the *but* for a full thirty seconds. It didn't come. She'd expected Sawyer to point out her faults—the way Brett always had. "You liked it?"

"Yes. You hit every point I wanted to emphasize." His praise exhilarated her. "Brett couldn't have done a better job."

A wave of guilt blindsided her. She took the file from him and dipped her chin. Her husband was the last person she thought of when Sawyer looked at her with approval in his eyes. She scanned the pages and then stared at him in surprise. "It will take me less than five minutes to make these changes."

"Like I said, it's good." He folded his arms and appraised her for several tense, silent seconds. She squirmed in her chair. "Care to explain how you knew what to put into a promo flyer?"

"Not really."

His jaw set. "Wrong answer."

Brett would have laughed himself into a hernia if he'd ever found out, but Sawyer's direct gaze made her feel like an insect pinned to an entomologist's board. She suspected he wouldn't let her leave until she gave him the information he wanted. "Brett kept all of his old college textbooks in the attic. I read them."

His brows lowered and his lips thinned. "You read the texts and learned this on your own?"

His carefully neutral tone made her clench her teeth. Was he setting her up only to cut her down? She lifted her chin. "Yes."

He muttered what sounded like a curse under his breath, straightened and circled around behind his desk, stopping on the opposite side. He leaned forward, bracing himself on straight arms. The hair on the back of her neck rose at the anger burning in his eyes. "He said you flunked out. That you…weren't cut out to be a student."

Brett had certainly told her often enough that he didn't think she was smart enough to attend college. *I don't want to waste my money,* he'd said, and he'd probably reported as much to his brother. "I didn't have time to study, and my grades weren't good, but I didn't fail."

"Then why did you quit?"

Her husband had resented the time she spent studying and every moment she spent outside the house, but she wouldn't tell him that. "Brett believed that my studies were interfering with our marriage."

He narrowed his eyes and a muscle twitched in his jaw. "He made you quit?"

She didn't want to tarnish his image of his baby brother. "The final decision was mine."

He snorted in disbelief. "Once we're married, you can go back to school. You don't have to work."

A lump formed in her throat, and her neck muscles knotted. Oh, how she wished she could take him up on that offer, but she'd been down that road before and learned a few hard lessons. Once Brett started working for Sawyer, she'd quit her job to attend college the way they'd planned. Not only had she become almost a prisoner in her own home, she'd given Brett the right to demand she justify every penny of his money that she'd spent. That his brother might try to hem her in the same way made her skin feel two sizes too tight. No matter how much she yearned to get an education she refused to repeat that error.

She closed the folder with a snap. "I want to work."

"It's not necessary."

"For me, it is."

His brows dipped. "Lynn—"

"Sawyer, I never planned to be unemployed. Except for the years I was married, I've worked since I was fourteen years old." Her father had been a firm believer in the Idle Hands Make Mischief theory. Sawyer's eyes narrowed, and she rushed on before he could object. "I want to work until the baby comes. Afterward, I'd still like to work at least part-time. If you don't want me here, I'll find a job elsewhere."

His fists clenched and his jaw muscles bunched. "My not wanting you here is not an issue. You used to dream of going to college. I thought you'd want to stay home with the baby or go back to school. You can do both. We'll hire someone to watch the baby while you're in class."

What he proposed sounded too good to be true—like Brett's offer had years ago, but her rose-colored glasses were gone, and she wasn't stupid enough to get her hopes up again. Some lessons you didn't need to learn twice. "I do, but—"

"Think about it. We have plenty of time to make those decisions." He pulled his date book forward, effectively ending the discussion. "Once you've made the changes to the brochure, we'll go to the courthouse to apply for the marriage license. We have an appointment to be married Wednesday afternoon at three o'clock. If you'd like to invite any guests, feel free.''

The butterflies in her stomach turned into 747s. He was moving too fast. Her head spun. "I don't have anyone except my aunt, and she's not well enough to travel.''

He closed his date book with a snap. "Okay. Your rooms are finished. You can start moving your stuff in this evening.''

She swallowed hard, trying to subdue her rising panic. "This is kind of sudden, isn't it?''

"Why wait?'' He dug in his pocket and offered her a key. "Here's a key to my house.''

When she hesitated, he caught her hand, pressed the key into her palm and closed her fingers around it. The metal had absorbed his body heat, and the hand enclosing hers was every bit as hot as she remembered. Her muscles locked. Before she could come up with a logical reason to refuse the key, Opal tapped on the door and then stuck her head inside the gap. "Ms. Riggan, your real estate agent is on the phone.''

Sawyer released her and motioned for her to take his seat behind the desk. He moved to stand beside the window. "Put him through, please, Opal. Lynn will take the call in here.''

Lynn's knees shook so badly she could barely stand and walk around Sawyer's desk. She sank into his high-backed leather chair. Unlike Brett's stiff seat, this chair had been broken in. It cradled her in soft, supple leather. Sawyer's spicy scent surrounded her. Her mind tumbled back to the night on the stairs and the way he'd smelled when she'd buried her face in his neck.

Her heart hammered triple time and her palms grew

damp. How could just thinking about Sawyer have this effect on her when actually being with her husband never had?

The light on the phone blinked, drawing her from her unwelcome thoughts. She lifted the receiver and listened to the agent with numb acceptance. They'd had an excellent cash offer on the house. Could she be out by the end of the month?

Panic swelled inside her. Doubts tumbled through her mind. Everything inside her screamed *No,* but with foreclosure and Brett's debts hanging over her head she had no choice. She said yes.

Hanging up the phone, she parked her elbows on Sawyer's desk and dropped her head into her hands. Like it or not, she'd committed to marrying Sawyer and to moving into his home.

Dear God, please don't let this be another mistake.

Five

___

Sawyer would be here any minute, and Lynn wasn't ready—but then, she'd probably never be ready to get married again. The thought saddened her, since a large family was the one thing she wanted most.

She set her hairbrush down on the bathroom counter and pressed a hand below her navel. This child would be her family. No, it wouldn't be the number of children she'd once yearned for, but it would be enough. It would have to be.

Yanking the wedding ring Brett had given her from her finger, she threaded a thin gold chain through the plain band. Her hands trembled so much that she could barely fasten the catch behind her neck. The necklace would be a talisman to remind her that this would be a short-term marriage of convenience, a business deal lasting only until Sawyer could buy her share of the company. Love had nothing to do with it. She dropped the ring into the scooped neck of her dress.

She'd spent hours with Brett's journal last night, rereading his cryptic notes and trying to find a way out of this wedding. Brett had mentioned money he'd made, but she'd found no trace of it in their accounts. And then his derogatory comments about her had made her sick to her stomach, and she'd put the journal aside.

How could she not have known he never loved her? And why, then, had he married her? How had he fooled her so completely? And what did he mean by, "As long as he held what Sawyer valued most he held the upper hand?" She'd have to go back to the journal, not a prospect she relished, but there was something in it that she couldn't quite figure out. Some of the comments seemed to be written in some code or something.

The doorbell rang and her stomach lurched. She clenched the countertop until the nausea passed and then slowly made her way downstairs.

She opened the door to find Sawyer on her welcome mat. Her pulse jumped. He looked devastatingly handsome in his black suit, blinding-white shirt and pewter tie. He'd pinned a single ivory rosebud with a sprig of baby's breath to his lapel. His jaw gleamed from an afternoon shave, and his hair had been freshly trimmed. Any outsider would believe him to be an attentive groom.

His cobalt gaze slid over her slowly, thoroughly, and her skin tingled in its wake. "Where's the Mercedes? Whose car is in your garage?"

She swallowed to ease the dryness in her mouth. "I traded the Mercedes in last night for something more practical."

His brows dipped. "Brett gave you that car for your twenty-first birthday."

"Yes, he did, but I'd prefer to drive something I don't have to make payments on." If she hadn't traded it in, the bank would have repossessed it. She'd been lucky to find a decent used car for the amount of equity she had in the convertible.

His lips thinned. "You loved that car."

Yes she had. The sports car was everything she wasn't: fun, sporty, classy and sexy. But she wasn't up for a debate over her debt-ridden vehicle when she had a wedding to worry about. Her nerves were rattled and her mind in turmoil. "Sawyer, it's just a car, and the sedan is much more practical for carrying a car seat."

He acknowledged her point with brisk nod. "Are you ready?"

"As ready as I'll ever be."

The softening of his expression warmed her. "Lynn, we'll make this work."

She wished she believed him, and as Tina Turner sang, "What's love got to do with it?"

"Let's go."

She grabbed her purse from the hall table and followed him out into the summer heat. Ten minutes later her heart skipped a beat when he parked in front of the historic stone church. Her mouth dried and her stomach knotted. She'd expected a quick, anonymous civil service like her last marriage.

The fabric of her pale-peach sundress clung to her suddenly damp skin, and the matching lace jacket chafed her neck. She plucked at the collar and fingered her necklace.

Sawyer circled the front of the vehicle, opened her door and extended his hand. Her muscles went rigid.

She wasn't sure she could force herself to walk up the sun-dappled, cobblestone path to the arched and elaborately carved front doors. His shuttered gaze held hers. With her nerves quivering like harp strings, she placed her palm over his. The warmth of his grasp enclosed her cold fingers as he gently tugged her from the SUV and shut the door.

Her knees knocked. She concentrated on conquering the telling motion. Her mouth dried. Sawyer opened the back passenger door and then closed it again, but she didn't look to see why. She focused on the steeple, the future and all the reasons she'd agreed to this farce. Security for her child. A roof over her head. Enough money to get an education and start over. Sawyer's touch on her arm startled her.

"These are for you." He offered her a bouquet of cream-colored roses intertwined with ivy and baby's breath.

Brett never bought flowers unless guilt was involved, but no guilty secrets lurked in Sawyer's direct gaze. The unexpected and thoughtful gesture brought tears to her eyes. She hid her emotional reaction by inhaling the heady scent. "You shouldn't have."

He shrugged. "I wanted to, and I guessed from all the roses in your yard that you like them."

"They're my favorite flower."

Two vehicles pulled into the lot and parked. Opal climbed from the closest car and a broad-shouldered, dark-haired man Lynn had never met climbed from the other.

Sawyer transferred his hand to her waist and guided her toward the flagstone sidewalk. The heat of his touch penetrated the thin linen of her dress, and her stomach muscles clenched. "Lynn, this is Carter Jones, my college roommate. Opal and Carter will be our witnesses."

She tried to think of something polite to say, but her brain refused to stumble past the fact that she was standing outside of a church with marriage on her mind. She shook Carter's hand and managed to croak out, "Hello."

He nodded briskly. The coolness in his steely eyes was as hard to miss as the disapproving set of his mouth.

"Shall we?" Sawyer swept a hand toward the church.

Her legs moved forward in jerky, disjointed steps. Sawyer had bent over backward for Brett, and he'd do the same for the child she carried. She thumbed her bare ring finger and then touched the necklace thumping against her breastbone. For her sake—*for her baby's sake*—she needed to be strong.

The inside of the church was cool and dark after the hot and humid June afternoon. The dramatic change in temperature made her grateful for her lace jacket, but she shivered nonetheless. Colored light filtered through the stained glass windows, painting the candlelit front of the church in Monet colors. The preacher waited there.

Lynn's first instinct was to run. One loveless marriage had been enough to last a lifetime, but her first marriage had begun with love—at least on her part. This one lacked even that illusion. Maybe that was a good thing. They both knew where they stood. Hearts wouldn't be broken.

Sawyer introduced the preacher and the two men quietly discussed the formalities while Lynn waited and tried to still the shaking of her bouquet.

Opal touched her sleeve. "You look lovely. Doesn't she, Sawyer?"

Lynn's heart flip-flopped. Her gaze met Sawyer's and a spark ignited in her midsection at his thorough head-to-toe inspection. She thought she saw a corresponding flicker in his eyes, but then he blinked and it was gone. "Stunning."

Her breath caught. "Th-thank you."

The preacher beamed. "Are we ready?"

No! Lynn swallowed the lump in her throat and forced a smile. "Yes."

"Do you have the rings?"

Her heart nearly tumbled from her chest when Sawyer withdrew his parents' beautifully engraved wedding bands from his pocket and laid them on the preacher's open Bible.

Her throat closed up and tears stung her eyes. Her sham of a marriage would be sealed with a Riggan family heirloom.

She felt like a fraud.

The service was brief and to the point. Sawyer clasped Lynn's cold hand in his and eased the gold band over her knuckle and into the groove left by his brother's ring.

The preacher instructed him to kiss his bride. Lynn's face turned a delicate pink and she dampened her lips. Sawyer's mouth dried. He wasn't supposed to desire her, but today she looked more like the woman he'd wanted years ago and less like the flashy woman he'd known as Brett's wife. Her summery dress floated over her slim curves with a subtle sexiness that revved his heart into a higher gear, and her hair draped over her shoulders like champagne-colored satin.

Damn, he wished she'd kept the sex-kitten wardrobe. Her sexy, seductive clothing had reminded him that she belonged to Brett and made it easier to resist her.

His chest constricted at the dampness in her eyes. She still grieved for his brother, and he'd railroaded her into marriage. Short of a court order, he hadn't had a choice if he wanted to keep her from fleeing to Florida and carrying her baby with her.

Sawyer cupped her elbows and leaned forward to touch his mouth to hers. Her sweet honeysuckle scent wrapped around him, and instead of one brief kiss, his lips lingered on the softness of hers until her cool flesh warmed and became pliant under his. The urge to pull her close and plunder her mouth raced through his blood like a forest fire, nearly consuming him. It took all he had to muster the strength to release her. He studied her flushed cheeks and damp lips, and his groin tightened.

How could she kiss him like that if she still loved Brett? Or was she thinking of his brother when she closed her eyes? Acid burned his stomach, and his suit coat felt too tight. He shifted his shoulders.

In the anteroom Sawyer signed the document the preacher put in front of him, and Lynn signed her name beside his—the same name she'd signed after marrying Brett. The burn in Sawyer's gut increased. He'd married his brother's wife, become his brother's temporary replacement. After so many years of thinking of Lynn as taboo, she suddenly wasn't, in a legal sense, but she hadn't married *him* out of love and, like her name, their relationship wasn't going to change.

Outside, while Opal fussed over Lynn's bouquet, Sawyer followed Carter to his car. Throughout the service he'd felt Carter's disapproval. His best friend and his brother had never gotten along, and Carter had been vocal in his arguments against this marriage when Sawyer had called to ask him to be his best man. Given Carter's objections, his willingness to stand beside him today meant a hell of a lot.

"Thanks." Sawyer offered his hand.

After a brief hesitation, Carter grasped it. "I hope you know what you're getting yourself into."

"Brett would have wanted me to look out for Lynn."

Carter snorted. "Brett only wanted you to want her. Look, man, you know I love you like a brother, but you have a blind spot where Brett's concerned. Keep your eyes on Lynn. She might have an ulterior motive for agreeing to this marriage."

"She's pregnant." Sawyer ground his teeth at Carter's I-told-you-so expression. He didn't dare reveal the whole truth—not even to his best friend.

"You can count on me…no matter what." Carter climbed into his Mustang and drove off in a spray of gravel.

Sawyer returned to the women and was struck anew by the fact that Lynn was now his wife. *His* wife. His beautiful, sexy-as-hell wife. And he couldn't touch her except in a platonic way. Adrenaline raced through his bloodstream, making his heart pound and his chest tighten. Get over it, Riggan.

He placed his hand on her waist and faced Opal. "You know how to reach me. Lynn and I will see you on Monday."

Lynn's spine stiffened beneath his fingertips. Her wide blue eyes stared up at him with a touch of panic in their depths, and her teeth dug into her bottom lip. He hadn't clued her in on their so-called honeymoon plans. She swallowed, drawing his attention to the wildly fluttering pulse in her throat. The memory of pressing his mouth there while he'd been buried deep inside her blindsided him. He barely heard Opal promising to limit her calls to emergencies before she left.

He escorted Lynn to his vehicle, returned her bouquet to the box in the back seat and then leaned in once she'd climbed inside. The sun bounced off his father's wedding band with a blinding light as he reached for her seat belt, and his mother's ring glistened on Lynn's finger when she reached at the same time. His hand met hers over the buckle.

"I can get it." She shook his hand off and clicked metal to metal. "Why are we taking the rest of the week off?"

He shoved his hands in his pockets and studied the top of her head when she didn't look at him. "Because it'll give us the time to get you settled in my house."

She closed her eyes briefly and then lifted her gaze. "I wish you'd warned me."

What was the problem? She'd avoided moving any of her belongings into his house, even though her rooms had been finished for days. He wanted the job done. He wanted Lynn in his home. He couldn't explain the sudden surge of protectiveness and possessiveness welling up inside him. "Isn't the estate agent coming to pick up the rest of your furniture tomorrow?"

"Yes, he says he can get a better price if he takes everything back to his showroom to display and sell."

He shrugged. "Now you have time off to supervise him."

Her fingers knotted in her lap. "But I haven't earned any paid vacation days yet. It was bad enough that I had to take half a day off today. Can we stop by the office so I can pick up some work? I can read over the intern applications at home. Otherwise, I'll have more time to make up.''

He didn't know what kind of objections he expected, but Lynn not wanting time off wasn't even remotely close. Brett had never called her lazy or stupid, but he'd implied it when he said she was a great wife as long as he kept her in her place—the kitchen or the bedroom. Sawyer shifted uncomfortably at the thought of Lynn in Brett's bed.

''You're on salary. It's not an issue.'' It had been an issue with his brother, who'd missed as many days as possible. Picking up his slack had become part of Sawyer's and Opal's regular workload, but Brett was a marketing genius so Sawyer had overlooked his slack work ethic.

Lynn looked ready to argue. He held up his hand. ''Carter and a couple of other guys are meeting us at your place in an hour. We'll move the bulk of your belongings to my house tonight.''

He wished he could erase the cornered look from her eyes. ''I'm sure Carter's thrilled about that.''

He sighed, regretting that Lynn had picked up on the undercurrents. ''Give him time. He'll come around.''

She didn't look convinced. ''Does he know this is a temporary marriage?''

''No, and I'm not offering explanations to anyone. It's none of their business.''

She sighed, laid her head back on the headrest and closed her eyes. She looked tired. He fisted his hand on the urge to trace the lavender circles beneath the fan of her eyelashes.

''Don't worry about anything except keeping you and your baby healthy.''

''And the company.''

He ground his teeth on the reminder that Lynn had agreed to this marriage for monetary reasons. "Right. But the company's health is my problem."

Her lids lifted and the wariness she'd worn since that night in her foyer was back. "I don't have much to move. I'm only keeping the furniture in my—the guest bedroom, my clothes and the boxes of household stuff that I couldn't sell."

"Then tonight you'll sleep in your own bed in my house. There's plenty of room for the rest in my garage." The thought of Lynn sleeping down the hall made him feel restless. He loosened the knot of his tie. Moments ago he'd stood in church and promised to love, honor and cherish her for the rest of his days.

Would the lie send him straight to hell or would the next twelve months just feel like it?

Ill at ease, Lynn stood on the fringe of the big farmhouse kitchen. She was used to RSVPs and formal parties, the kind of stilted affair her husband had preferred.

The boisterous group of four men and three women circled around Sawyer's kitchen island and dove into the pizzas as soon as the delivery man left. They settled at the table or on bar stools at the island, ate off paper plates and drank their sodas or beers straight from the can. They didn't expect Lynn to wait on them or to clean up after them. They expected her to pull up a chair and join them. After years of isolation, it was a bit intimidating...even without Carter's constant scowling.

"Lynn, you need to eat." Sawyer's quiet voice in her ear startled her out of her introspection.

After the ceremony he'd changed into a gray sleeveless T-shirt and a pair of cutoff denim shorts. She hadn't been able to take her eyes off him as he loaded her meager belongings into his friends' trucks. The bunching and flexing of his muscles had reminded her of his strength the night he'd held her and—

She interrupted the forbidden thought, looked away from his bulging biceps and wiped her palms on her slacks. Sawyer wrapped a big hand around her upper arm and tugged her across the tile floor toward the table. The warmth of his touch remained even after he set a plate of pizza and a can of her favorite soda in front of her and returned to the bar to retrieve his own dinner.

Brett had been a charmer, but he never could have picked up the phone and had friends with pickup trucks cheerfully agree to move furniture. Sawyer's friends had brought girlfriends, and in two short hours this crew had packed and loaded her belongings into their vehicles, driven here and unloaded. They asked for nothing in return.

She kept waiting for the catch.

The men had installed her brass bed upstairs in Sawyer's renovated guest suite. The women had complimented her on decorating the suite so beautifully, but she wasn't the one responsible for the soft-buttery-yellow walls or the Dresden-blue wood trim. Sawyer had chosen the paints to complement the hand-stitched quilt she kept on her bed. Why would he be so thoughtful? She couldn't help but be leery of his generosity. Brett's good deeds had always come with strings attached.

''Where's Maggie?'' one of the women asked.

Maggie? Had Sawyer been involved with someone when he'd suggested this marriage agreement? Brett had often remarked on the parade of women through Sawyer's life, and he'd often speculated on just why

Sawyer couldn't stick with one woman more than a few months. A chill washed over Lynn. Would she have a second husband who cheated on her? Sawyer had said he wouldn't. Not that it mattered, since this wasn't a love match, but she would prefer not to be humiliated.

"I put her in the laundry room while we had the doors propped open. Mind if I let her out?"

"No," the group answered as one.

"Lynn?" Sawyer's hand cupped her shoulder and his warmth seeped into her skin.

Okay, so Maggie wasn't a woman. "Who or what's Maggie?"

"My neighbor's dog. Rick found her on a job site and brought her home, but he's working out of town for a few weeks, and he asked me to keep an eye on her. Mind if I let her out?" he repeated.

"No, I love dogs." She'd wanted one for years, but dogs soiled expensive, white-carpeted houses and immaculately landscaped backyards, so a dog had been out of the question.

Sawyer crossed the kitchen to open the door. A long-haired rust-colored, mostly Irish setter waddled out, crossed the room and settled on a rug by the door. Lynn's mouth fell open. "She's pregnant."

Sawyer grimaced. "Very. And if Rick doesn't come home soon I'm going to be a father instead of an uncle."

The others laughed and teased him, but Lynn's gaze held Sawyer's and her breath caught. The similarity between her life and the dog situation was too obvious to miss. Would Sawyer be a father or an uncle? Did he want her baby to be his? The possibility of spending the rest of her life tangled in this sexual tug-of-war each time her child had visitations with Sawyer made her shiver.

Sawyer pulled a barstool up to the table and set his plate beside Lynn's. He looked at her untouched food. "Would you rather have something else?"

The concern darkening his eyes pulled at something inside her. She wanted to believe—oh, how she wanted to believe—in the picture of domestic bliss he painted, even if it was only temporary.

"No, this is really good." She wasn't referring to the pizza which she'd yet to taste. Years ago, when she'd imagined married life, this loud and friendly get-together with a big, old house and a dog was exactly what she'd pictured. Her fantasies bore absolutely no resemblance to her marriage—she gulped—her *first* marriage. The ring currently on her finger signified a new start—one that she'd never anticipated and didn't know how to handle. This new relationship scared her, because Sawyer made her feel things that Brett never had, and he made her hope. She'd learned the hard way that hopes led to disappointments.

Her stomach grumbled, making her aware that she was indeed hungry for the first time in months. She bit into the gooey cheese and listened to the good-natured teasing going on around her. Laughter bounced off the high, beamed ceiling and the tile floor. She could almost imagine the noisy, happy sounds of children playing in the room while their mother rolled sugar cookies on the long kitchen island. Sawyer had installed all new appliances, so cooking for a family would be a joy—a joy she would never experience.

It seemed a little odd that, with the exception of Carter, Sawyer's friends had accepted her into their midst without question, despite the fact that less than a month ago she'd been married to his brother. For the first time in her adult life Lynn felt as if she belonged, and she had Sawyer to thank for that. He'd taken her into his home and drawn her into his circle of friends.

He laughed at one of Carter's remarks. The sound rippled down Lynn's spine. He shifted and his thigh and shoulder brushed hers. Her breath caught. He treated her as if she were the woman he loved and not just an obligation he'd assumed.

This was what marriage was supposed to be.

Too bad it was a sham, and a temporary one at that.

Alone on their wedding night.

The door closed behind the last of their guests, and a deafening silence descended over the house. Lynn shifted on her feet in the front hall under Sawyer's watchful gaze. Her heart pounded hard in her chest. Time to find out if his kindness came with strings. She wiped her damp palms on her slacks. "Your friends are nice."

"Yeah. They liked you too, but—" Sawyer snapped his jaw closed and turned away.

She braced herself. After each of their rare social engagements Brett had engaged in a postmortem of her faux pas. An uncomfortable prickle crawled up her neck, and she dug her nails into her palms. She wanted to get this over with. "But what?"

He sighed before facing her. "You overdid it."

Did he mean she'd laughed too often? Talked too much? Or that she looked like a hag? She studied her reflection in the antique mirror hanging in Sawyer's foyer and grimaced. The khaki slacks and pale-pink blouse she'd changed into after the wedding were wrinkled and soiled. Her makeup had faded and wisps of her hair had escaped the barrette restraining it to hang around her face and neck, but it had been a long and emotional day. Would he fault her for looking a little ragged?

He stepped closer until her shoulder brushed the middle of his chest and the mirror framed them both. The warmth of his body reached hers, spreading down the length of her arm as effectively as a caress. Her pulse leaped and her mouth dried. Her skin suddenly seemed more sensitive to the weight of her clothing and the whisper of his breath on her temple.

A frown puckered his brows. He lifted his hand, hesitated and then tucked a lock of hair behind her ear. Goose bumps raced over her skin. "I shouldn't have let you do so much."

His softly spoken words made her jerk up her chin and squint at him in surprise. She'd expected condemnation and instead she got...*concern?* "Are you kidding? Every time I lifted something bigger than a shoebox one of your friends took it away from me." And then realization dawned. "They know, don't they?"

He didn't blink. "Yeah."

She closed her eyes, swallowed and then lifted her lids again. "What did you tell them?"

"That you're expecting."

She pressed her cold hands to her hot cheeks. "What must they think of me? Either they'll believe I've shackled one man to be a father to his brother's baby or that I've cheated on my husband."

Irritation flashed in his eyes, but his gaze held hers and his hand settled low on her belly. Warmth spread from his palm outward, and she could feel the imprint of each long finger. "My friends are not the kind to make judgments, and even if they were, I don't care what anyone else thinks. I will be a father to this child. I'll be there when he or she is born and for every Little League game or ballet recital thereafter. God willing, I'll be there for graduations, a wedding and the day I become a grandfather.''

Her throat closed up. She couldn't breathe. She ought to be alarmed by the possessive tone of his voice, but he painted the picture she'd yearned for most of her life, what she craved for her baby. Her parents hadn't been there to see her graduate from high school or for her weddings. Neither her parents nor Sawyer's would be around to cradle their first grandchild. Tears stung her eyes, and she blinked furiously to banish them. Tears were a sign of weakness, and each time she'd cried in front of Brett, he'd gone for the jugular.

"Shhh. Don't.'' Sawyer turned her into his arms, cupped his hand over her hair and pressed her face to his shoulder. His heart beat steadily beneath her cheek. She hiccuped with the effort to hold back the sob his unexpected tenderness evoked and fought the urge to burrow into him and absorb his strength. His scent wrapped around her and his kindness softened her bitter heart. Yet she heard a warning in her head—don't get your hopes up.

He lifted her chin with a fingertip and swept her tears away with his thumbs. "I didn't mean to make you cry.''

With his head tipped toward hers, his mouth hovered just inches away. His breath swept her face, making her yearn to rise on her tiptoes, press her lips to his and find the oblivion he'd given her that night. She wet her lips, and his eyes traced the movement. Heat flickered in his eyes, and the fine hairs on her body rose. Her fingers flexed in anticipation of stroking the five-o'clock shadow on his jaw. He leaned closer.

Maggie squeezed between them, whimpering to go out. Shocked by her behavior, Lynn took a hasty step back. She petted the dog and silently thanked her for the interruption. Kissing Sawyer would have been a colossal mistake. Relinquishing control always brought consequences. She'd been down this road before and could be carrying Sawyer's child as a result. Sucking in a sharp breath, she straightened her spine.

Sawyer shoved a hand through his hair and grabbed Maggie's leash off the credenza.

She eyed his rigid shoulders suspiciously. Was he angry that she'd rebuffed him? Had his gentleness been an attempt to soften her up to get her into bed? That was the kind of thing Brett would have done. Hadn't she learned that men could separate lust and love?

The difference was that Sawyer roused her emotions. He made her feel needy and hungry and cherished in a way his brother never had. She wanted to make love with him again, to feel that heady rush of feminine power, but she wouldn't because she could easily see herself falling for him if he kept up this subtle attack on her senses. Getting her heart involved would be a huge mistake. They were roommates, nothing more.

He attached the leash to Maggie's collar and faced her. The tension deepening the laugh lines on his face didn't look like anger. "Lynn, this is your home now. If you need anything, help yourself. I'm going to take Maggie for a walk. Good night."

He led the dog out the front door and shut it behind him with a controlled click. Very unlike his brother.

Lynn stared after him. What did he want from her? He had to want something. Other than the baby she carried, she couldn't think of anything Sawyer stood to gain from this relationship.

Before she could figure it out, the cumulative effects of the day hit her, weighing her limbs with exhaustion and muddling her thinking. She dragged herself up the sweeping semicircular staircase and went to bed alone on her wedding night.

An emotionless, temporary marriage was exactly what she wanted. Why did she feel so empty and alone?

Six

Sawyer's coffee mug slipped from his grasp and crashed on the tile floor. He swore, and Maggie scrambled under the kitchen table. Had having Lynn in his house turned him into a klutz?

Discounting his mother and the dog, he'd never lived with a female before. Not even his former fiancée had wanted to set up house, and that was a good thing, since Pam had broken their engagement the minute he'd stated his intention to file for custody of his sixteen-year-old brother.

Sawyer grabbed the dustpan and broom and swept up the shattered mess. Lynn's bedroom door creaked, signaling that he'd woken her. Damn. Her steps raced down the stairs. She skidded to a halt inside the doorway as he emptied the dustpan into the trash.

His breath lodged in his throat. With her flushed face and short, silky, leg-baring robe, she looked sexy.

Damned sexy. Desire slammed him with the force of a Mack truck.

Wide-eyed, she shoved back her tangled, rumpled hair with one hand and clutched the lapels of her robe together with the other. "I'm sorry. I overslept. If you'll give me a couple of minutes I'll have breakfast ready in no time. Tell me what time you'd like to eat tomorrow. I promise I'll have it waiting when you come downstairs."

He frowned at her rushed words and nervous tone. "I don't expect you to cook my breakfast."

Her brows dipped. She eyed him cautiously. "You don't?"

"I can feed myself." He tapped the box of Frosted Flakes sitting on the counter.

The wariness left her by slow increments, easing the tight set of her mouth and shoulders and relaxing the stiffness of her spine. She blinked and then her gaze glided over his bare chest to the waistband of his gym shorts—which he'd pulled on only because she was in the house—and down his legs. His blood raced in the same direction as if she'd stroked him with her hands. His body jerked to life under her perusal—something his thin shorts couldn't hide.

Color flooded her cheeks. She took a hit-and-run glance at his face from beneath her gold-tipped lashes and then turned her head, hugging her arms around herself. "I heard a crash."

"Dropped my mug. Sorry I woke you." His voice came out gravelly. He cleared his throat. He hadn't intended to embarrass her or himself, but his body reacted like a compass to the North Pole whenever she was near. He hadn't had this problem before that night in her foyer, but now that he knew how she tasted and

how the hot clench of her internal muscles would surround him, his control had crashed like a virus-infected
hard drive.

"I should be up already. You didn't cut yourself?"
He caught another brief glimpse of her blue eyes before
she ducked her chin and busied herself with tying the
belt of her robe.

"No. We aren't going into the office today, so you
can take it easy. Lie by the pool or put your feet up
until it's time to meet the estate appraiser."

"Is that what you're going to do?" She lifted a hand
to smooth her hair, and her robe slipped off the opposite
shoulder, revealing the spaghetti-thin strap of whatever
she wore underneath the slippery fabric.

Oh man, he did not need to think about what she
wore—or wasn't wearing—beneath that robe. He
couldn't swallow, couldn't breathe. Gritting his teeth,
he pinched the slick material and dragged it back up to
cover her creamy skin. Damn his overactive libido.
Clenching his fist, he retreated to the toaster before she
noticed just how strongly she'd affected him.

She'd asked a question. He glanced back over his
shoulder but kept his hips facing the counter. "I'm going to stain the wainscoting in the dining room this
morning."

She nibbled her lip and shifted on her long, bare legs.
"Would you like some help for a couple of hours?"

An extra set of hands would make the job go faster,
but only if he could keep his mind on his work. "Your
choice. The stain's nontoxic, and the room's well ven-
tilated. If you can stand the smell, I wouldn't refuse the
help. This is a big house and it's taking me a long time
to restore it one room at a time."

"Then count me in. If I'm going to live here, then the least I can do is help with your renovations. You've done a beautiful job so far."

"Thanks. Breakfast first?"

She looked tempted. "I should get dressed and put on my makeup before inflicting myself on you. I only came down because I thought you might be hurt."

He'd have to get used to someone worrying about him again. Other than Opal's occasional motherly advice, nobody had in ten years. And then her words sank in. *Inflicting herself on him?* What did she mean by that? Her averted face gave no clues.

"Lynn, this is your home, not a hotel. You don't have to get dressed or paint your face before you leave your room. Hell, you can walk around in your pajamas all day if you want." He hoped she didn't. He was all too aware that there were only a couple of layers of silk between him and bare skin. Would the rest of her skin be the same creamy shade as her upper thighs?

Get your brain out of your shorts, Riggan. "Eat something before you get sick. Toast?"

Maggie ambled over and pressed her snout into Lynn's hand. Lynn knelt to pet the dog, and her robe rode up to the top of her thighs. Sawyer nearly swallowed his tongue. He could practically feel her smooth skin against his palms. He bit back a groan. However long it took him to raise the money to buy her out was going to be too long.

"Okay." Lynn looked longingly at the coffeepot. "I'm going to miss coffee."

"We'll switch to decaf," he choked out and shoved two slices of bread in the toaster with more force than necessary.

"I probably should avoid caffeine, but I was thinking more along the lines of coffee isn't going to agree with me for a while."

He jerked his gaze back to her face. Now that she mentioned it, her color had faded, and she looked a little green. He didn't want her to be sick. Weird thought. Pregnant women got sick all the time, but for some reason it bothered him to see Lynn suffer. He grabbed a glass out of the cabinet and set it on the counter in front of her. "Juice and milk are in the fridge. Help yourself."

She hovered indecisively. The toast popped up. He dropped the slices onto a plate, set them on the breakfast bar and nudged the dish toward her. He turned back to add more bread to the toaster. The pang he felt over losing his brother battled with a jealous burn in his belly. Brett had shared four years' worth of breakfasts with Lynn—years of seeing her sleepy, mussed and sexy first thing in the morning. Or had she always come downstairs dressed and made up for the day? If so, then why? She didn't strike him as the vain type of woman who never strayed far from a mirror. He ought to know. He'd dated his share of those.

He took a bracing swig of coffee before facing her. "If you don't want strawberry there're other kinds of jelly in the fridge. I have cereal and there are some eggs on the top shelf."

"Toast is fine." She washed her hands and then opened the refrigerator. The teasing twinkle in the smile she flashed over her shoulder slammed the breath right out of him. "You have a sweet tooth. The cereal was a hint, but your jelly collection is a dead giveaway."

He poked the knife clear through his bread, and the

cold strawberry preserves blobbed on his palm. "Yeah, and I maintain a gym membership to support my bad habit."

She laughed and the sound stopped him in his tracks. He'd forgotten Lynn's laugh. Sure, she'd chuckled a couple of times over pizza last night, but that wasn't the same as her throaty, full-bodied, sexy-as-hell laugh. The sound reminded him of those nights four and a half years ago when he'd walked her home after work and stolen kisses in the shadows where the moonlight and streetlights didn't penetrate. He gulped more coffee and scalded his tongue.

She poured herself a glass of orange juice and slathered a thick layer of grape jelly onto her bread. He gestured to her breakfast. "Looks like I'm not the only one with a sweet tooth."

The corners of her mouth, dotted with purple jelly, turned up. The urge to lick that sticky substance from her, to taste the heat and the passion of her mouth, made his heart pound. He moistened his dry lips, pulled in a slow breath and lifted his gaze to hers.

Her smile faded, and awareness arched between them. Her nipples peaked beneath the thin robe, and her breasts rose and fell on a slow breath. She broke the connection by reaching for a paper napkin and wiping her mouth.

He clenched his hand around his mug, shifted to relieve the pressure in his groin and prayed for strength to ignore the attraction between them. He'd had his chance with Lynn years ago, and she'd made her choice when she ignored his letter and married his brother.

But, damn, he wanted his wife in the worst kind of way.

* * *

"Stop. Back up." Sawyer's command halted Lynn at the threshold of the dining room. "You can't wear that to paint."

She looked down at her coordinated exercise outfit. Brett had insisted she always look presentable—even when cleaning the house or sweating to one of the two dozen exercise videos he'd bought her. The lavender shorts and shirt were the most casual clothes she owned. "This is all I have."

"I'll loan you something." He swept past her and into the laundry room, returning with a gray T-shirt and shorts like the ones he wore.

Lynn jogged upstairs, changed and returned.

Sawyer's gaze scanned over her from top to toes. His jaw tightened and his nostrils flared. He jerked a nod. "Put on the gloves."

Ten minutes later she admitted that borrowing Sawyer's clothing was a mistake, especially on the heels of this morning in the kitchen when his every glance had been as hot as the glide of his hand over her skin.

Her body flickered to life, magnifying the slide of loose cotton against her breasts and the sweep of the oversize drawstring shorts around her thighs until she wanted to moan. Her reaction was ridiculous. Okay, so she was as sexually attracted to Sawyer as she had been years ago, but nothing had come of it then and nothing would now. This relationship was temporary, and she wanted to keep it that way. No more broken hearts for her.

From her kneeling position on the floor, she took out her frustrations on the rag in her hands, scrubbing away the stain Sawyer had applied to the waist-high wainscoting with his brush.

"Hey, easy there. Leave a little behind." Sawyer set

down his brush, knelt behind her and braced his left hand on her shoulder. He reached around her and covered her right hand with his, his thighs bracketing hers. If she leaned back even a smidgen his groin would cradle her buttocks. She felt surrounded, warm and very aware of herself as a woman.

"Like this. Just wipe off the excess. Applying a hand-rubbed finish takes a little practice, but you'll get the hang of it." He patiently demonstrated removing the excess stain with softer strokes along the wood grain.

The friction of his firm pectorals sliding against her shoulder blades made it difficult for Lynn to concentrate on technique. Her pulse drummed in her ears and her breath lodged in her chest. When she finally filled her lungs, it wasn't the wood stain she smelled. The scent of Sawyer's minty breath combined with his spicy cologne overwhelmed her senses and made her dizzy.

She couldn't blame the airlessness of the room on poor ventilation. Sawyer had positioned one fan in the open window to suck the stain fumes out and another at the entrance to force fresh air into the room. The breeze did nothing to cool her overheated skin.

"I'm sorry. I messed up," she wheezed, hoping he'd retreat to his end of the room.

He shrugged. She didn't see it; she *felt* it—the slide of his chest against her back. "Not a problem. I'll slap on more stain and nobody will ever know the difference."

He picked up his brush and applied more stain and moved back to the next section a short yard away. Her clenched muscles relaxed. Again he'd surprised her. Brett would have lectured her about how long it would take him to fix her mistake—not that he would ever have been caught doing manual labor in the first place. He paid others to do his dirty work.

Sawyer, she was beginning to discover, didn't have as much in common with his younger brother as she'd thought. He didn't belittle, and his generosity apparently didn't come with expectations of repayment. He took in stray, pregnant dogs…and stray, pregnant women. Sawyer Riggan was a genuine nice guy.

She touched her wrist to the ring hanging between her breasts. Don't get attached. Your judgment is faulty. Look how wrong you were last time. Shaking off the negative thoughts, she asked, "Why restore an old house when buying a new one would be so much easier?"

"We lost our house after Mom and Dad died and had to move into a cramped apartment. This neighborhood reminds me of the one Brett and I grew up in. There's nothing wrong with newer homes, but the old ones have a history and…" He shrugged.

"Character," she finished for him.

Their eyes met. "Exactly."

Lynn nodded. "I know what you mean. I love older homes, the mature gardens, the tall trees and the big yards."

"You are a plant lover, aren't you?" he asked with a crooked smile.

"I'm sorry. I can get rid of the house plants, if you like."

"Lynn, I like having green stuff in every room. It makes the house feel…like a home. Lived in. Cared for. Since you're such a green thumb, feel free to knock around outside in the garden."

"Don't you have a landscaping service?"

"Heck, no. What's the point of having a yard if you don't get out in it?"

Brett had hired a landscaping service and ordered her not to tamper with the expensive foliage he'd had installed. She hadn't been allowed to cut roses from her own yard. Luckily, she'd made friends with Lily the landscaper, and Lily had not only brought her blossoms each time she'd tended the yard, she'd taught Lynn tricks to keep her houseplants healthy. "But those beautiful flowers—"

"Came with the house. So did the blueberry bushes along the back edge of the property. We'll have a good crop come July. So why did you and Brett buy a new home?"

"He liked new things."

His brows dipped. "What about what you liked?"

"He was paying for the house, so he got to choose."

Sawyer set aside his brush. "I don't work that way. If you live here—even temporarily—then you have an interest in the decisions we make."

"You sound like you mean that." But talk, she'd learned the hard way, was cheap, and traps were subtly set.

"Lynn, I say what I mean, and I mean what I say. I expect people to show me the same courtesy."

She pushed a stray hair off her face with her knuckle. "I'll keep that in mind, but since I won't be here long, I don't want to sway your plans."

"Even after you leave, your child will be visiting." His gaze sharpened. "You smeared stain on your nose."

Grimacing, she looked at her hands encased in the plastic gloves. Messy. She dropped the dirty rag and searched for a cleaner one with no luck.

"Here, let me get it." On his knees, he edged closer, lifting the hem of his T-shirt as he approached. She caught a quick glimpse of the ridged muscles of his abdomen seconds before his belly brushed hers. Her breath hitched. One of his hands—decidedly cleaner than hers—settled on her nape, holding her stationary, while he used the other to blot the stain from her skin with his shirttail.

The heat of his stomach against hers caused a riotous response. She closed her eyes for fear he'd see her melting inside. When he stopped scrubbing but didn't release her, she slowly lifted her lids. His cobalt-blue gaze lasered in on hers, heated and then dropped to her mouth. Paralyzed by the sudden overwhelming need inside her, need which she saw reflected in Sawyer's eyes, she inhaled shakily and dampened her dry lips.

She wanted him to kiss her, to sweep her into that mind-numbing swirl of sensation where her worries vanished and she felt womanly and desirable. Only Sawyer could do that.

His fingers tightened in her hair, and his breath brushed her skin. She shivered and closed her eyes, and his mouth covered hers. His arm banded around her waist, pressing her hard against the hot length of him, and his tongue sliced through her lips to tangle with hers. He gently tugged on her ponytail, angling her head for a deeper penetration, and then he devoured her.

Her hands grew damp in the sticky plastic gloves. She wanted to peel them off and curl her fingers into Sawyer's supple flesh, but she kept her fists balled by her sides. Her skin tingled, and desire coiled in her belly. She ached for him to lay her down on the floor and make love to her right here on the rough, canvas drop cloth he'd spread across the hardwood floor. The knowledge shocked her. She couldn't afford to lose control. Panic stiffened her muscles and squeezed the air from her lungs. She shoved against his chest.

So much for platonic roommates.

Sawyer immediately released her. A muscle knotted in his jaw. He jerked his gaze back to the stain dripping down the wall. Tension radiated from every taut line of his body, and his breath rasped as harshly as her own.

Snatching up his paint brush, he put several yards between them. "If we want to finish in time for a swim before lunch we need to get back to work."

His rough baritone sent a flurry of goose bumps over her skin. Her heart pounded, but she nearly laughed out loud at the irony. He'd kissed her into a tailspin, then returned to work as usual. She swallowed hard and picked up the rag. Her hands trembled.

Sawyer wanted her, but he wasn't happy about it. Heaven help her, she wanted him, too, and the knowledge appalled her. She'd never been the kind of woman who gave her body lightly…except for that one time in the foyer. Until Sawyer, Brett had been her only lover, and what a nightmare that had been. Besides, if she made love with Sawyer again, she'd probably freeze up the way she always had before, and the experience would disappoint them both. If she doubted that, then all she had to do was read more of Brett's journal to find out what an abysmal example of womanhood she was.

She'd been young and stupid when she'd married Brett, but she was older and wiser now. She would keep her body and her heart to herself.

* * *

Living with Lynn was going to short-circuit his hard drive.

Sawyer laid the paint brush on the porch railing to dry in the sun. He reeked of stain and turpentine, and he couldn't wait to jump in the pool and rinse the odors from his skin. The cool water wouldn't hurt his libido, either. *That kiss.* Hell. Desire had tackled him like an NFL linebacker and ground him to a brainless pulp. Would he ever get enough of the taste of her?

She was off-limits to him, so why did his mind plague him with memories of the sweetness of her mouth and the softness of her bottom against his palms? Since he'd crossed the line, he couldn't seem to keep his mind on his side of the fence.

The back door opened, and Lynn, swaddled in an oversize towel, walked out, crossed the patio and dropped her towel on the concrete apron flanking the pool. He swallowed a groan. Trading in her flirty wardrobe for less-revealing clothing obviously hadn't included swapping her swimsuit. Sweat erupted on his skin, but the moisture had nothing to do with the summer heat and humidity and everything to do with the woman in front of him.

Lynn's lemon-yellow bikini top lifted and cupped her breasts the way his hands itched to do, and the high cut-bottom molded her tight butt like a spooning lover. Her muscles were slight, but firm and well formed. He traced the length of her endless legs with his gaze and then backtracked to her smooth belly. The hunger to have *his* child growing there surprised him, but he'd do right by the baby whether it proved to be his or his brother's.

The knot in his chest rivaled the tension in his groin.

He couldn't pry his eyes away as she arced into the pool and punctured the surface with almost no splash. She sliced through the water, quickly covering two laps. Maggie parked herself by Lynn's towel, apparently as fascinated by her new mistress as he.

Would Lynn like being pregnant? The wives of two of his team members had relished every aspect of pregnancies, and they'd shared more details than he'd wanted at the time. Swollen ankles. Shrinking bladders. Increased sex drive. *Like he needed to think about that right now.* The women had grabbed his hand and pressed it to their bellies, eager to share the power of their "little kickers."

Would Lynn let him feel her baby's movements? Since there was a chance the baby might be his, didn't that give him the right? He wanted to be a part of the pregnancy, the delivery and everything that came afterward. Would Lynn try to push him away?

Emptiness opened up inside him. His child wouldn't have the kind of family he'd had growing up. The love, the teasing, the sibling rivalry. As devastating as it had been to lose his parents and his baby brother, he couldn't regret the time they'd shared or the memories they'd made. Unless he and Lynn changed their agreement, then siblings were out of the question.

The desire to make love with Lynn butted against the hands-off sign that should be hanging around her neck. He'd wanted her from the day he'd met her, but getting his company off the ground had required days, sometimes weeks on the road. Before he'd left for California to clinch the contract guaranteed to keep his company afloat for years to come, he'd written a letter to Lynn explaining that once he landed the account, he hoped to see more of her. He'd given the letter to Brett to deliver, along with an apology for having to cancel at the last minute, but Lynn obviously hadn't been interested in waiting for him. He'd returned home two months later to find her married to his brother.

He still remembered the rock in his gut when Brett had grabbed her hand and waved her wedding band in his face. His plans for the future had crashed and burned at his brother's feet. He'd done his best to hide the fact that he lusted after his brother's wife. He'd dated so damned many women in the past four years that he couldn't even remember their names. Controlling his lust for Lynn had become easier when she'd turned into the kind of high-maintenance female he usually avoided, but now, with the old Lynn making a come-back, he was in serious trouble. Fresh-faced women with contagious grins and mile-long legs were his weakness.

He turned the water hose toward his face, drenching himself in frigid well water. After shutting off the spigot, he dried his face with his discarded T-shirt and then headed for the back door.

"Aren't you coming in?" Lynn called from the pool. She'd propped her arms on the edge of the pool. Her voice sounded breathless, no doubt winded from the half-dozen laps she'd swum.

"I'm going to check in with the office, and then I'll get a head start on clearing the garage."

She vaulted out of the water, startling Maggie back under the wrought-iron table. "I...I haven't decided where to put everything yet."

Snatching up her towel, she wound it around her lithe body, but not before the sight of her tight, pebbled nipples hit him like a punch in the gut. Her hair dripped in tangled strands over her shoulders, and she wore no

makeup. He couldn't remember the last time he'd seen
her unprimped before today. Had she ever looked better
than she did now with her honey-colored skin damp,
bare and glistening and with water droplets sparkling
on her gold-tipped lashes? He didn't think so.

She looked young and innocent, too much—for his
own his own piece of mind—like the girl he'd once
hoped to claim for his own. "Finish your laps. I'll
tackle the boxes while you're out this afternoon."

She hurried across the patio and stepped between him
and the door. "Sawyer, I have personal stuff packed in
them. I'd really rather deal with all of it myself."

She focused on a spot over his left shoulder rather
than meet his gaze, leaving him to wonder if the kiss
had made her uncomfortable, or if there was something
more.

Rivulets of water snaked from her hair over her
shoulders and breast bone to disappear into the shadowy
space between her breasts. His pulse accelerated. He
swiped a hand over his chin. "You shouldn't lift anything heavy. Tell me where you want the boxes, and
I'll move them for you while you're gone."

"I'm pregnant, not injured."

"Until you see a doctor and find out exactly what
your limitations are, I'd rather play it safe."

"Sawyer—"

"This one's nonnegotiable, Lynn."

She looked ready to argue and then sighed. "Just put
everything in the nursery. I'll dry off and make lunch."

He reached for the doorknob, but her touch on his
arm stopped him. "Sawyer, just so you know, I would
never consciously do anything to hurt this baby. Things
may not have turned out exactly how I planned, but I'm
looking forward to having someone to love."

Her gentle smile and the protective hand she placed on her tummy parked a lump the size of his SUV in his throat.

She wasn't talking about loving him.

Seven

It seemed eerily appropriate to hide her darkest secrets at the witching hour of midnight. Rising from her perch on one of the boxes Sawyer had stacked in the nursery, Lynn clutched Brett's journal to her chest, slinked back into her bedroom and quietly closed the door.

The journal made her feel exposed and unwanted, but until she could unravel Brett's weird notes she couldn't throw it away. If he had money stashed somewhere, then she needed to find it to cover his debts. It was frustrating because it was almost as if he'd written in some kind of code that only he could understand. She wished she could ask for Sawyer's help in deciphering the puzzling remarks, but doing so would reveal all of her faults. The old brass bed creaked when she pushed the book all the way to the sagging spot between her mattress and box spring.

The hour she'd spent with the journal had rattled her

nerves and made her stomach churn. She'd never get to sleep in this state. A glass of milk might help. Opening the door to the hall as quietly as possible, she winced at the hinges' squeak and then tiptoed down the stairs and into the kitchen. While her milk heated she checked on Maggie. The dog, curled on a pile of blankets in the laundry room, looked as restless as Lynn felt. After filling her mug, Lynn leaned against the counter, sipped and grimaced. Nasty stuff but supposedly good for insomnia and the little one she carried.

A shaft of light shone through the partially open door of Sawyer's study, drawing her like a moth to a flame. Sawyer, wearing the khaki shorts and polo shirt he'd put on before dinner, sat on the leather sofa with a large open book propped on his knees. A half tumbler of dark liquid sat on the coffee table beside a stack of more large books. Photo albums? He lifted his head and stilled before she could make herself scarce. His gaze raked from her face to her toes before slowly tracking back up to her eyes. Her body stirred.

A lock of dark hair had tumbled over his forehead, and beard stubble covered his jaw. "Trouble sleeping?"

The gravelly edge to his voice gave her goose bumps. She crossed her arms over her chest to hide her tightened nipples. Why hadn't she worn her robe? Her silky, short, slip gown revealed too much. A wise woman would retreat to her room. "I came to get a glass of milk to help me sleep. That nap this afternoon confused my body clock."

That was only part of the story. Watching the estate salesman cart off her belongings that afternoon had been difficult, like hammering the final nail in the coffin of her dreams. Four years wasted. The contents of those two rooms upstairs represented her entire life and all her worldly possessions. Not much to show for twenty-three years.

Leave Sawyer alone with his memories. Go back to bed.

Sawyer lifted the tumbler, drained it and looked down at the album in his lap. "He's been gone a month."

His pain-laced voice halted her retreat. "I know."

"This is his kindergarten graduation." He gestured to the picture in front of him.

Lynn wanted to escape, but Sawyer was hurting. He wanted to remember Brett as much as she wanted to forget his brother and the hard lessons he'd taught her. Talking about Brett was a natural part of the grieving process, and maybe by letting Sawyer talk she could understand why she'd fallen for Brett, how she'd been fooled by him. The knowledge could keep her from repeating her mistakes.

Edging closer, she stood by his side and looked over his shoulder at the grinning picture of Brett. Even then his eyes had danced with devilry, with promises of fun and laughter—promises he hadn't kept after the wedding. She sank down on the sofa beside Sawyer, keeping several inches between them, but his scent, mingled with the tang of bourbon and the warmth of his body reached out to her. She gulped her milk, hoping to settle her agitated stomach.

Sawyer turned the page. "This is the day he started first grade."

Brett looked so zestful and carefree with his white-blond hair. Beside him, Sawyer looked every inch the protective older brother with his serious expression and neatly combed dark hair. Would her child resemble one of them? The shame of not knowing which man had fathered her baby heated her cheeks. She wasn't promiscuous, but not being able to name the father of her child made her feel that way.

She tamped down the unpleasant feeling. "How old were you?"

"Twelve. There are—there *were* six years between us." Sawyer turned the pages, adding a line of explanation here and short story there. They finished one photo album and moved to another as the hour passed. Sawyer's love for his brother was evident on every page and in the tales he told, but the man he described wasn't the one she'd woken up to after her marriage.

Brett had possessed a darker side that he'd hidden from his brother, and she wouldn't tell Sawyer because she didn't want his memories of his brother to be tainted. Family was the most important thing in the world, and she'd learned the hard way that when memories of loved ones are all you have left, those memories need to be the type to keep you warm at night instead of the kind that haunted your dreams.

The Brett Sawyer described was the one Lynn had fallen in love with, and she felt a little less stupid knowing she wasn't the only one Brett had fooled. When he'd been sweeping her off her feet, Brett had shown her nothing but his charming side. She'd fallen in love with the idea of love and with a man who'd promised to make her dreams of home, hearth and family come true. But it had all been sheer fantasy. After the wedding he'd changed. She'd excused his neglect first by blaming it on the pressure of final exams and his upcoming graduation, then on his new job. And then she'd realized that the problem was her. She'd disappointed him in some way.

The photo albums revealed an ideal family, one that traveled and played together. The Riggans' obvious solidarity made her heart ache for those kinds of bonds—the involved parents, the dedicated sibling—for her child, but she'd never have them if she and Sawyer stuck with their marriage-of-convenience agreement. Her child would be a lonely, only child like her. Could she and Sawyer remain friends for their child's sake after they divorced? Could they have a family without love to complicate things?

"I envy you," she confessed.

He jerked his gaze to hers in surprise. "Why?"

"Because you have these." She touched an album. "After my mother died, my father was so hurt and angry he burned our pictures. I only had Mom for eleven years, and so many of my memories have faded. You had twenty-two years with your parents, and when you lost them, you had these and your brother to help you get through your grief."

"You told me your memories were here." He brushed her temple with a featherlight touch, and her skin prickled. "What do you remember most?"

"When I close my eyes, I can still see her smile. My mother was always happy and usually singing. My father would come home from work tired and beaten down, but my mom always put a smile on his face. After she died, I tried to do the same, but I couldn't." She'd never admitted her failure before and didn't know why she did now. Maybe it was the lateness of the hour or Sawyer's willingness to share his own memories.

He covered the hand she had fisted on her knee, silently offering support. Her throat tightened. "What do you remember most about your mom?"

A sad smile curved his lips. "Questions. She always asked questions. Maybe it was the university professor in her, but she made you look beyond the surface. We were never allowed to accept anything at face value. We had to know *why* it was that way.''

''Which explains how you became a computer expert.''

''Wanting to know how things work was only part of it. The rest was a career decision. You already know Carter and I roomed together during college. What you don't know is that he's like another brother to me. We were both computer geeks. We'd planned to get our degrees and join the U.S. Marines together and let the government turn us into computer experts. We pictured ourselves as computer-age secret agents.''

Another facet she hadn't known about the man she'd married. ''I didn't know you'd been in the military.''

''I never made it. My parents died on the way home from my graduation dinner. Carter and I were supposed to enlist the following week, but I backed out. I needed to take care of Brett.'' The clipped delivery of the words hinted at emotions he wasn't sharing.

''I doubt Carter faults you for that.''

His jaw set. ''I'd promised to stand beside Carter, and I don't believe in breaking promises. The company he operates now was supposed to be our company. We both followed our dreams, but separately instead of as a team.''

''You could hardly go off to fight in who-knows-where and have Brett lose you, too, Sawyer. You were all he had left.''

''My fiancée didn't agree. She took off when I refused to make him a ward of the court.''

Lynn turned her hand over and laced her fingers through his. ''I'm sorry.''

He shrugged. ''If she'd loved me enough, she would

have stayed. Love doesn't quit when the going gets tough.''

Sawyer closed the album and returned it to the stack on the coffee table. ''Our child will have two parents who love him, and we'll make memories that count.''

''I know, but it won't be the same when we're dividing holidays and shuffling *her* back and forth between us.''

His eyes twinkled and her insides warmed. ''You know something I don't know?''

''No, but I don't know anything about raising boys, so I'm hoping for a girl.''

''And I don't know anything about raising girls. I guess we'll have to learn together.'' The tenderness of his gaze hypnotized her and made her wish for what would never be.

A mournful howl raised the hair on the back of Lynn's neck. She sprang to her feet. ''It's Maggie. She sounds like she's in pain.''

She raced to the laundry room, and Sawyer, hot on her heels, bumped into her when she jerked to a halt on the threshold. He grasped her waist to steady them both.

Lynn's breath caught at the warmth of his touch through her thin gown and at the wonder unfolding in front of her. ''She's having her puppies.''

The first puppy slipped free. Maggie licked and cleaned it. Sawyer made a choking sound behind her. Lynn looked over her shoulder. He looked nauseated. ''Are you okay?''

He grimaced and swallowed hard. ''Yeah. I don't know anything about dogs in labor. Do you?''

''No. Do you think we're supposed to help her?''

In other circumstances she would have laughed at his

horrified expression. "I have no idea. I'll call Rick's vet."

"It's one in the morning. The vet's office is closed."

"I'll leave a message with his answering service, but there's no telling how long it will take for the vet to call back. Boot up my computer. We'll do a Web search for instructions on delivering puppies."

"Shouldn't I stay with Maggie?"

"I think we should know what we're doing before we interfere. Give me two minutes to make the call, and then I'll help you search."

Lynn raced back to Sawyer's study and turned on the computer. She pulled up an article and hit the print button.

Sawyer returned. "I left a message. The operator didn't think birth was an emergency since Maggie's not a pedigreed pooch."

"I found instructions." She nodded to the pages spewing out of the printer. Another howl from Maggie made them both jump.

Sawyer rubbed the back of his neck and paced as he read the article. His gaze met hers. "We can do this."

"I'm glad to hear it."

Two hours later Sawyer stood beside Lynn in the laundry room watching the fifth slimy little puppy come into the world. Unlike the last four, Maggie didn't immediately wash this one. After one sniff, she ignored it.

"Come on, Maggie," Lynn urged. Her grip on Sawyer's hand tightened. He didn't remember when she'd taken his hand, just that it seemed right to be holding hers while they watched the birth. "What are we going to do? Do you think it's alive?"

They'd read online about stillbirths, and he'd been prepared...or so he thought. He willed the tiny creature to wiggle and then it did. Ignoring his protesting stomach, he moved forward, picked up the slippery pup, and laid it at Maggie's paws. Maggie nosed it away. His gut clenched, and he looked over his shoulder. Lynn's eyes silently beseeched him to fix this, and his gut knotted.

"Go back to that Web site and find out what to do with an abandoned puppy."

Worry clouded her eyes. "You think she's rejecting it?"

He offered the fragile baby to Maggie again, and again she pushed it away. "Yes."

He broke the sac enclosing the pup and used the edge of the blanket to wipe him clean. The pup made tiny, helpless noises and Sawyer's heart clenched. It was just a dog, damn it. Why was he choking up?

The phone rang and Lynn answered it. "It's the vet."

"About time. Tell him what's going on. Ask him to walk me through whatever I have to do."

Lynn relayed the information, leading him through cleaning and warming the pup. Her expression made him feel as if he were accomplishing a most heroic feat. He didn't want to let her down or remind her that the odds were against them. He wanted to save the puppy for her.

When she finished the call, Sawyer rose, placed the tiny critter in her palms and then cradled her hands in his. Tears welled up in her eyes, and a lump formed in his throat.

He stroked the pup's stubby little nose and ran his finger over his wet rust-colored fur. "The Supercenter is open all night. I'll take the list the doc gave us and go buy supplies."

She chewed her bottom lip and looked at him. Concern darkened her eyes and furrowed her forehead. "I'll keep an eye on this little fella and Maggie, too. I can't believe she didn't want her baby.''

He shrugged off the residual bitterness. His gaze dropped to Lynn's belly. He couldn't imagine giving up his child. ''It happens all the time. Puppies, people. Brett was adopted. His mother decided she couldn't handle him. She dumped him in a church when he was two.''

She gasped. ''I didn't know. He never said anything.''

''I hope he didn't remember being unwanted. He was almost three when he came to live with us. We were damned glad to have him, and we tried to make it up to him.''

''But you two were so close. I never would have guessed...''

''There's nothing I wouldn't have done for Brett. Adopting him made my mother happy. She'd been pretty torn up by several miscarriages and she wasn't able to have more kids.'' He washed his hands and snatched up the shopping list. ''Keep him warm. I'll be as quick as I can.''

Sawyer grabbed his keys and disappeared. Lynn sat in the darkness cradling the puppy. Brett had been abandoned. Was that why he never cuddled her, never touched her and never loved her?

A steady thump woke Lynn. She snuggled into her pillow and tried to ignore the sound, but her pillow wasn't soft. Neither was her bed. Her legs were cramped and bent and... She opened her gritty eyes and blinked. She wasn't in her creaky brass bed.

''Ready to go upstairs?'' Sawyer's quiet baritone banished the remnants of grogginess from her brain. She jerked upright on the sofa. She'd been asleep, curled against Sawyer's chest with his arm draping her shoulders and the puppy in her lap. Only the dim light from the front hall penetrated the darkness. Her heart raced and her skin flushed.

"I'm sorry. I didn't mean to mash you." She hid her embarrassment by checking the pup's tiny warm body and repositioning the towel and hot water bottle. The last thing she remembered was Sawyer passing her the puppy after he'd fed and massaged it with such gentleness that her heart had melted.

"You didn't mash me. Are you ready to go to bed?" His husky voice made her wonder if he'd also been asleep.

She licked her dry lips. "No. I'd like to stay with the puppy. The vet said the first twenty-four hours are critical. What time is it?"

"Almost six." He tucked a lock of hair behind her ear. The gentle touch of his fingertip made her shiver. "Lynn, you're dead on your feet. Go to bed. I'll keep an eye on the pup."

Sawyer had stepped in and taken control tonight. He'd clearly been a little nauseated by the entire birth process, but he hadn't hesitated when the pup needed help. Would he be as bold and fearless with their child?

Their child. Her heart skipped a beat. Until tonight she'd considered the baby she carried to be hers and hers alone. Sure, she'd thought about having Sawyer around as a father figure in a vague sort of way, but she hadn't allowed herself to visualize him parenting her child. He'd be so gentle, so loving. Was she wrong in refusing to try to form a real family with him? Could she and Sawyer replicate the live-together, love-together family Sawyer had grown up in, and if so, could she keep her heart intact?

He took the sleeping puppy from her and set it in a towel-lined box on the hearth. Her heart softened at the careful way he handled the fragile puppy. "He's adorable."

"Yeah and he's a fighter—a real trooper." The pride in his voice made her smile.

"Trooper. That's what we should name him." Lynn touched his arm. "He would have died if not for you."

He shrugged and she laughed. "You don't want to be a hero? Well, too bad. You are." She closed the distance between them and kissed his cheek. Her breast brushed his biceps. She felt the contact deep in her womb.

He sucked in a sharp breath. His arm banded around her shoulders holding her when she would have pulled away. Their gazes locked, and awareness arched between them. Her skin prickled from head to toe. The banked fire in his eyes made her pulse pound and the tender place between her thighs tingle. She wanted him to kiss her, wanted him to make her feel the way that only he could make her feel. Desirable. Wanted. She dampened her lips and swallowed to ease the dryness in her mouth.

He cupped her jaw in one large, warm hand and leaned forward until only an inch separated their mouths. "Lynn, tell me you want this," he whispered roughly.

She couldn't speak, so she touched her lips to his. Her lids fluttered closed.

He groaned and slid his fingers into her hair, curling and flexing them at her nape. A shiver skipped down her spine and goose bumps swept over her flesh. His mouth pressed down on hers, and the slick heat of his tongue parted her lips, making her dizzy with desire. He sampled her mouth, teasing her, tempting her to reciprocate, and then he suckled her tongue when she dared to kiss him back. She clutched his shoulders for support, stroking and kneading his taut muscles.

His free hand settled at her waist, scorching through her thin gown as he stroked her hip, her thigh. Easing her backward on the sofa, he stretched out beside her, aligning her body with his. Their bare legs tangled, and his thigh slid between her knees. His wiry leg hairs teased her skin, and his arousal, thick, hard and hot, branded her hipbone with scalding insistence. The tension in her lower belly increased. She twined her arms behind his neck and bowed her back, pressing against him in an attempt to ease the excruciating emptiness yawning inside her. His hungry kiss intensified until she could barely breathe.

He tunneled a hand beneath the hem of her gown, tracing an agonizingly slow upward path with his fingers. Cupping her breast, he scraped his thumbnail over the sensitive tip, and she thought she'd go up in flames. She yanked her mouth free to gasp for air. Sawyer's touch was gentle—so gentle it made her hungry and impatient for more. She pushed herself greedily into his palm and touched her lips to his throat, licking him and savoring the saltiness of his skin on her tongue and letting the scent of him fill her senses.

With a groan, he eased his hand beneath her panties and found her wet center. The pleasure was extreme, unbearably so. She bit her lip, trying to hold back the moans multiplying in her chest, and then he plunged his fingers deep inside her, and she couldn't keep silent. His slick fingers circled on the tender seat of her passion, and she bucked involuntarily against his torment-ing touch. With skillful strokes he wound her tighter and tighter until she snapped, crying out as ecstasy rip-pled through her. She'd feared her passionate response the first time had been a fluke somehow connected to her unstable emotional state, but that wasn't the case tonight.

Sawyer soothed and petted her, sipping from her lips and kissing her brow, and then he eased his hands from her body and clutched the hem of her gown in his fists. He tugged the fabric over her head and sat back to study what he'd uncovered. Even in the dimly lit room she felt self-conscious and lifted her hands to cover herself.

"You're beautiful." His hoarse words stopped her.

She almost believed him. *Almost*. But she'd had years of Brett telling her that her breasts weren't large enough to turn on a real man. Desire ebbed. She turned her head and the chill of the night air crept over her.

"Lynn, look at me." His command made the fine hairs on her body stand at attention. Afraid she might see disappointment in his eyes, she hesitated before lift-ing her gaze to his. He looked as if he could eat her up bite by tantalizing bite. "No regrets this time."

Surprised, she blinked at him. Did that mean he still wanted her? *Her* with the barely B-cup breasts and less-than-plump lips? The desire dilating his pupils, flaring his nostrils and making his chest rise and fall like a bellows said he did. A dark flush swept his cheekbones, and a nerve twitched in his jaw. He looked like a man teetering on the edge of control, trembling with the force of holding back. *For her.*

A spark of womanly confidence reignited the embers within her. She lifted her hand and stroked her fingertips over the dark stubble bristling his jaw. "No regrets."

Blood pooled in Sawyer's groin, and his chest tightened to the point where he could barely breathe. Slow down. Take it easy. Don't rush her this time.

Easier said than done. His heart hammered against his rib cage, and a ravenous hunger urged him to feast. Now.

He stood, hauling his shirt over his head, but he couldn't tear his gaze from Lynn. Her lips were damp and swollen, and hunger burned in her blue eyes. Her breasts were firm and round with tightly puckered rosy tips, the perfect size to fill his hands and leave no waste. Shadowy blue veins showed through her milky skin, and he couldn't wait to trace each one with his tongue. His fingers flexed in anticipation and his mouth watered.

He dropped back down on the sofa beside her and fought the demons inside that urged him to drive them both insane as quickly as possible. He could always take it slowly *next time.*

Beneath the glide of his fingertip, her bottom lip was as soft as silk and damp from his kisses. His hand trembled when he stroked down the cord of her neck, bumping over the fine gold chain she wore on his way to the pulse fluttering wildly at the base of her throat. The chain had fallen behind her, becoming trapped between her body and the arm of the sofa. The gold links cut into her delicate skin. He dragged his finger back up, hooked it beneath the necklace and tugged.

The dismay in her eyes registered a split second before the liberated charm hanging from the necklace dropped between her breasts.

A wedding band. Brett's wedding band.

A chill washed over him, immediately extinguishing the raging fire in his blood. There were areas where a man didn't want to play second string to his brother.

Bed topped the list. He clenched his fists and sucked in a sobering breath to stave off the monster of jealousy.

Sharing the pup's birth tonight, having Lynn curl up and sleep in his arms had made him want what he couldn't have. Lynn was grieving and on the rebound. The ring said it all. Her heart still belonged to Brett.

She clutched her gown to her chest. "Sawyer, I'm sorry."

Sorry for what? Pretending he was his brother?

The regret in her eyes opened the acid floodgates in his stomach. Anger and hurt raged inside him. How stupid was he to fall for Lynn a second time? And just like before, Brett got the girl.

He shoved himself to his feet. "I'm not into three-somes. Don't come to me again until Brett's not the one you see when you close your eyes."

Eight

The puppy was missing. Instantly awake, Lynn sprang up in the bed, shoved the hair out of her eyes and turned on the bedside lamp. It wasn't her imagination or a trick of her tired eyes. Trooper's box wasn't beside her bed.

Sawyer must have taken him, but she hadn't heard him come into her room. Had he stood beside her bed and watched her sleep? Goose bumps rose on her skin. She shoved back the covers, raced through her morning rituals and yanked on red shorts and a matching top. She ran down the stairs, checked on Maggie and her pups and then stopped by the patio doors. Through the glass she saw a lone swimmer slicing through the pool with swift, efficient strokes. The puppy lay curled in his box on top of the wrought-iron patio table. Her worry drained and she gave a relieved sigh. She'd been afraid something had happened to the pup. He wasn't beyond the danger zone yet.

Lynn poured herself a glass of juice and went outside. She sank into a chair beside Trooper, sipped her juice and watched Sawyer swim. Her stomach tightened. If they were going to have an honest relationship, then she had to explain about the ring. It wasn't fair to let Sawyer believe she'd found him deficient in any way. She knew from personal experience how debilitating that emotion could be.

After another fifteen minutes, Sawyer heaved himself from the pool. Water cascaded over his wide shoulders, his deep chest and his muscular abdomen, molding his brief black trunks to the contours of his masculinity before sluicing down his legs.

Lynn's breath caught and her pulse raced. Her mouth dried and her breasts tingled. How could merely looking at this man make her feel feminine and fluttery? And why had her body chosen to awaken so easily for Sawyer when during her first marriage she would have given anything for even a fraction of this arousal? The more she'd worried about her lack of response to Brett the more tense she'd become.

Sawyer stalked toward her, stopping a short yard away. "Did you get enough rest?"

"Yes. I'm sorry I slept so late."

He reached for his towel. His gaze traced her face, making her wish she'd taken the time to do more than slash on lipstick and comb her hair. "We were up most of the night with the furball. You needed to catch up."

She tried not to stare as he dragged the fabric over his skin, but the bunching and flexing of his muscles fascinated her. The dark hair on his chest sprang into tight curls as it dried.

She wrapped her fingers around the edge of her seat and cleared her throat. "Sawyer, about last night—"

His face closed up.

"I need to explain." She took a bracing breath. "I wasn't thinking about Brett when you kissed me."

His lips flattened to a thin line. He leaned his hip against the table and folded his arms over his chest, but despite his casual pose, every tense muscle in his body belied his attempt to appear calm. A nerve jerked in his freshly shaven jaw, and he stared so intently that she could see the lighter shards in the cobalt blue of his eyes.

She smoothed a hand over her hair and took a shaky breath. "I wear... I *wore* the necklace for only one reason—to remind me that this is a marriage of convenience. Neither of us went into it expecting hearts and flowers, but I..."

She'd faced rejection so many times in her life she feared this confession would lead to another one. First her father, so blinded by pain, had shut down his emotions and sealed himself off from her after her mother's death, and then her high school friends had turned on her when the scandal about her father had broken. Next Sawyer had tired of her, and then Brett had decided she wasn't worth the effort. She felt exposed, but she had to make Sawyer understand.

"But you...?" he prompted.

"I like you, Sawyer. I like your kindness, your friends and the fact that you painted my bedroom to match my grandmother's quilt. I think it's amazingly generous that you're willing to baby-sit for a friend's pregnant dog and to become a surrogate dad to an abandoned puppy. I love that you put your loyalty to your brother ahead of everything else. In fact, I like everything about you."

Her heart raced and she thought she might hyperventilate. She braced herself for his reaction, but other than a slight narrowing of his eyes and flaring of his nostrils he didn't respond. She plowed on, but her throat closed up and she had trouble forcing out the words. "You need to know that I don't plan to fall in love again. *Ever.* I don't need another broken heart. I wore the ring to remind me that love is…complicated. But I wasn't pretending you were Brett. You're so—" superior to Brett in every way "—different from Brett."

She pressed her cold hands to her cheeks, exhaled and tried again. "I'm sorry. I'm rambling. What I'm trying to say is that I think we could have a good marriage based on mutual respect and friendship. I'd like to try to give this child the kind of upbringing you had."

Without breaking eye contact, he pushed off from the table and moved closer. Leaning forward, he braced himself on the arms of her chair. Her stomach dropped and her palms dampened.

His sharp gaze held her captive. "Would falling in love with your husband be such a bad thing?"

"Yes. Love ends." And it ends painfully with hard words that couldn't be taken back or forgotten.

His eyes softened. He knelt in front of her. "It doesn't have to, Lynn. My parents had twenty-five years of marriage and died loving each other."

He brushed the hair off her cheek with the back of his hand, tucked a strand behind her ear and curled his long fingers around her nape. His thumb settled over the pulse galloping at the base of her throat. "What do you say we keep the doors open and see where this year takes us?"

The heat in his eyes turned her muscles into liquid and robbed every speck of moisture from her mouth.

Goose bumps marched across her skin, and her nipples tightened painfully. She couldn't breathe and barely managed to nod in response to his question.

He rose, tugged her to her feet and slowly lowered his head until she could feel the warmth of his breath on her lips. He rested his forehead on hers and nuzzled her nose with his. Their mouths brushed, butterfly light, parted and touched again. And then he drew back until his cobalt gaze lasered into hers.

"I want to make love with you, Lynn, but only if you're certain you have no doubt who's sharing your bed."

Her heart thumped against her rib cage. She had doubts, but not the kind he meant. Her doubts were personal. What if she froze up, became dead from the neck down and disappointed them both? It hadn't happened last night or in the foyer, but those were two incidences versus four years of painful and humiliating misery.

She swallowed hard. Could they be lovers—not *in love*, but lovers? Yes, of course. Although she was only twenty-three, she was mature for her age. She could handle a purely physical relationship, and as long as she kept her heart tucked safely away then she wouldn't be hurt when it ended. "I could never confuse you with your brother."

She tipped her head back and parted her lips, but instead of the devouring, thought-blocking kiss she wanted—*needed*—he nestled his face in the side of her neck and inhaled deeply.

"You smell delicious…like honeysuckles and summertime." He opened his mouth over her pulse point, bathing her with his tongue.

"It's my—" her breath hitched and her stomach clenched when he nipped her "—shower gel."

"You use it all over?" he asked against her jawline. His chest brushed hers, teasing her sensitive breasts.

She couldn't stop trembling. "Yes."

A groan rumbled in his chest and then he captured her face with both hands and took her mouth with such scorching intensity that she felt woozy and weak-kneed. The persuasive pressure of his lips coaxed hers apart for the seductive invasion of his tongue. His hands swept down her spine to cup her buttocks and pull her flush against him. The hard evidence of his need pressed her belly, drawing her blood like a magnet draws iron filings. She shivered, slid her arms around his waist and curled and flexed her fingers into the muscles of his back like a cat being stroked. The dampness of his swim trunks saturated her shorts, but she didn't care. The kiss turned carnal, feverish.

Sawyer tugged her shirttail from her shorts and tunneled his hands beneath the fabric to encircle her waist. His fingers burned her skin from her spine to the bottom of her rib cage. He stroked upward, and the muscles of her midriff contracted involuntarily. With a flick of his fingers, the front closure of her bra snapped open and his hot palms cradled her. Breaking the kiss, she gasped.

Breath whistled between Sawyer's teeth. He snatched up the towel and wrapped it around his hips, but the thick material couldn't camouflage his condition. "Let's take this upstairs. I'll get the pup."

Uncertain and afraid that she might be making a huge mistake, she hesitated. Sawyer must have read her mind. Wedging the box beneath one arm, he caught her hand in his and led her up the stairs and into her room. He carefully set the puppy's box on the floor and faced her.

"Second thoughts?" His gaze held hers.

Making love with Sawyer could move her one step closer to having the family she'd always dreamed of. "No."

He stepped closer. His hips nudged hers, and then he brushed his lips across her brow, her temple. His hands skated from her waist to her stiff nipples, where he circled and teased until she whimpered. He peeled her shirt over her head, revealing her unclasped red bra, and groaned.

"Lynn, I don't want to rush you." His husky voice and searing eyes made her skin hot and tingly. Brett had never looked at her with such intense hunger, not even the first time.

"Rush me," she whispered. Please rush me. Don't give me time to think of the past or worry about the future. Don't give me time to wonder if I'm making another mistake.

And then contrarily, he did exactly the opposite. He eased her bra from her shoulders, inch by excruciating inch, and then stepped back, catching her hands in his and breathing heavily. He backed toward her bed, sat down and pulled her between his spread knees. His hands shook as he leisurely traced her areolas with blunt fingertips, and then he dipped his head and repeated the process with the scorching tip of his tongue.

She'd never experienced this deliberate, intense buildup of passion before, and it was driving her crazy. Shifting on her feet, she squeezed her thighs together, trying to ease the ache. She dug her nails into his shoulders, but he wouldn't be rushed. He feasted first on one breast and then the other, licking, nibbling and finally drawing her into his mouth. Her knees buckled. He caught her in his arms and kissed her deeply, hungrily.

The world tilted and spun. But the quilt against her back grounded her in reality as he laid her down on the bed. She and Sawyer were going to make love. Need twisted inside her, making her eager and impatient for the act in a way that she'd never been before. This wasn't duty, and it wasn't the desperate act of a woman on the verge of a nervous breakdown. This was elemental—man and woman and their driving hunger for each other.

It wasn't love. She wouldn't let it be.

He reached for the button on her shorts. Her skin jumped at the brush of his knuckles against her navel, and then the waistband gave way. The zipper quickly followed. He eased the fabric down her legs and over her ankles, leaving her red bikini panties behind. For several seconds he drank in the sight of her in the bright flaw-revealing sunlight bathing her bed.

She curled her fingers into her palms and fought the urge to cover herself, focusing instead on the hard ridge expanding behind his zipper. That telling sign, combined with the smoldering desire in his eyes told her Sawyer wasn't cataloging her faults.

He knelt on the mattress, bracing himself above her on straight arms. Slowly he lowered until his chest hair tantalized her breasts, her belly. She arched her back to intensify the contact. He captured her mouth. One mind-boggling kiss led to another and another. He abandoned her mouth to leave a trail of hot, openmouthed kisses from her neck to her collarbone and then her breasts. He sipped the crests, laved the undersides. Traveling lower with each sip and nip, he forged a path down her breastbone to her belly where he rimmed her navel with his tongue as he inched her panties down her legs.

After the wisp of fabric cleared her ankles, he cupped

her buttocks in his warm hands and descended farther still. Her muscles locked. She'd never experienced this part of lovemaking before, but then he gently parted her curls and found just the right spot to preempt her objections.

Lynn clenched her fists in the quilt, and when he focused on a particularly magical area, she dug her fingers into his hair, certain she couldn't withstand such extreme pleasure. Sawyer intensified his ministrations until her climax rocked her with such force that she called out his name and her body bowed off the bed.

He planted successive kisses on her tummy, her breasts, her lips, and then he stood, quickly stripping off his swim trunks to reveal the blatant thrust of his masculinity.

She had another moment of doubt. The man was perfect. Why settle for her? But she shoved the negative thought aside, sat up and reached for him. She curled her fingers around his thick, silky shaft and bent her head.

"Stop," he ground out, tangling his fingers in her hair and halting her one scant inch from her target.

She frowned up at him. His jaw muscles bunched, and the tendons of his neck strained as if he were in pain. "Don't you need me to…?"

His passion-clouded eyes locked with hers. "Baby, if I get any closer to your mouth it's going to be over. As it is, your breath on my skin is about to kill me."

His rough voice made her shiver, and surprise made her fingers go lax. "But—"

"Another time. Lie back and let me love you, Lynn."

She fought to catch her breath, eased back and extended her hand. He yanked the quilt from beneath her, pressed her back onto the cool sheets with a scorching kiss and then knelt between her thighs. Bracing himself on one arm, he leaned forward until his thick shaft probed her entrance, testing her dampness. He stroked her where their bodies would soon join, and her breath came in jerky gasps as tension built. Her lids fluttered closed.

''Don't.''

She blinked at him in confusion.

''Don't close your eyes.'' He lowered his head and brushed his lips against hers. She'd never kissed with her eyes open, and it was a strangely intimate feeling as if he could see into her soul. The soft sweep of his lips over hers sent a tingle through her and weighted her lids. She fought to keep them open but lost the battle when his tongue traced the inside of her bottom lip. ''Look at me and say my name.''

Although her pulse pounded and her body craved his, her heart ached. How could he believe she'd be thinking of Brett when he was so much more? She curled her hands around his hips and urged him closer. ''Sawyer, please. I need you.''

He thrust deep and groaned, ''Again.''

Her memory of that night in the foyer hadn't done him justice. His thickness filled her more than she was accustomed to, but her body adjusted and welcomed his. Making love with her eyes open was a new experience, but Sawyer's eyes reflected the same passion and need that raged inside her, and it empowered her. He wanted *her,* needed *her.*

She chanted his name and lifted her hips, meeting him stroke for stroke. Tension coiled inside her, tightening until her muscles trembled under the strain. She dug her nails into his back and pulled him down, hungering for his mouth. The wiry curls on his chest teased her, incited her, and then she snapped, convulsing with wave after wave of pleasure. He swallowed her cries and pounded into her as his own release undulated through him.

He collapsed to his elbows. Their sweat-slicked chests and bellies rose and fell in unison as each panted for breath. Warm and sated, Lynn held him close, stroking the damp skin on his back and savoring the fact that she hadn't been cold or unresponsive. She felt whole— like a real woman.

He rolled sideways and reluctantly, she let him go, but instead of shutting her out and going straight to the shower as she expected, he pulled her into his arms, tucked her head beneath his chin and held her close. His fingertips skated down her spine with a touch so light that the fine hairs rose on her skin. The need she'd thought he'd satisfied rekindled.

With every touch and every scorching look, Sawyer made her feel sexy and desirable instead of inadequate. Hope filled her heart, and she was very afraid that she might be setting herself up for another heartbreak.

If he hadn't known better, Sawyer would have sworn Lynn lacked sexual experience. She wasn't a virgin by any means, but she'd seemed surprised by ninety percent of what they'd done in the past three hours.

He tucked his T-shirt into his jeans as questions rolled through his mind like a summer thunderstorm. It was obvious she knew how to give pleasure, but she'd seemed surprised to receive it. The thought took him in a direction he didn't want to go, making the muscles between his shoulder blades knot and raising questions for which he didn't want answers. He couldn't think about Lynn with Brett—not when his skin still smelled of her and not when he still battled the guilt over sharing the future his brother should have had with her. The water in the bathroom turned off and the shower door clicked open. He shoved the unpalatable feelings aside and leaned against the doorjamb to enjoy the view.

She hadn't spotted him yet. She stood in the glass shower cubicle surrounded by a cloud of steam. Her damp skin glistened in the sunlight filtering through the lace curtains. One slender arm reached for the towel hanging on the rack. She snagged the fabric and dragged it over her hair, her neck, her back. Her breasts jiggled with each move, quickening his pulse and heating his groin. Guilt kicked him in the teeth when he noticed the spots of beard burn scattered about her fair skin and the love bite on her neck.

She stepped out onto the bath mat and bent to dry her long legs. He groaned at the view of her sweetly rounded hips. Startled, she straightened abruptly and shielded herself from his hungry gaze with the towel. "Did you need something?"

"No, I'm just enjoying the view."

A blush deepened the warm flush already on her skin from the hot shower. "You don't have to say that."

"You expect me to lie?"

"Sawyer, I'm flat-chested and skinny."

"You're kidding me?" He stepped forward, tugged the towel from her hands and dropped it on the floor. He cupped her breasts, stroking his thumbs over the tips. His body saluted when her nipples pebbled and her breath hitched. "You're incredibly beautiful, and these are perfect."

Disbelief filled her eyes. How could she doubt her beauty? As much as he wanted to convince her, to push her back under the hot spray and lose himself inside her again, he forced himself to kiss the tip of her nose and step back. The passion marks on her body proved he'd ravaged her enough in the past few hours. "I have to swing by the paint store this afternoon. Want to tag along to look at nursery decorations?"

Interest flashed in her eyes, but then she glanced at the bed and bit her lip. "I should probably tackle the boxes."

He swallowed his disappointment. After last night he'd thought they didn't stand a chance, but then today she'd surprised him. He had a feeling he was moving too fast for her, but they'd made headway today. She claimed she didn't want love, but he wanted her love. Until her grief faded he'd have to be happy with whatever she would give him.

Lifting the tray from their late lunch, he told himself he shouldn't be greedy. He'd never spent half a day in bed with a woman before, but he hadn't been able to get enough of Lynn. Watching the surprise in her eyes and the aroused flush on her cheeks had kept him chained to the bed more securely than a pair of handcuffs. His blood heated and he shook his head. If he didn't get out of here now, then he'd never leave and no doubt she needed a break after the workout he'd given her.

Dipping his head he stole another kiss and then drew back and grinned. The flush tinting her cheeks couldn't be blamed solely on her steamy shower. "Trooper's been fed. Maggie and the other puppies are taken care of. I'll be gone a couple of hours."

Optimism added a spring to his steps as he descended the stairs. Lynn desired him and she *liked* him. He grinned at the adolescent thought. They would make this marriage work. If Brett's ghost couldn't keep them apart, then nothing would come between them.

The feeling of rightness as Lynn draped her afghan over the back of Sawyer's sofa and arranged her knick-knacks on his shelves stirred hope within her, but if there's one thing she'd learned it was that if a situation felt too good to be true then it wasn't going to last.

It was time to regroup, to reassess and rebuild the walls around her heart. The need for a reality check drove her back to Brett's journal.

One frustrating hour later she slammed the book closed. What did Brett mean when he wrote, "He had the upper hand as long as he held what Sawyer valued most?"

What did Sawyer value most? What could Brett possibly have that Sawyer wanted? The rings? The pocket watch? She didn't think so. Whatever it was, she needed to find it and return it. Why couldn't she figure it out?

She'd read the journal several times from front to back since Brett's death, but the only thing she'd succeeded in doing was make her head and her stomach hurt. Parts of the journal seemed to be written in half sentences with words out of place. Was it code? She couldn't be sure, but she had a feeling Brett had been anticipating something big in the months preceding his accident, and then whatever-it-was had happened. His tone had been quite smug in those last few entries. But what was he writing about?

The crunch of tires in the driveway jerked her out of the past. She jumped off the chaise, shoved Brett's journal back under the mattress and tried to shake off her funky mood, but it clung to her like skunk stench.

She met Maggie at the bottom of the stairs just as

Sawyer entered the front door. Lynn wished she could blame the quickening of her heart on her run down the steps instead of acknowledging where it really belonged—on the man in faded jeans and a snug T-shirt shouldering his way through the door.

This morning had been a revelation. Sawyer had made her feel cherished with everything he said and everything he did. He'd spent hours pampering her and pleasuring her. She'd never been so spoiled in all her life, and she'd certainly never thought of herself as a sexual being. Now she did. Brett had been wrong about her being frigid. What else had he been wrong about?

Part of her wanted to throw caution to the winds, to believe in the fairy-tale image Sawyer created and to let him work his mind-numbing magic so she could forget the past and not worry about the future. But she'd been burned by the last knight who'd swept her off her feet.

A teasing grin eased over Sawyer's face and sparkled in his eyes. "I like my women waiting for me at the door."

She wet her lips and took a steadying breath, but her insides quivered. When he looked at her as he did now with heat and hunger in his gaze she felt attractive, and when he touched her... Instead of freezing, she melted. His touch had soothed the hurts inflicted over the past few years, and after the last hour with Brett's journal, she desperately needed that balm again.

Sawyer set down the paint cans, hooked a hand behind her neck and kissed her slowly, thoroughly. Her stomach fluttered and her heart filled with hope...and then clenched. *Reality bites, remember?*

She wasn't falling in love with Sawyer, was she? No. Absolutely not. She didn't need to review Brett's condescending and cryptic notes to be reminded of what had happened last time she'd loved someone. Love had made her vulnerable. She'd become a powerless victim of Brett's whims. For her baby's sake she couldn't—*wouldn't*—let that happen again. But this isn't a love match, she reminded herself. This is a friendly cohabitation. She would come out of this marriage financially secure and hopefully still friends with the man who would share custody of her child.

See where this year takes us, Sawyer had said. He wasn't thinking beyond the term of their original agreement. She shouldn't, either.

He drew back and pulled a stack of booklets and brochures from beneath his arm. Lynn frowned at the familiar logo. "What's that?"

"I stopped by the university admissions office and picked up a course catalog. The baby's not due until February. You can enroll in classes for the fall semester. The campus also offers programs that would allow you to study at your own pace from home after the baby is born."

What he offered drew her, but at the same time the offer slipped over her shoulders like a straitjacket. She hungered for an education, for a way to stand on her own feet and support herself and her child with a decent job. But first she had her independence to establish. "We've already been over this, Sawyer. I don't want to quit my job."

His features tightened. "When we were dating you couldn't wait to start at the university. Brett took that opportunity away from you. I want to give it back."

"I have to settle Brett's estate and get ready for the baby."

His jaw set in a determined line. "Then perhaps I should make enrolling a job requirement."

"You can't order me to take classes."

Muscles flexed in his jaw. "Dammit, Lynn, you have a knack for marketing. What you did with the flyer and with no formal training blows my mind. Consider how good you'd be if you had experts teaching you the tricks of the trade. You'd be phenomenal, even better than Brett, and he was a marketing genius."

His praise warmed her. "But I need my salary to pay off Brett's debts." She bit her tongue and prayed he'd miss her slip.

His eyes narrowed. "Brett's debts?"

"I meant the estate's debts."

Questions filled his eyes, but he didn't argue the point. "You can be a work-study student like our interns. Take a light course load and work part-time. I'll cover your tuition and book expenses. I only want what's best for you."

A chill slithered down her spine, chasing away the warmth of his praise. Brett had used that phrase with regularity—right before he'd told her something she didn't want to hear. "Don't ever say that to me."

He frowned at her sharp tone, and she grimaced. Reading the journal had sucked her right back into that negative place she'd been before Brett's death. She should have ignored it and finished unpacking the rest of her boxes. Maybe one of them contained the mysterious item Brett believed Sawyer valued so highly. "I'm sorry. I know you mean well, but I can't handle this many changes all at once."

His expression made it clear that he couldn't understand why she'd refuse the education she'd once passionately wanted, and she couldn't explain how trapped she'd felt during her marriage without tarnishing his mental picture of Brett.

Finally he shrugged and offered her a plastic shopping bag. "We're going out tonight. Wear this."

He'd hit another hot button, and her hackles rose again. What would she find in the bag? A skintight outfit like the ones crammed in her closet upstairs—the ones so tacky even the consignment shop wouldn't take them? Would Sawyer dress her up and parade her in front of his friends the way his brother had? God, she'd hated the way men looked at her in those skintight dresses. And the women... Dressing as if you might be interested in luring away someone's husband didn't exactly win friends and encourage lunch invitations.

She balled her fists by her side and refused to accept the bag. "I prefer to choose my own clothing."

His frown deepened. "Do you want to tell me what has you so edgy that you're ready to start a fight over a softball jersey?"

The knot in her stomach loosened. "A softball jersey?"

"The company team has a game tonight. I thought you might enjoy getting out and meeting some of the team members' spouses."

She winced and briefly closed her eyes. "I'm sorry."

"Lynn, what's going on?" His direct gaze and the stubborn set of his jaw said he wouldn't move until he had an answer.

Maggie, evidently sensing the tension between them, danced around their feet. Stalling for time, Lynn bent and scratched the dog. She couldn't tell Sawyer that reading his brother's journal had ripped the scab from all her insecurities and reminded her of what a fool she'd been in the past. She looked forward to the day when she could burn the book, but in the meantime, Sawyer needed an explanation.

"Brett used to choose all of my clothing."

She could almost see the Rolodex in his brain flipping through the suggestive clothing she'd worn with a different perspective. "And you don't want me doing the same."

"No."

"Because it reminds you that he's not here to do the job or because you don't want me dressing you like a sex kitten?"

Embarrassment scorched her cheeks at his harsh but accurate description, and she hated putting a chink in Sawyer's image of his brother. "It's time for me to make my own choices, including my clothing and my future."

"In most cases I'd agree. Lynn, you're a beautiful woman. You don't need to flaunt your assets to bring a man to his knees, and I sure as hell don't have any business choosing your clothes. But I want you to reconsider going back to school, for yourself, not for me." He tossed the university materials on the antique hall table and dropped the bag on the floor. "If you want to go to the game, I'm leaving in half an hour."

"What about Trooper?"

"He'll have to go with us." He turned on his heel and headed for the door, calling over his shoulder. "Come on, Maggie. Let's go for a walk."

The door closed. The course catalog drew Lynn like a magnet. She stroked her hand over the cover. What Sawyer offered sounded too good to be true. Did she dare trust him and take him up on his offer?

If she wanted to regain control, then getting the education Brett had denied her would be the first step. She would not let her past ruin her future.

Nine

The woman was a mass of contradictions. As soon as Sawyer thought he'd decoded the mystery of Lynn, she did something to confound him. Good thing he liked riddles.

What had happened during his two-hour absence? He'd left her soft, sexy and amenable, and then he'd returned to a porcupine. Everything he'd said had earned him a jab from her quills. But a porcupine only used its quills as a defensive measure. Did she regret making love? Or did she feel as if she'd betrayed his brother?

The more he learned about his brother's marriage, the less he realized he knew. It wasn't what Lynn said but what she didn't say that planted the questions in his mind and opened the acid floodgates in his stomach. The facts didn't add up.

He loaded the softball equipment and the water

cooler into the back of his Tahoe and mentally ticked off what he'd learned. Half the time Lynn seemed to be bracing herself. For what, he didn't know, but the tense set of her shoulders and the wariness in her eyes were hard to miss. And the way she responded like a flower turning toward the sun at even a hint of praise made him wonder if she'd not had much of it.

The yearning in her eyes when he'd offered her the university course catalog contradicted her stubborn refusal to enroll. Why refuse when he was willing to foot the bill, and why did she deny that Brett had made her drop out? What did she stand to gain by covering for his brother?

And then there were her clothes. Brett had dressed her in a way designed to make other men want her, and yet Lynn didn't have the confidence of a sex kitten. How could a woman with a body like hers not know her effect on men? It was obvious from her shyness and the self-contained way she moved that she didn't have a clue that rooms full of men suffered whiplash when she walked past. She didn't play to an audience.

And the biggest question nagging him: she didn't seem to be mourning his brother, and yet she'd been trying to have a baby with him. Did it have something to do with her I-want-a-marriage-but-not-love deal?

How could he woo his wife if he didn't understand her?

The back door opened, and Lynn, wearing shorts and the baseball jersey he'd brought her, stepped out on the porch. Her legs were long, lean, tanned and bare. Being tangled in them was as close to heaven as he'd ever been. Her all-American-girl freshness that was ten times more dangerous for his peace of mind than her knock-'em-dead clothing. Given the attraction between them, their basic belief in family and his love for her, he'd assumed that they could make this marriage work with a little effort. Now he suspected there might be several hidden obstacles in his path. "Ready?"

She jogged down the steps. Excitement and nervousness mingled in her eyes and pinked her cheeks. "Yes. I've never been to a company softball game."

"Brett didn't play." Come to think of it, Brett always managed to have a conflicting engagement whenever company events were scheduled. He didn't remember him bringing Lynn to any company functions, and Brett had rarely brought her to the office. Many of the folks she'd meet today would be strangers. Only a few of his employees' spouses had ventured to the funeral and even then, Lynn had kept to herself.

A line appeared between her brows. "No. He wasn't into sports. I'm not that athletically inclined, either."

An image of her sleekly muscled body flashed in his mind and heated his blood. "You swim like a fish."

Shadows filled her eyes. "I prefer it to exercise videos for keeping in shape."

Damn it. What wasn't she telling him? The strain in her voice told him there was more to the story, and he intended to learn all of Lynn's secrets—even if he didn't like the answers.

He opened her car door and assisted her inside. Once she'd settled herself in the seat, he leaned across to buckle her seat belt and kissed her. He reveled in the slickness of her tongue, the softness of her lips and the sexy little whimper she made when he cupped her breast. By the time he pried himself away they were both breathing hard, and his heart was trying to pound its way out of his chest.

He stroked a finger down her nose and over her damp

lips. "If this game wasn't part of the league championship, I'd drag you back upstairs." His words came out a little ragged.

He loved the way she blushed and the bashful way she ducked her head to hide her face. She'd been married for four years. How could she still blush over a kiss and a little flirtatious banter?

He nudged up her chin. "I packed snacks and drinks in the cooler. Eat before you get queasy."

"Sawyer—"

"I know. You can take care of yourself. Humor me. Let me get Trooper and we'll go." Sawyer shut her door, fetched the puppy's box and set his bundle on the floor behind the front seat. He settled in the driver's seat with a wry smile on his face. What was this? Practice for the baby and a car seat? Yeah, he liked the sound of that.

Before he knew it, the entrance to the city park loomed ahead. Unlike most of the women he'd dated, who filled every moment of silence with chatter, Lynn had remained mute during the ride. He pulled into a parking space behind the dugout and turned in his seat. "You want to tell me what upset you earlier?"

Lynn stared at her knotted fingers. "This morning was a little…intense."

His muscles clenched. "Regrets?"

She lifted her gaze to his and, sure enough, the wariness was back full force. "No. No regrets."

He released the breath he'd been holding, extracted his new family from the car and headed for the field.

Lynn nearly dropped Trooper's box when Sawyer put his fingers to his mouth and let out a shrill whistle.

Within seconds two dozen people surrounded them beside the bleachers. Sawyer set down the equipment bag and rested his hand on her shoulder. "Folks, this is Lynn. My wife."

Sawyer introduced her to the people she didn't know with a short descriptive phrase of who they were or what they did at Riggan CyberQuest. She'd met a few of the employees since starting her job, but names and positions swirled in her head. She'd never be able to keep them straight let alone remember all the spouses' names especially since *everyone* wore a red team jersey.

Sawyer hadn't bought her the jersey to make her stand out. He'd wanted her to fit in. Once more he'd included her in his circle as if she had every right to be there. The knowledge rattled the barriers she'd worked so hard to fortify.

Folks fussed over the sleeping puppy, and then a little girl around two or three years old toddled over and held up her hands. Sawyer scooped her up without hesitation and showed her the pup. After admiring the dog she cupped Sawyer's face with dirty hands and pressed a sloppy kiss on his cheek. He didn't object. Brett would have been horrified, and now that she thought back on it, Lynn wondered how she'd ever fooled herself into believing Brett would be a good father. Sawyer would be.

"Annie, you're getting Sawyer dirty." One of the women reached for the child.

Sawyer gave her up reluctantly, it seemed, and turned to Lynn. "Sandy and Karen can recommend obstetricians. Lynn and I are expecting."

He said it with a gentle smile in her direction that made Lynn's heart jolt in an irregular rhythm.

The umpire interrupted, telling them if they wanted to get this game in before the storm hit they'd better take the field. Off in the distance the sky had turned gray and threatening.

Sawyer escorted her to the bleachers and waited for her to settle. "Will you and Trooper be okay?"

"Of course."

He looked to the woman sitting on her right. "Sandy?"

"Got it covered."

Lynn stared after Sawyer as he jogged to first base. She tried not to notice how his white baseball pants hugged his firm backside and his thighs, but one thing led to another, and she recalled the taut firmness of his buttocks and thighs beneath her fingers and the unselfish way he'd pleasured her over and over until she'd begged him to stop. She marveled at the warm, tingly feeling in her stomach and the heat gathering beneath her skin. The fantasy pulled at her, but she tamped it down. This was not love. This was not a marriage made in heaven. There wasn't a happily-ever-after card in her deck.

She looked at the woman beside her. "Did he just ask you to baby-sit me?"

Grinning, Sandy bounced the toddler on her knee. "Pretty and smart. Guess Sawyer knows how to pick 'em."

Lynn laughed. She could hardly take offense.

The woman named Karen parked her stroller with a sleeping infant inside next to the bleachers and settled on Lynn's left. She gazed at the puppy in the box at Lynn's feet. "When's your baby due?"

"February, I think."

"You think? You haven't seen a doctor?"

"Not yet. We just found out." She refused to confess the shameful secret that she didn't know who had fathered her baby, and if these women knew about her marriage to Brett they were too kind to mention.

Sandy smiled. "Sawyer will be a great dad."

"I think so, too." Lynn felt like a teenager with a crush, sitting on the sidelines and cheering on the team captain. It was a new experience.

The women chatted about pregnancy and babies throughout the first three innings, pausing midsentence to cheer for the team and then resuming as if there'd been no interruptions. They made Lynn feel as welcome as an old friend. The instant acceptance was something she hadn't had in her adult life.

Children gathered around while she fed Trooper and then dispersed when she finished and returned the sleepy pup to his bed. Karen's baby awoke and lay in the stroller cooing and blowing bubbles.

Karen looked up and smiled. "You'll have one of your own soon."

The thought both excited and terrified Lynn. She touched her stomach. "Yes, I can't wait."

About halfway through the game another woman joined them, sitting down on the row above them. Sandy leaned forward. "Lynn, this is Jane. Her husband's on third base. Jane, this is Lynn, Sawyer's wife."

"Newlyweds, huh?" Jane arched her dark brows. "I can't blame Sawyer for rushing you to the altar. He's put his life on hold for that no-good brother of his. With Brett out of the picture Sawyer can make up for lost time."

Lynn's blood ran cold. She couldn't move, couldn't think, couldn't reply.

"No need to get catty, Jane," Sandy said with a nervous glance toward Lynn.

"Who's catty? I'm stating facts. Brett was a liability.

He never did his part of a project on time. Jim always complained about him, and God knows how much over-time Sawyer had to put in to get Brett's share of the work done. Poor Sawyer, it's a wonder he had any life at all since he was always cleaning up after Brett.''

Lynn's nails bit into her palms. Her stomach churned. She hadn't known Brett shirked his work. In fact, he'd often claimed to be working late. *He'd probably been with his mistress.*

The game played on, but Lynn's enjoyment of the evening had vanished. She struggled to focus on the men and women on Sawyer's team and tested herself on their names—anything to keep from dwelling on Jane's words. Was she just another cleanup job Sawyer had assumed?

Despite the heat and oppressive humidity of the early-June evening, a cold sweat beaded on Lynn's upper lip. She felt sick. Sick at heart. Sick to her stomach. She turned to Sandy. ''Could you tell me where to find the rest rooms?''

Sandy rose, ''I'll show you. Karen will watch the puppy.''

By the time they made it to the small building housing the facilities, the churning in Lynn's stomach had subsided to a manageable discomfort. She splashed cold water on her face and sagged against the counter. Sandy hovered nearby, washing the worst of the dirt from her little girl's hands and face.

''Should I get Sawyer?''

''I'm already here.'' Sawyer loomed in the doorway.

Lynn's heart skipped a beat. He'd been covering for Brett for years. Was that what he was doing now by marrying her? Finishing a job Brett hadn't completed? Tears stung her eyes. She blinked them back.

She loved him.

"Don't you have any respect for the sign on the door?" She winced at her peevish tone. He'd done nothing to deserve her anger—nothing except make her fall in love with him.

"Not when you're in trouble."

"You're missing the game—a *championship* game."

He shrugged. "I was in the dugout when I saw you bolt up here. Are you sick? Do we need to go home?"

Sandy scooted past him. "We'll just leave you two alone. Take as long as you need. We have the puppy covered."

Lynn tried to return Sandy's sympathetic smile, but her lips quivered. "Thanks, Sandy. Tell the team Sawyer will be right back. I'm okay now, Sawyer. Go back to the game."

He stepped forward. "What happened?"

Her heart ached. She wanted to ball her fist and beat his chest. Why had he made her love him? She knew what would happen next. She turned on the faucet, splashed water on her face to hide her tears and then buried her face in a fistful of paper towels. "It's just the usual not-morning sickness."

He took the damp towels from her and gently wiped her face. From the black on the paper, she guessed her mascara was history. "Come and sit in the dugout with me."

She wanted to sob at the tenderness in his eyes. It looked real, but it couldn't be if she was an obligation. Brett had fooled her so many times with his false sincerity that she didn't dare believe. "I can't do that."

He smiled and pressed a kiss to her forehead. "Sure you can. Being the boss comes with perks."

Her time with Sawyer would end. All her relationships did. But until it did she could soak up every moment of every day storing up memories in her own mental photo album.

He laced his fingers through hers and led her back toward the field. They detoured by the bleachers to pick up Trooper and kept going. In the cool shade of the dugout he settled her on the bench and handed her a pack of crackers and a cold drink from the cooler. He sat beside her, wrapping his arm around her shoulders as if she had every right to be there, and he stayed until it was his turn to bat. Every moment was bittersweet.

Tears pricked her eyes as he stepped into the batter's box. How could she help but love him? Sawyer made her feel wanted and cherished in a way no one had since before her mother's death. He made her feel smart and beautiful and sexy. She leaned against the solid block walls and pressed the ice-cold soda can to her cheek.

Twenty minutes later thunder rumbled and then lightning flashed, closer now than before. The umpire called the game, and the players left the field. Sawyer and his teammates jogged back to the shelter to gather their gear.

He brushed a hand over her hair. "Stay put. I have to help put the equipment away and then we can go."

The rain began to fall. Sawyer left the dugout and waved the others toward their cars. They left him to pick up the bases alone. By the time he had everything locked in the storage building the rain poured. Lynn hugged herself as the temperature dropped in the deeply shaded concrete shelter.

Wet but smiling, Sawyer reentered the dugout and settled on the bench beside her, lacing his fingers through hers and stretching his long legs out in front of him. "Let's give it a few minutes and see if the rain lets up."

For several minutes they sat in silence. She debated asking him if she was just another of Brett's burdens, but decided she didn't want to know the answer.

Sawyer lifted her hand onto his thigh. He traced a distracting pattern on the inside of her wrist with his thumb, drawing her out of her dark thoughts. She glanced at him, but his eyes were closed and his head rested against the back wall of the structure. He seemed unaware of the havoc his careless caress created inside her. And then his lids lifted, and she caught her breath at the smoldering desire in their depths. Maybe he wasn't as unaware as she'd thought.

"Ever made out in a dugout?"

The wicked twinkle in his eyes set off a chain of tiny explosions in her bloodstream. She sucked in a surprised breath, and her stomach muscles fluttered. Sawyer may not love her, but he wanted her, and she was greedy enough to soak up his attention while she could. "No."

One corner of his mouth tipped up. "Want to?"

She scanned what she could see of the now-deserted park, and a thrill raced over her skin. "We can't. It's a public place."

His brows waggled and his expression said, "So?"

Her heart was breaking and he made her laugh. "You make me feel like a naughty teenager."

"Is that a problem?" He slid closer and cupped her jaw.

"I don't know. I've never been one." Her words trailed off when his lips brushed hers.

His brows rose. "The captain of the baseball team never put his moves on you?"

"No. I wasn't very popular in high school," she admitted hesitantly. She didn't want to explain about the rumor that made her friends desert her in her junior year.

Disbelief filled his eyes and slowly turned to heat. He stroked the pulse at the base of her throat with his thumb, and then bent and sipped from her lips again. Drawing back a fraction of an inch, he met and held her gaze. "Let me show you how much fun we can have with our clothes on."

Her skin flushed and her body tingled. Fun? Sex had never been fun before. It had always been serious, intense and unsatisfactory business. Until Sawyer. She marveled at the way he could arouse her with nothing more than words. Why hadn't she experienced this before today? And would she ever again once this marriage ended? "Okay."

He kissed the corners of her mouth, her nose, her chin, making her desperate for his deep, drugging kisses. She chased his mouth with hers and finally caught his face in her hands and kissed him. She felt his smile against her lips, but he stubbornly waited until she licked the seam of his lips before opening his mouth over hers and letting her taste the slickness of his tongue. A duel ensued. Hot, long, wet kisses followed one after the other as she stockpiled memories.

Sawyer's fingertips skimmed her ankle, her calf, the sensitive seam behind her knee and then her thigh, sliding with agonizing slowness beneath the hem of her shorts. The tip of his finger eased beneath the elastic of her panties and her senses spun. She dug her nails into his back, wanting him to touch her, to recreate the magic he'd made this morning, but the fabric of her shorts impeded him. She'd never wanted to rip off her clothes before, but she did now and it surprised her.

His other hand skated over the slick fabric of her jersey, approaching her breast at a snail's pace. She fought impatience and dragged her nails up his back, urging him forward with a slight pressure. His wet shirt pressed against her chest and she gasped. "You're cold and soaked."

"And I'm going to get you hot and wet." He flashed a lethal grin and captured her breast in his hand, kneading her and plucking at her nipple.

Her breath hissed through her teeth as pleasure spiraled inside her. A shiver raced over her. Her breasts were overly sensitive from the attention they'd received that morning, but it was a good kind of tender. She pressed her hand over his, stilling him. He leaned back, his expression quizzical. "Tender."

He lowered his forehead to hers, pulled his fingers from beneath her shorts and captured her hands in his. "I'm a selfish SOB. I never considered that today might have been too much for you."

"No. I want you, Sawyer. I want this…" Her words dried up when she realized what she'd said. The words had come from her lips before. Brett insisted that she tell him she wanted him. But she hadn't meant it. Now she did. She wanted Sawyer, ached for him deep inside. She needed to feel the way only he could make her feel, and she wanted to look in his eyes, to watch him battle for the control and know that she had the power to push him over the edge.

She wanted to make love with him knowing she loved him.

"But?"

She'd never openly asked for what she wanted, she

realized, and that made her lack of physical pleasure before Sawyer at least partly her own fault. *Take control of your life. Take control of your passion.* "I want to touch your skin. I need to feel it pressed against mine."

She bit her lip at her boldness, but instead of offending him, passion flared in his eyes. His chest rose as he took a deep breath. "Let's go home before we get arrested for what I'm thinking."

He stood and pulled her to her feet. After covering the puppy's box with a towel, he put it in her hands and then slung the equipment bag over his shoulder and grabbed the cooler. His naughty wink sent her stomach plummeting. "Race you to the truck."

They were both drenched by the time they'd stowed their load and climbed into the front. Sawyer reached across the seat, snagged a hand behind her neck and kissed her until they were both panting. He cranked the engine and headed home. The sun, riding low on the western horizon, broke free from the clouds as they turned into the neighborhood. Sawyer pulled into the driveway, parked and silenced the engine.

Lynn's blood hummed in anticipation. She climbed from the vehicle before he could open her door, but he quickly caught up with her, took Trooper's box from her and set it on the patio table under the umbrella. He linked his fingers with hers and led her toward the pool.

She frowned. "Where are we going?"

"You wanted skin." His wet shirt clung to the muscular wall of his chest, revealing his beaded nipples. She didn't need to look down to know hers did the same. His white baseball pants were soaked and practically transparent. She could see that he wore nothing but his jock strap beneath.

"Yes, but…" Her words died when he pulled off his

shoes and dropped his keys inside of one. Her mouth dried when his shirt landed on top of them.

"Take off your shoes, Lynn." The husky rumble of his voice made her shiver.

Swallowing hard, she looked over her shoulders toward the neighboring house. "We're outside."

"Rick's not home and there's nothing but a hundred acres of woods on the other side of those magnolias. Nobody can see us." His baseball pants and socks landed on top of his discarded shirt.

The splendor of his naked, fully aroused body took her breath. Could she make this marriage work? Did she dare wish for more than the twelve months stipulated in their agreement? Hope flared inside her. She dug deep inside for the courage to do as he asked and toed off her shoes. He helped her peel the red jersey over her head, and then he outlined the lace edge of her bra. With a flick of his fingers the front clasp gave way. He dragged the straps over her shoulders, and her bra hit the ground. He unbuttoned her shorts and pushed those and her panties over her hips when she hesitated. She stepped free of the fabric and hugged herself.

In a swift move, Sawyer swept her into his arms and leaped into the pool with a whoop. The warm pool water, combined with the heat of Sawyer's skin, instantly banished the rain-damp chill. Her gasp of surprise turned into a sputter of laughter when she surfaced. The mischievous glint in his eyes made her smile. He wanted to play and so did she. With a swift kick, she ducked under the water and raced for the ladder at the end of the pool. He caught her three strokes later, encircling her ankle with his long fingers and tugging her back into his arms. She didn't fight hard.

Slick and wet, he slid against her. Their legs tangled.

Their bodies melded, hard chest to soft breast. His arousal prodded her belly and heated her blood. Knotting her fingers in his hair, she dunked him, twisted out of his arms and kicked free. He chased her toward the shallow end, but yanked her back into his arms before she could find her footing. Lynn's pulse accelerated, not out of fear or exertion but out of excitement.

Banding his arms around her waist, he backed her up against the cool wall of the pool. She couldn't touch the bottom, but he could. He stepped between her thighs. His thick, hard shaft pressed against her curls, and he flexed his hips. His hard shaft stroked her cleft and she gasped. Twining her arms around his neck, she depended solely on him to keep her afloat.

His hips pinned hers to the wall and his hands roamed freely, gently over her breasts, her buttocks, between her legs. Each hurried but tender touch expanded the need inside her. She mirrored him gesture for gesture. He stole a carnal kiss and caught her legs in his hands, winding them around his hips.

Surely he wouldn't be such a generous lover if he didn't feel something for her?

"Lynn." His voice sounded strained, like a man on the verge of losing control. For her. The knowledge glowed inside her. If she affected him half as strongly as he affected her, then maybe, maybe they had a future together.

She cradled his face in her hands. "Sawyer."

As if she'd whispered the magic word, he filled her with a slow, deep thrust. Her head tipped back against the smooth surround of the pool, and a moan escaped her lips. He devoured her neck, sucking hungrily as he withdrew and plunged again and again. With each thrust the pressure inside her intensified.

She caressed his slick skin, kneaded his taut muscles and his tiny beaded nipples. She fed off his ravenous mouth, and tension grew inside her. Hope grew. Love grew. She loved him. Loved him. Loved him. Waves of pleasure crashed over her, radiating out until even her toes tingled. And then Sawyer threw back his head, groaned and emptied himself deep inside her.

She feared this temporary marriage would lead to a permanent heartache.

Ten

The doorbell rang. Sawyer eased off the sofa, taking care not to wake Lynn from her Sunday-afternoon nap. He covered her with a knitted throw that she'd unearthed from her boxes.

She loved him. She hadn't said so yet, but surely love would explain the softness of her eyes and the tenderness in her touch. Of course, he hadn't confessed his love, either, but he would tonight over dinner.

He strode into the front hall and yanked open the door. Carter stood on the doorstep with a briefcase in his hand. The serious expression on his friend's face told Sawyer this wasn't a social call. Carter had found the thief. Adrenaline pumped through Sawyer's bloodstream. He motioned for Carter to come inside and then led the way to his study.

"Where's Lynn?" Carter asked.

"Taking a nap."

"Good." Carter closed the door, and the hair on the back of Sawyer's neck rose. He'd never known a more cool-headed person than Carter, but his friend was clearly nervous.

"Who?" The single word was all he could choke out through the tightness in his throat.

Carter faced him. "I triple-checked everything."

"And?" He moved behind his desk, grasping the edge and bracing himself.

"It's an inside job."

Sawyer swore. "Why would my staff want to steal from me? We have great morale and they're well paid. I know statistics support an inside job, but not by my team. We're like family. You must have made a mistake."

"I have the proof." Carter set his leather briefcase on the edge of the desk and flicked open the brass latches.

Pain over the betrayal filled Sawyer. Fast on its heels came rage. "I want the SOB's name. I want to know every time he accessed those files, every time he screwed me and with whom. I want to know who he sold the program to and how much they paid for it."

"It's all in my report." Carter hesitated until Sawyer wanted to shake the rest out of him. "Sawyer, I'm sorry. Brett was your mole."

Sawyer recoiled in shock. Denial screamed inside him. He went cold, but sweat popped out on his brow and upper lip. "You're wrong. Somebody laid a false trail and framed him."

"I found substantial deposits in his bank accounts coinciding with the dates you gave me—the most recent one and the one two years back."

He didn't want to know how Carter had gotten confidential bank information, but it didn't matter since *he was wrong.* "My brother would never steal from me."

Carter sighed. "You have to admit the competitive drive Brett had toward besting you with cars, homes, possessions, *Lynn,* could easily extend toward your business. He wanted what was yours."

"We had a healthy sibling rivalry. That's it." But what about the pocket knife, the ID bracelet and the rest of the jewelry? What about Lynn? He crossed his arms over his chest. "Why would Brett steal from the company that supported him?"

"Your brother owed money all over town. As far as I can tell, the bank had turned down his recent loan applications, and his credit cards were maxed out and past due. The only way he could get more money was to squeeze it out of you, but asking for it would have meant admitting he was in financial trouble, thereby losing his battle of one-upmanship."

The stack of bills he'd seen at Lynn's house substantiated Carter's statements, but he wouldn't believe Brett would betray him. "I know you didn't like Brett, but I never expected you would maliciously blacken his name."

Carter's face hardened. "Don't shoot the messenger, man. You've said yourself there's nothing I can't track. I wish I could pin this on somebody else. God knows I tried, but every lead circled back to Brett. As far as I can tell, he acted alone, selling trade secrets to one of your competitors."

Sawyer ground his teeth and turned his back on Carter. Why would Carter lie? But he *had* to be lying.

"Do you think it's easy for me to tell you this?"

He whirled around. "Then why did you if you're such a damned good friend?"

Carter exhaled heavily and held out his hands. "I almost didn't, but I didn't want you worrying about the security of your company. With Brett out of the picture you can go ahead and launch your other projects without fear that those will be pirated, too."

Sawyer shoved a hand through his hair. He'd done everything he could for Brett. He'd skimped and saved, budgeting to keep a roof over their heads and to put Brett through college. He'd given him a job and a share in his company. Brett would not betray him.

"Do you think Lynn knew what he was doing?" Carter asked.

Sawyer sucked in a sharp breath at the unexpected attack. Every muscle tensed. "No."

"I know you've always had a soft spot for her, but you've got to face facts. Lynn benefited from Brett's excessive spending, and she sure as hell married you before the dirt settled on his coffin."

"You're wrong." Anger tightened his chest. He fisted his hands and fought the urge to punch Carter's lights out. Why would his friend try to separate him from the two people he loved most? "I don't know why you're determined to pin this on Brett or to drag Lynn into it, but you've screwed up your perfect investigation record. I'll write you a check for your services, and then I want you to get the hell out of my house."

"You know I wouldn't lie to you about this." Carter withdrew a thick file from his briefcase and tossed it on the desk. "Here's my data. When you're ready to pull your head out of the sand, you can read the facts for yourself."

He wouldn't believe it. Couldn't believe it. "Get out."

A tense moment passed. "When you're ready to talk, you know where to find me."

"That won't happen."

Carter turned on his heel and stormed out of the house.

The slamming of the front door jerked Lynn out of her horrified stupor. The raised voices had woken her, but the words had chilled her to the bone. *Brett was the thief.* How could she not have known?

The illogical ramblings in Brett's journal suddenly made sense. For whatever reason he'd fabricated in his irrational mind, Brett had felt justified in taking away what Sawyer valued most. He'd wanted what was due him, he'd written. Brett wasn't like Sawyer. He never took the hard way when an easier one presented itself.

Lynn's breakfast raced for her throat. She slapped a hand over her mouth and raced upstairs to her bathroom where she emptied her stomach. When her nausea finally subsided, she rose, washed her face and brushed her teeth. Sagging against the bathroom counter, she hugged herself.

What was she going to do?

Would Sawyer's love for Brett turn into hate? Would that hatred extend to Brett's baby and her? Since Brett was adopted, there wouldn't be any blood tie between Sawyer and Brett's child. She laid a protective hand below her navel and prayed that she carried Sawyer's child—not only for her child's sake, but for Sawyer's sake. He valued family above everything, and he needed this child to be his. He needed a family to love. She'd fallen in love with him. She didn't want to leave, but he had every right to order her out just as he had Carter.

If he kicked her out what would she do? The money

she'd expected from selling her share of the company back to Sawyer wasn't rightfully hers. She couldn't take it if Brett had stolen from Sawyer. She wouldn't take anything more from him. She laid a hand over her breaking heart and blinked back tears.

"Are you all right?" Sawyer's voice startled her. She jerked around to find him standing in the bathroom doorway.

"Yes. Are you?" She knew exactly how it felt to have your precious memories poisoned. Her heart ached for him.

"You heard." His assessing gaze swept over her.

"It was hard to ignore the yelling."

"I'm fine." Just as he had after the funeral, he tried to hide his pain from her, but it was there in the shadows of his eyes, the furrow in his brow and the rigid set of his shoulders.

She'd wanted to protect him from Brett's dark side and she'd failed because she'd underestimated Brett's treachery. Covering the distance between them, she wound her arms around his waist and laid her cheek over his heart. His stiff spine slowly relaxed and his arms encircled her. "I'm sorry."

"Carter thinks Brett was the thief." The pain and disbelief in his voice made her eyes sting. "Why would my best friend lie about something like that?"

The crack in her heart widened. This morning she'd believed she and Sawyer had a chance to make this marriage work. She loved him. He liked and desired her. Now, building on that foundation looked like an impossible dream. But she couldn't let Brett continue to rob Sawyer by costing him his best friend.

The only way to stop the destruction of the friendship was to share the damning journal that described her faults in excruciating detail. Once Sawyer read what a failure she'd been as a wife and as a woman, he wouldn't want anything to do with her. But did she have a choice? Carter had been with him longer, whereas she was only an obligation he'd assumed, another of Brett's messes to clean up. As much as it hurt her to do so, she had to sacrifice her love for his bond with Carter.

"He isn't lying. Brett did steal from you."

Sawyer abruptly released her and stepped back. "What are you saying?"

Why did the possibility of losing Sawyer hurt ten times more than Brett's cheating? Had she ever really loved Brett or had she been in love with the idea of love, enthralled with the picture of home and family he'd painted, back when he'd swept her off her feet? There was no comparison between the superficial emotion she'd felt for Brett and the deep, soul-pervading love she felt for Sawyer.

Lynn reached under the mattress and pulled out the cursed journal. "I found this after Brett died. In it he writes about 'holding on to what Sawyer values most' and 'getting his due.' There are dates—probably the same dates you gave Carter—where Brett talks about his ship coming in."

When Sawyer wrapped his fingers around the journal's leather binding, Lynn silently said goodbye to her hopes and dreams for a happy marriage. "Brett has already taken enough from you, Sawyer. Don't let him drive a wedge between you and Carter."

His eyes turned hard. His lips thinned into a flat line. "You knew what he was doing and you covered for him."

Her blood ran cold. Suddenly dizzy, she staggered to

the door frame for support. She didn't know what to say. There were no magic words to change the past.

"You covered for him because you still love him," he accused.

No! But she couldn't tell him she didn't love Brett or that on that fatal night she'd almost hated his brother for what he'd done to her and hated herself for what she'd surrendered to her marriage. His disgust made her stomach threaten another revolt.

She swallowed her nausea. "I didn't tell you because I didn't want to ruin your memories of your brother. Brett's gone. His crimes ended with his death. Your company is secure."

He cursed, paced to the window and spun to face her. The agony in his eyes made her gasp. "You betrayed me. Just like my brother."

She pressed a hand to her chest. "Sawyer, I would never do anything to hurt you. I love you."

He recoiled as if she'd struck him. "Do you think I'll believe that now? You're trying to cover your ass. You love my brother enough to lie for him even after he's gone." He shoved a hand through his hair, and that curl that she loved fell onto his forehead. She yearned to pull him close and brush it back, but he wouldn't welcome her touch now.

"Did you have sex with me after the funeral to cover your bases? Maybe you hoped to trap me into protecting you. And, fool that I am, I sapped up the story that this might be my child."

The knife in her heart gouged deeper. "You know that's not how it happened, and it *might be* your baby."

"I don't know what to believe anymore. I thought I took advantage of you, but it looks like I had that backward."

"No, I—"

"The people I trusted most in the world have cheated and lied to me."

"I didn't know until—"

"You knew Brett was screwing me and you didn't tell me. That's all that matters." He turned his back on her. The tension in his shoulders revealed his battle for control. "I'm going to take Maggie for a walk."

"But—"

"I need to get out of here, to figure out where our marriage stands." He turned and headed out the door.

Tell him.

"Sawyer, wait." He didn't pause. His steps clattered down the stairs. He whistled for Maggie, and then the front door slammed on all her dreams.

Sinking onto the chaise, she didn't try to stop her tears. Should she stay and fight for her marriage or scurry to her aunt's in Florida like the timid little mouse she'd pretended to be for the past four years?

Get out of Sawyer's house and his life before he kicks you out, the coward in her urged, but the fighter in her reminded her that her daddy had always said nothing worth having comes easy. Fearing rejection, she'd let Brett run roughshod over her dreams, and she'd paid for her cowardice. She'd lost herself, her soul in her first marriage. If she loved Sawyer she had to tell him the truth—*the whole truth*—and risk rejection.

And then Trooper whimpered. Lynn dried her eyes and tended to the puppy, because no matter how bleak things looked, life went on. And she wasn't a quitter.

How in the hell had he been so blind?

Sawyer dropped Brett's journal onto his desk and buried his face in his hands. How could he not have seen the malice in his brother? He and Brett had always been competitive, but the actions Brett had boasted about in his journal—using many of the secret code words the two of them had developed as kids—went far beyond a healthy rivalry. His brother had been willing to lie, cheat and steal to best him, and it hadn't mattered who got hurt in the process.

Lynn. Sawyer clenched his teeth until his jaw ached. Brett hadn't loved Lynn or cherished her the way she deserved. He'd used her, possessed her, dressed her and flaunted her like a trophy. All those puzzling clues finally made sense. No, she didn't know how to receive pleasure. No, she'd not been given any praise. Yes, she'd been bracing herself for an attack. Had Brett limited himself to verbal abuse?

Nausea roiled in his stomach and anger fired his blood.

What in the hell had she endured as a pawn in Brett's game of tormenting Sawyer with what he couldn't have? And why hadn't she ever spoken of the misery she must have faced behind closed doors? Had she really fallen for his brother's sappy apologies? Brett bragged that she did, but Lynn was too smart for that.

How could she love such a monster? But she must love him or she wouldn't keep covering for him. Sawyer rubbed the ache in his chest. *She still loved his brother.*

Brett's derogatory comments sickened him. His brother didn't think Lynn was smart enough, sexy enough or pretty enough. Sawyer had never met a smarter, sexier woman, and Lynn was beautiful inside and out. God, he loved her laugh, her thirst for knowledge, the way she'd turned his house into a home in just a few short days.

Brett had called her frigid. Had his brother been crazy? Lynn was the most responsive lover Sawyer had ever had, but how could she melt all over him if she still loved Brett? His mind tumbled with the contradictions of what he'd once thought versus what he now knew. What was fact and what wasn't?

He blamed himself. He'd found Lynn first, and if he'd spoken directly to her before leaving town four and a half years ago instead of trusting Brett to deliver a letter—a letter he suspected Lynn never received— she wouldn't have suffered the indignity of having the man she loved tell her she wasn't woman enough for him without plastic surgery. He silently applauded Lynn's bravery in refusing to go under the knife, but what had her refusals cost her? The journal had revealed a vindictive side to his brother that he'd never seen.

Bile burned the back of his throat. He'd once threatened that if Brett ever hurt Lynn he'd make his brother pay. Brett had hurt her all right, over and over, and then he'd done whatever it took to hold on to what Sawyer valued most. *Lynn.*

He'd been too blind to see his brother's machinations.

Sawyer rose and stared out the window. He loved Lynn with all his heart, but he'd let her down. First by failing to protect her from Brett and then by forcing her into a marriage she didn't want when she still loved and grieved for Brett.

Though it hurt more than anything he'd ever faced before, he knew what he had to do. He had to set Lynn free.

He headed for the door on leaden legs and found her in the kitchen preparing dinner. Her eyes were puffy and rimmed with red. Her face looked drawn and her bottom lip swollen as if she'd been chewing on it. Her hands trembled as she set the dishes on the table. After one hit-and-run glance, she wouldn't look at him.

He shoved his fists in his pockets and fought the urge to hold her. "I'm sorry."

She stopped in her tracks and lifted her gaze to his, but she remained mute, clenching the back of a chair until her knuckles turned white.

"I'll see my attorney first thing in the morning to arrange for a divorce."

She inhaled sharply, paled and after a moment nodded. "I understand."

"I'll get a loan to buy your share of the company."

"I won't let you do that, Sawyer. Brett has already stolen from you. You shouldn't have to keep paying for his mistakes. I'll sign my share over to you."

He wouldn't let her do that, but he didn't want to argue now. "I'll pay you a monthly allowance, and I'll pay child support, but I'll relinquish my paternal rights."

He tried to ignore the tears pooling in Lynn's eyes and then streaking down her face, but each one burned him like acid. He cleared his throat, but the knot remained stubbornly in place. "I don't know where I went wrong with Brett or what I could have done to make him hate me. I don't understand what he thought he'd gain by destroying the company that paid his salary. Hell, another incident like this and Riggan CyberQuest would have folded. He would have been out of a job. Maybe that's what he wanted—to destroy my dream. I don't know where I went wrong," he repeated.

"You didn't," she whispered.

He snorted his disbelief. "If I messed Brett up this badly in only a decade imagine what I could do to your child in an entire lifetime. It scares the hell out of me."

"Sawyer, you can't blame yourself for Brett's greed."

"I won't inflict myself on you or the baby you're carrying."

She crossed the kitchen and laid a hand on his forearm. "I can understand why you'd shun Brett's child, but if this is your son or daughter, then he or she deserves the right to know you. Don't let Brett's actions make you believe you'd be anything but a wonderful father."

Stunned, he gaped at her. "You'd be willing to risk me turning your kid into a felon?"

"That wouldn't happen. Brett didn't hate you, Sawyer. He worshipped you, and he wanted to be just like you. Only, Brett was lazy. He wasn't willing to work for what he wanted. He took shortcuts. That's not your fault."

Even now she covered for Brett. Jealousy and pain threatened to choke him. He shook off her touch, because it only made him want to hold her more, and scrubbed a hand across his face. "He abused you verbally. Did he ever hit you?"

"No. Never. If he had I would have left."

"He treated you like crap, Lynn. Why cover for him?"

"Because family is the most important thing in the world, and I didn't want your memories of Brett to be tainted. When memories are all you have left, those memories should keep you warm at night instead of haunting your dreams." She paced to the back door, turned and faced him.

"You knew my father was a cop and that he was killed in the line of duty. What you probably didn't know was that the ensuing investigation turned up a suspicion that he'd been a dirty cop. He was never cleared but never found guilty, either. That didn't stop the papers from crucifying him or my aunt and me since he was already gone. All of my memories of my daddy have been poisoned. When I think of him now, instead of remembering a man who loved my mother so much that he almost died when she did, I remember those last days. The detectives took our house apart. They went through every closet, every drawer. *They went through our trash.*"

Tears rolled freely down her cheeks, and the knot in his throat thickened until he could barely breathe. "I remember being told the man I thought was a hero was really a crook who took advantage of the people who counted on him to take care of them. I didn't want you to suffer like I did."

She looked so shattered and vulnerable. He stopped fighting his need to hold her and pulled her into his arms. He kissed her hair and rubbed his cheek against the soft strands. Her honeysuckle scent filled his senses. "I'm sorry."

She shrugged and pulled free.

"How could you still love Brett after the way he treated you?"

She looked away and then her shoulders sagged. When she met his gaze again, his stomach clenched at the pain in her eyes. "I didn't."

"What?" He grabbed her shoulders. "Tell me the truth this time. All of it. Don't try to pretty it up to save my feelings."

She hesitated so long he thought she'd refuse. "Brett and I had been having trouble for a long time. I'd already talked to a lawyer about filing for a divorce, but Brett convinced me that his bad attitude was caused by job stress. He promised he'd get better, and he dangled the chance to start the family I'd always wanted in front of me. I wanted a baby so badly that I was stupid enough to give in.

"That night, after we made love I found out he'd been cheating on me *with Nina.*"

Sawyer swore. He should have suspected something when Brett hired an assistant whose bust measurement was higher than her IQ.

Lynn took a deep breath. "We had a huge fight. I lost my temper and screamed at him to get out of the house. I told him I would file the divorce papers the next day. An hour later he was dead. So while you're hating Brett, you might as well save a little of that hatred for me. If I hadn't lost my temper, he might still be alive."

"Lynn, he was driving ninety miles an hour in a thirty-five-mile-an-hour zone. You can't blame yourself for that. We're damned lucky he didn't take somebody out with him. And from the garbage he's written in his journal, I think you were entitled to lose your temper."

"You still blame yourself for the accident that claimed your parents."

"Yes."

"What's it going to take to get through to you? The other guy was *drunk.* It was dark. *He* ran the light, *he* didn't have on his headlights. You're not being logical."

Some of the weight lifted from his shoulders. "Yeah. I guess you're right."

Lynn headed for the stairs. She had to get out of here before she lost control. A sob burned deep in her chest, and in two more seconds she'd be bawling like a baby.

"Why do you care?" Sawyer's question halted her on the bottom step.

What did she have to lose? She'd already lost it all. Without turning she said, "Because I love you, and I believe you're the one who said, 'Love doesn't quit when the going gets tough.'"

Quick steps crossed the tile floor and then his hand trapped hers on the newel post before she could retreat to her room. "Dammit, Lynn, don't you dare tell me you love me and then walk out on me."

She stiffened her spine and bit down on her quivering bottom lip.

He stroked her spine and she shivered. "Look at me. Please."

Slowly she turned. Her position on the bottom stair put them at eye level. What she saw in his deep-blue eyes made her tremble.

"You read Brett's journal. You must know that I love you."

She couldn't breathe; her head spun. "There's nothing in that journal about love. It's filled with hate and what a horrible wife I was."

One corner of his mouth lifted in a sad smile. Tenderness softened his eyes. "You're a perfect wife. Fun and sexy and so damned hot in bed that you make me lose it like an adolescent every time."

A spark ignited in her womb and radiated outward. She tried to snuff it out, because hope brought disappointment.

Sawyer's fingers drew tiny circles on the back of her hand, and the fine hair on her body rose. "Brett wrote that as long as he held what I valued most he held the upper hand. What I valued most was *you*, Lynn."

Her knees buckled. Sawyer caught her in his arms

and carried her into the den. He sat down on the sofa with her in his lap and stroked a finger down her cheek. "When we met five years ago I knew you were special. What we had was amazing. But you were young, barely nineteen, and I had to spend so much time on the road trying to grow the business that I thought we should wait. When I was called out of town unexpectedly with an offer for a contract that could get the company off the ground and keep it running for years to come, I knew I finally had something to offer you, and I didn't want to wait any longer.

"We had a date that night, but I couldn't reach you to cancel it. I asked Brett to meet you, instead, to explain and to give you a letter that I'd written for you."

Lynn gulped air. She wanted to believe what he said so badly, but she was afraid to get her hopes up. "Brett didn't give me a letter."

"I suspected as much from what he wrote in his journal. He must have opened it and read it to know how I felt about you. In the letter I wrote that I loved you, and that I wanted to spend the rest of my life with you. I wanted to see you as soon as I returned home, but I knew I'd be gone for months. I asked you to wait for me."

A sob rose in her throat. Lynn slapped a hand over her mouth to contain it.

"And then I returned home to find you married to my brother." The honesty and pain in his eyes convinced her he told the truth.

She leaned her cheek against his and stroked his bristly jaw. "I thought you'd dumped me. Brett said... He said you told him it was fun while it lasted, but that it was time for a taste of California girls. I turned to him on the rebound. I let him charm me out of my heartache. I feel like such a fool.''

''We were both fooled.''

''I'm sorry.''

''Me, too. Now, would you tell me the truth about enrolling at the university?''

She sighed. ''Most people see education as a chance to spread their wings, to gain freedom. For me it became the opposite. When I quit my job, Brett made me account for every penny of his money I spent and for every second of my time outside of the house. He sabotaged my study time. My grades suffered. Eventually he made me doubt whether or not I was smart enough to be a student.''

Sawyer swore. ''And you quit.''

''Yes.''

He laced his fingers with hers and kissed her fingertips. ''Lynn, I railroaded you into this marriage. If you want out, if you want your freedom, I'll let you go, and I'll pay for your education.''

Her heart swelled. ''I don't want out. I want to stay with you and raise a family with you. But, Sawyer, you need to understand that I'll love this baby even if Brett is the father.''

He palmed her belly, and her blood pooled beneath his hand. ''I will, too, because it's a part of you. I love you, Lynn.''

''And I love you.''

Epilogue

Sawyer pushed open the front door. Trooper barked and danced around his feet. "Yeah, buddy, your momma's home and so is your new baby brother. Calm down. You're deafening me."

Behind him Lynn laughed. She did a lot of that these days, and it grabbed him every time. Grinning, he dropped the house keys back into his pocket. His breath caught and his heart swelled the way it did every time he looked at his wife and his son. *His* son. Lynn took a step forward, but he stopped her. "I didn't do this the first time I brought you home as my wife."

He swept her and her precious bundle into his arms. She squealed. "I'm too heavy."

"You're perfect." He carried her over the threshold and set her down in the front hall.

She gasped. "Oh, my gosh. What did you do? Buy

out the florist? There must be a hundred red roses in here.''

''Happy Valentine's Day. And there are six dozen roses—one dozen for each Valentine's Day we should have spent together.''

She smiled that tender, you-shouldn't-have smile that turned him to mush on a regular basis. ''You have to stop showering me with gifts. You don't owe me for the past.''

He bent and kissed her gently, tamping down the hunger that gnawed at him, and then brushed his lips over the pale-blue cap on JC's head. ''Spoiling you is my job.''

Gravel crunched as Carter's car pulled into the driveway. Trooper streaked outside to greet the newcomer and then barked even louder as Maggie and Rick strolled through the magnolias. Rick pitched a tennis ball, and both dogs streaked after it.

''So, did you make it through the delivery without hurling or passing out?'' Rick asked as he and Carter climbed the front steps. The dogs charged past them and settled on the rug in front of the blazing fireplace.

Sawyer grimaced. ''Near miss.''

Lynn's chuckle skipped down his spine like a caress. ''You did wonderfully once you settled down. It was the hour after my water broke that had me worried. Thanks for driving us to the hospital, Rick. Sawyer was a little nervous until we arrived and the doctors convinced him everything was proceeding as planned.''

Rick laughed. ''A little nervous? He was a basket-case.''

Carter stepped forward. ''So, let's see the little guy.''

Lynn angled the baby toward them, and Sawyer tugged the knitted cap from his son's head revealing a shock of black hair. A moment of stunned silence greeted them.

Carter frowned, looked at JC, at Sawyer and then back again. "He looks just like you."

Discovering that he was the baby's father had been a wonderful surprise. They'd never explained about their forbidden encounter in the foyer. Lynn had been afraid his friends would think less of her for sleeping with him on the day of Brett's funeral. And if that was the way she wanted it, then his lips were sealed, despite his desire to shout the news of his son's birth from the rooftop.

Her smile and the happiness in her eyes put a lump in Sawyer's throat. He couldn't speak.

"Yes, he does," Lynn said quietly. "He looks exactly like his daddy. He has those Riggan blue eyes and that straight little nose, and I'm guessing that's going to be the same stubborn chin. I have Sawyer to thank for helping me through a very difficult time and for giving me this very special gift."

Carter was the first to recover, but he didn't voice the questions in his eyes. "So what does JC stand for, anyway?"

Lynn laid his son in the bassinet beside the sofa and slowly unwound the extra blankets the cold weather required. "Joshua Carter. Joshua after my father and Carter after the man who agreed to be his godfather."

Carter swallowed hard and then turned his head. Sawyer saw him blink a few times before he faced them again. "So does this make me an honorary uncle?"

Sawyer clapped him on the shoulder. "You bet it does. Both you and Rick. Lynn and I figured we'll give you all the practice you need at baby-sitting and diaper changing so you'll know how to handle your own kids when the time comes."

Rick jumped back with an appalled expression on his face. "Whoa. Don't be shoving me down the aisle. I like being a bachelor."

Lynn just smiled. "You'll change your tune as soon as you get that promotion. Just wait and see. You'll want someone to share that big, rambling house of yours."

"I have Maggie, and the mutt is the only female I need living under my roof."

Sawyer pulled Lynn into his arms and looked deep into her eyes. He kissed her brow, her cheek and her nose. "Trust me, guys, once love grabs ahold of your heart, you'll change your tune. And you won't ever regret it."

Rick groaned. "Here they go again. Come on, Carter, let's see what we can rustle up for dinner. If I know Sawyer, he probably planned to serve the new mommy Frosted Flakes."

Carter and Rick headed for the kitchen.

Sawyer wasted no time in capturing Lynn's sweet lips. She kissed him back, and suddenly the six weeks until they could make love yawned like six years. He brushed a strand of golden hair from her cheek, eased her coat off her shoulders and tossed it over the back of the new rocking chair. "Thank you for being the best thing that ever happened to me."

She gave him a watery smile. "Thank you for showing me what love is all about."

"My pleasure." He reached into his pocket, withdrew his mother's silver-heart locket and then flicked it open to show her the pictures inside.

Her teary smile put a lump in his throat. "My two

men. You and JC. I love you, Sawyer, more than I ever thought possible.''

"And I love you.'' He looped the chain over her neck. "We'll have to keep trying for that daughter, but for now, why don't you hold on to this?''

"It's only fitting because you are in my heart.''

"And you, Lynn Riggan, are in mine.''

* * * * *

PERFECTLY SAUCY
BY
EMILY McKAY

For my wonderful family. For my father,
who taught me to do the right thing, my mother,
who taught me how to have fun, and my sister,
who is always there for me.

Prologue

10 Things Every Woman Should Do
—Excerpted from *Saucy* magazine

1. Find Your Fling— After all, when was the last time you had an affair to remember?
2. Don't Be a Homebody— Fly away from your nest to live abroad.
3. Go Tribal— Get a tattoo or piercing to channel the wild thing inside.
4. Release Your Inner Dominatrix— Buy a leather skirt and wear it proudly. Whip, optional.
5. Be a Diva in Bed— Don't just ask for what you want, demand it.
6. Drop the Drawers— He'll go crazy when he finds out you're going commando.
7. Live in the Fast Lane— Relive the thrill of the forbidden by having sex in the back seat of the car.
8. Just Admit It— Own up to a big mistake. After all, confession is good for your soul and guilt is bad for your skin.
9. Shake Up Your Space— Because life should be shaken, not stirred.
10. Conquer It— Overcome your greatest fear and you'll know you can do anything.

1

Alex Moreno was the first person Jessica Summers had ever heard say the F-word out loud. By the time she'd heard him say it in the eighth grade, she was fairly certain he'd already done…it several times.

Even at fourteen he'd had his pick of girls and the girls he'd picked were almost always older, more experienced and willing to do all the things Jessica only whispered about at sleep-overs. In high school he'd been the kind of boy girls fawned over, boys picked fights with and teachers disciplined just to prove they were in control.

Apparently things hadn't changed much. Two weeks ago Jessica had seen him for the first time in more than ten years. He'd been walking down the street with a kind of lazy confidence that declared he was back in Palo Verde to stay and there was nothing anyone could do about it, short of arresting him and physically hauling his ass out of town. Again.

Even after all this time, they were still polar opposites. He was the son of migrant farm workers. She was the daughter of the town's most prominent family. He was wild, reckless and brash. The ultimate bad boy.

She, on the other hand, seemed doomed to a tragically boring, spinsterlike existence. Unless she did something drastic.

Jessica glanced down at the delicate silver watch on her wrist. Four forty-five. Alex would be here soon and the next hour was going to go either very well or very badly.

Turning, she paced the length of her kitchen, the three-inch heels of her shoes *rat-tat*ing across the tile floor, echoing the pounding of her heart. She reached the arched doorway to her living room and kept going, the plush cream carpet muffling the clatter of her heels as she strode toward the sliding-glass door that looked out onto her back patio and pool. She stood for a moment, watching the surface of the water ripple in a breeze and wishing she wasn't perpetually early. Today, fifteen minutes seemed like an eternity.

Her telephone rang, its shrill clatter piercing the silence. She spun around, lunging for the cordless phone she kept on the coffee table, sure it was Alex calling to cancel their appointment.

Her heel caught on the carpet and she kicked off her shoes, nudging them under the table as she grabbed the handset. For a second she clutched the phone, exhaling sharply so she wouldn't sound like such a nervous wreck. Would she be disappointed or relieved if he couldn't make it?

Mustering her courage, she punched the talk button and tried to sound casual. "Hello? Sumners residence."

God, why did she always sound as though she was answering her parents' phone?

"What are you wearing?" demanded a feminine voice.

"Patricia?"

"No, it's your great-uncle Vernon. Of course it's Patricia." Her voice practically rang with exasperation. "He's going to be there soon, right?"

"Maybe ten, fifteen minutes."

"So don't waste my time with pleasantries. If you'd re-sponded to my e-mails at work today, we wouldn't have to do this at the last minute. Now, what are you wearing?"

Jessica had made the mistake of telling Patricia over lunch about her plan to meet Alex this evening. The other woman had ignored work all afternoon, peppering Jessica with frantic e-mail questions. Most of which Jessica had ignored. "Why does it matter what I'm wearing?"

"You're going to see Alex for the first time in how many years?"

"Ten."

"And you don't think it matters what you're wearing?" She didn't give Jessica a chance to answer but plowed right ahead with the conversation. "Just tell me it's not one of your god-awful, prissy little sweater sets."

"No," she said through gritted teeth as she made her way to the entry hall. "It's not one of my practical and com-fortable sweater sets. I'm wearing a simple black silk sheath dress."

"Is it tight?"

Jessica paused in front of the hall mirror just long enough to shoot herself a piercing look. "No."

"Is it low-cut?"

"No." She felt a sinking sensation deep in her belly. Had she worn the completely wrong thing?

"It's at least short?"

Jessica extended her leg to get a better look at the length. "Four, maybe five inches above the knee."

"Good. That's good. Your legs are your best feature."
Please, Dear God, let Alex be a leg man.

"Okay," Patricia barked, clearly moving beyond the clothing issue. "So what's your game plan?"

"Game plan?"

"What're you going to do? Just invite him in and proposition him?"

"No, of course not!" When she'd spoken to Alex on the phone earlier this afternoon she'd said something inane about wanting to hire his construction company to do work on her house. But she'd had no idea how she would segue from "Want to remodel my kitchen" to "Want to go out sometime?" Or, after a date or two, to transition to "Want to tear off each other's clothes and have mad, passionate sex? Often?"

To Patricia she said, "I just…"

"Just what?"

"I don't know." She spun on her heel and stomped back to the kitchen, suddenly irritated with herself. "I don't really have a plan."

"Exactly. *You* don't have a plan. That's what worries me. You *always* have a plan."

"That's not—"

"Did you or did you not just send everyone in our team a detailed plan of what to do in case of a tornado?"

"I'm the floor safety manager now. It's my job to—"

"We live in California. There are no tornadoes in California."

"But—"

"Ever."

She started to explain that she was just trying to do her job well. That she took her new responsibilities at work seriously. But wasn't that the problem? She always took everything so dang seriously.

Before she could put any of that into words, Patricia babbled on. "So, yes, it scares me that you have no plan. This is just so unlike you. Inviting Alex Moreno over so you can seduce him or whatever is just so…so…"

"Like something you would do?"

"Exactly. This is what concerns me. You are acting like me."

"Well, you can stop worrying. I'm not going to seduce or proposition him. I promise. I just want to see him again."

To see if any spark of attraction still lingered between them.

And if it did?

Well, she'd worry about that when the time came.

"See him *again?*" Patricia asked shrewdly. "There wasn't something going on between you two back in school, was there?"

"No," she said dismissively. And it wasn't entirely a lie.

"I didn't think so. I mean, I'd heard the rumors, but I never thought they were true."

"Rumors?" She'd certainly never heard any rumors connecting the two of them.

"That you were secretly in love. That you were going to run away together. I figured it was nonsense. I mean, you and Alex Moreno? It was more absurd than that rumor about the giant snake living in the second-floor bathroom."

"What's that supposed to mean?" she asked, more than a little offended about the snake comparison.

"Just that you weren't each other's type. You were such a Goody Two-shoes in high school. And he was always in and out of trouble. And on top of all that, your father was the judge. How ironic would that have been? The daughter of a judge dating a guy who'd been arrested at least a dozen times."

"Hmm. Very," Jessica said noncommittally. Of course, the real irony was that, although the rumors had been false, at the time, she would have given anything for them to be true.

"But I guess you must have had a crush on him then," Patricia continued blithely. "Or else you wouldn't be thinking of having your passionate fling with him now. Not that I blame you. He was scrumptious even at eighteen. And just so bad."

Patricia's inflection on the word "bad" made it clear she thought "bad" was a very good thing.

And Jessica supposed she knew what Patricia meant. Even a Goody Two-shoes like her could appreciate the thrilling appeal of being naughty. But that was never what had drawn her to Alex.

It wasn't his bad-boy charm, his many arrests or the titillation of shocking her parents and her peers. No, what appealed to her most about Alex Moreno—even now—was all the things about him no one else saw. His strength. His kindness. His integrity.

Well, all that and his sizzling raw sex appeal.

For now she needed to get Patricia off the phone before her friend's circuitous logic drove her absolutely batty.

But before she hung up, she couldn't help but ask, "What I don't get is this. If you're so worried about what I'm doing, why did you want to make sure my clothes met with your approval?"

"Well, sure, I'm worried. That's all the more reason for you to look drool-worthy. If you're going to make a fool out of yourself, I at least want you to look good while you do it."

Buoyed by Patricia's "encouragement," Jessica poured herself a splash of wine and gulped it down. "Thanks, that's very helpful."

"I'm sorry I'm not more optimistic." But Patricia didn't

sound the least bit contrite. "Look, I can understand you wanting to get some—I mean, lately you've been living like a nun—but, come on, Alex Moreno? Going from celibacy straight to him is like deciding you need to work out more often and starting by climbing Mount Everest."

"Pffft," Jessica muttered dismissively. But was Patricia right? Was Alex the Mount Everest of men? Was she insane for thinking he might be interested in her? Was she crazy for thinking he'd even remember her?

"Jess, you can 'pffft' all you want, but he's the baddest bad boy this town has ever known. You could get into serious trouble with a guy like him. And if you're doing this just because of that silly list…"

On her way back from a nine-week-long business trip to Sweden—a trip during which she'd worked her butt off and still hadn't gotten the promotion she'd been promised—she'd picked up a copy of *Saucy* magazine in Gatwick Airport. The cover article was "10 Things Every Woman Should Do." Have an Affair to Remember was at the top of that list. And Alex Moreno was at the top of her list of men she'd want to have a passionate affair with.

"Patricia, you only think The List is silly because you've done all of the things on The List."

"Well—" She chuckled, sounding just a tad smug. "I guess I have."

"Exactly," Jessica growled.

"Hey." Patricia sounded falsely cheerful. "It's not like you haven't done *any* of the things on the list."

"One. I've done one. Live Abroad. That's the one and only thing on The List that I've done. And that hardly counts since I did that for work."

"All I'm saying is," Patricia countered, "you want to do some of the things on The List? Fine. But start with something smaller. Something a little less traumatic. Less likely to come back and bite you on the ass. Why not buy a leather miniskirt? That was on the list, too, right? Or get a tattoo."

"Get a tattoo? You think permanently scarring my body would be less traumatic than sleeping with Alex?"

"Okay, traumatic maybe wasn't the best word. Drastic is more what I meant. I just don't think you need to do anything quite so drastic."

And that was exactly what Patricia—who'd done all the things on the list numerous times—didn't get. Drastic was just what Jessica needed.

"I've worked for Handheld Technologies for six years now," she pointed out. "For the past two years, I've been working my butt off for a promotion to team leader. Instead of promoting me, they made me floor safety manager—the schmuck in charge of keeping the first-aid kit stocked and evacuating the floor in case of a natural disaster."

"It's almost like a promotion," Patricia murmured in placating tones. "It's a sign they trust you."

"No, it's a sign they think I'll look okay in a bright orange vest. I'm tired of settling for floor safety manager. I'm tired of settling, period. I'm ready to start living my life."

And—silly or not—she'd begin with that list of ten things every woman should do. As soon as she'd seen it, she'd pulled out her Day-Timer and copied each item onto her Priority Action sheet. She'd start at the top and work her way down. And at the top of her list was Alex Moreno.

"Look, I've got to go," Jessica said.

"Just remember to sway your hips when you walk. And lick your lips a lot. And—"

"Patricia—"

"And...and, good luck!"

Jessica punched the off button and returned the phone to its cradle. Luck? She didn't need luck. She was a *Saucy* woman now. Or she would be soon. Once she checked all the items off The List.

STANDING ON THE doorstep of Jessica Sumners's quaint, ranch-style house, Alex Moreno felt as nervous as he had standing in her father's courtroom a decade ago.

Not for the first time since he'd moved back to Palo Verde, did he doubt his sanity. He'd moved home to prove to this town that he'd changed. That he wasn't the wild, reckless kid he'd been back in high school. He was now a successful businessman and upstanding member of the community. A damn paragon of responsibility.

All of which would have been a hell of a lot easier to prove if someone would actually hire him. He needed this job.

Despite that, he hated that his first job would be from her.

In the past decade he'd imagined seeing her again more often than he cared to admit. He'd pictured them meeting as equals, he casually mentioning the jobs he'd worked on in L.A. and the Bay Area, her suitably impressed by his success. Never once had he pictured standing on her doorstep, praying she'd hire him and thus resuscitate his dwindling bank balance.

As he rang the doorbell he caught a flash of movement through the leaded glass of her front door. His stomach turned over in anticipation.

Through the window, he saw her walk toward the door and swing it open. Her eyes flicked up the length of his body then came to rest on his face. Her smile faltered and he watched her struggle to keep it in place.

She looked nervous, but even nervous, she still took his

breath away. She wore a simple black dress, with her hair pulled back. A pearl hung from a silver chain around her neck. Her strained expression undermined the elegance of her appearance. Maybe she was dressed for a funeral. Either way, he saw a flicker of anxiety in her eyes. As if he was the cause of her heightened emotions.

"Alex." She murmured his name, almost caressing it with her mouth.

The sound of his name on her lips sent a wholly inappropriate shiver of pure lust through his gut.

Then she cleared her throat, swung the door open wide enough to let him in and held out her hand for his. "Thank you for coming on such short notice."

"No problem." Her hand felt small and warm, her handshake surprisingly firm. He pulled his hand from hers then held out the portfolio describing his experience and listing his references.

Jessica blinked in surprise at the folder, then finally took it. She barely glanced at it before laying it on the marble-topped table beside the door. Her gaze traveled down his length to settle somewhere near his feet.

"You wanted me to look at your kitchen," he reminded her. He'd come straight from work. His shoes, his clothes—hell, everything about him—carried the dust of a hundred construction sites. He worked for a living—hard, manual labor. That never bothered him...until this instant, standing on Jessica's doorstep.

"Oh, yes." She blushed, stepping aside so he could enter. "It's this way."

She gestured for him to follow her, then turned and walked through the wide doorway to the living room. Her hips swayed gently as she moved. The movement dragged his gaze down the long length of her legs to her bare feet.

Her little black dress did nothing for him...but, man, oh man, the sight of her bare feet twisted him into a few knots.

Her feet were narrow and delicate, but not tiny. The feet of a tall woman, with long, graceful toes and high arches. Pale...and perfect. Perfectly manicured. Perfectly buffed. The pampered feet of a rich woman.

He glanced down at his own dirt-crusted work boots.

She swiveled back toward him, one foot planted firmly on the ground, the other leg bent slightly at the knee, exposing the arch of her foot and accentuating the curve of her calf.

Between them stretched a good ten feet of pristine cream carpet. Carpet he would track dirt all over the second he crossed her threshold.

"It's through here." She pointed through the living room toward the west end of her house.

"Right." He wiped his feet on her doormat, but it didn't do much good. Giving up, he stepped through her doorway, excruciatingly aware of the dried mud that flaked off his boots onto her floor. Yep, some things never changed.

He'd aged ten years since he'd last seen Jessica Sumners. He'd traveled halfway across the country and back. He'd opened and run his own business. Built houses for people who could buy and sell the Sumners. But the second he'd stepped foot back in this town, he'd felt like a dirty *moja-dito*. Completely unworthy to even stand on her doorstep, let alone do or say any of the things he yearned to.

Jessica Sumners was the closest thing their little California town had to royalty. She came from a world of wealth and privilege, he, from one of dirt and sweat.

Not that Jess had ever treated him like a wetback. No, she'd treated him with the same cool but equable friendliness she'd treated everyone at their high school.

Except for a few short weeks in his senior year when their relationship had evolved into something more. Something he still couldn't define or explain. Something that still sometimes kept him up at night.

But based on her cool reception, he wasn't even sure she remembered those weeks. Either way, he'd be damned if he tracked dirt across the floor of the one person in this town who'd never treated him like filth. He reached down and tugged loose his laces, then toed off his boots. Grime ringed his white socks where his boots met his ankles, but there was nothing he could do about that.

He followed her into the kitchen, trying not to notice the seductive rhythm of her hips as she moved. Her long legs accentuated the length of her stride. No pretension or seduction there. Which made the pull even stronger.

"Well, this is it." She gestured broadly to the kitchen like a game-show hostess revealing the prize behind door number two.

Taking in the room, he frowned. White-painted cabinets, white appliances and dark green laminate countertops in a simple galley-style kitchen. Dated, but functional.

Scratching his chin, he asked, "What exactly were you looking to have done?"

She crept closer. Standing almost shoulder-to-shoulder, she studied the kitchen, head tilted slightly toward him. "I don't know." She shifted, her bare shoulder brushing his sleeve as she faced him. "I was hoping you'd have some ideas."

"On the phone you said you wanted to meet as soon as possible. You implied it was an emergency."

Her gaze shifted nervously away from his. She appraised the kitchen, her forehead furrowing in a frown, before saying, "Haven't you ever made a decision and wanted to act on it as soon as possible? Just wanted to get it over with?"

Those words, coming from any other rich white woman, would have irritated him. But somehow, coming from her, they didn't sound selfish or childish, but...frustrated. And very human.

They hinted at the girl he'd known all those years ago. Was the sensitive and kind girl still buried inside this gorgeous creature? The way his hope leaped at the idea made him chuckle.

Dang, but he was susceptible to her.

Her gaze snapped back to his. "You think that's funny?"

"No, I just..." His hasty reassurance caught in his throat. Her eyes—startlingly blue at this close range—were wide and vulnerable. "It was just unexpected."

She frowned. "In what way?"

"I don't know," he admitted. "Back in school you were always the perfect rich girl. The perfect student. I guess I never pictured you as the impatient type."

A hint of a smile tugged at her lips. "I'm surprised you bothered to picture me at all."

Oh, man, she had no idea. If she knew how many times and how many ways he'd pictured her back then, she wouldn't want him putting his hands anywhere near her kitchen. He could guaran-damn-tee it.

Keeping his mouth firmly shut on the subject, he said, "I'll tell you what—" He pulled his tape measure off his belt and his notepad out his back pocket. "I'll take some measurements, make some notes. We'll see what we can come up with."

Just holding the tape measure made him feel more at ease. Jessica may have money, but he had skills. He'd come a long way from the boy he'd been back in high school.

Moving from one end of the kitchen to the next, he measured the length and width, noting the depth and locations of each of the cabinets. He put his pad down on the countertop and began making a quick sketch of the kitchen as it was. She stood beside him, closer than was necessary, throwing off his concentration. And damn, she smelled so good he could barely think.

He shifted away from her, propping his hip against the countertop. "Are you willing to give up storage space? Maybe a wall?"

"What do you think?"

What did he think? He thought she was standing awfully close for someone who just wanted her kitchen remodeled.

Think about the money, he ordered himself. If she wanted to drop forty or fifty grand on a whim, he'd be happy to help her do it.

Think about *that*. Not about how she smells—fresh and clean, yet spicy. Like Ivory soap mixed with something decadent.

He cleared his throat. "If you're going to do it, do it right."

"So you think I should…"

"Knock out that wall." He pointed to the wall separating the kitchen from the living room. "You open up this space, the kitchen and the living room will feel bigger."

"Really? You can do that?"

"Sure." He crossed to the wall and rapped on the drywall beneath the upper cabinet. "We tear out this wall, put in a structural beam to support the ceiling and you've got a whole new kitchen. What'd you say?"

Come on, baby, take a bite. Just a little nibble.

She glanced at him, then back at the wall. Her eyes glazed over, just a little, as if she were trying to imagine what the room would look like. "It'd look great. I—"

She seemed to catch herself just short of saying yes. Shaking her head as if to clear it, she smiled shyly. "I should probably think about it first."

He'd almost had her. Then, bam, she was gone. Just like that.

Just his luck.

And if his luck didn't turn soon, he'd be flipping burgers down at the Dairy Barn. Work was scarce in Palo Verde. Scarce, if your name was Alex Moreno.

When he'd moved back here, he hadn't anticipated the animosity people in this town still harbored against him. But he was determined to prove he wasn't still the pain-in-the-ass kid he'd been back then. He'd do just about anything to prove it. He'd damn near beg if he had to.

"I'll tell you what… While you're thinking about it, I'll work up a few drawings. Give you an idea of what I'm picturing."

She looked unconvinced. And again it struck him as odd that she seemed so interested in him, yet so uninterested in her kitchen, when she'd been so insistent on the phone. If she'd been any other woman—anyone other than perfect Jessica Sumners—he'd have assumed she was hitting on him.

The Jessica he knew from high school was smart and fair and always treated people with dignity. And she absolutely did not invite guys she barely knew over to her house for a quick tussle in the sack.

She stepped even closer and placed her hand on his arm. She moistened her lips in a movement that somehow looked both outrageously sensuous and slightly embarrassed all at the same time. "Or maybe we could talk about it more over a drink." Her voice trembled and her hand felt surprisingly warm against his bare skin.

His gut clenched at her touch. He sucked in a deep breath and the air around him seemed laden with her scent.

Then her words hit him. A drink? She wanted to go out for a drink? Damn, she *was* hitting on him.

He jerked his arm away from her touch. "By 'go out for a drink,' do you mean, go out on a date?"

She shrugged, her shoulders shifting in a movement of graceful self-doubt. "I just thought…well, yes. I'd love to catch up with you. If you're interested."

He shook his head, laughing bitterly. Did he want to go out on a date with Jessica Sumners? Hell, yes.

But there was a gleam in her eyes that told him this wasn't just for old times' sake. How in God's name had he been so wrong about her?

One by one, the implications hit him square in the chest. She'd asked him here to hit on him. Which meant she wasn't interested in hiring him. Which meant he wasn't going to get the job he desperately needed. Finally—and strangely, this was the blow that hurt the worst—she wasn't the sweet, open girl he remembered. She was, however, the kind of woman who liked to order in a little blue-collar fun for the afternoon.

The pisser was…he was tempted.

Staring down into her eyes, breathing in her scent, *and* the heat of her touch still burning his arm… Yeah, he was tempted. Jessica—rich, beautiful and damn near saintly in the eyes of this town—was hitting on him. If the look on her face was any indication, she wanted more from him than just a drink.

The temptation to give it to her, to toss his dignity out

the window, to pull her into his arms and explore that luscious mouth of hers almost overwhelmed him. Not just because she was beautiful, but also because kissing Jessica…hell, pulling off her expensive dress and nailing her right here in her kitchen…would be the ultimate teenage fantasy brought to life. Making it with the most beautiful, well-respected girl in town. The girl he'd wanted so bad it had made his teeth ache.

The temptation was too strong. Finally giving in to what he'd wanted ever since walking through that front door— hell, to what he'd wanted all his life—he reached out and ran his fingertips down her cheek to her jawline and nudged her chin up. His thumb brushed against her moist lower lip, tugging it open.

"Is this what you want?" he asked. He inched closer to her, a little surprised when she actually swayed toward him, instead of shying away.

"Yes."

Her bare knee brushed against his jeans, her foot nudged his. He glanced down. The simple intimacy of the touch, her bare foot against his sock, struck him. Her perfect, pampered foot nuzzled up against his dirty work sock.

He dropped his hand from her face and stepped back, angry with himself for wanting what he couldn't have. And with her for making him want it.

"That's why you called me, isn't it? That's why you needed me to come over right away?"

She blinked, her eyes wide with surprise, and maybe confusion. "No." Her no wasn't forceful enough to convince even herself. "Maybe."

"You don't really want to have your kitchen remodeled, do you?"

Her gaze shifted nervously from his. "No. I just…" She

took in a noticeably shaky breath and pressed her palm to the countertop as if she needed something to hold her up. "I just thought…"

"What? That it would be fun to jump in the sack with the manual laborer?"

"No!" Her spine stiffened.

"Then what?"

"It's complicated," she insisted, her voice now firm. "This was obviously a mistake."

"Right. Obviously." He ripped the top page out of his notepad and crumpled it into a ball. "Did it ever occur to you that this is my job? This is how I make my living?"

She arched one perfect eyebrow. "Did it ever occur to you that I might honestly have wanted just a date? That not every woman wants to jump in the sack with you?"

If he hadn't been so angry, he might have laughed at her bravado. From the way her voice stumbled, he'd be willing to bet good money she'd never used the phrase "jump in the sack" before in her life.

"Not interested, huh?" Before she could protest, he wrapped his hands around her arms, pulled her to him and kissed her.

He told himself he was doing it to prove a point.

But the second he felt her body against his, he knew he'd lied. The only point he wanted to prove was that she was as kissable as she looked. Man, was she ever.

Her lips were warm and smooth beneath his. She tasted like red wine, which surprised him, because he would have sworn she was the kind of woman who drank white wine.

When her tongue darted out to brush against his lips, surprise was the least of his reactions. Hot, aching desire hit him hard in the gut.

Abruptly he pushed her away. She looked as shell-shocked as he felt. She pressed her fingertips to her mouth, glaring at him.

"That was rude," she finally said.

He laughed out loud, gathering up his notepad and measuring tape before heading for the door. "It's rude to kiss someone who's clearly asking for it, but not rude to interrupt the middle of someone's workday and waste their time?"

She trotted after him. "I didn't think you would mind. I—"

He spun back around to face her. "Well, I do. Apparently you have nothing better to do on a Friday afternoon but jerk people around. But I've got work to do." She flinched as if stung by his criticism, but he didn't stop. As he shoved first one foot and then the other into his boots and tugged them on, he continued. "Real work, princess. Not imaginary work that bored debutantes make up because they want a playmate. Work I'll get paid for."

"You don't think *I* work?"

Shaking his head at her indignation—*her* indignation!—he snapped, "I don't care whether or not you work. I don't care if you're bored or lonely or horny or whatever it is that made you decide you wanted someone to come over and play. I care that you're wasting my time. Goodbye, princess."

AND WITH THAT, he was gone. The door slammed behind him hard enough to actually rattle the windows.

For a second she stood there, fuming at the closed door and shooting angry glares around the empty foyer. Then she propped her hands on her hips and said—to no one in particular, "You are the last man I'd invite to come over and play, even if I was bored or lonely or—" she sputtered, then forced herself to say the word "—horny. Which I am not."

Except she was.

It was as if her body had come alive again at Alex's touch. And as if it had gone through electric shock treatments at his kiss.

She felt hot and tingly. Exposed.

She spun on her heel and stomped to the kitchen where she poured herself another glass of wine. She sipped it slowly, making sure she was perfectly calm before taking the last sip. Then she carefully poured herself some more, even though what she really wanted to do was to throw the goblet to the floor.

Halfway through the glass, she set the crystal aside, propped her elbows on the countertop and buried her head in her hands.

How in the world had that gone so wrong?

How had she so drastically underestimated how she'd respond to him? She'd just wanted to see him again. To size up his potential as a "Passionate Fling-ee." Instead he'd made her all googly-eyed and she'd practically attacked him. No wonder he'd gotten the wrong impression.

He was a different person than he'd been in high school. Taller, for one thing. And he'd lost some of his wiry thinness. Now, he was lean, but muscular. Powerful. And so handsome, it made her ache.

One thing was sure. Seeing him answered the question of whether or not he still got to her. From the moment she'd opened the door, she'd felt his pull deep in her gut.

When he'd asked her what she'd wanted, her mind had just gone blank. She'd wanted him. Some part of her had always wanted him.

And now he'd probably never talk to her again, which was going to make apologizing very difficult.

She straightened and turned around. Propping her back against the counter, she reached for her glass of wine. From the corner of her eye, she saw the crumpled ball of paper Alex had tossed aside.

She picked it up then flattened it with her hand to work out the wrinkles. There was a black-ink sketch of her kitchen, surprisingly accurate, with measurements written on the side in Alex's masculine handwriting.

The seriousness with which he'd approached the project only humiliated her. Shaking her head at her own stupidity, she carefully folded the note in quarters.

Yep, she owed Alex an apology. And if she knew him half as well as she thought she did—

No, scratch that. She clearly didn't know him at all. But she suspected he wasn't going to make it easy on her.

She crossed to where her Day-Timer sat propped in one of the kitchen chairs and opened it to her Priority Action sheet. There was The List.

1. Find Your Fling.
2. Don't Be a Homebody.
3. Go Tribal.
4. Release Your Inner Dominatrix.
5. Be a Diva in Bed.
6. Drop the Drawers.
7. Live in the Fast Lane.
8. Just Admit It.
9. Shake Up Your Space.
10. Conquer It.

Number one—Find Your Fling—taunted her. How could she have a passionate fling without Alex, when he was the one man she felt passionately about?

Then she scanned down to number eight: Just Admit It. "Own up to a big mistake."

Well, it looked as though she'd soon be able to cross one of the items off The List after all.

2

THE THOUGHT OF SEEING Alex again made Jessica's stomach twist into nervous knots.

At least, that's what she told herself. Those knots in her stomach were knots of dread, not excitement. And the jittery feeling she got at the thought of seeing him again had nothing to do with the way he'd kissed her. The way his roughened palms had made the bare skin of her arms tingle. The way he'd smelled unlike any other man she'd ever known—an appealing mix of sunshine, dust and sweat.

She blew out a long, slow breath.

Yep. Just nerves. That was it.

She'd armed herself with his business card and an outfit less likely to attract snide "princess" comments—black capri pants and a black, boat-necked T-shirt. It was as good an outfit as any to grovel in.

According to the card she'd salvaged from the portfolio he'd given her, Moreno Construction operated out of his home, which turned out to be a small bungalow-style house on the outskirts of town. Finding the house was not nearly as difficult as finding the courage to walk up the overgrown path to the door. But, she conceded, owning up to mistakes was not supposed to be easy.

She rang the doorbell, waited a full minute then rang it

again. The front door was open, and through the screen door, she caught glimpses of the darkened interior. But no sign of Alex himself.

Then from deep within, she heard a male voice shout, "Come in."

She opened the screen door, stepped over the threshold and closed the door behind her. The entry opened straight into the living room, which ran the width of the house. A collection of standard-issue bachelor furniture sat clumped in the center of the room. Moving boxes flanked the walls in stacks three or four high. From where she stood, she caught a clear view of the dining room and the kitchen beyond. More bland furniture, more boxes. Only the kitchen looked lived in, with a couple of cereal bowls on the counter and a pizza box wedged into a trash can.

From somewhere at the back of the house, a power tool roared to life, so she followed the sound down the hall to a back bedroom.

And sure enough, there was Alex. He stood on an A-frame ladder, straddling the peak. The stance accentuated the muscles of his long legs. With one hand, he held up a sheet of drywall, with the other, he used a cordless drill to drive screws into the sheet.

With the exception of the spot where Alex worked, the walls had been stripped down to the studs. Chalky dust from the drywall hung in the air, making her cough.

He turned at the sound and stared at her for a second. Disbelief and then suspicion registered in his eyes before he turned back to the drywall and drove in three more screws.

Watching him move, Jessica found herself fascinated by the way his broad shoulders shifted under the threadbare cotton of his white T-shirt. By the hole in his jeans that bared his knee and the worn patches of denim along the length of his thighs and down his zipper.

She was used to seeing men dressed in Dockers and button-down Oxford shirts. Three-piece suits and tuxedoes. Clothes designed to advertise a man's wealth and social position. Funny how none of those clothes spoke of a man's strength—a man's ability to work with his hands— the way Alex's worn jeans and grimy T-shirt did.

Funny how she now noticed how appealing those qualities were. How they made her skin tingle with excitement.

When he swung one leg over the peak of the ladder and climbed down, she averted her eyes, trying not to gawk. After all, he'd made it clear he just wasn't interested. As he nodded in greeting, he dusted off his hands, then wedged them into his back pockets. Not the warmest reception, but about the best she could hope for under the circumstances.

"I wanted to apologize for yesterday. And to explain."

At her words, the suspicion in his gaze seemed to flicker and go out, but his eyes were dark and mysterious regardless, so she couldn't be sure.

Stepping to her side, he stopped just short of touching her and instead gestured toward the door.

"It'll be less dusty outside."

As with most houses in Palo Verde, the backyard sloped away from the house, up toward the foothills. A patch of overgrown fruit trees lined the far fence and crowded against the detached garage. A picnic table sat proudly in the center of a lawn of close-cropped weeds. It was a far cry from her own neatly manicured, obsessively maintained backyard.

When she turned her gaze to Alex, she found him

watching her carefully, as if gauging her reaction. Once again she found his inscrutable dark gaze unsettling.

"It's nice," she said, carefully lowering herself to the bench seat of the picnic table.

He stared at her in blank disbelief.

"Come fall, you'll really enjoy the apples from those trees."

"My parents have worked in the apple orchards for over thirty years. I hate apples," he said flatly as he sat opposite her.

Wow. Could this go any worse?

He crossed his arms over his chest and eyed her speculatively. And though she felt her pulse leap at his perusal, there was little flattering in his expression. "So, did you come here to talk about my landscaping or did you just think it'd be fun to waste another of my afternoons?"

Just when she was starting to hope someone would come by and shoot her with a tranquilizer gun just to put her out of her misery, she noticed his lips twitching.

He was enjoying this. Not out of cruelty, she was fairly certain, but he seemed to like having her at a disadvantage. That should have annoyed her, but it didn't. Something in his smile short-circuited her synapses. "As I said, I came here to apologize," she said again, trying to be blunt. Get this over with as quickly as possible. After all, he may enjoy flustering her, but she didn't enjoy being flustered. "I think you got the wrong impression yesterday."

He arched an eyebrow in speculation. "You mean you *do* want me to remodel your kitchen?"

"No. But you seemed to think I invited you over just to…sleep with you. But that's not why I called you."

"So you don't want to sleep with me?"

"No!" A second too late, she saw the teasing glint in his gaze. He was toying with her.

"You'll think it's stupid."

"Tell me anyway," he coaxed.

And, oddly enough, she wanted to. It'd been like that when they were in school, too. Something about Alex Moreno made her believe she could trust him implicitly. That she could tell him anything. And he'd never hurt her. Of course, it didn't help matters that he seemed so much less angry than he had yesterday. Even less than he had when she'd arrived. Her apology had gone a long way toward softening him up. Score one for *Saucy* magazine.

"It all started with this list." No, that wasn't right. "Actually it all started with my trip to Sweden."

"Sweden?" he asked, his mouth set in an inexplicably grim line.

"For business. I write software for PalmPilots. Companies hire us to write programs for them. Software that tracks sales, shipping, delivery, that kind of thing. So I went to Sweden to install it and train them to use it. I went with the understanding that when I came home, I'd have this big promotion."

"Let me guess. You didn't get the promotion."

"Three days before I came home, they gave it to someone else. You know the really ironic thing? The whole time I was in Sweden, everyone kept talking about how hard I worked. That I did the work of three people. Everyone was amazed. But you know what? I didn't work any harder there than I do here. But that's when I saw The List."

"'The List'?"

"In a magazine I was reading on the flight home. '10 Things Every Woman Should Do.' I decided right then and there that I was going to do everything on that list. I know it sounds silly, thinking that some list from a magazine will change your life, but I'm tired of settling for doing the work without the recognition. I'm tired of putting my life on hold while I wait for some promotion that may never come."

She studied his face, looking for some sign that he found this as silly as she did, now that she heard herself saying it out loud. But his expression was carefully blank, so she said with a shrug, "I know it's just a list, but it's a start."

"So how do I fit into all this? What exactly is on this list that you think I can help you do?"

The question she'd been dreading. But he certainly deserved her honesty, if nothing else. She swallowed hard, embarrassment burning her cheeks. The idea of discussing sex with Alex made other less visible parts of her burn, as well. "Number one on the list is 'Find Your Fling.'"

He nodded and for a second she thought he wasn't going to respond, but then he asked, "And you thought I'd be a good candidate?"

She shrugged, wishing desperately he wasn't so blasé about this whole thing, as if women propositioned him all the time. Though, for all she knew, they did. For all she knew, she was just one in a long line of lonely women who wanted to have a passionate fling with Alex.

And if that was the case, no wonder he'd been so annoyed with her yesterday. Of course, she still hadn't owned up to her mistake, not completely. So she sucked in a deep breath and said, "Yes, I thought you'd be a good candidate. And not because I wanted to fool around with the hired help."

Something in his eyes caught and held her attention. Once again she felt the gut-level tug of attraction. Passion, yes. But something more. Something more unsettling than that.

She waited a moment, hoping he'd say something. When he didn't, she moved to leave. "I should go."

But he grabbed her arm to stop her. "Wait—"

For a moment they simply sat there, his palm warm against her arm, the delicate skin at the crook of her elbow sensitized to the touch of his work-roughened fingers.

In that instant she knew—she hadn't come here to apologize. She didn't want him to forgive her. She'd come here hoping… Hoping what?

That he wanted her as much as she wanted him?

That the kiss they'd shared yesterday had been more than just a kiss?

That it had kept him up all night—hot and wanting—as it had her?

Yes, yes and yes. What she'd really wanted was for him to touch her again. After a lifetime of being coddled and cosseted by men with soft hands, she wanted this rough man—these hands—to touch her. Just once she wanted to know how that felt.

Too bad he didn't seem to want the same thing.

Okay, maybe he was a little interested. After all, that kiss in the kitchen had been pretty hot. But she wanted more. She wanted the kind of passion he couldn't walk away from.

She never again wanted to settle for less than that.

ALEX WATCHED HER as she scooted off the bench and stood. She made it about three steps down the driveway toward her car before he stopped her. He didn't know why, but he didn't want her to leave like this.

"Wait, Jessica."

She swung back to face him, her spine unnaturally stiff, her chin a notch higher. Outwardly she seemed so together. Cool and in control. But there was vulnerability there, too. *That* was what he couldn't walk away from.

"Why me? When you decided you wanted to have a passionate fling, why'd you pick me?"

He was an idiot for asking. But he wanted to spend more time with her almost as much as he wanted to take her to bed and do all kinds of sinful things to her body.

Jessica didn't answer right away. For a long moment she just studied him, her head tilted at an angle that let a lock of her hair fall across her cheek. Her expression was cautious, as if she were trying to decide whether or not to tell him the truth.

Finally she said, "I had a crush on you in high school. I was a junior, and you were a senior. It all started one day when—" Her gaze darted away from his and the barest hint of a blush crept into her cheeks. "You probably don't even remember it."

"Try me."

But he did remember. He knew exactly which day she meant.

"I was walking home from school alone one day. A couple of boys cornered me by the old Dawson house, where I used to cut across the creek. One of them was that Morse boy. Ronald, I think. His brother had been picked up for drunk driving. This was back when my father was still a judge and he'd just sentenced Ronald's brother. He was a repeat offender. My father had no choice. But Ronald was looking for someone to blame. I guess I was an easy target."

The way she said it—so simply, with no resentment or anger in her voice—made him wonder how often that kind of thing had happened. How many of her fellow students had resented her, hated her even, because of the power her father yielded?

"So there I was, all alone with these three guys, when you came along and—"

"Saved you." He finished the sentence for her because he couldn't stand to hear the hero worship in her voice.

Her gaze snapped back to his. "You do remember."

As if it were yesterday. In vivid detail. And he remembered all the things she was leaving out and skimming over. Her "a couple of boys" had been three huge guys. Football players, if he remembered right. Big, dumb and just looking for an excuse to pin Jessica Sumners up against a tree.

Which was exactly where they'd had her when he'd come along. She must have been terrified, but there hadn't even been a glimmer of emotion in her eyes. She hadn't begged or cried out or even fought them, as if she'd instinctively known that would only incite their rage. Instead she'd stood there, her gaze as calm and steady as her voice as she'd talked to Ronald.

Her tone so soft, Alex hadn't caught much of what she'd said. Something about how this would be for the best. How his brother could get the help he needed.

Alex had stood there, half hidden by the fence, his blood pounding, waiting to see what would happen. Unable to leave her to fend for herself, if the guys didn't walk away, he'd have to do something. But jeez, they were huge. And he'd been in enough fights to know he hadn't stood a chance, not against all three.

"It all happened so fast," she mused. "One minute I was all alone, the next I was surrounded." She looked up now, her eyes finding his. "And then you were there."

When he'd seen Morse lean in toward her, he'd acted instinctively. He'd called out her name. Not Jessica. Not Sumners, which was what Morse had been calling her. But "Jess."

"You called out to me," she said, still studying him with that pensive expression that made him so uncomfortable. "It must have surprised them, because they all three turned around and I was able to get away."

She'd run straight to his side. Without thinking, he'd put his arm around her shoulder. Together, they'd walked through the Dawson's yard to the street. At the sidewalk, he'd dropped his arm, but kept walking beside her, not wanting to let her out of his sight. Especially when he'd glanced over his shoulder to see all three guys standing in front of the Dawson house, watching them.

After they'd turned the corner and were out of sight of the football players, she'd slipped her hand into his. He'd felt her palm damp against his and her fingers trembling, and only then had he known how scared she'd been.

When they'd reached her block, he'd stopped and tried to pull his hand away, but she'd held tight. All he could think at the time was that he'd never imagined he'd ever find himself holding Jessica Sumners's hand. And he sure as hell had never imagined it would feel that good.

Then she'd looked up at him, her eyes bluer than any he'd ever seen, her expression so serious. Not distant and reserved, as it had been the few times their eyes had met while passing in the halls, but warm and filled with emotion. Gratitude, sure, but something else, as well.

An awareness of him. As if she was seeing him for the very first time. Hell, maybe she was. Girls like Jessica— good girls—didn't notice him. And for all he knew, she'd never really looked at him until that moment.

She'd stood so close to him that when the breeze picked up, a long strand of her hair fluttered close to his face and he'd caught the scent of her. She'd even smelled rich. Clean and fresh. Not like strong perfume, the way his sisters did.

In that instant he'd been distinctly aware of two things. First, he'd wanted to kiss her. Desperately. He'd wanted to press his lips to hers to see if she tasted as rich as she smelled.

Second, he shouldn't even be touching her.

Jessica Sumners was perfect. She never got into trouble, she never got her hands dirty, and she sure as hell never kissed guys like him. Not in darkened cars late at night when no one could see her and certainly not in the middle of the day forty feet from her front door.

Less than a month before, he had stood in her father's courtroom and been ordered by Judge Sumners to "keep his nose clean and stay out of trouble."

He'd suspected making out with the judge's daughter would get him into a great deal of trouble.

Despite that—or maybe because of it—he'd pulled his hand from hers and shoved it into his pocket. It had been one of the hardest things he'd ever done.

When she'd opened her mouth to say something, he'd interrupted her. "I'll stay here and watch until you're inside." She'd nodded. "Don't walk home alone again. Wait to walk home in a group. The bigger the better."

"I'll have our maid pick me up at school until this blows over."

Of course. Her maid. Why hadn't he thought of that? "Good idea."

She'd seemed to want to say something else as she'd watched him with those huge blue eyes. Eyes that seemed full of something perilously close to hero worship. Hell, that had been the last thing he'd needed. Jessica Sumners getting a crush on him.

Damn, that'd screw up his life but good.

"Go on." He'd nodded toward her house. Keeping his tone bored, he'd added, "I got things to do."

Her gaze had flickered as she'd turned and hurried toward the imposing mansion. She hadn't looked back. Hadn't seen that he'd stood on the corner, watching her house for nearly thirty minutes, belying his comment about having things to do.

Now, all these years later, as Jessica stood in his driveway, he thought again about how nothing had changed. She was as out of his reach now as she had been on that long-ago spring afternoon. And she still seemed unaware of how much he wanted her.

"I looked for you the next day at school," she said. "I guess I wanted—" She shrugged. "I don't know."

She may not have known what she'd wanted all those years ago, but he had. She'd wanted to recapture that connection they'd both felt standing on that street corner, her hand in his and the rush of adrenaline still pounding through their veins.

She looked at him now, her expression unguarded. When she looked at him like that, he felt like a hero. Ironic, given the very unheroic things his libido was urging him to do.

"So that's why you came to me? Because I saved you from some bullies?"

She frowned, looking very unsure of herself. "Not exactly."

"Then what?" When she didn't answer, he leaned forward. "I didn't do anything anyone else wouldn't have done."

Now her eyes met his with a flash of annoyance. As if it irritated her to hear him belittle his actions.

He sighed. "Look, Jess, it sounds to me like all these years you've been walking around thinking I'm some kind of a hero. But that's just not true. I didn't rescue you. I wasn't a hero. To tell the truth, I wasn't even a very nice guy."

"I don't believe you," she snapped. "What you did might not have meant anything to you, but it did to me."

"A momentary lapse in judgment."

Shaking her head, she exhaled loudly. "Would it really be so bad?"

"What?"

"Would it really be so bad to let people know that under your rebellious, tough-guy exterior, deep down inside you're actually a nice, decent human being?"

His heart swelled at her words—but it only reminded him of another body part that tended to swell around her. Not sure how much more hero worship he could take, he purposely lightened the mood.

He reached over and chucked her gently on the chin. "That's where you're wrong, Jess. Deep down inside, I'm just like I am on the outside."

She stiffened. "I don't believe you. You wanted people to think you're despicable, but you weren't."

"Despicable?" He laughed. "Honey, villains with big mustaches in old silent movies are despicable."

The irritation flashed in her eyes again but quickly disappeared. However, it wasn't as easy to hide the blush his teasing had brought to her cheeks. She pressed her lips into a thin line. "Okay. So not despicable."

Sensing he was close to having her exactly where he wanted her, he pressed his advantage. "No. Not despicable." And because he just couldn't resist touching her, he reached for her hand. Instead of taking it in his, he flipped it over, exposing her palm to his touch. "I'm much worse than despicable. You know what I was thinking about the whole way home?" She shook her head. "I was thinking about how I wanted to kiss you."

"But—"

He didn't let her finish. "There you were thinking I was some kind of a hero and all I could think about was how to get in your pants." He didn't look at her, didn't take his eyes away from her palm, which he couldn't seem to stop touching. It was so incredibly soft and warm under his fingertips. "I would have nailed you in a minute if you'd given me the chance."

She pulled her hand away. "I don't believe you."

This time he couldn't stop himself from meeting her gaze. He studied her face, but for once found it almost impossible to read her expression.

"As you pointed out," she said. "There I was, thinking you were a hero. If all you'd wanted was to—"

When she hesitated, he supplied the words for her. "Nail you."

She nodded. "If that was really what you wanted from me, you could have had it then."

At her near-whispered words, blood surged through his groin, nearly destroying the last of his control. But her calm and steady gaze assured him of her seriousness. He laughed ruefully. "It's probably a good thing I didn't know that then."

Now she was the one to laugh, clearly embarrassed. "And here all this time, I assumed you did know and just weren't interested." He shot her a questioning look and she shrugged sheepishly. "I looked for you all that next week at school, but every time I saw you, you were with friends. Or that girlfriend of yours. What was her name?"

Alex had to search his memory. Funny, he'd dated "that girlfriend of his" for months, but he could barely remember her name, let alone picture her. Yet he still remembered the expression on Jessica's face when she'd put her hand into his. And the color of the shirt she'd been wearing. And the way she'd smelled. And—

"Sandra," he finally supplied.

"Right. Sandra. Every time I saw you that week, you were with her. At first, I thought you were avoiding me on purpose."

"I was. It wouldn't have been in either of our best interests if people thought there was something going on between us."

He'd known even then how impossible a relationship with her would be. Even a friendship would have caused problems. She was the a straight-A student and the daughter of the county judge. He was the son of a migrant farm worker, already a grade behind in school, in and out of more trouble than she could imagine, his police record already burgeoning. None of that had kept him from wanting her, but it had damn well kept him from acting on it.

He'd avoided her so effectively that she'd eventually resorted to slipping a note in his locker. Three simple lines thanking him for coming to her rescue, in neat, cursive writing on pale pink paper.

"I thought that you knew I'd developed a crush on you and were trying to discourage me," she said now.

"I was."

Her gaze darted to his, her eyes a vivid blue that he seemed to have no defenses against. "Then why did you write me back?"

Because he'd just plain been unable to resist.

He shrugged. "I don't know."

His response, slipped through the vent of her locker during fifth period, had started a flurry of notes. She wrote him every day, often more than once, about things both wonderful and absurdly out of the realm of his experience—a low score on a chemistry exam, the shoes her mother had had dyed to match for some party dress, the fight she'd had with her parents over whether or not she'd go to tennis camp over the summer.

He'd written her less often, but with almost unbearable attention to detail. He'd penned his notes to her in the library, hunched over the dictionary, carefully checking his spelling, scouring the thesaurus for words he thought would make him look smart. Words like "supposition" and "eradicate."

Those three weeks that they'd exchanged notes had been some of the happiest of his young life. Then one day he'd received a note from her asking if he wanted to take her to the prom.

He'd known he couldn't do it, but God how he'd wanted to. And he hadn't had the heart to say no. So he'd just stopped writing to her.

"I know you thought I was just some annoying kid," she said now. "But I loved getting those notes from you. I'd pretend, just for a little while, that I was your girlfriend, instead of Sandra." She paused for a heartbeat, lost in some long-ago memory. "It was like you couldn't keep your hands off her. Did you know, I even saw you kissing her once?"

He did know. He remembered the moment vividly. He'd been avoiding Jessica all week, but she hadn't taken the hint when he'd stopped answering her notes. Every time he'd turned around, there she'd be. His patience and his willpower had started to wear thin. She hadn't ever caught him alone, but he'd been sure she eventually would. He'd been sure she'd look up at him with those impossibly blue eyes and that when she did he wouldn't be able to resist doing something incredibly stupid, like kiss her.

So he'd done something he was sure would scare her

off. He'd kissed Sandra in front of her. Not an innocent little peck on the mouth, either, but a full-bodied, openmouthed, I-can't-wait-to-get-your-body-naked kiss.

"I'd never seen anyone kiss like that," Jessica admitted
with a little laugh. "Not in real life anyway. That kiss…it
was like something out of movie. And I remember thinking, 'So that's passion.' I'd never been kissed like that." She
laughed nervously, the pink returning to her cheeks. "I still
haven't."

"Jess—"

Her hands were clasped tightly together and she was
staring pointedly down at them. "All my life and I've
never been kissed like that. Never felt that kind of passion.
Or had anyone feel that kind of passion about me."

The sheer yearning in her voice finally wore him down
and he reached out and put his hand over hers. "Jess," he
said again.

This time she looked up at him. Her eyes held none of
the emotion he'd expected to see. Just a glimmer of resignation. Nothing more.

But she pulled her hand out from under his. Then she
turned, hitching her purse strap up on her shoulder as she
made to leave. "Don't feel sorry for me."

"I don't," he protested. "But if you think no man's ever
felt passion for you, I think you may be seriously under-
estimating the effect you have on men."

Her gaze narrowed and she shook her head dismissively. "I don't need your pity. And I certainly don't need
you to massage my ego. I only brought it up because I
didn't want you to think that yesterday was just—what was
that phrase you used?— me wanting to screw around with
the hired help. I don't think of you that way. I never have."

She continued down his driveway toward the street,

but only made it a few feet before he stopped her. "Then what was it?"

"I guess I just wanted someone to feel that kind of passion for me." This time, when she turned to leave, he just let her go.

Because if she stayed any longer, he might break down and tell her the truth. That he did feel that way about her. That he'd wanted her badly even back then. That, apparently, he still wanted her now.

And that she *had* inspired the kind of passion she'd spoken of.

That day back in high school, when she'd seen him kiss Sandra, it wasn't Sandra he'd been kissing. Oh, it had been Sandra's body pressed to his and Sandra's mouth under his lips. But when he'd closed his eyes, it had been Jessica's face he'd seen. And Jessica's scent he'd smelled. It had been Jessica he'd wanted to kiss.

He'd known then he couldn't have her, but that hadn't kept him from wanting her. And it didn't now.

3

"SO WHAT YOU and I need to do," Patricia said as she pulled Jessica through her front door a week later, "is find you another man to have a wild fling with."

As she was dragged toward Patricia's bedroom, Jessica tried to protest. "I don't want to find another guy."

Patricia paused to prop her hands on her hips like a drill sergeant. "You want to do all the things on The List, don't you?"

"Yes, but—"

"There's no 'yes, but' about it. If you want to complete the list, you need another guy. Which is why you and I are going clubbing."

"Clubbing?" She narrowed her gaze suspiciously. "I thought you said we were just going to hang out."

"We *are* just going to hang out. At a club."

"Do we have to?"

"Yes, we have to. If we don't go out, you can't meet men." Patricia ticked off her points on her fingers as she spoke. "If you don't meet men, you'll never be able to do all the things on that list." Her voice dropped to a low growl. "You're not giving up on The List are you? Are you?"

Feeling even more like a young recruit at boot camp, Jessica snapped to attention. "Sir, no, sir!"

Patricia eyed her shrewdly for a second before cracking a smile. "That's more like it." She clapped her hands together. "Now we just have to find something for you to wear."

Jessica looked down at her clothes. "I can't wear this?"

"Um...no. You look like you're going to an English tea party."

"But—"

"Trust me when I tell you that where we're going, you'll look out of place." With that, Patricia disappeared into her closet. A few minutes later she peered around the door. "Do you trust me?"

Uh, oh. This didn't sound good.

Jessica hesitated, but then she thought of The List and nodded firmly. "I trust you."

"Great!" Patricia emerged, her arms laden with clothes, the fingers of one hand clutching a pair of knee-high, black patent-leather boots. They looked like something a superhero would wear along with a bright red spandex outfit.

Jessica eyed the boots warily. "Seriously?"

"You trust me, right?" Patricia's lips curved in a mischievous smile. "You said you did."

"Maybe."

"The boots go with the outfit." Patricia tossed the boots onto the bed and began sorting through the clothes. "You're not weird about wearing other people's shoes, are you?"

Other people's shoes? Maybe a little weird. Other people's superhero boots? That was a whole 'nother bag of Skittles.

"I'm not sure we wear the same size," she pointed out.

Patricia planted her foot on the floor beside Jessica's. "Close enough. Besides, they're big on me. They should be perfect on you."

Eyeing the boots with trepidation, she murmured, "Great."

Patricia snorted with laughter. "Here, put this on."

She tossed a tank top at Jessica, who caught it automatically then let it dangle by the straps from her fingers. "This? You want me to wear this?" She was a good four inches taller than Patricia. "This won't fit me."

"Yes, it will. It's stretchy."

"That's not reassuring."

Next, she tossed Jessica a skirt. A very tiny skirt.

"No. No way."

"You said you trusted me."

"I lied."

"You'll look hot. Besides, it's leather."

"So?"

"Wasn't one of the things on The List something about wearing leather?"

Yes, but Jessica chose to ignore the question. "I can't wear this. I'll look ridiculous."

Patricia thrust out her hand in a I-don't-want-to-hear-it gesture. "When was the last time you went to a club?"

"Last weekend."

"Not the country club. An actual club."

"College," she admitted.

"Okay, so you haven't been to a club in ten years—"

"Seven."

"Whatever." Patricia waved her hand in exasperation, then rolled her eyes, in case the hand-waving wasn't enough. "Think about why you're doing the things on this list. You don't want to settle for being plain, boring ol' Jessica Sumners anymore, right? You want to be saucy. Like the magazine. Then be *Saucy*."

"Okay. Be *Saucy*," she repeated resolutely as she tugged on the clothes. The tank top fit better than she would have thought. The neck draped loosely, skimming the tops of her breasts. The hem just reached the low-slung skirt, teasing but not revealing.

She picked up one of the boots and studied it speculatively. "With a miniskirt? Really?"

"You'll look hot."

Still doubtful, but determined to be saucy, she tugged on the boots before standing and looking down at her outfit. The skirt was a good ten inches shorter than anything she'd ever worn. The tank top exposed glimpses of her midriff every time she moved. And the boots… Well, let's just say, if her mother ever saw her wearing them, she'd faint dead away into her martini glass.

Patricia sighed. "Alex would be on his knees begging if he could see you now."

"That would be nice," she said with a chuckle.

Patricia came to stand beside her. Shoulder to shoulder, they stared at their reflections in the mirror.

"Well, forget about Alex," Patricia said. "You look so good you'll have to pry men off you with a paint scraper! And I say, we don't leave that club alone. We'll definitely find you the perfect guy for your fling."

Despite Patricia's bravado, Jessica had her doubts. What she wanted was someone who would:

A. Drop everything to have a wild passionate fling with her.
B. Want her so passionately, he forgot everything but her. And,
C. Make her forget all about Alex.

Yep, that about summed it up. In other words, she wanted a freakin' miracle. She didn't need superhero boots, she needed Dorothy's red shoes.

ALEX HAD NEVER BEEN one to find redemption at the bottom of a bottle. Then again—he mused as he tipped the longneck back—he'd never really looked for it there.

He emptied the beer then set it down on the faux wood tabletop. The condensation and the slight tilt of the uneven table legs pulled the bottle closer to the edge, but his brother, Tomas, grabbed it before it could crash to the floor.

The table—like the rest of the decor—was a little too slick for his taste. Music blasted from the bar's sound system and a mile-long row of bottles lined the mirrored wall on the other side of the gleaming, polished bar. This wasn't a real bar, it was bar lite. Purified for the yuppies. But Tomas was buying and it was Alex's first night out since he'd arrived back in town. Who was he to complain?

"What do you think?" Tomas gestured at the room with his beer.

Alex hid his smile and his sarcastic comment. "It's great. You come here often?"

Tomas took a sip from his bottle, but couldn't hide his own mischievous smile. "Never been here before. I think it's absolute crap. But thanks for lying."

"If you think it's crap, why'd you bring me?"

"You seemed like you needed to blow off a little steam."

Even as he protested, he knew Tomas was right. He appreciated his brother's efforts, but he wasn't sure how much good it would do. The bar was little more than a pickup joint catering to Palo Verde's growing yuppie population. The beautiful women were plentiful and scantily clad. And if he'd been interested, he probably could've snagged one.

But, right now, the only woman he wanted to take to bed was Jessica Sumners.

He told himself she was all wrong for him. They had

nothing in common. Sleeping with her would get him nothing but a few moments' pleasure. None of that mattered. None of that had driven her from his thoughts.

And—so far—neither had the beer he'd been drinking.

He picked up the empty bottle. "You want another one?"

Tomas nodded. "Sure."

A few minutes later he was working his way back through the crowd, holding a pair of longnecks, when Jessica walked in. The way she was dressed, he almost didn't recognize her, but her posture gave her away. Even in a bar, she had the bearing of a princess. The sight of her jerked him to a standstill.

She was with a friend…someone shorter and curvier with platinum-blond hair. Beside her friend, Jessica looked like a goddess—one of those water sprite things he'd read about in school, tall and willowy. Her honey-blond hair tumbled over her shoulder in gleaming waves. Her eyes widened and shifted nervously as she glanced around the room.

Then, almost as if she sensed him watching her, her gaze drifted to his. She took half a step back and bumped into the door behind her. Her eyes darted from his as she frowned and tugged on her shirt.

The action called his gaze to her clothes and his hands clenched the necks of the beer bottles. Her outfit was no more revealing than the clothes of any other woman in the bar and less so than many. Neither her clothes nor the gorgeous body underneath held his attention—though the combination packed a powerful punch. But, oh, man, her expression nearly ripped his guts out. A beguiling mixture of innocence and seduction. Of temptation and redemption. He raised one of the bottles to his lips and took a long, slow drink.

He lowered the bottle and watched her trail behind her friend toward the bar. A line from one of those sappy romantic movies his mother loved to watch drifted through his mind. Of all the bars in the world, why did she have to walk into this one?

His heart thudded in his chest while he waited for her to reach him, but before she did, she touched her friend's elbow, said something he couldn't hear over the music, then steered her friend to the far end of the bar.

He couldn't believe she'd shown up in a dive like this. Even more surprising was the fact that no one else seemed to have noticed the princess of Palo Verde slumming in this joint. But maybe no one recognized her. After all, the bar's clientele seemed a far cry from the country club set she most likely usually hung out with.

He took another swig of beer, then worked his way back toward his brother, telling himself he was glad she'd avoided him. Just because she'd taken the leading role in every sexual fantasy he'd had in the past seven days didn't mean he wanted to run into her. Not with her dressed like that. And certainly not with his self-control so threadbare.

Plunking the bottle down in front of his brother, he scooted onto the opposite stool.

"Thanks, man." His brother took a swig of beer, then gestured with the bottle. "It's the damnedest thing. While you were up getting the beer, these two women walked in and I would've sworn one of them was that Sumners girl. You remember her from school?"

"No." He lied, because he didn't want to get into it.

"Man, she looks hot. Do you think she looked this hot back in school?"

"Nope." Hell, she hadn't looked this hot a week ago. And a week ago she'd been pressed up against his body, begging to be kissed, which had drastically increased her appeal.

Tomas took a fortifying drink, then set down the bottle and stood.

Alex reached out and grabbed his arm before he could get more than a step away. "Where're you going?"

Tomas pointed to the end of the bar where Jessica and her friend now lingered. Her friend, dressed in a skin-tight bright-red dress that crisscrossed her chest and left her belly bare, sat perched on the edge of a stool. Her elbows were propped on the bar behind her, a position that arched her back and thrust her breasts forward. Jessica stood off to the side, looking uncomfortable but still sexy as hell.

"I'm going over to say hello." Tomas grinned. "It'd be rude not to."

"Sit." He tried to keep the irritation from his voice, but didn't succeed.

"What?" Tomas asked. "You want a shot?"

At Jessica? Nope. He wasn't sure he could resist temptation again this soon.

"Look," he began hesitantly. "Jessica is—" Before he could fumble through an explanation, Tomas cut him off.

"Jessica, is it? You do remember her."

"She's thinking about having her kitchen remodeled. That's all."

Tomas raised his eyebrows. "That's all?"

Alex forced himself to nod, though he was tempted to do something considerably less benign. That was the kicker about family. They knew how to push your buttons. Tomas, the brother he was closest to both in age and temperament, certainly knew how to push his.

"If that's all it is, then you shouldn't mind if I go over to say hello." Tomas's smile broadened. "Should you?"

His desire to keep his brother away from Jessica battled with his instincts not to give in to Tomas's teasing. "Let it go, Tomas," he warned.

Tomas cocked his head in the direction of the bar. "Looks like I'll have to. Missed my chance."

Alex shifted in his chair to look over to where Jessica and her friend stood. While he and Tomas had been talking, the two women had drawn a small crowd.

A sinking feeling settled in his stomach. A guy so slick and glossy he looked like a magazine cover model wrapped his hands around the waist of Jessica's friend and lifted her to the bar. The woman smiled gamely, then swung her legs up onto the bar and stretched out. Propped up on her elbows, her chest thrust forward and her head tilted back, she commanded the attention of nearly every male in the room.

But not his. Alex's gaze went immediately to where he'd last seen Jessica. Thank God she was trying to move away from the bar instead of toward it. But the growing group of men crowded closer to where her friend lay sprawled and waiting...for tequila, no doubt.

Then, sure enough, the bartender approached with a bowl of limes and a bottle of the potent liquor. But Alex wasn't concerned about the girl on the bar. What worried him was the burly guy dressed in denim and flannel leering at Jessica.

A sinking feeling in Alex's gut told him that if he didn't step forward to stop it, the next woman lying across that bar would be Jessica.

4

"YOU'RE NEXT, sugar," a low voice growled in her ear.

Jessica jerked her gaze from the horrifying sight of Patricia balancing a shot of tequila on her belly for the next man in line.

The man wiped a dribble of liquor from his chin with the back of his hand. His still-moist lips twisted into a toothy smile.

Jessica pressed her fingers to her throat. "Me?"

"Yep, sweet thing, you're mine."

She stepped back, but bumped into the mass of men behind her. Scooting to her left, she tried to dissuade him. "Oh, I'm not sweet at all."

The redneck barked with laughter. "That's just fine. I like my women tart."

He reached for her and she darted to her right, barely eluding his grasping hands. "I'd really rather—"

A beefy hand grabbed her arm and yanked her toward him. "Now don't be shy."

Though her arms were trapped between them, she pressed her palms against his chest to leverage herself from his grasp. His shoulders were impossibly wide and he towered over her. Beneath her hands, his muscles felt like raw steaks, soft yet unyielding. Not raw steaks, she mentally corrected. Like an entire cow carcass. Huge, immovable and frankly rather nauseating.

She straightened her arms, straining to wiggle from his grasp. "I don't really like tequila," she protested.

He released another bark of laughter as his hands closed in on her waist. "You won't be drinking it," he said, as if that was reassuring.

He lifted her effortlessly and spun her toward the bar. She gasped as she landed on the hard—and somewhat sticky—wooden surface a few feet down from where Patricia still lay. Patricia's performance was drawing quite a crowd and almost no one noticed Jessica—or the redneck. Unfortunately the redneck's attention was riveted on her.

"Lonnie," the redneck called to the bartender, "another shot down here."

"Oh, my." She tried to scootch off the bar, but the redneck stood too close.

The bartender nodded to indicate he'd heard, but was busy pouring another drink. The delay bought her a few seconds to consider her fate. She patted the pocket of her Bolero jacket, where she'd stuffed two twenties, her keys and her pepper spray. She could talk her way out of this pickle, but she wanted it handy. Just in case.

But before she could even try the diplomatic approach, Alex elbowed his way toward her. He moved through the crush of people with the controlled grace of someone used to slipping through the unlit corners of the world.

For an instant, when his gaze met hers, she forgot where she was. The crowd, the redneck and even the impending tequila shot faded to little more than background noise as she watched him. For the first time since he'd come back, he seemed like the angry young man he'd been when he'd left. Wild and dangerous.

She jerked her gaze away and reality snapped back into place.

The bartender slapped a saltshaker, a bowl of limes and a shot glass down on the bar beside her hip. Tequila sloshed over the rim of the glass onto the bar and her bare thigh.

The redneck grabbed the bowl of limes and held it out to her. "Here ya go, honey."

The salacious gleam in his eyes churned her stomach. She pushed the bowl back toward him with her palm. "Thank you, but no."

Before the redneck could utter another word, Alex grabbed the bowl of limes from his hand.

"What the—"

"She's with me," Alex said, his voice hard and tight.

She tried to catch Alex's eye, but he didn't even glance her way.

The redneck bristled, his chest swelling with indignation. "She didn't come in with you."

Alex was lean, wiry. Even though he had to be nearly six feet tall—several inches taller than she was—the other guy dwarfed him, not just in height, but in width and mass, as well. Still, Alex didn't back down. Didn't even blink as he said, without glancing in her direction, "Jessica, tell him you're with me."

The redneck shot her a questioning look.

Talk about situations Emily Post never covered.

Any reply she might have made caught on her tongue and, ultimately, she could only nod mutely.

The rest of the bar carried on—loud and raucous, a turbulent whirl of people. Tension bounced between the three of them. They were like the quiet, deadly eye of the storm. Silent, tense and coiling for an explosion.

Her breath quickened and caught as she waited for one of the men to move. For one of them to back down. But neither did.

It was all she could do not to squeeze her eyes closed so she wouldn't have to watch. Alex was tough—she knew that—but this guy was huge. He was going to trample Alex. He would beat him to a pulp. He would—

Abruptly the guy shrugged, then shuffled a step back. He gave one last glance in her direction. "You sure you're with him?"

Before she could answer, Alex stepped forward. "Sure, she's sure." He placed his hand on her leg, just above her knee. "Aren't ya, honey?"

He didn't give her a chance to answer. Automatically her legs opened as he stepped between them. Bracing his hands on her hips, he pulled her toward him and gave her a hard, fast kiss. Just as she began arching into him, he pulled back, then ducked his head to nuzzle her neck.

Under the guise of nibbling her ear, he whispered, "What are you doing here?"

His lips felt divine against her skin and she shivered. Forcing herself not to arch into the caress, she struggled to focus on his words. And his exasperated tone.

"What are *you* doing here?" she countered.

"Saving your ass from Paul Bunyan, that's what."

Of course. He was rescuing her again. It wasn't that he'd changed his mind. It wasn't that he'd suddenly realized he found her irresistible. Annoyed with the way her pulse leaped at his touch, when clearly he wasn't affected at all, she snapped, "My ass doesn't need saving, thank you very much."

"You're in over your head," he insisted. She shoved at his shoulders. He didn't budge.

"I don't need to be rescued anymore. I was handling this just fine before you showed up." She'd hissed the words, so only he could hear.

He pulled back just far enough to look into her eyes. "You want to do body shots with Paul Bunyan, be my guest."

Paul Bunyan, it seemed, had been watching closely. He grabbed Alex's arm and pulled him around.

"I don't think she wants you here, after all."

Alex shrugged, his expression uninterested. "Well, Jess, what do you say? You want me to do the shot or you want him—" Alex tipped his head in Paul Bunyan's direction "—to do it?"

Her gaze darted from Alex's to Paul Bunyan's. Alex raised his eyebrow in question, Paul Bunyan looked torn between eyeing her hopefully and scowling at Alex.

What a choice!

No choice at all, really. She wasn't going to let Paul Bunyan put his moist, fat lips anywhere near her body, and Alex knew it. Damn him.

She watched him through narrowed eyes, wanting nothing more than to wipe that smug expression off his face.

Oh, you think you're so clever, don't you? Well, think again, mister.

He may have her backed into a corner, but that didn't mean she couldn't take him down with her.

Mimicking a move she'd watched Patricia pull earlier, she dropped her chin a notch so she gazed up at Alex from under her lashes. Twirling a single lock of hair around her finger, she said, "Alex, honey, of course I want you." He sucked in a breath of air and she blinked innocently up at him. "To do the shot, I mean."

She ran the toe of her boot up the outside of Alex's leg, smiling benignly up at Paul Bunyan. "You don't mind, do you? You'll still get to watch."

Paul Bunyan grinned broadly. "Just don't forget I'm here if you change your mind."

When she glanced back at Alex, she found him glowering at her. His grim expression almost made her laugh. That's what he got for trying to manipulate her.

Quickly on the heels of that thought came another.

She'd just manipulated him into doing a body shot off her in the middle of a crowded bar. Which was worse? The fact that he'd be kissing and licking her bare skin? Or the fact that he'd be doing it in public?

Well, she'd wanted to be bad. But how could she have known it would feel so good?

Glaring at her through narrowed eyes, he muttered, "Fine. Let's get this over with."

Pleased she'd gotten under his skin, she replied, perhaps a little too smugly, "Whenever you're ready."

Only when he quirked an eyebrow did she realize he was waiting for her to do something. For an instant her mind raced frantically. Patricia was the only person she'd ever seen do a body shot. She'd stretched out on the bar and had the salt poured on her bare belly. The stranger who'd done Patricia's shot had done a lot of licking. Something Jessica couldn't quite imagine letting any man do in public. Surely that wasn't the only way to go. After all, she'd seen those billboard ads for body shots...other body parts had been involved.

Determined to wing it, she slipped her jacket off her shoulders. She grabbed a lime from the bowl beside her and placed it on the hollow of her collarbone. She was less sure of what to do with the shot glass. So she merely held it in one hand and the saltshaker in the other.

She almost felt proud of herself. Until Alex stepped closer and licked the side of her neck. Instantly desire washed over her, sweeping away any other emotion she'd been feeling.

His tongue, moist and hot, swept down the side of her neck, lingering on the hollow at her collarbone. Then he grabbed the saltshaker from her hand and shook a generous sprinkling onto her neck. After the heat of his tongue, the salt felt surprisingly cool against her skin, which was so sensitized she seemed to feel each individual grain as it landed on her flesh. Heat pulsed through her body, settling low in her belly. Her skin prickled, ready for the touch of his tongue.

The crowd faded away as he pulled her closer, his hands firm and warm on her hips. Her eyes drifted closed as the heat of his breath washed across her skin. Time seemed to slow, the earth seemed to still, as she waited for him to lick the salt from her neck.

She'd expected a single swipe at the salt. Fast, like she'd seen that other man do on Patricia. Quick, like pulling off a Band-Aid. But, Alex, it seemed, was not a fast-and-quick man. He moved slowly, his tongue returning to her neck again and again in tiny passes, removing each grain of salt one at a time.

The room spun around her. She felt inexplicably unstable, as if she sat on a swing high above the crowd, rather than on the solid wooden bar. Her free hand automatically clutched at his shoulders as she sought to balance herself. But his assault on her senses continued and a single handhold couldn't keep her from slipping off the swing and plunging into the crowd. She clenched her knees together, pulling him closer, grounding herself in the moment.

His tongue lingered on her neck, prodding her pulse point over and over in a movement reminiscent of a much more intimate act. She shivered and gasped, arching toward him, nearly begging him to stop. Or to never stop, she wasn't quite sure which.

Then the licks turned to gentle soft kisses, no less potent. And then he stopped. For a moment he pressed his temple against her jaw. She could feel his thundering pulse beneath her chin, his ragged breath against her neck.

Abruptly he pulled away. His body tense and his movements sharp, he ducked his head to her collarbone and grabbed the slice of lime in his teeth. His lips brushed her shoulder as he bit down on the lime and a single drop of cool lime juice trickled onto her skin. He straightened, leaving the now-bruised lime still resting on her shoulder, and reached for the shot glass.

He tossed back the shot with a single drink, then slammed the glass down beside her on the bar. The clang of the glass against wood—which sounded remarkably loud in the already loud room—snapped her senses back into place.

As if waking abruptly from a dream, she was instantly aware of everything around her. The hum of dance music, the scents of stale perfume and staler beer, the mass of people around them—some watching their display, most unaware of their existence. And of Alex…standing so close, his expression taut and his normally dark eyes nearly black.

Worst of all, she was aware of her own position, perched on the bar, her legs nearly wrapped around a man who was—for all intents and purposes—a stranger.

Oh, my.

Oh, my goodness.

This may not have been on The List, but it should have been, because she definitely felt *Saucy* now.

She wanted to pull Alex back into her arms and lick off whatever tequila still clung to his lips. To hell with propriety. To hell with society's expectations for Jessica Sumners.

Before that kernel of rebellion could muster enough force to even mount a protest, Alex's eyes narrowed.

He didn't step away from her. Didn't so much as move an inch, but she felt his withdrawal just the same.

Grabbing her hips, he lifted her from the bar as if she weighed no more than the shot glass. He set her on the ground, then grabbed her hand. "Come on, let's get out of here."

But she sensed from his clenched jaw and brusque attitude that this was not the start of the hot fling she'd been hoping for. She might have tempted him, but now he was back to rescuing her. More's the pity.

Still, she had more sense than to protest, and let him pull her blindly along toward the door. He stopped just short of the door to talk to a man seated at one of the tables. She assumed he was one the brothers Alex'd mentioned, since he had the same high cheekbones and piercing eyes as Alex. Desperate to regain some of her usual control, she moved around Alex and extended her hand. "I'm Jessica. I don't believe we've met."

Tomas stood, smiling, and took her hand. "Tomas. Alex's brother."

"I figured." She smiled in return, secretly thrilled he didn't bother to hide his appreciation.

Alex, however, seemed less than pleased. "You can let go of her hand now."

Tomas's smile broadened as he released her hand. "A bit of a bully, isn't he?"

She smiled. "Most definitely."

To Alex he said, "You go on. I'll be fine here."

Alex nodded, "Thanks."

He pulled her just a few steps toward the door before she protested. "I came with Patricia. I drove her here. I can't just leave without her."

"I suspect Patricia will be just fine on her own."

"But I can't leave her," she stated again. There were probably all kinds of protocols that she didn't know about going clubbing with single friends. But even if that protocol said it was okay to leave your friends stranded at a club, she just couldn't do it.

"Fine." The word came out as little more than a growl. "Go find her."

For a moment Jessica stared at him, eyes wide. Alex felt the energy that had been buzzing back and forth between them all night—hell, since he'd walked into her house last week—intensify like the thrumming feedback of an amplifier turned up too loud. Then she spun on her heel and disappeared into the crowd.

Just let her go, his mind begged. *Just let her walk the hell away.*

He didn't even bother to argue with himself over it. No way would he leave her here alone. Not with this crowd, already rough, on edge and more than a little drunk. Not when he knew what every guy here was thinking. He knew what they were thinking, because he was thinking the same damn thing. In vivid Technicolor detail.

But there were two major differences between him and every other guy in here. One, his fantasies were fueled by the memory of what it was like to actually taste that beautiful skin. And two, he was the only man in the room determined to keep his distance.

5

THOUGH THE CROWD was thick, he easily kept her in his sights. Her blond hair was too distinctive to miss. She wasn't the only blonde in the club, but she was the only one on whom the honey tones looked natural. He caught up with her just in time to send a warning scowl at one of the fools lumbering toward her.

She stopped just short of the dance floor. Standing on her tippy toes, she strained to see over the crowd. Pointing to the far corner of the room, he said, "Over there."

He knew the instant she spotted her friend in the throes of a complicated bump and grind between two guys, because she recoiled and stumbled into him. She'd tried so hard to be tough and worldly tonight. And she was failing so miserably.

An unexpected wave of protectiveness washed over him. She didn't belong here any more than he belonged in her world. And he could only imagine how he would feel at one of her society parties. He battled the sudden urge to carry her away from all this. To protect her.

But from what? From his world? From himself?

Before he could do—or say—anything stupid, she straightened her shoulders and marched onto the dance floor. He could do nothing other than follow. She approached the dancers with a confused but determined expression on her face.

Finally she brushed past one of Patricia's male admirers to tap Patricia on the shoulder. Patricia smiled broadly as she greeted Jessica.

From this noisy corner of the dance floor, he couldn't hear what the two women said, but their body language spoke clearly enough. Jessica suggesting they leave. Patricia brushing aside Jessica's offer for a ride. Repeat as needed.

Finally, Jessica turned back to him. Bracing her hand on his upper arm, she stood on her toes to speak into his ear. "She doesn't want to go."

"Obviously." He grabbed her hand, ostensibly to lead her toward the door, but also to keep her from touching him. There was only so much a guy could take.

But she stood firm. "I can't just leave her here."

Ah, crap. Here we go again.

He was just about to launch an argument when he spotted Paul Bunyan watching them from his perch near the bar. Great. Just what they needed.

Alex tightened his hold on Jessica's fingers and pulled her closer. "Dance with me."

"What?"

Before she could pull away, he wrapped his other arm around her waist and pressed her to his chest. Thrown off balance, she leaned against him. His hands settled low on her hips, instinctively pulling her closer.

His body leaped to life at her nearness and the erection he'd just started to get under control strained against his jeans. His mind flashed back to how her lips had felt under his. For a moment all he could think of was how damn good it would feel to let his hands slip down to the hem of her skirt. To ease that hem up and expose the silky skin of her thighs to his touch. To make love to her right here.

To lose himself so completely in her that he forgot they were in a public place.

Trying to distract himself, he started dancing, slowly shifting his feet. However, Jessica's feet remained firmly rooted to the ground.

She stared up at him, her wide eyes filled with confusion. "What are you doing?"

What was he doing? "Dancing. You can't stand in the middle of the dance floor arguing. People notice." He nodded in the direction of Paul Bunyan. "I didn't want our friend over there to get any more ideas."

She glanced back over to the bar. "Oh."

"You know, this dancing thing will look more convincing if you dance with me."

Slowly her feet shifted back and forth between his. The action created just enough friction between their bodies to drive him crazy. He forced himself to continue the conversation they'd been having before he'd spotted Paul Bunyan. "If Patricia doesn't want to come with you, you don't have a choice." He sounded far more reasonable than he felt.

"The thing is, she has it in her head that she doesn't want to leave alone, you know? She made me promise that we wouldn't leave until we'd both picked up guys. I tried to tell her that you hadn't really picked me up—that you were just taking me home—but she didn't believe me."

Well, at least he knew where he stood with her now. To her, going home with him didn't count as being picked up. "So leave her here." He practically ground the words out.

She pressed her palms against his chest to push away from him. "I still can't leave her here."

"Jessica—" He growled the warning.

"Look, you don't want to stay? Fine. Don't stay. But

I'm not leaving without Patricia. So if you'll kindly let go of me..."

Even though she was a good three inches shorter than he was, she managed to look down her nose at him. How the hell she could stand there, dressed like that, and still look like the princess of some snotty European principality he'd never know.

The only thing he did know was that he sure as hell wasn't going to leave her royal highness alone in this bar. "Fine. I'll get Tomas to take her home," he muttered, dragging her away from the dance floor toward Tomas's table.

"But—"

"Don't worry. He'll get her home safely and without bruising her ego."

A few minutes later he shoved Jessica into the empty chair beside a smirking Tomas. "Wait here. I'll go get Patricia." To Tomas, he said, "Don't let her out of your sight."

Tomas's smile broadened.

Alex scowled and resisted the temptation to knock his brother off the chair. He wasn't feeling any friendlier when he finally extracted Patricia from her admirers and dragged her back to the table twenty minutes later.

Tomas and Jessica sat side by side, their heads bent toward each other as they talked. From across the room, he saw Jessica tilt her head, turn her ear closer to Tomas, concentration written clearly on her face. Her eyes widened in surprised amusement as she got the punch line to whatever joke or story Tomas was telling her. Then she laughed.

A full-bellied, throw-your-head-back laugh.

Watching them together, something ugly and unpleasant twisted in his stomach. Something very unbrotherly.

Something he definitely shouldn't be feeling in connection with a woman who meant nothing to him.

His relationship with Tomas had all the standard childhood crap that came with a large family. But even at its absolute worst, he'd never felt like this. This gut-wrenching jealousy. All because Tomas had made Jessica laugh.

Only when he felt Patricia pulling on his arm did he realize he'd stopped walking. The sight of Jessica and his brother had literally stopped him cold.

"Aren't we going?" Patricia trilled loudly.

Angry with himself for being jealous in the first place and for being so damn transparent, he snapped, "Sure."

He deposited Patricia unceremoniously into Tomas's care and dragged Jessica out the door without waiting to see if they would follow. Stopping short outside the door, he scanned the parking lot for the cherry-red Beemer he'd seen parked in her driveway the other day. He found it, parked all alone in the far corner, as if the car had been afraid of catching cooties from the other cars.

He stomped off in the direction of her car, assuming Jessica would follow and almost too irritated to care if she didn't. What the hell was wrong with him?

He was still asking himself that same question as Jessica began insisting on driving, but he ignored her.

"Fine!" she finally said, throwing open the passenger door and climbing inside.

Once behind the wheel, he felt a moment's hesitation. Why couldn't she have driven a Toyota or Volvo? No, the princess had to drive a top-of-the-line convertible M3. The damn thing was worth more than his house.

Scanning the interior of the car, he struggled to orient himself with the different controls of a foreign vehicle. He'd borrowed a friend's Yugo once in L.A., but that was as close as he'd gotten to a German-engineered automobile. The fine-grain leather seat cradled his body and, once he'd eased the seat back a couple of notches to accommodate his longer legs, he realized this was going to be—hands down—the most comfortable, most exhilarating drive he'd ever take.

He glanced at the gearshift, straining to see it in the dimly lit interior. Six Speeds. Damn. Forget comfortable. This was gonna be a blast.

"I told you I should drive," she muttered as if reading his mind.

"I can handle it," he muttered as he slipped the car into Reverse and backed out of the spot. The bar was on the far outskirts of town and they were a good twenty or thirty minutes from either of their homes.

After a moment of silence she said, "So, you never told me how you got into construction."

"You never asked," he pointed out. A little of his irritation began to slide away. Jessica clearly found the situation awkward and it amused him that she was trying to make polite conversation.

Her lips curved downward. Frowning, but more irritated than annoyed. "Are you always this difficult?"

"Are you always this nosy?"

"Only when I'm uncomfortable," she blurted.

He took his eyes off the road long enough to glance in her direction. In the flickering light of the street lamps, he noticed her stiff posture, her tightly clenched hands. She met his gaze and he cocked an eyebrow in question.

"Conversational sleight of hand," she said with a nervous laugh.

"Excuse me?"

"You ask people questions, get them talking about

themselves." At his pointed look she added, "My parents had political aspirations since before I was born. I grew up needing to know how to make conversation." She shifted to look out the window, so he almost didn't hear her sigh. "The easiest way to keep people entertained is to keep them talking about themselves."

He pondered that for a minute, wondering what it must have been like to grow up under those circumstances. Wondered if that was why she'd been so serious as a teenager. Their lives had been so different. And for the first time he considered that hers—for all its wealth and acceptability—might not have been easy.

"That must have been a hard way to grow up," he found himself saying.

"I suppose it was." Then after a minute she added, "I think it was easier on my brother. He made a great politician's son. You know, class president, football hero, that kind of thing. But I would have been happier just sitting on the sidelines and staying out of the limelight. Thus the need for the conversational sleight of hand."

Her words were so different from what he would have expected of her. And yet, was it really that surprising? The girl who had left notes in his locker all those years ago had seemed unsure and a little shy. She had talked, even then, about wanting to escape from the shadow of her father's presence. She had spoken of parents who loved her but whose reputation and expectations were stifling. He'd known all too well what that was like.

Because he didn't know what else to say, he answered the question she'd asked earlier. "My uncle worked in construction. Carpentry, actually. He lives in Sacramento, but he did work here in Palo Verde, also. Remember when the country club was remodeled back in the eighties? He did a lot of the woodwork on that."

"So after graduation you went to work for him?"

"I started working with him when I was twelve. Over the weekends, during the summer."

"That isn't legal!" She sounded outraged.

"Probably not." He shrugged as he slipped the car into a higher gear. "At a busy construction site, people don't notice a boy doing odd jobs, hauling away scraps and carrying lumber."

"And your parents let you do this?"

"My father insisted." She understood so little of what his life had been like, so he tried to explain. "Migrant farm workers don't make a lot of money. A lot of kids go to work at ten or eleven to help out. But my parents wouldn't let any of us drop out of school. Even when they finally let me start working, they wanted me to have a skill."

"I…" Her voice cracked under the weight of her obvious remorse. "I didn't know. I'm sorry."

"Don't apologize."

"But I didn't mean to imply—"

"Look, I'm not ashamed of my parents. I'm proud of all they did. They worked hard. And they kept us together. They made sure we got an education. They wanted us to have the sort of success they'd never had. I don't want to do anything to jeopardize that."

"When I said I was sorry, I wasn't apologizing for your background, I was apologizing for my ignorance."

He nodded. Again she'd surprised him. He didn't like how off balance he felt around her.

As if trying to put distance between himself and his desire, he slipped her car into sixth gear, enjoying the thrum of the engine responding to his command.

"You like it, don't you?"

He shot her a suspicious look. "Like what?"

"Driving the Beemer." In the light of a passing street-lamp, he saw her smile...the first genuine smile she'd given him all night. "You're enjoying the power, aren't you?"

He did enjoy it. Handling this high-performance car gave him a bigger thrill than he ever would have imagined. Part of him wanted to remember every second of this drive, knowing he'd never again get the chance to put his hands on a car quite like this one.

And part of him knew he'd trade the experience in an instant for the chance to get his hands on Jessica again.

She intrigued him unlike any woman he'd ever known. She seemed a mass of contradictions. One minute so serious, the next so sexy. He wanted to peel back the layers of her personality to reveal the true Jessica, almost as much as he wanted to peel back the layers of her clothes. What few layers she still wore.

Pulling his thoughts back to the car he said, "Actually, I'm surprised you enjoy driving the Beemer. You don't strike me as a standard kind of girl."

She laughed. Unlike the laughter she'd shared with his brother, this laugh didn't sound amused, but tinged with relief.

"Funny, that's what my mom said." She raised her voice and spoke in a snooty tone. "Do you really have to drive that—that sports car? How would it look for your father if you were stopped and given a speeding ticket?"

He shifted the car into a lower gear. If her mother thought it would look bad getting caught speeding, he could just imagine how she'd feel about Jessica's car being pulled over with Alex Moreno driving.

"So you never speed," he observed.

Her smile broadened and mischief glinted in her eyes. "I just never get caught."

"Good planning."

"It's all about knowing where the cops are." Her voice sounded dreamy, as if she ached to be behind the wheel now, zipping along at eighty miles an hour. "The cops spend the whole weekend patrolling the highway between Sacramento and Lake Tahoe. Which leaves the northern part of the county free. There are some great back roads up in the foothills. If you get out there early enough on Saturday or Sunday morning, there's not a soul around."

"Rock Creek Road."

Her head snapped toward him. "You know it?"

"I used to go driving there when I was a kid." He stopped at a light and turned to look at Jessica. In the moonlight her hair seemed even paler. The light changed and he forced his attention back to the road.

"When you were a kid?" she asked.

"Well, teenager."

"In your '69 Camaro."

"That's right." It'd been a rusted-out piece of junk when he'd bought it, in such bad shape even he'd been able to afford it.

"Man, I loved that car." The day he'd scraped together the money to buy it had been one of the proudest of his young life.

"I know," she murmured. "The speed. The power. It's like flying."

Her words were filled with pure, unadulterated joy. He could picture her, in his mind, speeding along the hairpin turns of Rock Creek Road, the top down on her car, the wind blowing through that glorious blond hair of hers. The bright noonday sun shining down on her.

His own experiences on Rock Creek Road had been very different. And not just because he'd been driving a beat-up old Camaro instead of a high-performance, sixty-thousand-dollar luxury car.

He'd always gone at night—the darker the better. For him, there'd been no joy in driving along Rock Creek Road. Only escape. Disappearing in the darkness. Driving had been an act of rebellion. And of freedom, yes. But not of joy.

He struggled to put that into words and, in the end, gave up. His emotions seemed so…ugly compared to hers. "For me it was the solitude."

"The solitude?"

"Six kids in a three-bedroom house."

"Oh." She looked horrified, but tried to hide it. "I hadn't thought… That's a lot of people under one roof. I guess you needed the escape, too."

Escape, too, she'd said, which left him wondering what exactly *she* was escaping from. That wonderful life of hers? That life of wealth and privilege that he'd always assumed was so perfect, but apparently wasn't?

Even though he knew it was a mistake to bring it up, he still found himself saying, "So, going to the club tonight…was that another thing from your list?"

"Yeah, I guess so."

"But…?" he prodded.

She twisted to look out the window. "There is no but."

"You're working your way through that list like there's no tomorrow. This can't just be about some magazine article."

"No, the magazine article just made me realize how tired I was of settling for less than what I want."

"Tell me something, Jess. Do you like your job? Are you good at it?"

"I'll be a great manager. If I ever get the promotion."

"No. The job you do now. Do you like that one?"

"Programming?" She sounded surprised by his question. "Yes, I do. I'm good at it. Writing code and debugging it appeals to me."

"If you like what you do now, why are you so determined to get that promotion?"

"I—" She broke off, and he could sense her confusion.

After a long, thoughtful moment, she answered him. "Just expectations, I guess. I'm nearing thirty and I don't feel like I've accomplished much."

He raised his eyebrows. "You went to college. You have your own house. You're good at a job you like doing. What more do you want?"

"It's not that simple. Not for a Sumners anyway. My father was a judge by the time he was thirty. He went on to parlay that into a career in politics and now he's a senator. My brother owns his own consulting business. He was worth over a million dollars by the time he was thirty. It's a lot to live up to."

"And you think your parents love him more because of all he's achieved?"

"No," she said quickly, but then added, "Not exactly. They've always been proud of his accomplishments. But with me it was different. I was always their little girl. They were always trying to protect me. As if I couldn't handle things on my own."

"And you always hated that," he murmured, without meaning to say it out loud, and he felt her stiffen beside him.

"Yes, I did. How did you know that?"

"From the, um—" he cleared his throat "—the notes you wrote. There was one about some concert in Sacramento they wouldn't let you and some friends go to. You were pretty pissed at them."

"I can't believe you remember that."

Even without so much as glancing in her direction, he felt the intensity of her stare. Uncomfortable under her scrutiny, he shrugged it off. "It just came back to me now."

But in truth, he remembered every note she'd sent him—seventeen in all—almost to the word. He'd reread them dozens, maybe hundreds, of times. Late at night, after the rest of his family had gone to bed, he'd sneak out to his car, turn on the dome light and reread her notes. As he'd sat there in that grungy, beat-up, piece-of-junk Camaro he'd loved so much, he'd imagine her writing those notes to him. He imagined her sitting in the middle of her bed—one of those fancy, ruffly, four-poster jobs— propped up on mounds of pillows, her soft blond hair loose around her shoulders, looking like some princess from one of the fairy tales his mother made him read in English to his younger sisters.

"I remember the things you wrote me, too." Her words spilled out quickly. As though she was embarrassed by the admission. "You never complained about your family."

"Not much to complain about." At least, not much that she'd have understood. Or that he could have told her without revealing how dirt poor they really were. He couldn't tell her how tired he'd gotten of eating rice and beans. Or how he'd dreaded the end of apple season when his family would pick up and move to Arizona for a couple of months each winter. So instead, he'd crafted his notes from his hopes and dreams.

"You always talked about the places you wanted to

travel," she said. "The things you wanted to do when you got out of school. I think that's why I loved your notes. Your future was wide open. No expectations. No settling."

But that had been big talk back then. What he wanted now was so much simpler than that. Just a decent job that made decent money and that people respected him for doing.

Wanting to shift the focus back to her, he asked, "But what about what you want? You said you don't want to settle. So don't."

She drifted into silence and he wondered if he'd offended her. Then suddenly she chuckled. "Thank you."

"For what?"

"For trying to make me feel better. And for getting me out of there."

Glancing into his rearview mirror to make sure there were no other cars on the road, he slowed down and pulled off the main highway onto a darkened side road. As the car came to halt, he shifted into neutral and set the hand brake.

He turned in his seat to face her. "Jess, you shouldn't ever have to settle."

Jessica twisted in her seat, tucking one foot behind the calf of her other leg. The movement was intrinsically classy. A reminder she was a princess, despite her clothes. And way out of his league.

But that didn't stop him from wanting her. An odd intimacy settled over them, brought on by the close confines of the car and dim dashboard lighting. His headlights stretched out into the night outside, but inside, the world seemed to contract to include just the two of them.

"I..." She bit down on her lip and he thought there was a glimmer of tears in her eyes. "Thank you."

Her intense vulnerability damn near broke his heart.

He exhaled a deep, slow breath, then brushed his thumb against her chin, working up to her lip. With a gentle tug, he pulled her lip free from her teeth. "Ah, Jess, you're killing me."

He hadn't meant it as an invitation, but nor did he stop her when she leaned forward and pressed her lips to his. Her kiss was tentative and shy. And unbelievably erotic.

She tasted sweet and hot with just a hint of mint. Like she'd brushed her teeth before leaving the house and the flavor still lingered. Proof she hadn't even had a drink at the bar. This close, she smelled faintly of limes, a scent he'd never considered erotic until now. But the scent called up the memory of how her skin had felt beneath his tongue. Smooth and silky. Far more potent than the shot of tequila.

6

HE'D HAD ENOUGH trouble keeping his hands off her when he'd made himself think of her as a rich, selfish princess. Now that he knew the truth, he didn't stand a chance.

He knew in an instant if he didn't pull away now, he'd be in serious trouble. No matter how much he wanted her, he couldn't have her. She was all wrong for him. And there was no way he could get involved with her without destroying any chance he had of making this town believe he wasn't the reckless and wild boy he'd been when he'd left ten years ago. Worse still, the decent man Jessica thought he was would walk away from her right now.

That thought alone gave him the strength to pull away from the temptation of her kiss.

He gripped her upper arms, gently setting her aside. "We can't do this."

She looked up at him, her eyes wide, pupils dilated in the dim lighting. "Why not?"

"Look, Jessica, don't think I'm not interested, but I really can't." He held her gaze, hoping she'd see the truth in his eyes. "I'm trying to run a business. I've got enough going against me as it is."

She frowned, looking adorably confused. "I don't understand."

No, she probably didn't. She was blind to the inequality in Palo Verde. Not because she purposely ignored it the way so many people did, but because she just didn't think that way.

"How do you think people would feel about me if we were together?" he asked her.

"I don't know." She cocked her head to the side considering. "I don't think I care. Surely you don't, either. That kind of thing has never mattered to you."

"Fifteen years ago, you'd have been right. But things are different now. I've got a business."

"You think being seen with me would hurt your business?"

He laughed, a chuckle half amusement, half resignation. "Soil the reputation of Senator Sumners's precious daughter? Hell, yes, I think that would hurt my business."

"But why? I don't understand."

"People like you, Jessica. They feel protective toward you. It's like you're the freakin' town mascot or something."

She scowled, looking seriously displeased with the analogy. "Maybe you're wrong. Maybe being with me would help. I know a lot of people in this town. Besides, people here have better things to worry about than my social life."

"Maybe. But there's a good chance it would just piss people off. I don't want to make it harder than it has to be."

"No offense, but if it's so hard, why are you doing it? Why start a business here? Why move back here at all?"

Wasn't that the million-dollar question? Alex exhaled slowly. "Making it here, it's just something I have to do. Something I have to prove to myself. When I left town after high school, it wasn't by choice."

She nodded, her expression serious but without censure. "I always wondered if the rumors were true."

"Rumors?"

"That after high school you'd been arrested. For fighting. And that you had pulled a knife on the guy."

"Actually, I just had a pocketknife. The police found it when they patted me down. Who knows if that would have factored into the charges."

"But instead of filing charges, they just brought you before the judge…"

Her voice trailed off. Either she didn't know what had happened after that, or she didn't want to say, so he finished the story for her. "He suggested I leave town."

"'Suggested'? That doesn't sound like Daddy."

"Daddy?"

She blushed and averted her eyes. "The judge. It was him, wasn't it? This was before he ran for Senate when he handled cases like this."

"It was him. And you're right. 'Suggested' probably isn't the right word. He said I'd be better off starting over some other place."

She frowned. "I'm not sure I understand. 'Some other place'?"

"Some place where I had less of a history."

More importantly, some place where he'd had less of a history with the judge's daughter. It had gone unsaid back then, and so he left it unsaid now. There was no reason to make Jessica feel bad over something that had happened years ago. Something she'd had no control over in the first place.

She puzzled over his words for a minute, then said, "So my father wanted you to leave town so you could get a clean start somewhere else?" She studied him, then added, "But you don't think that's the real reason he did it, do you?"

He wanted to prevaricate, but found it difficult to do so with her watching. "Let's just say I think he may have taken other issues into consideration and leave it at that."

"'Other issues'? What other issues?"

Other issues such as Alex's relationship with Jessica. "Let's leave it at that," he repeated.

Not that he and Jessica had had a relationship back then. It was all speculation and gossip. Speculation and gossip that might have become public record if Alex had ever gone to trial. Could he really blame the judge for using his power to make sure that hadn't happened?

The judge had made it clear he thought substantiating the rumors about their relationship would ruin Jessica's life. Maybe he'd been right.

Jessica studied him, as if trying to decide how far she could push it or whether or not she should leave it at that. Thankfully, she let it drop. Sort of.

"My father, for all his faults, is a fair man. Dictatorial, yes, but fair. He may have genuinely thought he was acting in your best interests." She must have seen the doubt in his eyes, because she rushed on before he could interrupt. "And taking care of the people of this town has always been his top priority."

"My parents are migrant farm workers. Don't assume your father thought of me as one of this town's citizens."

"I don't believe that. My father—"

"Your father saw me the same way everyone else in town did. As a wild, reckless pain in the ass that would probably end up in jail someday anyway."

She studied him, her gaze serious and relentlessly probing. "Is that why you moved back here? To prove they were all wrong? To prove to everyone that you made something of yourself and you didn't end up in jail?"

"Yeah, I guess so."

Suddenly she looked up, her expression brighter. "But you said you're having trouble finding work."

"All I need is one really good job," he said with more bravado than he felt. "Construction is like any other business. It's all about networking. One job leads to the next."

"What about the courthouse?" she asked, her tone bright.

"The county courthouse?"

"Yes. In the last election, the county passed a bond to renovate the building. I know all about it because Daddy had me working overtime at the country club to campaign for support. It's a huge job. If you got it, you'd be set."

He'd been running some numbers in his spare time, but knew getting the job was a long shot. And that was if he could convince the powers that be he was a reformed man.

And then there was Jessica, staring up at him with her bright blue eyes. Whether she knew it or not, every flicker of her gaze, every flutter of her well-manicured fingertips transmitted a sensual promise. He'd like nothing more than to peel off her clothes and explore every inch of her sleek little body.

But those were not the actions of a reformed man.

Besides, she wanted a plaything. A check on her list. Nothing more. He told himself he wanted her just because she was available. Just because nailing her would bring that teenage fantasy of his to life. Yet, deep down inside, he was afraid it was more than that. And if there was one thing he knew about rich girls, when they tired of their playthings, they tossed them aside.

Since she still seemed to be waiting for an answer, he said, "I'm already looking into it."

She watched him carefully, as if gauging his reaction. "You don't think you'll get, do you?"

Because she was right, he didn't answer directly. Instead he asked, "Why do you say that?"

"All those things you said about how hard it's been for you to start a business in this town... You were talking about bidding the job for the courthouse, weren't you? That's what you meant."

Seeing the determined glint in her gaze, he admitted what she already knew. "It's harder than I thought it would be. I didn't realize how many people here still think I'm worthless."

"Not worthless," she protested. "Just wild."

"Too wild to finish a job."

"I could help you. Put in a good word with my father. *He* could help you."

"Helping me is the last thing your father will want to do. Trust me on that."

"Look, he has his faults, believe me, I know. And I may not always agree with the way he and my mom do things, but if I ask him to, I'm sure he'll help. He can convince people you've changed..." Her voice trailed off, as if she'd become lost in thought. After a moment she said, "But it wouldn't help if people thought we were sleeping together, would it?"

He shook his head. "Nope."

"I see." Twisting in her seat, she shifted her leg back to the floor and turned as if to look out the window.

Watching her in profile, he could see her struggle to breathe and knew she was as affected by this intimacy as he was. He, too, twisted back in his seat. He shifted the car into first and executed a perfect three-point turn before he realized how tightly he was gripping the steering wheel.

Forcing his hands to loosen, he said, "After tonight, we probably shouldn't see each other again."

From the corner of his gaze, he saw her nod stiffly. "Of course."

As he pulled back onto the highway, the frustration eating away at him mingled with anger. Anger at himself.

Kissing Jessica had been a mistake. A big one.

Kissing her only made him yearn for all the things he couldn't have. And right now, she topped that list.

But he'd said it himself. She should never have to settle. And if the two of them ever did get involved, they'd both be settling. She'd have to settle for a man who wasn't good enough for her and he'd have to settle for being just the man she slept with. He didn't want either of them to make that sacrifice.

7

CUTIE PIES held the dubious honor of being Palo Verde's most popular restaurant. Located on Main Street, half a mile west of the county courthouse, between Hansen's Hardware, est. 1894, and Cash Down Bail Bonds, est. 1987. Every morning the local apple farmers came in to eat breakfast and to complain about the codling moths. By lunchtime, the place was full of judges and attorneys. Directly across the street sat the Palo Verde Hotel, the oldest continually operating hotel in the Northern Valley where, occasionally, celebrities stayed on their way through town to Lake Tahoe.

So while Cutie Pies made its money selling pastries, coffee and light lunches, its real trade was in gossip. Something every girl born and bred in Palo Verde knew quite well. But Jessica had spent her entire life being immune to the local gossip mill—not because her character was so sterling, but because she, quite frankly, had never done anything interesting enough to warrant gossip.

What Alex had said about the way the town viewed her had got her thinking. What if everyone did just see her as Judge Sumners's precious daughter? What if that was part of the problem? Maybe she'd been such a good girl all her life simply because everyone always treated her like a good girl.

That had certainly been true back in high school when boyfriends had always brought her home from dates at nine fifty-five and no one ever invited her to keg parties. But was it still true?

She'd never done anything to change the way people viewed her. Until now.

So when she walked into Cutie Pies just after ten o'clock on Saturday morning, she missed the way the restaurant went silent. She also ignored the inquiring look from Mrs. Frankfort, the sixty-year-old woman who ran Cutie Pies and taught the local tai chi class. Nor did she notice the pointed way the waitress asked her how her morning was when she ordered her latte and her low-fat oatmeal muffin. In fact she didn't notice anything until she turned to leave, her muffin tucked safely in a white paper bag, and saw Alex sitting at a far table with his brother Tomas, the remnants of bacon, eggs and a short stack sitting in front of them while they finished their coffee.

Her heart leaped at the sight of him, but her feet simply stopped moving. For a moment she just stood there, clutching her coffee and her little white bag.

She'd spent a lot of time the previous night thinking about their conversation in the car. Oh, he was attracted to her, all right. After that tequila shot, there was no way he could deny it. He wanted her.

Ultimately she was right back where she'd been before she'd gone to the bar. With one exception. Now she knew what she wanted. Alex. And she wasn't going to take no for an answer.

She had briefly considered his concerns about the town thinking he'd "corrupted her," but then dismissed them. He was wrong about that. She knew the people of this town much better than he did. Being with her would do far more to help his career than to hurt it.

She wanted—no, needed—to see where this thing with Alex would lead. She needed to know if she could ever be the kind of woman he couldn't walk away from.

He'd said she wasn't his type, but that could change. She'd just have to discover what his type was.

Determined to do just that, she crossed the diner to Alex's table. His expression tightened and he didn't look particularly pleased to see her. Tomas, however, immediately stood and asked her to join them.

As she lowered herself to one of the vacant chairs, Alex's frown deepened. "I don't think this is a good idea."

"It's just breakfast," Tomas said.

But Jessica knew what Alex meant. It wasn't a good idea because people might gossip about them, gossip that might hurt his chances of getting work. But Jessica had a plan to change all that.

Before she could reassure Alex, Tomas said, "I think I'll head back over to the house. You can stay here and finish your breakfast."

Before Alex could protest, she smiled brightly and said, "Thanks. That'd be great."

Alex scowled at her but waited until Tomas was out the door before leaning forward, propping his elbow on the table and saying in a low voice, "Jess, this isn't a good time."

"Don't worry. I have a plan."

He gazed at her from under half-lowered lids, clearly suspicious. "What plan?" he asked.

"I want you to remodel my kitchen." Feeling smug, she pulled her muffin from the bag, then refolded the paper flat and set the muffin on top.

"Why? A week ago you couldn't have cared less."

"A girl can't change her mind?"

"Let's just say I suspect your motives."

"Fine." She carefully peeled back the paper baking cup and broke off a piece of the crunchy top. "That's fair. But you need the money. And I need change."

"Pity? You're doing this out of pity?"

"I hadn't thought of it like that." She tilted her head to the side and considered that as she nibbled on her muffin. Then she firmly shook her head. "Well, it's not out of pity. Guilt? Maybe. But not pity."

"Guilt?"

"I feel bad for the way I treated you. Especially since you've been so nice to me."

He shifted uncomfortably in his chair, reaching for his coffee cup only to realize it was empty. He set it down with a loud thump and an irritated, "Humph."

A pretty young waitress zipped to his side with the coffeepot. "You want a refill, sugar?"

"Sure." But he didn't even look in the waitress's direction.

Jessica popped a bite of muffin into her mouth to hide her smile. Even when he was looking annoyed, it felt darn good to be the center of Alex's attention.

As soon as the woman left, he said, "I won't take your money. I don't care how guilty you feel."

"Ah, but you're the one who said I shouldn't settle."

Alex looked confused. "Huh?"

"Last night, you said I should never settle. Well, I've never liked the kitchen as it is now. It's boring and drab. So I want a new kitchen and I'm not going to settle for anything less than the best." She met his gaze with wide-eyed innocence. "You are the best, aren't you, Alex?"

He merely glowered at her, as if he knew exactly where this was going.

"Besides," she continued in a cheerful voice. "It's on The List."

"You expect me to believe that 'have your kitchen remodeled' is on *Saucy* magazine's list of '10 Things Every Woman Should Do'?"

She laughed, swatting at his arm. "No, silly. But number nine on The List is 'Shake Up Your Space.' I figure a kitchen remodel counts."

He sipped his coffee—black, she noticed—while studying her over the rim of the white ceramic mug. Finally he shook his head. "Can't let you do it."

"But—"

"If you spend all this money just because of some stupid list, you'll regret it in the end."

"I won't," she insisted. Planting her palms on the table, she leaned forward. "I need to do this."

"Why?"

"Because it's time. I haven't done a single reckless and irresponsible thing in my entire life."

He chuckled. "There's a sixty-thousand-dollar car parked out on the street that says differently."

"I bought it used and got a very good deal." Then she realized how ridiculous that sounded. "Okay, so maybe buying a used convertible and having my kitchen remodeled aren't the wildest things I could do, but it's a step in the right direction."

His lips curved in a sardonic smile, all trace of annoyance now gone.

"A very small step," she admitted. "Besides, if you're not working for me, no one will believe me when I recommend you for jobs."

"You're going to recommend me?"

"Naturally. You said it yourself. One job will lead to the

next. And I know a lot of people in this town. The right people."

"'The right people'?"

A flicker of disgust crossed his face and she wished she'd picked a different word. "The people who can help you get this job remodeling the courthouse. Look, the courthouse is classified as a historic building. That means everything about the remodel has to be approved by the historical society. The architect, the plans, the builder. Everything."

"Please tell me you're kidding."

"That's the bad news. The good news is, if you can win over the historical society, you're in."

"Trust me," he muttered, "that's not the good news."

"That's where I come in. I know these people. I can help. For example, see Mrs. Higgins over there?"

She pointed to a dour-faced, older woman seated at Cutie Pies's counter. He barely glanced in her direction. He knew exactly who Mrs. Higgins was. Of course, Jessica had no way of knowing that.

Mrs. Higgins had the plump figure of an archetypal grandmother, but the sour expression of an embittered piranha. No doubt she'd been trolling the waters here at Cutie Pies for hours looking for gossip to devour.

"This isn't going to work," he said warningly.

Mrs. Higgins pressed her lips into a disapproving frown as she studied first Jessica and then Alex. Her expression hardened into grim lines when Jessica waved her over, but Alex saw the ravenous gleam in her eye and knew she was more than happy for the excuse to observe them first-hand.

"Trust me," Jessica murmured through teeth clenched behind a tight smile. "Mrs. Higgins is the president of the historical society."

Mrs. Higgins stopped beside their table, her hands

clenching the handle of her wicker shoulder bag as Jessica introduced them. Alex didn't bother to stand to shake her hand, knowing she wouldn't extend hers to him.

"Mrs. Higgins, Alex is remodeling my kitchen. He's the owner of Moreno construction."

"Hmm." She raised an eyebrow in outright specula-tion. "Yes, I know who Alex Moreno is."

She looked at him as if he were no better than a cock-roach. One she very much wanted to squash. Under her disapproving, sanctimonious stare, he felt the remnants of his teenage rebellion stirring.

"I'm sure you do," he muttered as he stretched his legs out in front of him, slumping into the pose of a slacker as he draped his arm across the back of Jessica's chair.

He didn't take his gaze from Mrs. Higgins and did noth-ing to tamp down the resentment he knew simmered there. Even without glancing in Jessica's direction, he felt her stiffen and from his peripheral vision saw her shoot him a glance as she nudged him with her elbow.

Ignoring the undercurrents, Jessica plowed ahead. "Well," she said cheerfully, "then I'm sure you've heard about the great work his company did in L.A. and at the Hotel Mimosa in Marin County."

Listening to her rattle off his most recent jobs, he could barely keep himself from gaping at her in confusion. Ap-parently she'd looked up the references he'd included in that portfolio he'd given her that first day. She'd done her homework.

Mrs. Higgins didn't look impressed. He'd known she wouldn't be.

She sniffed loudly, finally pulling her indignant gaze from his face. Looking down her stubby nose at Jessica, she said, "Some people will hire just anyone." She turned as if to leave, then looked back over her shoulder and added, "Dear, you might want to check his references a little more closely. You'll find there are quite a few people who don't think he's up to par. Then again, maybe it isn't his skills in construction you're interested in."

As Mrs. Higgins swept from the restaurant, Alex had to clamp a hand onto Jessica's shoulder to keep her from catapulting out of her chair and storming after the woman.

"Let it go, Jess," he murmured, struggling to keep his expression blank, all too aware of the attention they'd attracted already.

"But—" she sputtered.

"Let it go."

"I've never seen her be so rude before! To imply I'd hired you just to sleep with you."

"You almost did," he pointed out. But he couldn't keep a smile from creeping onto his face. He felt absurdly pleased by her passionate defense of him.

She stiffened. "That's hardly the point. She treated you like you were slave labor or something. And not even good slave labor at that. What does she think this is, 1910?"

"Some people are just bigoted."

"Well, it's unacceptable." Suddenly she shot him a look of annoyance as she waved her hand in his direction. "And you. Don't even get me started on your behavior."

With a wince, he removed his hand from her shoulder. "My behavior?"

"Women like Mrs. Higgins put a lot of stock in propriety. You didn't even stand to shake her hand when I introduced you. Instead you just lounged there looking like some insolent delinquent."

"Trust me, I could have stood on my head to shake her hand and she wouldn't have treated me any differently."

"I don't believe that. I've known Mrs. Higgins my whole life and I've never seen her treat anyone like that. Why, I went to school with her son and—"

She broke off, a frown drifting across her face as she studied him. Her gaze open and assessing, her head slightly tilted in that way she had.

"No," she mused. "*We* went to school with her son. That's it, isn't it? Something happened between you and— What was his name?"

"Albert."

"Right. Albert." She nodded, as if remembering an important detail. "He's the one you got into that fight with right before graduation, isn't he?"

He nodded, his mind on autopilot taking him back to that day Albert—one of the boys who'd been picking on Jessica just a few weeks before—made some comment about her. Alex couldn't even remember what the comment had been now, but at the time it had made him furious.

Her frown deepened, as if she sensed there was much more he wasn't saying but wanted to. "Tell me about that day."

He shrugged and took a sip of his now-cold coffee. For the first time, he realized how coffee was like regrets, the longer you held on to them the colder and more bitter they became. "Nothing to tell. We fought. I got arrested. He didn't."

"There has to be more to it than that. Otherwise why would she still resent you?"

"Mrs. Higgins is a bigoted old fool. Sure, it doesn't help that I beat up her son, but even if that fight had never happened, to her I'd still be a dirty *mojadito*."

Jessica's expression tightened. "But that's not fair."

"Women like her never are."

She fumed for another minute before taking several deep breaths and making a visible effort to control her anger. "That's all the more reason to accept my job offer. Mrs. Higgins may be president of the historical society, but she's just one person. If you can't win her over, you'll have to work harder to convince the others you're right for the job."

Thinking back to the way she'd rattled off his last job, he asked, "What makes you so sure I am right for the job?"

She straightened, looking a little smug. "I did my research."

"Your research?"

"When you came to the house, you gave me that great portfolio about Moreno Construction. You didn't expect me not to read it, did you?"

He quirked an eyebrow. "After the way things ended that afternoon? I figured you'd just trash it."

"Well, I didn't. And after I knew what projects you'd worked on before moving back to Palo Verde, it was easy enough to poke around online a bit and get an idea of the kind of work you're capable of." She leaned forward, a spark of admiration in her eyes. "From what I read, the Hotel Mimosa was months away from being condemned. Without the work your company did, that beautiful Art Deco hotel would have been lost forever."

Alex found himself unable to tear his gaze away from hers. The awe in her eyes tugged at something deep inside him, made him feel worthy. Whole.

He forced himself to shake his head, breaking the hold her gaze seemed to have over him. "Ah, it was nothing. With a job like that, ninety percent of your success comes from finding good workers."

But she wouldn't let him off the hook. "But isn't that your job? Isn't that what makes you good at your job? Finding and managing the workers who can do quality craftsmanship at the right price? Isn't that what being a contractor is all about?"

"Mostly," he reluctantly admitted.

As she leaned back in her chair, she sent him a smug little smile that said she knew she had him exactly where she wanted him. "You know you aren't doing a very good job of selling yourself to me. You're supposed to be convincing me that being a contractor is hard work and that you are absolutely worth all the money I'm going to pay you."

"Jessica, I'm not going to let you hire me out of pity."

"It's not pity. I really want to do this. Besides, I can't recommend you unless you've worked for me," she insisted.

Or maybe he only wanted to believe she was insisting. In the end, he gave in way too easily.

She had nothing to lose except her reputation. He, on the other hand, had everything to lose. Working for Jessica could save his career or ruin it.

Losing his business worried him almost as much as losing his heart. But at least the business was still up for grabs. His heart, he feared, was already hers.

8

CONVINCING HIMSELF—not to mention his body—that he didn't want to take Jessica to bed would have been a lot easier if he didn't see her every morning. And every evening.

Every morning when he faced the intimacy of her finishing her breakfast, rinsing out her coffee mug or brushing her teeth, he swore to himself he'd be out of there long before she got home from work. Yet every evening, he hung around, filling the time with odd jobs, while he waited for the sound of her Beemer in the driveway.

Pathetic.

Not to mention stupid.

And idiotic.

And moronically pleased when she strolled through the door and said, "Oh, good, you're still here," which was what she always said when she walked in.

She always followed with some question about construction. Some new countertop material she wanted his opinion on or some question about why dovetail joints made drawers stronger.

Today, a few weeks after she'd first hired him, was no different.

"Oh, good. You're still here," she said before the front door even closed behind her. "I've got a question for you."

Setting aside the cordless drill he'd been using, he dusted off his hands. "Shoot."

"What kind of woman are you attracted to?"

"Huh?"

He'd been expecting, "What makes a better backsplash, tile or granite?" or "Could we move the stove next to the fridge?" This question he just hadn't seen coming.

"Huh?" he repeated stupidly, then added, "Um, why?"

"I've been thinking about the kind of men I usually date. Guys I've mostly met through work. But that hasn't been successful for me. Those guys have turned out to be big, boring duds. Which was the point of going out that night with Patricia."

As she spoke, she moved farther into the kitchen. She set her purse on the table and then propped her behind against the edge. With her hands braced on either side of her hips, she stretched her legs out in front of her.

"But obviously that didn't work, either," she went on. "Clearly, Paul Bunyan isn't the kind of guy I want to attract."

He tried to listen to her words, but all he could think about was her legs. She'd kicked off her shoes at the door, as she always did. Her legs were bare from the tips of her hot-pink toenail polish all the way up to where her skirt hit her midthigh.

"Maybe I shouldn't have let Patricia dress me. That must be where I went wrong."

Maybe he shouldn't have been here when she got home. That's where he went wrong.

He should have been at his house. Drinking a very big shot of Scotch. While taking a cold shower.

Maybe then he wouldn't be thinking about her legs.

Who was he kidding? He'd been fantasizing about

Jessica's legs nonstop for the past two weeks. Whether or not she was around seemed to have very little impact on how often he thought about her.

All of which might not have been so bad under other circumstances. If, for example, he knew she'd been fantasizing about him, too.

If he wouldn't ruin his career by taking her to bed and spending, oh, the next month or so with those kick-ass legs of hers wrapped around his waist.

Or if he wasn't terrified that when that month or so was up, she'd walk away and he'd be left pining for a woman he couldn't have.

Under the circumstances he had to stop acting like a lovesick boy around her. Which meant he had to get his mind off her legs and onto her conversation.

"The thing is," she was saying, "today during lunch, I was making a list of what I want in a guy. When I was done with the list, I realized, I don't want someone like Paul Bunyan or like any of the guys from work. I want someone like you."

Like him?

Or him?

His attention snapped from her legs back to her words. He searched her face, looking for answers.

A second later she realized how he'd interpreted her words. She stiffened, straightening away from the table, as a streak of red crept up her neck.

"Not you, of course. Just someone like you." She gestured emphatically.

"Right." Of course, she wasn't interested in him. Wasn't that what he'd been telling himself?

"I'm not actually hitting on you. I just—"

"I get it."

She looked away, clearly embarrassed.

His gut clenched, but not with lust. He didn't want her pity. He'd had enough pity to last him a lifetime.

Besides, it wasn't as if he was the only one affected by this attraction between them. Wiping his hands on his pants, he crossed the room to her. He didn't stop until he stood closer to her than he should.

His hands itched to touch her, but he forced his muscles to relax and his arms to hang limply by his sides. He wanted to remind her that she was just as vulnerable to this as he was.

And he needed to remind himself that he could be in the same room with her and keep his hands off her. That he still had some control where she was concerned. That this attraction—no matter how gut-wrenching—was nothing he couldn't handle and no more serious than any other mindless, sexual pull he'd ever felt.

"What was your question?" he asked, keeping his tone light, only a little curious.

"I, um…" She swallowed and he was close enough to hear the little sound her throat made when she did.

How the hell did this woman make swallowing sexy? Or maybe it was just all the things he could imagine in her mouth when she swallowed.

"Well, I was wondering—" Her hand fluttered up to her head and she tugged on a stray strand of hair.

Charmed by how flustered she seemed, he supplied, "You were wondering what kind of woman a guy like me finds attractive."

She laughed nervously. "Yes, exactly."

"Are you sure a guy like me is really what you want? You think you can handle a guy like me?"

Her laughter faded and again she swallowed hard. He wanted nothing more than to run his mouth down the length of her neck and trace those contracting muscles with his tongue.

"No," she admitted. "I'm not."

"The problem is, Jess, you take everything so seriously."

She nodded and he imagined she swayed toward him. "Yes," she breathed. "I mean, I do. But—"

"And guys like me, well, we don't take anything seriously at all."

"Well, you see—"

"Guys like me like to keep things light. Fun."

"Light and fun," she repeated as if making a mental list.

"Casual," he explained. "Playful. Maybe even a little wild."

"Got it. Casual and playful. Maybe wild."

Despite the fact that her mere nearness had his blood pressure skyrocketing off the charts, he couldn't help smiling.

"What?" she demanded, eyeing him suspiciously.

"Nothing."

"You're laughing at me."

He shook his head, but said, "Yes, I am." Then he couldn't keep it down any longer and he chuckled. "You look like you're itching to take notes."

"I don't know what you mean."

But she did. He could see it in her eyes. "You want to take notes. You want to brainstorm ideas of how to achieve 'fun' and 'playful' and then write them down in that Day-Timer you're always carting around."

She fidgeted, her gaze skittering nervously away from his, so that he knew he'd nailed it.

As soon as the phrase "nailed it" slipped into his mind, he thought instantly of what else he'd like to nail. Or rather, who.

God, he wanted her.

And before he knew it, he was touching her. Just running his knuckle down her cheek in a whisper-soft touch that left him aching for more. The way she arched into his caress didn't help matters. The way her eyelids drifted closed, as if she'd been hypnotized and was completely at his mercy.

As if he wasn't having a hard enough time keeping his hands off her as it was. As if he wasn't already aching to take her to bed, where it'd be far more complicated than plain ol' ordinary sex. Plain ol' ordinary mind-blowing sex.

Way to keep it light and casual.

He should have known that would come back to bite him in the ass.

She had to know how much he wanted her. But with any luck, he could keep her from knowing that his feelings for her were anything but casual.

"Come on, Jess," he murmured. "You know you're dying to do it."

Her breath caught and her eyes fluttered open. "Do what?"

"Make a list. Analyze how to be fun and playful."

Only when she recoiled slightly from his touch did he realize there was a hint of challenge in his voice.

For a second he thought she was going to back down. Or be offended. Instead her eyes lit up in response to the challenge.

"I can be fun and playful."

"Yeah, right."

"You think I can't be fun and playful? Because I can *be* fun and playful."

"Sure you can, princess."

"I can!" she insisted.

"Tell me one thing you've done that's fun and playful, let alone wild."

She opened her mouth then an instant later snapped it closed. Her lips pursed and her forehead furrowed. After a long moment she said, "I went out to the club with Patricia. That was fun. I let you do body shots off my neck. That was wild."

"Don't forget. I was there."

"So?"

"So, I know how much you hated being in that club. And that body shot you did was the most ladylike, least-wild body shot I've ever seen."

It had also been sexy enough to nearly blow the top of his head off, but she didn't need to know that. The pathetic truth was, if Jessica ever did shed that pristine, princess facade of hers and get really wild, he'd be in serious trouble.

"But—"

"That body shot may have been wild for you, but by most standards, that was tame. Some body shots are poured straight onto a woman's naked belly."

He trailed a finger down the outside of her sweater to her stomach. He heard her quick intake of breath, felt the quiver of her contracting muscles.

"The tequila runs across her belly, pooling in her navel. You have to run your tongue all over to get it. It's sticky and messy and very, very hot."

And just the thought of doing that to Jessica—of running his tongue all over her—made his blood pound. But worse than his own reaction was watching hers.

Her breath was coming fast and shallow now. Her eyelids at half-mast, her body swaying toward him. All he had to do was touch her and she'd dissolve into his arms.

Just a single touch and she'd be his.

"Alex, I—"

He shook his head, not giving her the chance to finish her sentence. If she was going to beg him to take her to bed, he couldn't bear to hear it. "Sorry, Jess. You're just not going to convince me you're the type who likes it messy."

But if they ever had sex, that's how he'd want her. Hot, sweating and begging. And very, very messy.

Yeah, right. As if that was ever going to happen.

"You're just not the type," he said.

His words seemed to snap her out of her stupor and irritation flashed in her eyes. "You don't know that," she protested.

"Sure I do. You've got 'good girl' written all over you. Everything from your sensible shoes to the conservative clothes to the way you wear your hair."

She looked down at her clothes, as if to ascertain what was wrong with them. "You don't like the way I dress?"

He loved the way she dressed. So tailored, so conservative. So unswervingly prim and proper. Yesterday it had been a navy pantsuit. Today, slim black pants and a pale pink sweater set.

And as always she looked incredibly classy. Undeniably rich.

Everything about her appearance should have reminded him how out of his reach she was. Instead, her outward appearance only reminded him of the passions that lurked beneath her prim-and-proper surface. Passions that nearly boiled over every time he touched her.

All the more reason not to touch her.

Reminding himself not to touch Jessica was becoming a full-time job. One that would be a hell of a lot easier if she'd leave him in peace.

Hoping to placate her and to end the conversation, he said, "Hey, there's nothing wrong with the way you dress."

She didn't look placated. Frowning, she looked down at her clothes. "Nothing wrong except that you don't like it."

"I didn't say that," he pointed out.

"You didn't have to." Her frown deepened as she plucked at the hem of her sweater. "You don't like my sweater set." She shrugged out of the button-up sweater and tossed it onto the kitchen chair. Extending her arms to show off the tank she wore underneath, she asked, "Better?"

With her shoulders bare and the bulky top sweater removed, she looked unbelievably appealing. Her sweater tank fit snug across her breasts and clung to her narrow waist, yet somehow it was her bare arms he couldn't pull his eyes away from. Her upper arms were smooth and tanned, her shoulders gently curved. And the strap of her bra peeked out from beneath her sweater, a swatch of dark purple nestled against a faint sprinkling of freckles.

From just that glimpse of purple his mind filled in a thousand details. Her bra would be one those little half push-ups jobs. The kind that cupped a woman's breasts and offered them to a man like the most decadent of treats. Satin and lace, but cut down almost to her nipples.

Knowing Jessica, she'd have matching panties. They'd be cut high over her thighs or maybe even—God help him—a thong.

He swallowed the groan he felt threatening to escape, but he couldn't manage to banish the image.

"What?" Jessica asked. "Is it really that bad?"

"Huh?" was all he could mutter.

"You hate it, don't you? You hate the way I dress."

"No," he said too quickly. "I just…"

But what the hell could he say without sounding like a pervert? *I was just picturing you in a thong, could you repeat the question?*

"Hate the way I dress," she finished for him. "And why wouldn't you? I dress like my mother. I dress like a spinster."

"A what?"

"An old maid. So will you help me or not?"

"Help you do what?" Had he missed part of the conversation when he was fantasizing about Jessica wearing a thong? Because he had no idea what she was talking about.

"Go shopping. Will you help me pick out new clothes?"

Shopping? For clothes? What a nightmare. "Why would I do that?" He tried to keep the horror from his voice, but wasn't sure he managed it.

She looked a little hurt, but after a minute she said, "Okay, then. I guess I'll go alone."

Thank God.

"I haven't been to that new Galleria in Roseville." She cocked her head to the side in that cute way she did when she was thinking about something. "I'm pretty sure they've got a Victoria's Secret."

Victoria's Secret? Ah, crap.

With an expression of guileless innocence, she added, "You know, I've never even been in a Victoria's Secret. Not even once."

Thank God. That meant the bra strap he'd glimpsed wasn't part of some mind-blowingly sexy getup. He could stop torturing himself imagining it.

Then she smiled gamely. "Well, there's a first time for everything."

He did not need to know that.

Again the image of her in nothing but a dark purple bra and thong flashed through his mind. He ruthlessly shoved the image to the deepest corner of his troubled psyche.

Okay, this wasn't too bad. As long as he didn't have to see her wearing anything from Victoria's Secret, he could handle it. Besides, he was already picturing her in her lingerie anyway. It couldn't get much worse than this, right?

But then it did.

"I wonder," she mused. "Do you think the Victoria's Secret stores sell clothes like the catalogs do? I've always wanted to wear clothes like that."

"You have?"

"Sure. All those short little skirts and cute little shirts." He must have looked worried, because she hastened to reassure him, "That's not to say I won't shop for lingerie, too, of course. If I'm lucky, I can buy everything I need there. What do you think?"

What did he think? He was a dead man, that's what he thought. She was going to go shopping and come back dressed like his hottest, wildest fantasy.

There was no way in hell he could let her shop alone.

"Okay, we'll go shopping. But there's no way—no way in hell—I'm going in to Victoria's Secret."

She smiled brightly. "Okay."

He just stared at her for a minute while a feeling of dread sunk in. How the hell had she gotten him to agree to go shopping with her? And why did he feel as if he'd been manipulated by a master?

9

YESTERDAY, Alex had teased her about the lists she kept in her Day-Timer. Oh, if only he knew...

Her Day-Timer was now devoted almost entirely to Operation Be Saucy, which somehow had shifted focus from The List to her plans to seduce Alex.

Career goals had fallen away in favor of lists of seductive skills she wished to master. Tips she'd gleaned from *Cosmo* now filled the pages where business appointments had previously been listed. And on the very first page was her Priority Action sheet on which she'd written the characteristics he wanted most in a woman. Fun, casual, light, playful and wild.

And if that's what Alex found sexy, then by golly, that was what she would be.

Saturday morning, as she dressed for their shopping trip in tailored shorts and a snug-fitted T-shirt, she felt like a general preparing for war.

Armed with knowledge and determination, she marched into battle.

She would get him into bed. She would get her passionate fling. If for no other reason than to prove to herself just how saucy she could be.

And whenever doubts arose within her that there might be another reason for wanting to sleep with Alex, she squashed them ruthlessly.

Of course, actually getting him to the mall had been challenging, and if the way he was dragging his feet was any indication, it might take quite a bit of manipulation to get his honest opinion on clothes.

"What about this store?" he asked as they made their way through the mall.

She looked in the direction he pointed, then shook her head in frustration. He'd been making stupid suggestions like this all morning. "That store sells purses and belts."

"So?"

"You can't seriously want to help me shop for accessories." She slowed her pace to let a pack of noisy teenagers drift past. Once they were out of earshot, she leaned in closer and whispered, "But if it's leather you're interested in—"

Before she could finish the thought, he gripped her elbow and propelled her past the store. His expression taut and unyielding, he muttered, "Forget it."

"You don't like leather?" she asked innocently. The possessiveness of his hand on her arm thrilled her, sending little fissures of pleasure racing through her body and giving her the courage to be bold. "Because it is kind of wild."

"I said forget it."

"I'm just trying to be open-minded."

The hand on her elbow tightened convulsively then loosened. Instantly she missed his touch and the loss only renewed her determination.

A short while later, when Alex was pulling another one of his what-about-this? tricks—this time outside a store that sold hiking boots—she spotted it.

There, in the window of one of the trendy boutiques, was the perfect outfit. The skirt was short, but not tight like the one Patricia had picked out. Instead it fell in soft waves around the thighs of the mannequin, its pale floral print the perfect counterpoint to the sweater paired with it. The cornflower-blue sweater tank was miles away from the shell she'd worn just the night before. The knit was just loose enough to reveal glimpses of skin beneath. It scooped low in front and in back. The store had paired it with comfy, low-slung sandals, a chunky string of beads and a floppy woven hat. Now that was a playful outfit.

It was beautiful and feminine. She'd usually avoided floral prints. They seemed to require a delicate femininity that she'd never quite mastered.

But she could see herself wearing it. In fact, she yearned to rush into the store to try it on.

But what would Alex say?

She glanced in his direction. His face registered a look of horror. Either he hated the outfit or he loved it. But which?

"What do you think?"

He swallowed. "I, um… It's a little small, isn't it?"

He loved it. Definitely.

"Come on, I'll try it on, then you can decide if it's too small." She grabbed his hand and pulled him toward the entrance.

Yanking stubbornly against her hand, he protested. "What about that store?" He pointed across the fairway. "Those clothes look bigger."

She glanced toward the store in question, then sighed in exasperation. "Of course those clothes are bigger. Those are maternity clothes."

"Oh. Right."

She took advantage of his momentary shock and dragged him the rest of the way into the store. Ten minutes later, she shucked her Princess Jessica attire and slipped into the flirty little skirt.

The second she walked out of the dressing room and saw Alex's expression, she knew this outfit would drive him crazy. This outfit would wear him down.

He'd been sprawled in the chair, his long, denim-clad legs stretched out in front of him, his knees apart, his shoulders slumped as he chewed mindlessly on a toothpick.

The instant he saw her, he stilled. To an observer, he might have seemed relaxed. Bored even. However, she felt the energy coming off him in waves. His expression as he watched her—so studied and intense—was as erotic as if he'd crossed the room and begun to undress her. His gaze traveled down the length of her throat. It skimmed over the crests of her breasts, just barely visible above the scooped neckline of the sweater, down the skirt, to where the hemline ended midthigh. Then his eyes stopped and he just stared at her bare legs.

She shivered under the intensity of his gaze and had to look away. Nervously, she scanned the store, sure that the tension between them was attracting attention. But as she glanced around, the store seemed empty.

Tucked into the back corner of the store, with towers of clothes shielding them from view, they were virtually alone. With that thought, a kind of reckless confidence propelled her toward him.

As she approached his chair, he straightened. With that toothpick clenched tightly between his teeth, he looked tense enough to bolt. Stopping just between his outstretched feet, she twirled around so the skirt belled around her legs. Peering at him from over her shoulder she asked, "What do you think?"

He swallowed, then pulled the toothpick from between his teeth and tossed it into the wastebasket by the chair. "It's short."

Pretending she hadn't quite heard him, she moved closer, perching on the arm of his chair, stretching her legs beside his. "Yes, but do you like it?"

He stiffened, but didn't move away from her. So she crossed her legs, and running one foot up the back of his calf, she pressed, "Is it sexy?"

He all but jumped out of the chair to get away from her. "You know what's sexy? Long skirts."

"Long skirts?" she asked seriously, trying her best to hide her triumphant amusement.

"Yep. Long skirts." He pulled something off a nearby rack and thrust it at her. "Long skirts and bulky sweaters. And layers. Lots of layers."

As he spoke he pushed first one piece of clothing and then another into her hands. Within seconds, she had a chest-high stack of clothes, none of which matched, most of it the wrong size.

She dropped the clothes into the chair he'd abandoned and crossed to where he was holding up an oatmeal-colored fishermen's sweater easily big enough for him to wear. She moved in close so that only the width of the sweater separated them. It was a bulky sweater, but not that bulky, and she could feel the effect she had on him.

Knowing she'd turned him on—in public, for goodness' sake—nearly drove her crazy. "You don't really find this sweater sexy, do you?"

"Sure I do," he replied too quickly.

"It's big," she pointed out.

"That's what's sexy about it."

He was grasping at straws now. He had no idea what he was talking about. And she'd bet he hadn't even glanced at the sweater in question. Well, that was fine by her.

"I suppose," she said innocently, "that you're going to tell me that this sweater is sexy not because of how much it reveals but because of how much it hides."

"Sure."

"Because when a woman's wearing a sweater like this, the man has no idea what she's wearing underneath."

"Right. Exactly." But he sounded a little less sure now, anticipating her next words.

"Sure, maybe she's wearing a plain white cotton bra and panties." At the word "panties," his gaze darkened and her pulse kicked up a notch in response. "But maybe not." She could hardly believe how bold he made her feel. "Maybe she's wearing some sexy little lingerie set she picked out when you weren't watching. Or maybe she's wearing nothing at all."

"Nothing?" His voice sounded strained to the limit.

She nodded, smiling. "That's one of the things on the list."

His gaze darkened and he swallowed visibly. She felt an intoxicating surge of feminine power as he lowered his head as if to kiss her, but she stepped back before he could.

Keeping her tone light, despite the trembling need she tried to hide, she folded the sweater and said, "You're right, I think I will buy this sweater. Good choice."

It took all her control to walk away from him when— frankly—she would have preferred to pull him into the dressing room with her and have her way with him.

He might even have been agreeable to a little tryst in the dressing room, but she wanted more than that. She wanted him all to herself and she wanted all night long. No distractions, no complications, just the two of them.

And he wanted it, too. He just didn't want to admit it.

10

SOMETIMES A MAN should know when to keep his mouth shut. It was a skill Alex had never quite mastered.

Apparently the other day when he'd told Jessica he liked playful women, she'd taken it as a personal challenge. Big shock there. Now, as he packed up his tools after a long day tearing out her upper kitchen cabinets, she was treating him to a lengthy diatribe about all the fun and playful things she'd done in the past year.

"I didn't—"

He shook his head ruefully, cutting her off. "Whether you're fun and playful or not, being in the bar wasn't fun for you."

"But—"

"And that body shot definitely wasn't playful." To make matters worse, she was wearing the sweater he'd picked out. The damn thing was driving him crazy. Just as she'd predicted, he couldn't stop wondering what she had on underneath it. "You did that only because you hate to back down from a challenge."

"That's not true."

"Come on, Jess. I was there. If you hadn't been backed into a corner, there's no way you would have let me do that body shot."

She frowned. "So what you're saying is that men like

you are attracted to women who do that kind of thing. To women who do body shots in bars?"

Before Jessica? No, he hadn't been. But since that night? Hell, since then, all he could think about was how she'd looked perched on the edge of that bar. How her body had felt beneath his hands and how her skin had tasted. That was, when he wasn't wondering what she had on under that freakin' sweater.

All of which he knew he should damn well keep to himself. But he didn't. He was tired of her pushing his buttons. Tired of keeping his mouth shut. And before his common sense could kick in, the instincts he'd been suppressing for weeks now flared to life and took over.

"Am I attracted to women who do body shots in bars? No, not really." Relief flickered across her face, until he kept talking. "But if I'm going to drink tequila at all, I'd rather drink it off a woman's skin, not out of a glass." Her eyes widened at his words. And he couldn't help noticing how the color darkened, making them an even deeper blue. "I won't lie to you, Jess, ever since having you up on that bar that Friday night, I've been thinking about getting you up there again."

She opened her mouth to speak, but this time he was the one who stopped her.

"But I've never been much of an exhibitionist. So next time, it wouldn't be in a bar, it'd be private and preferably close to a bed. Just the two of us."

He was standing so close to her he could see every flicker of emotion that crossed her face. He saw the many layers of her heated response. The interest. The desire. The anticipation. Even the flicker of trepidation.

He saw her struggle to bring her reaction under control, but took pleasure in knowing it was no easier for her than it was for him.

She may want him, but he didn't doubt for a minute that all her desire was tied back to the damn list. For her, he was convenient. She wanted a passionate fling and thought he could give it to her.

To make matters worse, she was totally focused on the "passionate" part of passionate fling. But all he could think about was the "fling."

Flings, passionate or not, were short-lived. A week, maybe two, if he was lucky. But he wanted so much more from her than that.

He chuckled at the irony. "Maybe you're right. Maybe you could handle fun and playful just fine. Maybe it's the pure, gut-wrenching lust you've got a problem with."

He didn't know why he'd said it. Maybe hoping to scare her off. But he'd forgotten that nothing scared Jessica.

To his amazement, she didn't even look away. "Maybe you're right. Maybe that's part of the problem." Her nervous laughter told him she wasn't as unflappable as she appeared. "Maybe I do keep my distance from—as you put it—the pure, gut-wrenching lust. Or maybe the problem is that men always assume women like me just aren't interested in the pure, gut-wrenching lust."

This time, he was the one to back away. It was just a half step and not nearly enough distance to give him back his perspective, but just enough to keep him from reaching out to her.

It did not, however, keep her from closing the space between them. In an instant she was standing so close that her body was almost plastered against his. Her hand was hot on his arm as her lips tilted up to him.

Suddenly all the reasons why he shouldn't kiss her vanished. All the arguments against getting involved with her that had been running through his head for weeks now just disappeared. The only thing he could think about was how sweet and hot she'd taste and how good she smelled and how he wanted more than anything to touch her. And to keep on touching her.

He might have had the strength to resist her, but before he could muster any of that strength, she pressed her body to his. With one hand in his hair, she pulled his head down to hers and she strained onto her toes to kiss him.

The kiss was hot and deep. Pure gut-wrenching lust.

He tried to back away from her, but she followed him step for step until he felt the counter at his back. Only then did he give in completely, opening his mouth to her persistence. As soon as he felt her tongue dart between his lips and the sweet suction of her kiss, he knew he was a goner.

Why had he even been fighting it?

He ran his hands down the length of her, reveling in the feel of her soft curves beneath the bulk of her sweater. A sweater that looked demure, but didn't hide the heartstopping body beneath.

Besides, he knew the truth about Jessica.

For all she seemed like the perfect good girl, that was an act. Just beneath the surface lurked a fun and passionate woman who'd never be light and casual.

He only hoped she didn't see beneath his surface as easily as he saw beneath hers. Because she'd know that he didn't want light and casual. He only wanted her.

He wanted more than a passionate fling. He wanted more than just her body. He wanted her heart and her soul. And he wanted them forever.

ALEX WAS WRONG. This wasn't pure gut-wrenching lust. It was pure heaven.

Never before had a simple kiss made her ache with

need. Never before had the feel of a man's hands on her hips made her weak in the knees. Made her ears ring, for goodness' sake.

At least, she thought it was his kiss that made her feel that way. But maybe she was weak in the knees because she'd missed lunch. Maybe the ringing in her ears was just…

Just his cell phone.

She released her hold on him and tried to step away. He didn't let her go, but lifted his head and stared at her for a heartbeat, his eyes glazed with passion.

"Your phone," she said numbly, trying again to step back.

"Let it go."

Before he could lower his mouth to hers again, she pressed her palm against his chest and stopped him. "That's your work phone. You should answer it."

He looked ready to argue with her, but instead he yanked the phone from his hip and jabbed the button. "Moreno here."

Wanting to give him privacy for the phone call, she tried to pull away, but he kept his arm anchored firmly across her shoulders. Cradled against his chest, with the strength of his arm holding her firmly against him, she could only rest her head against his shoulder and relax.

At least she tried to relax. Tried to calm herself and her reaction to him. But she was all too aware of the tensing muscles of his chest and the thudding of his heartbeat beneath her hand. More than anything, she was aware of her own reaction to him.

Of the heat slowly burning its way through her. Of the heavy weight of her breasts and the need she felt to press them against his chest, as if that could ease the desire driving her wild.

She tried to ignore the half of the conversation she could

hear, but she caught a word or two. The name of a street not far from her house. The name Veronica. Information that barely registered in her mind before being helplessly dislodged when he slipped his foot between hers.

Her legs automatically parted, allowing his thigh to slide up to the juncture between her legs. Squeezing her eyes closed, she concentrated on not moving, even though her every instinct urged her to rock her hips forward, to rub herself against him, to ease the heaviness building inside of her.

His arm tightened across her back as the muscles beneath her hands tensed. She sensed him struggling for control and that only made it harder on her. She felt as if her skin were on fire and the only way to extinguish that fire was to touch Alex. To pull his shirt from the waistband of his jeans and to rub her palms over the muscles of his chest. To rid herself of her clothes and to rub her skin against his. To rip the phone from his hand, toss it aside and have her way with him this instant.

But she couldn't do that.

Enough of his conversation made it through the fog of her desire for her to realize this was most definitely not a personal call. This Veronica wanted him to come by to give her an estimate. And—unless she was mistaken— he'd just agreed to be there within the hour.

Tapping down an irrational surge of jealousy, Jessica tried to muster up some happiness for him. He didn't need to tell her what this next job could mean for his business. He'd mentioned more than once how much trouble he was having finding work.

And she knew how important making his business a success was to him. Until he did, he'd never really believe he was good enough.

With a sigh, she let her head drop back to his shoulder,

her aching need for him cooling with the realization that—whatever else happened tonight—she would not be ripping the phone from his hands, tearing his clothes from his body and having her way with him.

At least not tonight. And maybe not ever.

A few seconds later he ended his call and tossed the phone aside. Since the last thing she wanted was to listen to him make excuses about why he couldn't stay, she beat him to the punch.

"I know. You have to go."

He squeezed her shoulder again, resettling her against his body. "Thanks."

"For what?"

"For understanding."

Funny, she didn't feel understanding. She felt frustrated and annoyed. Mad at herself for wanting more than he could give and mad at him for not being able to give it.

Not wanting to sound as irrational as she felt, she still couldn't keep herself from muttering, "Why does this have to be so hard?"

He chuckled. "You want a scientific explanation?"

With the length of his erection nuzzled against her hip, she had no trouble interpreting his innuendo. A strangled laugh escaped her lips. "That's not what I meant."

"I know."

She felt his sigh ruffle the hair at her temple. This time, when she pulled away, he let her go. A few shuffling, backward steps later, she propped her hips on the opposite counter.

Even though several feet now separated them, her body still trembled with need and she felt the heat of his gaze on her skin as potently as she'd felt his touch.

"Look, I know your business is the most important

thing in your life right now. And I know you think getting involved with me will be bad for your business…"

She let her words trail off, watching him carefully to gauge his response.

Deny it, she thought. *Contradict me. Tell me I'm wrong. Tell me I'm crazy.*

But he offered her no reassurances. Instead, he met her gaze with a steady silence that spoke more loudly than words could. As far as he was concerned, a relationship between the two of them was still out of the question.

Not that she wanted to be more important to him than his business.

If this was just a fling, then she certainly couldn't expect to be the center of his universe. She couldn't expect him to make sacrifices for her.

And this *was* just a fling. Short term. No emotional commitment. Very *Saucy.*

That's what she wanted. Wasn't it?

Pushing her confusion and doubts aside, she said, "So, tell me about this job."

He hesitated, then said, "It's just down the street from you. A neighbor who saw the sign I put in your front yard, actually."

"But what kind of job is it?" she pressed. "A remodel? An addition? What?"

Instead of answering right away, he turned his back to her and started gathering up his tools. "Sort of an addition."

"'Sort of an addition'? What's that supposed to mean?"

"They want to add on an outdoor living space."

He loaded up the rest of his tools without once meeting her gaze. He was dissembling, which just wasn't like him. So she kept pushing. "An outdoor living space? Do you mean a sunroom?"

"No, not a sunroom. More of a—" He winced. "A deck."

"A deck?"

The tinge of red in his cheeks told her he was embarrassed—maybe even ashamed—by the job. And just like that, the intimacy between them evaporated. Damn, she should really learn to bite her tongue.

Torn between wishing she could take back the words and wanting to make him understand her meaning, she said, "Alex, you're a general contractor. I wouldn't have thought building decks was the kind of job you did."

His jaw tightened, a sure sign he thought she was overstepping some boundaries. "It's a job."

"Sure, it's a job, but I've seen the work you're capable of. You should be remodeling historic buildings, not building decks."

"I'm not in a position where I can turn down work."

"And if you get a reputation for building decks and fences, instead of remodels and construction, you never will be."

"I can't be that picky. It's good, honest work. There's nothing wrong doing manual labor."

"Well, sure." Her voice rose with the heat of the argument. "If that's your job, but you can do more than that."

"My parents do manual labor. They have for over thirty years now. It's how they put food on the table."

Great. And now she'd inadvertently insulted his family.

Resisting the urge to bury her face and groan, she said, "I'm sorry. I didn't mean—"

But he didn't give her the chance to backpedal. "I'm not ashamed of the way they made a living. And I'm not too proud to do the work they did."

His voice was thick with emotion. Emotions more complicated than just his anger of her inadvertent slip.

Maybe he actually was *ashamed of how they'd made their living*.

Feeling a bit like she was approaching a wounded bear, she crossed to him and placed a hand on his arm. She spoke with a soft voice, determined to make him understand. "I truly didn't mean to insult your parents."

He looked up at her, studying her for a long minute before nodding.

"There isn't anything wrong with doing manual labor. I admire the people who make their living that way. They work harder than I do, for less money. You're right to be proud of the work your parents did. But there's nothing wrong with wanting more than that."

She wanted him to know that she understood his mixed emotions, even if he didn't understand them himself. "Besides, you told me yourself that your parents wanted a different life for you. How do you think they'd feel knowing you were thinking of wasting your time on a job like this?"

For a second she thought she might have swayed him, but then he looked away from her and pulled his arm out from under her hand. "It's not wasted time if I'm paid for the work."

"But—"

"I'll be doing that job over the weekends." He unplugged an extension cord and began to loop it from his hand to his elbow. "You don't have to worry that it'll take time away from this project."

He was being so stubborn it made her want to howl with frustration. "You know that's not what I'm worried about. I couldn't care less when you finish this job. But what about your bid for the renovations on the county courthouse? If you're spending all your time building decks, when are you going to work on that?" He said nothing, but the grim set of his jaw told her everything she needed to know. "Oh, I see. You're not going to work up a bid for the courthouse, are you?"

"I didn't say that."

"You didn't have to." Shaking her head, she turned to leave the kitchen, only to spin back to face him a few steps later, unable to leave it alone. "I can't believe you let that woman bully you like this."

"If you're talking about Mrs. Higgins, I didn't let her—"

"Excuse me, but that's exactly what you did. The last time we talked about it, you were still planning on turning in a bid. You weren't optimistic, but you were going to do it. But all it took was a few thinly veiled insults from that meddling old cow and all of sudden you back down?"

"That meddling old cow—as you put it—has the power to veto any bid I turn in. I'm not going to waste my time working up a bid I know I don't have a shot at winning."

"So what are you going to do instead? Waste your time building decks?"

"It's a job," he repeated, his voice strained and slow, a sure sign he was as tired of this argument as she was.

But she still couldn't let it go. Not when she *knew* she was right.

"Sure it's a job, but it's a job that's beneath you. Look, don't get me wrong, there's nothing wrong with building decks or doing manual labor, but you are capable of so much more." She gestured to the work he'd done in her kitchen. "I've seen the work you can do."

He frowned. "How—"

"I went online and downloaded the before-and-after

pictures of the hotel you worked on in Marin County," she admitted, waving aside his question, hoping to move on quickly so that admission didn't make her sound like a stalker. "You did amazing work on that hotel. But then, it wasn't just you doing the work, was it? You admitted you had a whole crew working on that project. Not to mention subcontractors. Having that kind of job in your portfolio should have made your career."

Though there was a glint in his eyes warning her she was pushing too hard, he said nothing. The look itself almost stopped her. But she'd already angered him. What harm would it do to finish proving her point?

"But instead of parlaying that success into another career-defining job, you decided to move back here. Ostensibly to prove to the people of this town that you've changed."

That—finally—got a rise out him. "'Ostensibly'?"

But she ignored him and went on. "That you've made something of yourself. But that isn't what you've done. Instead of going after the one job that will prove exactly that, you're satisfied with remodeling kitchens and building decks."

"'Ostensibly?'" he repeated, his tone rising in irritation.

"Yes, ostensibly. You don't seriously think you're going to impress anyone building decks, do you? If you really want to show these people what you're capable of, you have to get that job remodeling the courthouse. You have to—"

This time, he cut her off, crossing to her in a few short steps and wrapping his hands around her upper arms. "You think I don't want this job? You think I haven't thought of this?" He tugged her closer, so that they were almost touching. "I *have* thought about it. Of course I want this job. But since I moved back here, it's been obvious there are some things I just can't have." He sucked in a deep breath. "Sometimes you just have to let it go."

And just like that, he released his hold on her.

Before he stepped away, she reached for him. "Sometimes you have to fight for what you want. You can't settle for what people are willing to give you. You can't just give up."

"I'm not giving up. I've still got work."

"But you're the best person for that job. You know you are. You can't settle for any less than you deserve. You just can't. Besides, if you're satisfied with whatever crappy and demeaning jobs the people in the town deign to throw your way, then the only thing you're proving to them is that they were right about you. That you really are good for nothing. Nothing important at least."

He jerked his hand out from hers. "I need to go. If I'm late, I won't get the job. Then it won't matter whether or not you think it's beneath me."

As he turned away from her, she saw that his gaze was dark and shuttered. His expression completely closed.

Dang it, why did she always manage to say the wrong thing around him?

"Alex, I didn't mean—"

She reached out to him again, but he neatly avoided her touch and cut her off at the same time. "What does it matter to you, anyway? What difference could it possibly make to you what this town thinks of me? Surely you're not worried about my reputation rubbing off on yours? Because that was the idea all along, wasn't it? That being with me would bring you down to earth a little bit. That sleeping with me would show people how wild you really are. Hell, I'd think the fact I'm a manual laborer would only enhance that."

"I just thought—"

"What? That because we kissed you had the right to stick your nose into my personal business? Well, you were wrong. That was just about sex, Jess. Nothing more."

"But—"

"See, that's exactly what I meant."

"Meant?" she asked numbly.

"About you. You take everything much too seriously, princess. You just don't know when to keep things light and casual."

11

THE FIGHT with Alex left Jessica in a sour mood. She'd told herself all along that all she wanted from Alex was a few nights of passion. And last night she'd nearly had it. She had nearly worn him down. If it hadn't been for that dang phone call, she might now be basking in some serious afterglow. Instead they'd fought.

If anything, she should be upset that her plans to seduce Alex had once again gone astray. Instead, it was the fight that nagged at her. He'd all but told her to butt out of his life.

Why did that bother her? She'd been telling herself all she wanted from Alex was a few nights of passion.

He'd made it clear he wanted nothing more from her than a light, fun fling. Which was all she really needed to check number one off The List. So why did she suddenly feel sick to her stomach?

She tried to bury her doubts while at work, tried to mask her fears. And she might have managed to do it, if she hadn't stopped by the break room to check her mail and run into Peter—Handheld Technologies's resident lothario.

She normally managed to avoid Peter altogether, since he worked in the marketing department. He'd also never before sought her out, which was fine by her—especially if even a fraction of the sleazy rumors were true.

But today, Peter's gaze skimmed the length of her body suggestively before returning to her face. "Hi."

She made a nonsensical comment on the weather while feigning interest in a United Way donation request, then headed for the door. She almost made it before he stopped her.

"Jessica, hold up a minute."

You've got to be kidding. Letting disdain drip from her voice, she said merely, "Yes?"

"I..." He smiled broadly at her, but clearly had to search for a topic of conversation. "I've been having some problems with the Carson account."

Assessing him through narrowed eyes, she looked for any hint of what he really wanted. Surely he wasn't going to hit on her. "I haven't worked on the Carson account in over three months," she said pointedly. "I was taken off the team when I went to Sweden. I can't possibly be any help."

"Right." He nodded, obviously looking for an excuse to keep her here. "Well, sure, but...you're so good, I bet you remember all about the account." He slanted her a greasy smile. "You probably still have some great insights. Have you eaten yet? Maybe we could talk about it over lunch."

"It's three-thirty. So, yeah, I've eaten lunch." She turned to leave, but he fell into step beside her as she made her way to her office.

"What about dinner?"

"What about you leaving me alone?"

He stopped her, grabbing her arm so she had to turn and face him. "Come on, Jessica, you can drop that good-little-girl charade you've got going." He ran his hand up and down her arm in a way he no doubt thought was provocative. "You don't have to pretend with me."

She shook his hand off her arm. "Pretend?"

"To be all prim and proper."

"I don't know what you're talking about." Her tone still dripping with disdain, she could only hope it hid her trepidation. She was afraid she knew exactly what he was talking about.

"You and Alex Moreno. Oh, come on, Jessica, surely you didn't think people wouldn't find out."

"There is nothing going on between Alex and me." Not that she hadn't been trying. "We're just friends."

"Don't be naive." The hard note of cynicism in his voice grated her nerves. "Guys like Alex aren't *friends* with women."

"What do you mean, guys like Alex? You don't even know him."

"I know all about him. I've heard all about his wild past, picking fights and getting into trouble. Causing—"

"That was in the past. He's grown up now. He's an adult. A concept you, apparently, haven't grasped."

"Keep telling yourself that."

"What's that supposed to mean?"

Peter shrugged but there was no hiding the insulting implication in his gaze. "It just seems to me that if a guy like that is fooling around with you, he must be doing it just to prove he can. It must be quite a thrill for someone like him to knock a prissy little good girl like you off her pedestal."

For a moment she merely floundered in her indignation. Finally she narrowed her eyes to a glare and stepped closer to him. "What bothers you, Peter? The fact that I'm slumming? Or the fact that I didn't come to you to go slumming?" As he stood there gaping mutely at her, she raked him with a dismissive stare. "I decided that if I was going to climb down off my pedestal, I wanted to do it with a real man."

Then she turned on her heel, walked the rest of the way to her office and waltzed inside before closing the door with a simple click. The second the door shut behind her, she sank against it.

What a mess. What a nasty, icky mess.

Of course, she'd always known Peter was a jerk, but today he'd sunk below even her expectations of him.

But that was the least of her worries. Peter may be a jerk, but what if he was right? After all, there was a certain logic to that. Alex had told her over and over again that she wasn't his type. What if Alex was attracted to her just because of the thrill of—what was the phrase Peter had used?—knocking a "prissy little good girl" like her off her pedestal?

Worse still, Peter's accusations actually hurt. A sign she was way more emotionally involved than she'd ever meant to be. A sign she might even be falling—

No. She was *not* falling in love with Alex.

Saucy women did not fall in love this easily. This was just a fling. Or rather, it would be if she could ever get Alex to cooperate, damn it!

JESSICA WAS HOME early. He heard her car pull into the driveway at a quarter to four. After glancing out the window to verify that it was her car, he crossed to the kitchen sink to wash the dust from his hands. When she still hadn't walked through the front door a few minutes later, he looked out the window again.

He found her sitting in her car, her arms draped on the steering wheel, her forehead propped on her arms. At first he thought she might be crying, but when she straightened, he saw a deep frown marring her forehead.

Finally she threw open the door to the Beemer and

stalked up the steps. Anger delineated every line of her body. Even through the glass, he could hear the tapping of her shoes on the pavement, followed by the sound of the key in the lock, the door clicking open. He waited for the resounding slam that was sure to follow. And waited.

He'd lived with women for most of his life. Every woman he'd ever known slammed doors when she was angry. But apparently Jessica, even well and truly pissed, did not.

After setting down the cordless screwdriver, he made his way to the living room, only to stop short when he found her leaning against the closed front door. Head tipped down, eyes closed, a frown entrenched on her face.

Dressed in a charcoal-gray dress and black jacket, black heels, her hair was pulled back into a twist, the way she always wore it. Her makeup pale and minimal. A single pearl dangled from the silver chain around her neck.

Like the pearl, Jessica was beauty without flash. Classiness almost to the point of delicacy. Lovely, but frail.

Then her eyes popped open.

No, not frail. Contained.

"You're home early."

"I wasn't getting any work done." She propelled herself away from the front door. Her skirt was tight enough to keep her steps small, but with each stride, her heels tapped crisply against the tile in the entry hall. She walked past him toward the bedroom, reaching to the back of her neck to open the clasp of her necklace.

"Wanna talk about it?"

She stilled, then spun on her heel, the necklace hanging from her fingertips. "Talk about what?"

"Whatever's got you so pissed off."

One perfectly sculpted blond eyebrow arched. Her chin

bumped up a notch and she managed to look down at him from across the room. "I don't know what you're talking about."

"Whatever." Angry women, he knew how to deal with. Chilly ones were something else entirely. So she made it three more steps down the hall before he added, "Your highness."

Her head snapped back around and she glared at him, her gaze no longer dismissive but openly confrontational. "What?"

That was better. If he diverted her anger toward him, he wouldn't worry about her snapping from the strain of keeping it under control.

"You were doing your princess impersonation. I just thought I'd play along."

She opened her mouth to shoot back a reply, but instead of skewering him, she sighed. "Sorry."

Propping his shoulder against the doorway between the kitchen and the living room, he asked again, "So, do you want to talk about it?"

She shook her head and he thought that would be the end of it. But instead of disappearing down the hall, she mimicked his stance, propping her shoulder against the doorway on the opposite side of the room.

"Tell me something, Alex, do you think of me as a good girl?"

"I'm not sure I know what you mean."

"I mean, do you think I'm a good girl?" She pushed away from the doorway and shrugged out of her jacket as she moved toward him. With each step, her hips swayed with the rhythm of her words. "A prissy, prim and proper good little girl."

He'd been right. Jessica was itching for a fight and there

was a seductive, sexual edge to her anger. Despite himself, he felt his body respond to her.

Since she was still waiting for an answer, he prevaricated. "I wouldn't say that."

"But you do think I'm a good girl, don't you?"

"What's your point, Jess?"

By now, she was standing directly in front of him, mere inches away.

"You think I'm a good girl. 'A princess,' you said. It's one of the things you find attractive."

"I—"

"I know you're attracted to me. I know you feel the same pull I do. Don't deny it, Alex." There was a pleading note in her voice. She all but begged him.

"I wasn't going to," he admitted.

Her eyes flashed with something like triumph. "So the only question, then, is, are you attracted to me just because you think I'm a good girl?"

Ah, so that's what this was about.

He had no idea what had brought this on, but he had to be honest with her.

"I do think you're a good girl, Jessica. But I also think you're more complicated than that. I think you're smart and funny. I think you're hardworking, and I admire that, because you've got enough money you don't have to be. I think—"

"The question is—" she cut him off, walking her fingers up his chest "—whether you're only attracted to the good girl in me. Because I'm tired of being good."

Her fingers traced distracting patterns on his chest, making it impossible for him to even think straight. She gazed up at him with those unbelievably blue eyes of hers and he felt something in him snap.

"I want to be naughty, Alex. I want to feel—what was it you called it?—pure gut-wrenching lust? That's what I want."

He struggled to get his body's response under control, but her fingers were driving him crazy. He backed away from her touch, trying to put some distance between them, but she followed him step for step until he felt himself bump into the kitchen counter behind him. He grabbed her hand in his to stop their progress across his chest.

"Jess, I don't know what brought this on, but with the mood you're in this would be a mistake. You'd—"

"I won't regret it. Promise. It's what I want. It's what we both want."

With her hand enclosed in his, she stepped closer to him, eliminating the space between them, trapping their joined hands between their bodies. She tugged their hands down so his knuckles brushed against her breast.

Her nipple puckered and hardened beneath his touch. Her eyelids drifted closed as her body arched into his.

"Come on, Alex, you've been a bad boy all your life. Stop trying so hard to be good."

12

SHE KNEW the instant his control snapped. One second, he'd been perfectly still, practically frozen. The next, she felt his hands everywhere. He grasped her around the waist and lifted her to the countertop.

His every touch sent shivers of pleasure through her body. The cool air against her skin, the heated touch of his rough and calloused fingertips. His were the hands of a worker. Strong. Used. Lived in.

She ached to feel them on other parts of her body. On her neck, her breasts. Between her legs.

She'd never wanted a man the way she wanted Alex. Never ached for a man this much. Never felt so incomplete without him.

She linked her calves behind his waist, pulling him even closer. Her dress bunched up almost to her crotch and the denim of his jeans scraped against the sensitive skin of her inner thighs. The sheer eroticism of having him between her legs had her gasping for breath. But knowing he wanted her as much was even more compelling.

He nuzzled her cheek, his mouth sliding slowly across her skin. When his lips finally met hers, his kiss was hotter and wetter than any she'd ever had before.

Heat and desire spiraled through her blood, pooling low in her gut and between her legs, making her ache with need. As if he knew exactly what she wanted, he grasped her hips and pulled her to him. She groaned as her tender flesh came into contact with him.

His penis was hard beneath the fabric of his jeans. Through the delicate silk of her panties she felt the ridge of his zipper and the heat of his erection.

Suddenly desperate to feel his skin against hers, her palms tingled as she tugged at the buttons of his plaid shirt.

The flesh she uncovered was hardened by years of manual labor, the muscles clearly defined. She couldn't help but marvel at the way they bunched and twisted beneath her hands.

His skin—so much darker than hers—was smooth except for a sprinkling of fine, coal-black hair across the vee of his chest.

No other man she'd ever been with had a chest like this, so dark and so hard. So used by life. Only Alex earned his living with these muscles, used them to destroy and to create. Only Alex.

The differences between their bodies fascinated her. His strength to her softness. The hard planes of his body to her curves. His dark tan to her pale skin. No one else so defined her by all that she wasn't. Only Alex.

Then she felt his hands on her back, at her zipper. He tugged it down in one smooth motion, baring her skin to his touch. She gasped as she felt his work-roughened fingers trace the length of her spine. Wanting to be closer to him, she struggled to free her arms from the dress.

When he tugged impatiently at her bra strap, she gently nudged his hands aside and undid the front clasp herself.

As she tossed her bra aside, she couldn't help but revel in his expression. His face was taut with desire as he looked at her bare breasts. For the first time in her life, she felt proud of her body, exhilarated by a man's reaction to it.

Once her arms were free, she braced her palms on the counter and lifted her hips as he pulled the dress down her legs and tossed it aside.

Sitting there, nearly naked on her kitchen counter, her breath coming in short bursts and her skin prickling against the cool air, she shivered, not from the cold but with anticipation, as he traced a single fingertip down her chest, then around her nipple. He brushed his thumb across the peak, his gaze focused intently on her response. She arched her back as her nipples hardened, all but begging for his touch.

"Please…" she heard herself gasp. Beg. "Please, Alex…"

His lips twitched. In an instant he went from so incredibly serious, to amused. "I like hearing you beg," he teased. "I could get used it."

So could I, she realized. Out loud, she said, "Please, Alex. Don't make me wait."

And he didn't. Ducking his head, he pulled her nipple into his mouth. She was nearly undone by the feeling of him suckling her breast, by the sight of his dark hair against her pale skin and his lush, sensual mouth on her breast.

Her legs clenched automatically around his hips, pulling him even closer. She bucked off the counter, rubbing her aching flesh against the length of his erection.

"Now, Alex," she gasped. "Please. Now."

He seemed not to respond, but continued lavishing attention on first one breast, then the other. His hands teasing her sensitive flesh, his teeth nipping at her skin, his breath warming her. Finally he looked up. Though his face was hardened with desire, his gaze hadn't lost that teasing glint.

"Tell me what you want," he ordered.

"You. I want you."

With one hand firmly on her back, the other traced a path down her belly, hovering just above her panties, which were moist with her desire for him. He slipped one fingertip beneath the elastic. "Be specific."

She nearly groaned. "You're enjoying this," she accused.

He had the gall to chuckle. "I'd rather hoped you were enjoying it, too."

Clutching at his shoulders, then his waist, she tried to urge him toward her. "You know what I want."

"Do I?" His finger withdrew to trace a path along her belly.

"Yes." She gasped as he rimmed the elastic at the leg hole of her panties before slipping his fingers inside to toy with the tender flesh. Arching against him, she moaned. "I want you."

"You want me to…"

"I want you inside of me. Please, Alex, make love to me."

She only had to ask once. With brusque movements, he fumbled for his wallet. She frowned, unsure what he was doing, frustrated that he'd stopped touching her, until she saw him pull a condom from the wallet before tossing it aside. As he tore the condom open, she reached for the closure to his jeans. She tore at the button and zipper, then pulled down his jeans and his boxers. Her hands trembled as she freed his erection. She had to concentrate to keep her movements gentle as she cradled him in her palm.

Almost reverently, she took the condom from him and eased it down his length. He seemed as affected as she felt as he pulled her panties down her legs and tossed them aside. Cradling her cheek with one hand and bracing the other on her hip, he kissed her long and deep before sliding her to the edge of the counter and thrusting up into her.

She shuddered as he filled her completely, pulling back from his kiss to gasp out his name. Clutching at his shoulders, her cheek pressed to his, she chanted, "Alex, please."

She gasped out the words with his every thrust. Tilting her hips forward, she accepted him more deeply inside her. It seemed he touched her very core, the heart of her. And with every thrust, he pushed deeper, driving her closer to the edge, until finally she dissolved around him as he thrust one last time, clutching her to him, gasping out her name.

JESSICA FELT SO GOOD in his arms, he hated to move. Still, he couldn't resist lowering his mouth to hers and kissing her one last time before leaving her bed. After making love to her in the kitchen, he'd carried her through the house to her bedroom where he'd loved her a second time. If he had his way, they'd never leave the bed again. Since that wasn't an option, he poured into the kiss all the emotions he couldn't share with her out loud.

When he finally pulled away from her, he had to clear his throat before speaking. "Didn't you say something about meeting your parents for dinner?"

For a second her expression remained soft and sensual. Then, as his words sank in and reality returned, she stiffened. "Damn."

Jumping to her feet, she swayed slightly before gaining her balance. Shaking her head as if to clear it, she stalked toward the bathroom. Stopping midstride, she swung around. "What time is it?"

He glanced at his watch, then rolled onto his side and propped himself up on his elbow to watch her. "A quarter to seven."

"Damn." She paused at the doorway. "I can be ready to go in ten minutes. Can you be ready to go by then?"

"You want me to go with you?"

"No! I—" She frowned. "I mean, will you be ready to leave when I leave. So I can lock up. But I guess you have my spare key, don't you?" Again she shook her head. Doubt etched the lines of her face where passion had been not so long ago. Doubt and something else, as well. "You don't…want to go. Do you?"

Whatever he might have said five minutes ago was irrelevant. He'd seen the absolute horror flicker across her face. She didn't want him to meet her parents. In fact, the very thought of him meeting her parents had drained the blood from her cheeks and shocked her system.

"No, I don't want to meet them."

"Good. I mean…they're not…it would be awkward, today since we just—" she waved her hand back and forth between them "—you know." Then, as if she'd just thought of it, she tacked on, "And they're not expecting you."

"I get it."

"You…" She hesitated. "You're not mad?"

"Not at all." The words stuck in his throat, but he forced them out.

She didn't even notice. She just sighed with relief and made her way to the bathroom.

He pulled on his clothes as he found them. Shoving his legs into his jeans, yanking on his shirt, ramming his feet into his work boots. Cursing himself every step of the way. What was wrong with him?

He didn't want to meet her parents. So why the hell was he so pissed off? Because it killed him that she didn't want him to meet them.

By the time she emerged from her bedroom, he was seated at the kitchen table, tying knots into his shoelaces.

"Have you seen my necklace? The pearl?"

She wore another one of her sleek, knee-length dresses, this one cream-colored with a long flowing scarf tied around her neck. Her hair was once again smoothed to the back of her head, her makeup once again flawless. The transformation from hot, sexy woman to icy princess was remarkable. And, just as she'd predicted, it had taken less than ten minutes. Hell, she ought to win some kind of an award for that.

"On the coffee table."

"Thanks."

By the time she fastened the necklace and picked up her purse, he was out the door and halfway down the walkway. When he heard her call out, he almost didn't stop.

"Alex, wait up."

But he did stop. Muttering a curse, he pivoted to face her. She turned the key in the lock then twisted the doorknob to verify she'd locked it before walking down the path to where he stood. Dusk had set in and the half light cast shadows across her face, highlighting the pure perfection of her bone structure as well as the frown that marred her forehead.

"When will I see you again?"

"I'll be back in the morning to finish knocking down the wall and to clean up the debris. After that, it'll be a couple of days before I make it back. The lumber and drywall won't be delivered until late next week."

"That's not what I meant. When will I see you?"

"What happened tonight was a mistake. We both know that."

She jerked back as if she'd been slapped. "A mistake? Alex, what are you talking about?"

He stepped closer and lowered his voice. "Come on, Jessica, you screwed around with the hired help. You've had your fling now. Don't tell me you thought this would develop into a long-term relationship."

"'The hired help'? Is that how you think I see you?"

He heard the surprise in her voice, but he was too pissed off to care. "It's pretty obvious how you see me." He took a step back, unable to stand being so close to her for much longer. "Look, it was fun, but I won't be waiting around for the novelty to wear off."

She grabbed his arm. "Alex, wait."

As tempted as he was to shake her off, he couldn't bring himself to do it. Not when she said his name like that. He looked down at her hand on his arm, then back up at her.

"I don't think that's fair. Not to either of us. What happened tonight was more than just a novelty." Doubt flickered across her face. "Wasn't it?"

Against his will, something inside him softened. "Do you really want to have this conversation right now? When you're already late for dinner with your parents?"

He'd been unable to keep the twinge of bitterness from his voice and her brows snapped together when she heard it.

"The dinner with my parents? Is that what this is all about?"

Now that it came down to it, he didn't want to say the words. And he sure as hell didn't want to hear her say them. But clearly she wasn't going to let this go. "Look, you don't want me to meet them. That's fine. Can't say I blame you."

"That's what you think? That I'm ashamed of you?" She didn't give him a chance to answer, but closed the distance between them and cupped his cheek in her palm. "It's not you I'm ashamed of. It's them."

"Your parents?" Jeez, he'd never thought she'd lie about it. "The senator and his wife? Right. They're the ones you're ashamed of."

"You don't know what they're like—"

"Spare me the excuse." He jerked away from her touch. "You're going to be late."

"No! Listen to me, damn it."

He stopped and leveled his gaze to study her. To really look at her for the first time since she'd left the bed. Her frown had deepened and her skin was even paler than normal. Her teeth worried at her lower lip.

"I'm serious, Alex. My parents can be...well, 'rude' is the nicest way to say it. And they've always been particularly nasty to my boyfriends. And given your history with my dad…"

He studied her face for signs she wasn't telling the truth but found none. And despite himself, he couldn't help being amused by the idea of Jessica trying to protect him. He smiled wryly. "I can take care of myself."

She smiled in relief. "I'm sure you can. But you don't know them. My father always grills men about how much money they make and how their retirement funds are doing. My mother's even worse. Just trust me. It's really not you I'm worried about."

Her eyes begged him to believe her. He almost did. But he watched her climb into her Beemer with a growing sense of dread. His instincts told him she was being honest, but he wasn't sure he could trust them. His instincts also told him to toss her over his shoulder, carry her back into her bedroom, lock the door and spend the next week making love to her.

And regardless of what his instincts said, a lifetime in this town told him sleeping with Jessica—no matter how pleasurable the experience might be—wouldn't solve anything.

She'd had her little fling with the town bad boy. She'd proven to herself that she wasn't boring, passionless or too good. For her, this had been nothing more than a means of self-expression. For him, it had been everything.

13

"DEAR, don't pick at your food."

Criticism number twenty-three. Not bad for less than thirty minutes. Among other things, they'd discussed, in nauseating detail, Jessica's clothing—too wrinkled, her hairstyle—too harsh, her job—too menial and her lip-stick—entirely too bright.

She didn't bother to tell her mother that she wasn't wearing any. Any color in her lips had been put there the old-fashioned way. It'd been kissed into them.

Looking around the country club's main dining room, she couldn't help but see it in a different light. This room made up most of the wing that had been added in the late-eighties. Alex's uncle had worked on this room. Chances were good Alex had, as well.

For the first time she studied the dark oak paneling. The country club had originally been built back in the fifties. During the renovation it had been redesigned to look as if it had been built at the turn of the century, to match the ar-chitecture of downtown Palo Verde. The transformation had been miraculous. And Alex had been a part of it. In some small way, he'd been a part of building something that would last.

Had she ever, in the entire course of her career at Hand-held Technologies, created something as wonderful?

"If you're not going to eat—" her mother's voice interrupted her thoughts "—just set your fork aside and be done with it. The way you're playing with it, you look like you've been afflicted by melancholia."

"Thank you, Mother, for your concern."

Her mother stiffened. "Jessica, is this really necessary?"

"What?"

"These occasional bouts of adolescent rebellion?"

"I don't know what you mean."

Her father cleared his throat, then shot a stern look in first her mother's direction and then in hers. Then he purposefully changed the subject. "So, Jessica, when are we going to see that boyfriend of yours again?"

She stilled instantly. "Boyfriend?"

"Yes, yes. Weren't you seeing someone from work before you went to Sweden?" Her father sliced off a bite of steak and popped it into his mouth.

"I went on a couple of dates, but it petered out long before I even left the country."

Her mother set down her fork with a beleaguered sigh. "I wish you'd told me. I've already bought tickets to the fund-raiser. I doubt I'll be able to return his."

"I did tell you." She had trouble keeping her frustration from her voice. "And the fund-raiser is for a good cause. I doubt an extra thousand dollars for cancer research will kill you."

Her mother at least had the good grace to look offended. "Well, of course not, but—"

"The campaign is going well." Jessica's father cut her mother off before she could continue. Not to avoid the argument, necessarily, but to turn the conversation back to him.

"That's nice, Daddy." Jessica sighed, wishing she

could return her attention to picking at her food. Frankly, she didn't care how the campaign was going, but not responding would create more trouble than simply listening.

Ever since he'd been elected to the senate, their conversations always felt as though she was being prepped for an interview. Midway through his dissertation on educational budget cuts, she interrupted him.

"What's your position on the new senate bill to help migrant farm workers?"

Her mother sighed. "Honestly, Jessica. Didn't you read any of the information I've given you about your father's platform?"

Refusing to be cowed, she met her mother's gaze head-on. "Actually, no I didn't."

Her mother bristled. "How many times— "

Her father placed his well-manicured hand over hers. "Now, Caroline…" He let his voice trail off, sending some silent, subtle message.

Her mother sipped her wine, but said nothing more.

"Well, Jessica, I'm glad you asked. As I'm sure you know, this is a complicated issue. Concerns for migrant farm workers must be balanced with the economic prosperity of the small family farm. Research shows that—"

She interrupted him again. "You have the opportunity to do wonderful things. How can you ignore that?"

Her mother slammed down her wineglass. "Is it really necessary to question your father's politics in public?"

Without giving her a chance to respond, her mother segued to another topic with an ease that left Jessica shaking her head. She wasn't allowed to discuss politics in public, but when was the last time she'd seen her parents in private? Months? Years?

At times like these, she felt as if she was only invited to these weekly dinners because it would look bad if conservative family man, Senator John Sumners, didn't see his daughter once a week.

But in her heart, she'd always felt that way. More a prop for her parents' political ambitions than a child. She knew now that they loved her in their own way…it was just a very distant, reserved way. But as a child, she'd yearned for her parents' affection. Except for all the times she'd been carted out for important social functions, she had few memories of her mother. The occasional whiff of Chanel No. 5 and vodka.

Jessica had fonder memories of their first housekeeper and cook, Mrs. Rivera, a comfortably round woman who dispersed giant hugs and homemade cookies with equal glee. Who smelled of homey vanilla mixed with the faint scent of exotic spices like cumin and coriander. Spices that never made it into the shrimp scampi or chicken cordon blue that graced the Sumners' dinner table.

Then one summer Jessica had been sent off to tennis camp, where she'd made no friends, learned almost nothing and repeatedly bonked her doubles partner with stray serves. She'd returned home to find Mrs. Rivera replaced by Mrs. Nguyen, a rail-thin Vietnamese woman whose French cooking was impeccable, but who smelled faintly of vapor rub and who never baked cookies.

For the first time in years, she thought of Mrs. Rivera, wondered what had happened to the woman once she'd left the Sumners household, and longed for a vanilla-scented hug. Almost immediately, she felt awash with shame. Why hadn't she thought of Mrs. Rivera in so many years? Why hadn't she cared enough to wonder what had become of the woman until now?

She hadn't lied to Alex earlier when she'd told him she was embarrassed by her parents. But she hadn't been entirely truthful, either. She was also embarrassed by herself.

She was at her worst when she was with them. In her deepest heart, she feared she could be just as pushy and self-centered and manipulative as they could be. It was something she didn't like to admit to herself. It was certainly something she didn't want Alex to know.

14

JESSICA STOOD on Alex's doorstep for a full three minutes before ringing the doorbell. It took her that long to muster up the fake, cheerful smile. If she'd waited to muster her courage, as well, she would have stood there until dark.

In the end, her fear of being discovered lurking on his porch outweighed her nerves. She hadn't seen him since they'd had sex, then fought about her parents immediately afterward. Not the best way to start a relationship—even a fling.

Showing up uninvited to a party wasn't the best start to a relationship, either, but here she was. When she'd left the house this afternoon, determined to smooth things over, she'd never anticipated stumbling into a full-blown bash.

Cars filled the driveway and overflowed to the curb to stretch the length of Alex's property and well beyond. Latin music, with a heavy beat and a seductive rhythm, drifted out through the open windows. Not at all what Alex usually listened to while he worked—which was jazz, surprisingly enough.

Finally the door swung open to reveal a middle-aged woman with graying hair and dark smiling eyes.

The woman asked a question in Spanish that Jessica had no hope of understanding.

Jessica choked out a surprised, "Hello," then frantically began sifting through her memory for any other scraps of sixth-grade Spanish.

The woman nodded, as if she understood Jessica's hesitation. "You are here to see Alejandro?" The woman asked in heavily accented English.

Ale-who? Jessica wondered for a second before her brain kicked in and she remembered Alex was the Anglicized form of Alejandro.

"Yes." Thank God, she hadn't been forced to respond with her limited Spanish vocabulary.

"Come in, come in."

As Alex's mother—who else could she have been?—led Jessica through the living room to the kitchen, she couldn't help thinking of her own mother, who received guests in the formal living room and who preferred to serve white wine and roasted Brie while strains of Chopin played softly in the background.

Today, the tiny kitchen was overflowing with women, most of whom had a child or two in tow. The scent of roasting meat and fresh tamales filled the air.

Alex's mom introduced her as merely a friend of Alex's and within minutes she'd met both of Alex's sisters and a bevy of cousins and children whose names she would never remember. Marisol—the oldest of his sisters—was petite and curvy, with sleek, cropped hair and sad, soulful eyes. Isabel—the younger sister—was nearly as tall as Alex with long, golden hair.

Within minutes of ringing the doorbell, Jessica had a drink thrust into her hand and was seated at the table with a child on her lap, like an old family friend. No one seemed to question why she was here, as if she'd been invited to whatever family gathering she'd stumbled into.

To make matters worse, she knew when Alex realized she'd arrived, he would not be happy. After all, if he'd wanted her here, he would have invited her himself.

As if her trepidation had conjured him, Alex appeared in the doorway an instant later. Through the open back door, she caught a glimpse of the backyard, men sitting around the picnic table, a couple of boys wrestling in the grass. A setting so cheerful and inviting she hated that she'd interrupted his day with his family.

If the expression on his face was any indication, he hated it even more.

She handed the child off to its mother and stood. "Hi. Sorry to bother you at home." Even as she apologized, she hated having to do it.

"No problem." He crossed the small kitchen and extracted her from the huddle of women before leading her into the living room. The moving boxes she'd seen on her first visit were gone and the furniture had been arranged around the fireplace on the far wall.

"It seems like you're having a party."

He nodded, and though he seemed reluctant to bring her into the loop, he explained, "My niece Miranda's ninth birthday."

Right. A family affair. Not the sort of thing to which one invites one's sexual partners. Well, she probably had that coming. She hadn't wanted him at the dinner with her parents. Why should he want her here?

"I just stopped by for a minute. I've got some news."

"Is it something about the house?"

"Sort of." She sat on the sofa, very aware of the voices in the kitchen, the buzz of curious women. Still, if he could be reserved and professional for the sake of his family, so could she. "Actually it's about your bid for the courthouse job."

He sat opposite her, legs stretched out in front of him. A flicker of annoyance crossed his face before he asked, "What about it?"

She reached into her bag and pulled out the pair of tickets her mother had given her. "The Annual American Cancer Society Gala at the country club."

She held her breath, waiting for his response. Which was not quite what she'd hoped for. Finally she said, "The annual gala is the one event no one misses."

"So?"

"So...the entire city counsel will be there. So will the county manager. More importantly, so will all the members of the historical society."

He continued to stare blankly at her.

"So...if you go to the gala you'll have the chance to schmooze with all the people who'll decide who gets the job."

Interest sparked in his gaze, but he quickly banked it. "You know I don't have a chance of getting that job."

"Why not? Someone has to get it, why not you?"

"Because this damn town—"

"Is not the same town it was fifteen years ago. But you have to give people the opportunity to see that you've changed, too."

He studied her face a moment before asking, "You really think going to this gala will do that?"

"Yes, I do. The city council and county manager are business people. They'll make their decision based purely on whether or not your bid is better than the others. But the historical society is something else entirely. If you come to the gala, it's going to impress them. If we're there together—"

"That'll just make it worse."

"Only if people think I'm ashamed to be seen with you. If we go to the party together, people will see you're not just the hired help I'm doing on the side. You're a businessman I happen to be dating." He still looked unconvinced, so she threw in, "Even if you don't get the courthouse job, you'll still meet people, potential clients. Come on, Alex. It can't hurt."

"I'll think about it," he finally agreed.

"Think about what?"

Jessica turned to see Alex's mother standing in the doorway, drying her hands on a dishtowel. Sensing a potential ally, Jessica stood and held out the tickets. "I'm trying to convince Alex to attend the American Cancer Society gala with me. He doesn't want to, but it would be very good for his business."

His mother raised her eyebrows, looking very much the way Alex did when he was skeptical. "What is this…" She hesitated, as if trying to wrap her tongue around an unfamiliar word. "…gala?"

"It's a big party. A lot of potential clients and influential people will be there."

Alex's mother frowned and the confusion in her eyes highlighted Jessica's mistake.

Anxiety knotted her stomach. She simply didn't know what words to use. "I mean—"

Before she could fumble any more, Alex finished the sentence for her in Spanish.

"Ah!" His mother nodded in understanding, then smiled at Jessica. "Sometimes my English is—" she held out her hand, palm down, twisting it in a so-so gesture "—not so good."

"Oh, no, Mrs. Moreno," she protested automatically. "It's excellent."

Alex's mother beamed. "Please, call me Rosa." Linking arms with Jessica, she led her back toward the kitchen. "My boy tells me *nada*. He doesn't want me to worry, he says. How can I not worry?"

Mrs. Moreno—no, Rosa—didn't give her a chance to reply. "You'll stay for dinner, *sí*?" In a voice filled with awe she explained, "Alejandro paid for José and I to fly up to Sacramento for Miranda's birthday. José and the boys are making *carnitas*. The girls and I are making tamales. You can help."

The decision was made before Jessica could even think of an excuse. In the kitchen, Rosa poured Jessica another drink and put her to work rolling tamales.

The other women smiled broadly when Rosa explained about the gala, but Jessica could see the questions in their eyes. They were all wondering who she was and what claim she had on their brother.

And Alex wasn't talking. However, his feelings about the subject were quite obvious. A scowl settled onto his face as he stood with his arms crossed over his chest and his shoulder propped against the door to the kitchen. Even after his mother shooed him out to the backyard with the rest of the men, Jessica could still feel his irritation looming over her.

Telling his mother about the gala may have bought her more time in which to convince him, but it had pissed him off. And sooner or later she'd have to deal with him. Frankly, she was hoping it'd be later.

HAVING JESSICA meet his family—his entire big, loud, pushy family—all at once was the last thing he'd wanted. That's why he hadn't told her his parents had come up for the weekend.

His family was bad enough in small doses. Not that he didn't love them…he did. But he was also painfully aware of how different they were from Jessica's family. Not that he'd met her parents, but he could imagine. In fact, he'd caught a glimpse of the senator and his wife on the local news the other night. At a thousand-dollar-a-plate political fund-raiser.

Shit. A thousand dollars a plate. He could feed his entire extended family for a fraction of that. While he'd watched that news clip he couldn't help imagining how that smiling, slick couple would react if they knew he was sleeping with their daughter. Him, the son of a dirt-poor migrant farm worker, a guy who made his living with his hands. A guy who couldn't even begin to pay a thousand dollars a plate to eat dinner with Senator Sumners.

He couldn't help thinking about the damn political dinner and wondering how many of those things Jessica had attended over the years. And how this cheap backyard barbecue couldn't even compare.

He spent the whole day waiting for her to make her excuses and leave. Surprisingly, she didn't.

She'd worn the sexy little skirt and sweater she'd bought the day they'd gone shopping together. The skirt accented her slim hips and long, shapely legs. Bright pink toenail polish peeked through the open toes of her sandals. As always, her hair was slicked back and knotted low at the back of her head, exposing the elegant length of her neck and the slender silver chain from which her pearl dangled.

He'd watched as she'd helped roll tamales. With each tamale, she'd scrunched up her eyes and bit her lip in concentration.

By the time his mother called them all for lunch, he'd been more than ready for her to leave.

He watched in dread as his mother led Jessica to the table and seated her between Isabel and Luis, who was back from college for the weekend.

"Don't look so worried," Tomas murmured as he slid into the chair next to him.

"I'm not worried."

Tomas laughed. "Yeah, right. Look, she's doing fine." Tomas reached across him for the salad bowl. "You, on the other hand, look ready to have a seizure. Calm down."

"That's easy for you to say. That wasn't your girlfriend out there drinking Uncle Sal's home-brewed beer."

Tomas clapped him on the back. "Don't worry. Uncle Sal's home brew has never killed anyone. Yet." As they'd watched, Jessica had taken a tentative sip of the beer. She'd blanched only for a second before pasting on a bright smile. "It takes a while to get used to. And she's probably not normally a beer drinker."

"Right. That's it."

"What? You think she's not enjoying herself?"

"Look around, Tomas," Alex mocked. "She's the daughter of a senator. They have their family parties at the country club. She's got a trust fund, for Christ's sake. Do you think this is her kind of party?"

"Hey, she's getting along great. You're the one who's uncomfortable."

And she did seem to be getting along great. As he watched, eighteen-month-old Beatrice, the youngest of Isabel's three children, toddled over to Jessica and held up her arms.

This would be it. The thing that pushed her over the edge and sent her running for the door.

He sat back, ready to go to her rescue. But before he could even stand, she set down her fork and reached for the child. She picked up Beatrice awkwardly, her inexperience clear in her stiff movements and worried expression. Beatrice didn't seem to notice. She curled up against Jessica's chest, grabbed a lock of blond hair with one hand and reached for a tortilla with the other.

Beatrice gummed the tortilla, drooling occasionally, but otherwise sat peacefully in Jessica's lap while Jessica made conversation with Isabel.

Beatrice didn't even look out of place in Jessica's arms, and Jessica even seemed to relax further, the longer the toddler was in her lap.

She fed Beatrice bites of *masa* and chunks of the pulled pork his father had roasted overnight. When Beatrice waved a greasy fist near Jessica's sweater, Jessica captured the girl's hand in her own. Alex waited, fully expecting her to hand Beatrice back to Isabel. Instead, Jessica brought Beatrice's tiny hand to her lips and nipped playfully at her fingers. Giggles erupted from Beatrice, mingling with Jessica's melodic laughter.

Watching her, he felt his heart fill with something that felt terrifyingly close to love. Not just the adolescent, lust-driven puppy love he'd been battling for so long, but something far more complicated. He was glad she'd come, yes, and he was glad she was getting along with his family. But it was more than that. He wanted her here. Not just today, but always. He wanted to stand here, to watch her feed bites of *masa* to *their* child.

He knew in that instant how completely he'd been fooling himself about his feelings for Jessica. This wasn't just lust. This wasn't even just infatuation. This was the real deal.

And that scared the hell out of him.

Beside him, Tomas took a long swig of beer. When he set down the bottle he said, "See? She's doing fine."

"For now," Alex admitted. Though she was doing far better than he ever would have imagined.

But maybe he should have expected this. After all, her father was a politician. She was probably very skilled at this kind of thing. She'd even had a term for it. What had she called it? Conversational sleight of hand.

No wonder she seemed to fit so easily into the family.

"Tell me something, Alex. What's got you more worried? The fear that she wouldn't get along with the family or the fear that she would?"

He shot Tomas an irritated look. "Don't you have anything better to do than annoy me?"

The sound of Tomas's laughter grated his already raw nerves. "As a matter of fact, I do. I promised the kids a game of basketball after lunch."

With that, Tomas collected his now-empty plate and rose from his chair. Alex didn't bother to offer to join in the game. He couldn't take his eyes off Jessica. And he didn't want to.

With Tomas's words echoing in his ears, he consider for the first time that he might have been wrong about Jessica. All this time, he'd assumed their relationship had no future outside the bedroom.

Yet she'd spent most of the day with his family. And she seemed to be enjoying their company.

Were these really the actions of a woman who wanted a quick, passionate fling and nothing more?

They didn't seem to be.

Until now, he'd assumed Jessica would never settle for a relationship with someone like him, someone from a poor family who worked with his hands for a living. But what was it she'd said earlier? That people would only look down on their relationship if they thought she was ashamed to be with him. Those words implied she *wasn't* ashamed to be with him. Was it possible that all his fears about not being good enough for her were all in his head?

Everything he knew about her indicated she wasn't interested in a long-term relationship. But what if everything he knew about her was wrong?

"—BUT, YOU KNOW ALEX. He would never let us fight our own battles. He was up at the dean's office giving them hell until things got sorted out."

Luis and Isabel both laughed at the story. Jessica played along, though laughing was the last thing she felt like doing. Alex's brother and sister had been regaling her with stories about him for the past hour. With every "You know Alex" they tossed out, she felt less and less that she did.

The worst was when they'd forget she was there and slip into Spanish. When they referred to him as Alejandro, she felt as if they were talking about someone she'd never even met.

Oh, they'd catch themselves, apologize and repeat what they'd said in English. But every time it happened was a reminder that she just didn't belong here.

As the afternoon had drawn on, more and more people had shown up. Cousins and friends mingled by the picnic tables. All part of a vibrant and complex community she hadn't even known existed in Palo Verde. Alex had stood under the trees talking to the uncle he'd worked for as a teenager. The yard was decorated with casual spontaneity, streamers thrown up into the branches of the apple trees, white Christmas lights draped from limb to limb. The card table set up by the back door sagged under the weight of the desserts and treats. The party was barely planned, but lovingly executed in a way none of her own childhood birthday parties had ever been. Hers had been implemented with all the detail and emotional warmth of military action in the Gulf.

She took another sip of the margarita someone had poured her and looked longingly toward the door. Would it be wrong to leave before the birthday girl finished opening her presents? Would it matter, since she didn't even have a present for Miranda?

And that was the problem with crashing a party. You never knew what to bring.

Before she could make her escape, Miranda interrupted them. "Daddy said to tell you it's time for cake," the girl said solemnly.

Isabel rushed away to find paper plates and plastic forks. Luis followed to help carry the cake. Which left Jessica alone with the little girl.

Miranda, a tiny, darker-haired version of her mother, was already striking. She had black hair, which fell in baby-fine ringlets around her shoulders. Her eyes were large, like those of a Disney cartoon heroine. And—faced with a stranger—she bit nervously on her lower lip. Her gangly arms clutched a fat hardcover book close to her chest.

Finally the girl thrust out the book for Jessica to see. "It was a gift from Tío Alejandro."

Jessica accepted the book and studied its cover for a moment before asking, "Do you like Harry Potter?" The girl nodded. "Then I'm sure you'll enjoy having your mother read the book to you."

Miranda stiffened. "I'll read it myself." She must have sensed Jessica's disbelief, because, as she snatched the book back, she explained, "I've already read all the others."

"I'm impressed," Jessica admitted, though she had no idea what books other nine-year-old girls read.

"I read very well for my age," Miranda stated proudly. "Tío Alejandro said my book was from you, too. But I think he was just being nice because you forgot my present."

Jessica winced. "Well, you know Alex."

Miranda stared blankly at her.

Suddenly inspired, Jessica reached for the clasp of her necklace. "Actually, I did bring you a gift. I just didn't wrap it." She held out the silver chain to Miranda.

For a long moment Miranda merely stared at her. Finally she shifted the book to one hand and with the other, reached out to touch the pearl with the tip of her finger. "It's pretty." Her wide gaze met Jessica's. "Is it really for me?"

She hesitated only a moment. "Of course. Turn around and I'll put it on."

Miranda carefully set her book down on the chair, then turned her back to Jessica and held her hair out of the way.

As she fastened the necklace around Miranda's delicate neck, Jessica felt an odd tug deep inside. Very similar to the tug of emotion she'd felt holding Beatrice earlier. Alex's family was getting to her. Much as the man himself had.

When she looked up, she found Alex watching her once again. Throughout the day, it seemed every time her gaze sought him, he was already looking at her. The look in his eyes—one of dark intensity—made her shiver.

For an instant she almost forgot that he hadn't wanted her here. That he hadn't wanted her to meet his parents and his family. For an instant, she was lost in the intimacy of his gaze. Then the moment passed and she shook herself back to the present.

Miranda had skipped over to her grandfather and was pulling him toward Jessica. Alex's father was shorter than any of his children by several inches. What he lacked in height, he made up for in presence. With his lean, muscled body and impeccable posture, he seemed a much bigger man than he was. Though she could see why Alex worried about him. He moved like a man who'd lived hard years, slowly and with caution. His sun-darkened skin a badge of the seasons he'd spent working in the apple orchards of the northern valley and the citrus orchards of Arizona.

"*Abuelo*," Miranda said. "Look at the necklace Miss Jessica gave me."

Though he moved slowly when he knelt beside his granddaughter, his eyes sparkled as he spoke to her in a flurry of Spanish that Jessica had no hope of understanding.

Miranda blushed and shook her head. Then, clutching her book in one hand and the pearl pendant between the fingers of her other, she turned back to Jessica. "Thank you, Miss Jessica."

"You're welcome, Miranda."

"Go get your cake," José said, then patted her on the behind as she scurried away to her mother. He watched her, smiling, until she was by her mother's side, then made his way to the chair beside Jessica.

As he lowered himself to the chair, her mind raced. She spoke almost no Spanish and he spoke very little English. Besides, she just didn't know what to say to him.

Lately she'd spent some free time at the office doing research online about migrant farm workers. But asking him how he felt about the use of pesticides in modern agriculture seemed inappropriate.

So instead, she said nothing.

He smiled broadly at her and she found herself smiling

back, hoping that could communicate how thankful she was to have been included today, how special his family had made her feel.

Finally, in halting English, he began to speak to her. "My boy, Alejandro...he is a good boy."

Her gaze automatically sought Alex in the crowd. At some point, the music had been turned up. Luis had pulled Marisol out into the yard and, along with several other couples, they danced beneath the lantern-strewn branches of the apple trees. Alex was out there dancing, as well. Holding Beatrice close to his chest, he danced her around the yard. The sight was so sexy, so heart-stoppingly masculine, her breath caught in her throat.

A good boy? Oh, he was so much more than that.

To his father, she merely said, "Yes, he is."

He nodded, seemingly satisfied with her limited answer. "I want Alex to..." He struggled for the right word, then settled on, "To do good."

She nodded her understanding.

Then he turned his gaze to her. "You will help."

"Yes," she said. "I will help." She was trying to anyway. If only he'd let her.

When she glanced back at Alex's father, she found him smiling slyly at her. Then he stood and extended his hand to her to help her up. Instead of releasing her hand when she stood, he draped it over his arm and led her to where the others were dancing to the heavy Latin beat. Their exuberant movements were a far cry from the sedate, mandatory dancing she'd done at the country club.

"Come. We'll dance."

When she pulled back, he stopped, looking at her with a raised eyebrow and questioning eyes, much the way Alex did so often.

"I don't know how," she explained. Not really a lie. She'd never before danced with such joy.

"*¿Por qué no?*"

"I don't know how." At his blank stare, she took an exaggerated, lumbering step and made to crunch his toes.

He laughed, nodding his understanding. Then shrugged as if to say "So, what?" He tugged again on her hand, but she refused to move.

With a sigh, he repeated her gesture, then tapped his fingers on her chest, just above her heart. "Here?" Then he tapped his fingers on her temple. "Or here?"

This time when he pulled on her hand, she allowed herself to be led out on the impromptu dance floor. Though the song was an upbeat Tejano tune, he held her as if they were waltzing. His feet moved smoothly in time to the music and, with his hand firmly on her back, she found it easy to let him lead.

But she didn't dance with Alex's father for long. Soon she was passed off to Tomas, who made her laugh so hard she really did step on his toes. Finally, he begged off and handed her to Alex.

Her breath caught when she felt herself wrapped in Alex's strong arms. They hadn't been alone all day. Though they were hardly alone now, the flickering lights from the tree branches created an intimacy that seemed to shelter them from the rest of the crowd.

His hand felt warm and strong against her back. It seemed the most natural thing in the world when he slipped his hand under the hem of her sweater to rest on her bare skin.

He cradled her hand closer to their bodies and she instinctively leaned in close to him. He smelled of sunshine and the roasted cumin from the *carnitas*.

"I saw you give your necklace to Miranda," he murmured, his words brushing against her ear. "You didn't have to do that."

She pulled back just enough to meet his gaze. "I didn't have anything else to give."

In the half light, his eyes looked pure black, his expression unreadable. Finally he nodded.

"I'll make sure Isabel knows its worth. Miranda will only wear it on special occasions."

She almost told him not to bother. Wasn't it more important the girl enjoy the necklace?

But that was the attitude of a rich girl…someone accustomed to buying and having expensive things. For the first time she considered that Alex's family might think such an expensive gift inappropriate from someone practically a stranger. So she said nothing.

One song passed into the next and then the next. Finally, when the burden of silence was too heavy, she spoke. "Alex, today's been nice. Your family is…" She let her words trail off, having no way to express how kind and welcoming they'd been.

"Crazy? Loud? Overwhelming?"

She laughed. "No. Well, yes. But wonderful."

As inadequate as that was, she didn't know what else to say. His mother, who treated her with such generosity. His brothers and sisters, who made her laugh and had been so kind. And his father, who with a few words of broken English had displayed more emotion than her father ever had, with the entire English language at his disposal.

To him, his family may be crazy, loud and overwhelming.

But to her? To her, they were a bit of Alex she never would have seen otherwise.

And her heart ached to think this was a part of him she'd never see again.

"WHERE'D YOU disappear to?"

Jessica started guiltily at the sound of Alex's voice. Slowly she turned to face him. Only the moonlight overhead and the faint light shining through an uncurtained window illuminated his form. He stood several feet behind her, midway down the driveway that ran alongside his house. His hands were propped on his hips.

She gestured toward her car, which was parked at the curb. "I thought I'd head out."

"You weren't going to say goodbye?"

"You were busy with your parents." She shrugged. The party in the backyard was still very much in full swing. She didn't want to demand his attention. Moreover, she didn't want to explain how lonely she'd suddenly felt among his family.

For a brief time, she'd felt a part of them. Though she knew that was only an illusion brought on by their friendliness, she couldn't help yearning to be a part of it for real.

"Thank your mom for making me feel so welcome," she said, slowly edging her way toward her car.

Alex followed her, the gravel of the driveway crunching under his feet with every step. "Stay and tell her yourself."

"No. I've stayed too long as it is. I've intruded enough."

"Don't go."

"Why would you want me to stay? You didn't want me here in the first place."

He ducked his head, a lock of hair falling across his forehead. "I never said that."

But he didn't deny it, either. "You didn't have to. You didn't invite me to meet your family."

Finally he caught her hand and held it, tugging it gently to pull her closer to him. At either end of the driveway, climbing roses grew up the sides of the house, shielding them from the backyard as well as from the street. "It's not that I didn't want you here. They can be…"

"Overwhelming? You said that earlier. I thought they were wonderful," she admitted. "I felt like part of the family."

He laughed ruefully. "The bad news is, now you practically are. Now that Mom knows we're dating, she'll inundate you. She'll call you. Bring you food." He interlaced his fingers with hers. "That's why I didn't invite you today. I didn't want them to scare you off."

She straightened her shoulders. "I don't scare easily."

But that wasn't necessarily true. The longing she felt when he talked about her being a part of his family terrified her. Despite what he said, spending a single afternoon with them didn't make her belong. Only Alex could do that, and she knew how unlikely that was.

Shoving that thought from her mind, she asked, "Have you decided about the gala?"

He stiffened and she sensed his withdrawal from her. "No."

"You really should come. It's the kind of thing that will make or break you."

"So you keep reminding me," he said, his tone harsh.

Sensing he was even more annoyed than he was letting on, she tried to explain. "I just meant that—"

"I know what you meant."

Yet, somehow she didn't think he did. She reached out to put her hand on his arm. Feeling his muscles tense beneath her touch, she added, "Alex, your family is very proud of you. They want you to be successful."

His gaze may have flashed with irritation, but the lighting was too dim and his eyes too dark for her to know for sure. She wanted to press him for an answer about the gala or to find out what she'd done to annoy him, but before she could, he closed the gap between them, then slowly backed her up to the wall behind her. The open kitchen window was just a few feet above her head. Through it drifted the faint Spanish of his family's conversation, interrupted occasionally by the clinking of plates and banging of pans.

"This is the first time we've been alone all day," he murmured. "Do you really want to talk about the gala?"

"Alex, don't." But there was no force behind her words. "Your family…" She looked up toward the window above her.

"Is all busy doing other things." He edged closer to her, nudging his knee between her legs. With one hand, he brushed a loose strand of hair away from her face. The other he ran up and down her arm.

His calloused fingertips felt deliciously rough against her bare skin. "They'll see us." But her protests sounded weak even to her own ears. She pressed her palm to his chest, trying to wedge some distance between them, but there was no strength behind her hand.

"They won't," he insisted, nudging her knees further apart, pressing into her body. "The roses block their view." He leaned in closer, barely kissing the corner of her mouth. "No one will see us. No one will know we're here."

She glanced from side to side. He was right. They were almost completely hidden by the climbing vines. Surrounded by dark green leaves, tiny white flowers and the fragrance of roses mingling with the intoxicating scent of warm male skin.

Her pulse kicked into high gear. The illusion of their solitude was enough for her body. She widened her stance, making room for his thigh to press against the juncture of her legs.

Part of her knew this was a mistake. Someone could walk around the corner at any minute. But at the same time, she didn't care. All she cared about was the burning ache inside her. The need to feel his body pressed against hers. The reassurances of how much he wanted her—physically, if not emotionally.

She tilted her chin upward as he lowered his mouth. She acquiesced immediately, opening her lips to his. His mouth was hot and impatient, ruthlessly coaxing a response from her. Not that he had to work hard.

A few hot kisses, the feel of his hands on her bare skin, that was all it took. When she felt him slide his hands up her ribcage to her breasts, she was gone.

Her passion hit quickly, unexpectedly. She'd spent the day cut adrift. Near him, but not with him. And as risky as it was to be with him right now, she needed it. Needed the affirmation that he still wanted her. That even while their relationship was rife with so many questions, this at least she knew and understood: he wanted her. Needed her, just as she needed him.

She clutched at his shoulders, rotating her hips to rub herself against him. She could feel his erection through his jeans, but her skirt was in the way. Almost without realizing what she was doing, she reached down and pulled her skirt farther up her thighs, giving her room to widen her legs. She moaned when she felt the hard length of his thigh come in contact with her crotch.

"Ah, Jess," he murmured in her ear.

"Please, Alex," she gasped. "Please tell me you have a condom with you."

He froze. Then cursed. "I don't."

She squeezed her eyes closed, trying to hide her frustration. "Can you come by tonight?"

"Yes." Then he cursed again. "No. My parents are staying at the house."

She nearly groaned out loud.

"Shh," he murmured. "It's okay."

His hand slid up her thigh, pushing her skirt further out of his way. He gently moved her panties aside to stroke the aching folds of her flesh. She gasped at the touch of his fingers.

"Shh," he murmured again as his other hand crept over her mouth, cutting off her panting gasps. She felt one finger and then another slide inside her. His thumb found her clitoris. His touch was soft, but his fingers rough.

The gentle stroking of his thumb edged everything else from her consciousness. As if from very far away, she heard a car pass on the street. The voices from the kitchen and yard faded to nothing. Soon, all she could hear was the faint rhythm of the music, the ragged tempo of his breath against her ear and the thrumming of her own blood.

All she could feel was the heat of his hands, the strength of his body and the touch of his fingers, pushing her closer and closer to the edge. As if her entire body and soul were condensed down to that one tiny nub of flesh. Balanced on a precipice. Waiting for him to push her over. And then he did. Her muscles spasmed around his fingers, her heart pounded against his chest and his mouth captured her moans of pleasure.

15

WELL, SHE'D WANTED to be saucy. Surely fooling around with a guy within earshot of his entire family ranked pretty high on anyone's list of saucy behavior.

Fooling around? the conservative prude buried deep inside of her asked. *That's a bit of an understatement.*

Ignoring the voice, she tugged her skirt down, pulling it back into place. She ran one hand, then both, over her hair, smoothing it and twisting it into a knot before she realized her bobby pins were scattered all over the ground, lost forever.

Through all of her efficient straightening of her clothes, she searched frantically for something—anything—appropriate to say. But she was woefully inexperienced in such matters and completely at a loss.

Alex, however, seemed relatively unfazed. He nudged her chin up with his knuckle, forcing her to look him in the eye. "Jessica, why don't you come inside with me? Stay for the rest of the evening?"

After what they just did? No way. Under the circumstances, she was having enough trouble meeting his gaze. Meeting his parents' would be impossible.

"No. Thank you." She reached for her bag, which she'd dropped at some point. "I'd rather just go home."

She'd expected more of an argument. Instead he nodded. "Okay." And fell into step beside her as she walked down the driveway toward her car.

When she climbed into the driver's seat, he braced his forearm on the roof and leaned in through the open door. "Jess, I—" He broke off abruptly, shaking his head ruefully. "I'll see you tomorrow."

"About the gala—"

"Don't worry," he said with a tired sigh. "I'll be there."

Then he planted a quick kiss on her mouth before straightening and closing the door. With his hands fisted on his hips, he stood on the curb, watching as she shifted the car into gear and drove down the street toward town.

As she made her way home, she couldn't shake the feeling that they'd left so much unsaid. Despite their intense physical attraction, they had almost nothing in common. Today more than proved that.

The obvious closeness and open affection of his family only made her uncomfortable. And at the same time, it made her ache with jealousy. In some ways, it seemed they spoke another language…in addition to the fact that they actually spoke another language. Beyond that barrier, so many other things differentiated them.

The thought left a sick feeling of dread deep in the pit of her stomach. As she pulled into her driveway and stared up at her own house, she realized she'd never even had her family over for dinner. Not once in the five years she'd lived here.

But as soon as she resolved to change that, an image of her mother popped into her head. She imagined her mother's lips curling in distaste as she said, "Really, dear, it's so much more convenient to meet at the country club."

By convenient, her mother would mean, less messy, both physically and emotionally. No dishes to clean up, no personal conversations to steer clear of. No one discussed emotional issues at the country club, so eating there was a way of keeping all of that at bay. More convenient, indeed.

Was this really the world she wanted to introduce Alex to?

Now that she'd talked the gala up both to him and his parents, did she have a choice?

"LET ME SEE if I've got this right. In the three weeks Brad and I were gone, you've given up your career goals, demolished your kitchen and hopped into bed with Alex Moreno."

Mattie sat cross-legged in the center of Jessica's bed. Her brown hair was streaked with blond from her time spent in the sun. Her arms were tanned, her nose and shoulders pink. She'd never looked better. Funny, how being loved did that for a woman. Made her bloom.

Watching Mattie, Jessica felt a pang of longing well up inside of her, but she ruthlessly squashed it back down. With a sigh, she rose from her bed and headed for her closet. "I haven't abandoned my career goals. I've just stopped obsessing on them. But otherwise, that about sums it up."

Mattie shook her head, either in confusion or exasperation. "I was only gone three weeks."

"Hey, I was gone for nine weeks and you fell in love with my brother. By the time I got back, you'd planned the wedding."

"That's different." Mattie stiffened. "Brad and I have a history."

"Well, Alex and I have a history."

"You had a crush on him in high school. That's it."

"That's not entirely true."

Mattie frowned, suddenly suspicious. "What else was there?"

As simply as she could, she told Mattie what had happened that day at the creek and explained how she and Alex had ended up exchanging notes. When she was done, she studied Mattie but couldn't gauge her reaction.

Mattie shook her head with a sigh. "And you never told me?"

Wincing at the accusation in Mattie's voice, she said, "There didn't seem to be much to tell. They were just notes." But even as she said it, she recognized how much more to her they'd been.

"Were you in love with him?"

"I hardly knew him. But in those notes, he was... different than I would have thought. Smarter and more sensitive. I wished I could have known him better, but he stopped writing to me. I couldn't hold his interest even then."

"Jess—"

Hoping to end the conversation, Jessica headed for her closet. "Do you want to borrow a dress for the gala or not?"

Mattie followed her into the closet, but didn't even glance at any of the gowns. "Okay, so you guys exchanged some notes, but that's not a history. At least not the kind of history you base a relationship on."

A relationship? No. But a wild fling based on pure gut-wrenching lust?

"It's not a relationship."

"Then what is it?"

Mattie's voice was filled with concern. Concern that normally would have comforted Jessica, but today just grated on her nerves. "It's just sex, okay?"

"Jessica—"

"Look, I know what I'm doing. I don't have any illusions about where this is going. I know it's based on sex and nothing else and I'm okay with that. You should be, too."

Patricia rushed into the room, breathless. "I hope it's okay I let myself in. I got here as quickly as I could. Are we looking at dresses yet?"

"We're trying to," Jessica muttered. Hoping Mattie would take a hint.

She didn't.

"I'm just worried about you, that's all."

Patricia's ears perked up. "Worried? Why? Because she's dating that really hot guy?"

"Yes," Jessica said, rolling her eyes.

"No," Mattie said at the same time. "I'm worried because you're not dating him. You're just sleeping with him. And I'm not sure you're capable of having a sex-only, no-emotion kind of relationship."

"But—"

Mattie cut Jessica off before she could even finish the thought. "Oh, I know you think you can. I'm sure you've got it all planned out how you're going to sleep with him, but stay emotionally detached and how it'll all work out for the best."

Patricia waggled her eyebrows speculatively. "Sounds to me like someone is speaking from experience."

"Exactly! It's no different than my big plan to seduce Brad as a way of getting over him. And look what happened to me."

"You fell in love, got married and are happy," Patricia pointed out.

"Yes, that's what I'm saying." She looked pointedly at

Jessica and, when she got no response, she turned her gaze on Patricia. "Help me out here."

Patricia merely shook her head. "I don't see your point."

"Don't…" Mattie practically sputtered in frustration. She looked back at Jessica, who finally took pity on her.

"Don't worry. I see your point. But you're wrong. I'm not in love with Alex. I'm not going to fall in love with Alex. I'm not. I promise. This is just one more thing to cross off my list."

Mattie threw up her hands in exasperation. "Don't even get me started on that stupid list."

"Hey, now." Patricia narrowed a steely glare at Mattie. "Don't be dissing The List."

Mattie rolled her eyes. "Seriously, it's just about the silliest—"

Before either woman could launch into a full-scale attack, Jessica interrupted them. "Look, Mattie, it's okay if you think The List is silly. But I don't." She grasped Mattie's hand, desperate to make her understand. "It's made me rethink my life. In a good way. It's made me try things I never would have done otherwise and that's exciting for me."

Mattie's frown deepened, then she sighed. "If you really feel like you need The List, fine. But it's not like you're doing *everything* on that list anyway. It's not like you're going to 'Go Tribal' and get something pierced."

"Actually…"

Mattie went white. "Dear God, don't tell me you got a tattoo!"

"No! You know I can't stand pain."

Patricia all but beamed. "Which is why I made her an appointment tomorrow to have Mendhi body painting done."

"Mendhi?" Mattie asked skeptically.

"It's temporary," Jessica hastened to reassure her.

"It's traditional Indian body painting done with henna to celebrate transcendence and transformation. As in, our little Jessica transcending her previous, boring existence and transforming into a *Saucy* woman." For a second Patricia sounded very serious and downright serene. Then she winked salaciously and added, "Besides, it's very sexy."

"So that's the last of The List, then?" Mattie asked.

"Just about."

In truth, there were several items left on The List—Drop the Drawers and Live in the Fast Lane she had plans for. Within the next forty-eight hours, she'd have done everything on The List, with the exception of number ten—Conquer It. Overcoming her worst fear.

The problem was, right now, her worst fear was that Mattie's words of caution had come too late. She was terrified that she already loved Alex.

As if she could sense Jessica's thoughts, Mattie's frown deepened. "Are you sure you know what you're doing?"

"I'm positive."

"Because—"

"I'm positive," she repeated firmly. But Mattie looked utterly unconvinced.

Actually, she looked about as unconvinced as Jessica felt.

As she, Mattie and Lucy dug through the dozen or so formal dresses she'd worn to country club events over the years to find one for Mattie to borrow, she kept trying to convince herself.

She did a decent job of faking carefree cheerfulness for their sake, burying her dread deep down inside. As her eyes drifted time and again to the red satin, vintage gown she'd picked out to wear to the gala herself, she chanted the words like a mantra. I'm not in love with Alex Moreno.

I'm not in love with Alex Moreno.

I'm not in love with Alex Moreno.

Once again, she found herself wishing for a pair of ruby-red slippers.

She eyed the high-heeled satin shoes she'd had dyed to match the dress. If she clicked her heels three times while chanting her new mantra, would that make it any more true?

16

HE'D NEVER WORN a tux before and frankly it was damn uncomfortable. But there were some things worth the discomfort of a starched shirt and rented shoes. The sight of Jessica poured into red satin was one of them.

From the front, the dress was relatively modest, cut well above her breasts, with thick straps that looped from her shoulders down to her waist. However, when she turned her back to him to lock her front door, the back of her dress was...missing. Soft folds of fabric puddled at the base of her spine, leaving her entire back bare.

Low on her back, she bore a small but intricate design drawn in reddish-brown ink. No doubt the henna tattoo she'd mentioned getting. He couldn't resist tracing the image with his forefinger. Her skin was unbelievably soft and he felt her shiver under his touch, making his pulse leap.

He didn't bother to stifle his groan. "You, um, look great."

She looked over her shoulder at him, and though her eyes darkened with desire, her smile teased. "Thanks."

She looked amazing. As if the dress had been made just for her. Something that only made him more aware he'd had to rent his tux. Most of the men she usually dated probably owned their own.

She straightened then tossed him the keys and nodded toward her driveway where the Beemer sat with the top down. "You want to drive?"

Hell, forget about the guys that owned their own tuxes. He was intimidated by the guys who owned cars nice enough to drive her in. His own beat-up work truck didn't qualify.

Still, she was with him. Not any of those other guys who could buy their own tuxes or buy her dinner at a thousand dollars a plate. Him. And that had to count for something.

As he walked her to her car, he automatically slid his hand to the small of her back. He nearly regretted it. Her skin was smooth and warm beneath his hand. With the fabric pooling low on her back, the tips of his fingers brushed against the dimples at the base of her spine.

"A dress this revealing makes a guy wonder what you've got on underneath," he said casually.

"Nothing."

He stilled. "Nothing?" His voice cracked on the word.

She merely smiled. Of their own volition, his eyes dropped to her breasts. He raised his gaze to hers and cocked an eyebrow. Biting innocently on her lip, she shook her head. He looked pointedly to the juncture of her thighs. Again, she shook her head.

"Number six on The List was 'Drop the Drawers.' The article promised it would drive you crazy. Is it working?"

Shaking his head as he opened the passenger door for her, he muttered, "You're killing me, Jess."

She slid into the car, smoothing the skirt of her dress. "Slowly, I hope."

They were several minutes down the road before either of them spoke. For his part, it took all his mental energy to concentrate on keeping the car on the road. Knowing nothing separated the silky fabric from her skin sent his head spinning. Didn't she know he was nervous enough about tonight as it was?

When they reached Main Street, Jessica broke the silence. "Let's not drive through town," she said. "We can take Rock Creek Road. Pick up the highway on the other side of the foothills and be there almost as soon."

That was an exaggeration at best. Taking Rock Creek Road would add a good fifteen minutes onto the drive. But he didn't argue with her. Why not postpone the inevitable?

So he turned left on Main Street instead of right. Drove away from town and from the country club. Away from the social and work obligations they'd both eventually have to return to. Eventually, but not yet.

Rock Creek Road met Main Street just west of town. From there it snaked north through the foothills of the Sierra Nevada. Like all country roads, the lighting was poor to nonexistent. The branches of the trees on either side of the road met overhead, intermittently blocking out the starlight. When the wind was right, the breezes carried the scent of the apple blossoms from the nearby orchards. On one of the hairpin turns, there was room to pull off. The surrounding trees had been trimmed, revealing a spectacular view of the town.

Making the drive, it seemed as if no time had passed. Following the curves of the road, Alex felt eighteen again. Young and stupid with passion. But this time he was stupid with love, as well.

It seemed he'd been waiting his whole life to drive up this road with Jessica beside him in the car. Nothing had ever felt more right.

As they approached the bend in the road, he slowed the car. "Do you want to stop?"

Looking at him from beneath her lashes, she nodded. "You bet."

He slowed the car to a stop, having turned off the road, then angling the car for the best view of the city before setting the parking brake. The surrounding trees were taller than he remembered.

"Funny," he said. "The view's not as impressive as I remember."

"Funny, I didn't think you came here to admire the view."

He laughed. "That's true. But the view helped."

"You sound nervous." She reached out her hand to his then toyed with his fingers where they rested on the gearshift. "Don't tell me you're worried about tonight."

"Nervous? No." *Terrified? Yes.*

Terrified that as soon as they arrived at the gala, he'd do something stupid to embarrass her. Or that he'd insult someone important. That even if he stood in the corner and didn't talk to anyone the whole night, that by the time they left, she'd know the truth about him. That he wasn't really all that different from the dirt-poor, reckless kid he'd been a decade ago. That he had no more right to be with her now than he had then. That she was way out of his league.

"Aren't you going to try to talk me into the back seat?" Her words were bold, but she blushed as she said them.

His control slipped a notch. She looked so lovely in the moonlight. Her hair gleamed, pulled back from her face and twisted into a mass of delicate curls high on the back of her head. Her very skin seemed to glow from within, pale and lovely, pink tingeing her cheeks and the base of her neck.

It'd be so easy to lean over and kiss her. To wipe away her memories of the boy he'd been. But he hesitated before finally forcing himself to ask, "Do you think that's wise?" He glanced at his watch. "The gala has already started. We'll be late as it is."

"You're right. It's not wise. Not at all. In fact, it's a very bad idea."

With a flick of the handle, she swung her car door open. She climbed out then fumbled for a second with a lever. Her seat sprang forward. She raised her skirt as she climbed into the back seat, revealing red high heels, sheer hose and just a glimpse of garters. She pulled the door closed behind her before settling into the seat and toeing off her shoes.

He warred with himself for only a moment, knowing it would be a very bad idea to show up at this gala fresh from making love to Jessica in the back seat of her car. But facing this temptation, logic simply couldn't win out. It took him mere seconds to join her.

He wanted to pull her immediately into his arms. To grind her mouth beneath his and to bury himself in her body. To make her completely his in the only way he knew how.

He may not have the money or the resources or the background that she deserved. But he did have this…this sexual connection to her. The ability to drive her crazy.

It might be all he had going for him. Maybe it wouldn't be enough. Or maybe it would.

He stopped himself just short of dragging her against his body. That wasn't how this was done. Up on Rock Creek Road, in the back seat of a car, a girl needed to be coaxed. Tempted into doing things she knew she wasn't supposed to. Push for too much too soon and you'd lose everything.

So instead of exploring her luscious mouth, he draped his arm across her shoulder and pulled her to his side. Easing back against the supple leather of the seat, he pretended to look at the stars.

"Do you know," she mused. "You were the first person I ever heard use the F-word out loud."

"The F-word?" he teased.

She nodded seriously. "Oh, yes. You must have been in the eighth grade. Mr. Menchero, the band teacher, caught you smoking behind the band hall. You told him to F-off."

He twisted slightly in his seat to better watch her face. Each time she said "F," she pursed her lips slightly. Proof that underneath that sex-goddess dress, she was still the judge's proper daughter.

On a hunch he asked, "Jess, have you ever said—" he hesitated, then borrowed her phrasing "—the F-word out loud?"

She scoffed. "Of course—" But her blush gave her away and she admitted, "Not."

Her skin seemed to glow in the moonlight. He couldn't keep himself from touching her. His fingers nearly trembled with need, but he merely stroked her shoulder, down the length of her arm to the inside of her elbow. "How old are you?" he asked. "Twenty-eight?"

She shivered, leaning closer to him. "Twenty-nine."

"Twenty-nine years old and you've never said the F-word?" Unable to resist the lure of her skin any longer, he nuzzled her neck. The scent of her perfume washed over him, no longer as foreign as it had been that first day he'd kissed her, but still exotic. Still intoxicating.

She gasped, then struggled for words. "It's always seemed like such an angry word."

He kissed her neck, her cheek, making his way to her mouth. As he kissed her, her words reached him through a fog of desire. *What was she talking about?*

Her mouth was hot beneath his. Hot and begging. But also, as always, just a little bit prim. That prim little mouth of hers was one of the things that turned him on the most.

That's right. The F-word.

Just the thought of hearing her prim little mouth say that word out loud made him hard.

He pulled her closer, dragging her half across his body. As he cupped her breasts, he murmured, "You're right. It can be an angry word." His hands found the open back of her dress. Pulling her even closer, he reveled in the softness of her skin. "But it can also be a sexy word."

She pulled away from his kiss, her expression a curious mixture of desire and wide-eyed surprise. "A sexy word?"

"Oh, yeah." He hooked his hands on her thighs and pulled her onto his lap so that she straddled him. "Sexy. Hot. And dirty." He bucked his hips against her. "Isn't that what you want, Jess? Sex that's hot and dirty?"

Biting down on her lip, she smiled, her eyes alight with enthusiasm. She twisted, reaching for her purse, which lay on the console between the front seats. From the red beaded bag, she pulled a single condom.

Oh, yes, this was what she wanted. This was what he could give her. Hot and dirty sex. A quick tussle in the back of a car up on Rock Creek Road.

The red satin of her skirt draped over them. He slid his hands beneath the fabric to her silk-encased legs. The stockings were smooth beneath his palms, her skin hot.

His fingers found the straps of her garter belt. The exquisite flesh of her thighs trembled beneath his touch as he ran his hands up the back of her legs to her bare buttocks. She hadn't lied about not wearing any underwear.

Groaning, he squeezed his eyes closed, desperate for

control. He sucked in deep breaths, one after the other. Even as he struggled to control his desire, he couldn't control his hands, which seemed to mindlessly explore her sensitive skin and the tender folds between her legs.

When he felt her hands unfastening his pants, his eyes flew open. In seconds she'd freed his erection and, with trembling fingers, eased the condom down its length.

He searched her expression in the moonlight. Her lips were red and glistening, her eyelids lowered, her gaze dazed by passion.

She massaged his penis through the condom, her hand hot and eager. She began to lower herself onto his length, but he gripped her hips, holding her above him.

"Not yet," he gasped.

She moaned in protest, her eyes fluttering open.

"Tell me what you want."

"I want you," she said simply.

He wasn't even inside her yet, but already he could feel his orgasm building low in his belly. It took all of his will to hold back. "What do you want me to do?"

"I want you to make love to me."

"No, Jess, this isn't making love. Making love is tender and sweet. This is hot and dirty."

Her eyes flashed with frustration, but then she caught on to the game and she smiled. "I want you to F-word me."

His fingers found the nub of her desire. Stroking her with his thumb, he insisted, "Say it. Come on, Jess."

She jerked and trembled at his touch. His body strained toward hers. Bracing her palms on his shoulders, she leaned over and whispered the words in his ear, demanding what she wanted. He surged up into her, gasping in relief. Driving them both over the edge.

But as he held her trembling in his arms, he realized

he'd lied. Whatever kick he'd once gotten out of the idea of nailing Jessica Sumners, the town's good girl, had long since given way to something much more complicated. With her, even when sex was hot and dirty, it was still making love.

17

As ALEX WATCHED Jessica walk across the floor of the country club's main ballroom, for the first time in his life, he felt completely at peace with himself.

He stood listening to one of the city council members—a guy who'd been friends with Tomas back in high school—but his attention was focused entirely on Jessica. She looked breathtaking, with her body encased in that amazing red dress, her blond hair now loose around her shoulders.

When she'd walked through the door, she'd had the attention of every man in the room. But that wasn't the only reason he was glad he had her by his side. She'd worked the crowd like a pro. Remembering everyone's names. Asking about their children and relatives. Their businesses and hobbies.

Conversational sleight of hand, she'd called it. Except now that he saw it up close, he realized it was more than that. She really listened to people. Really cared about them.

That surprised him, even though it probably shouldn't have. He should have known by now there was more to Jessica than met the eye.

The people at the gala surprised him, as well. He'd always pictured the country club filled with rich snobs. People in tuxedoes and glittering gowns looking down their noses at him.

It wasn't like that at all. Half the town had turned up for this thing. He saw people he'd gone to high school with or known as a child as well as people he'd done business with since he'd returned—Hank Hansen, who owned the hardware store, and even Steve Foscoe from the lumberyard. Not necessarily rich people or snobby people. Just people.

As he looked around the room, most of the men, like him, looked a little uncomfortable surrounded by this wealth and glamour. He saw very few men who looked rich enough to own their tuxes and none, other than her father, looked as though they could truly afford these expensive fund-raiser dinners.

He hadn't wanted Jessica to have to settle for a guy like him, a guy who worked in construction. He had worried so much about all the things he couldn't give Jessica. But, really, what could any of these guys give her that he couldn't?

Sure, some of them made more money. A couple of them maybe even could afford those thousand-dollar-a-plate dinners. But had she ever said she wanted that? No, she hadn't. But she had said she wanted him.

And even if he didn't have money or a prestigious job, there was one thing he could offer her that no other man in this room could. His love.

He knew without even a flicker of doubt that he loved her in a way no other man could. And if she was willing, he'd spend the rest of his life making sure she never settled for anything less than she deserved.

He searched the room, wanting to find Jessica, who'd somehow disappeared in the crowd. Needing to be with her, even if he couldn't immediately tell her how he felt. But before he could find her, Senator Sumners cornered him.

As soon as they were alone, he pinned Alex with a steely stare. It was the same emotionless look Alex remembered from the courtroom. And now that he thought about, it was the look Jessica had given him the few times she'd wanted him to keep his distance. The familiarity of it was calming. Sort of.

"It seems you're dating my daughter," the senator said flatly.

Alex wasn't sure if he'd heard disdain in the statement or merely imagined it. He tapped down the barest instinct to shoot off some smart-ass comeback. "Yes, sir, I am."

The senator's eyes narrowed for a second, no doubt gauging his sincerity. Finally his expression relaxed infinitesimally. "You've learned some manners since you were last in my courtroom."

He'd had manners then, he just hadn't seen the point in using them.

"Well." The senator cleared his throat. "No doubt Jessica's led you to expect some kind of inquisition from me."

"Actually, she has."

"Her mother and I tend to be a little overprotective where Jessica is concerned. Because of her good nature, we haven't wanted people to take advantage of her."

"Jessica is one of the most stubborn people I've ever met. I can't imagine anyone taking advantage of her."

The senator frowned. "No, perhaps you can't. Nevertheless—"

"Let me save you some time, Senator. This is the part of the conversation where you warn me off. You remind me that I can't give her all the things she's used to. Point out that we're from different worlds. You ask me to stay away from her. You wrap it up with a big speech about how I'm just not good enough for her."

Jessica's father stared blankly at him for a minute, then asked, "Are you done?"

"No, not yet." He probably should be, but he wasn't. He'd been expecting this speech since he'd walked into the ballroom tonight—hell, he'd been giving it to himself since he'd walked into her house—but in the end, he could think of only one response. "The thing is, sir, you're right. I'm not good enough for her. But the way I see it, who is? I'm not rich like some of the other men in this room, and I can't give her some of the things they can, but I can make her happy. Because I love her more than any other man ever will. And I think she cares about me, too."

"That was quite a speech." The senator studied him with a raised eyebrow. "Did you practice that long?"

"Ever since we walked in." Alex chuckled as he said it, the sound more nervous than amused. He hated standing in front of this man and feeling judged by him.

The senator nodded. "Well, I've been practicing mine a bit longer than that."

Now it was Alex's turn to raise his eyebrows.

"If I've been hard on the men my daughter dates, it's because I only want her to be happy. If you honestly think you're the man who can do that, you're welcome to give it a try. But I have to warn you, you were right about her being stubborn. If you really love her, I'm not the one you have to convince. She is."

"OH, JESSICA, what *were* you thinking?"

Jessica glanced down at her watch before turning to face her mother. Fifty-two minutes. She braced herself for the faux motherly embrace as a cloud of Chanel No. 5 surrounded her.

"Almost an hour, Mom. You're losing your touch."

Her mother blinked, managing to look both innocent and surprised. "I don't know what you mean."

"Fifty-two minutes. That's the amount of time that's passed since Alex and I walked in the door. Frankly, I would have thought you'd have rushed over to make some snide comment a lot sooner than that."

The surprised innocence flashed briefly to annoyance before settling into an expression of vague hurt. No doubt in case anyone walked close enough to overhear them. Her mother had shanghaied her on her way back from the rest room, which meant they were close to the flow of traffic.

"Really, Jessica, I can't imagine why you'd think I'd do such a thing...but now that you mention it, I was surprised that you didn't bring that nice man you were dating from work."

Biting back her frustration, she said, "I didn't bring him, because we broke up. Quite a while ago, actually. And you know that, because I've mentioned it twice. So why don't you just say whatever it is you're going to say about Alex and get it over with?"

Her mother sighed. "Yes, I know you broke up. I just had hoped you might have worked things out."

"I didn't want to work things out. I knew after two dates he wasn't the kind of guy I'd want to have a relationship with."

"But at least you would have had something in common with him and—"

"He wasn't someone I wanted to spend the rest of my life with. He wasn't someone I could have loved."

"So you're saying you love this Alex person?"

For an instant Jessica thought her heart had stopped beating. Was that what she was saying?

Across the crowded dance floor, her eyes sought Alex. He stood waiting in line at the bar, talking to her father. Both men seemed surprisingly relaxed. Apparently, Alex was fairing better than she was.

He looked comfortable, calm and unbelievably handsome. No one would guess he'd been nervous about coming here tonight. She knew, but only because she'd sensed it in the car. Sensed his desperation when they'd had sex. Sensed it and knew him well enough to understand why he was nervous.

Yes, it had been hard for him to come here tonight. To walk back into the country club he'd helped his uncle remodel. To face all the people—her father included—who'd made things difficult for him. And yet he'd done it. Not—she suddenly realized—because it would be good for his career, but because she'd asked him to.

From across the room, he glanced in her direction and caught her looking at him. His lips curved into a wry smile before he pointedly turned his attention back to the conversation, as if to show her he was doing his best.

"Are you?" her mother asked again.

She pulled her eyes away from Alex to stare blankly at her mother. "I don't know," she answered honestly. "I certainly didn't plan to fall in love with him."

Talk about the understatement of the century. She'd planned to have nothing more than a wild fling with him. Great sex, big passion and a chance to check number one off The List. Nothing more.

Her mother sighed in resignation. "Well, if you are, I don't suppose there's much we can do about it now, is there?"

"Sorry to disappoint you."

The annoyance in her mother's gaze was back. "Look,

dear, I know you like to see me as cold, heartless and manipulative. But I genuinely do want you to be happy. And I just can't imagine you being happy with someone like him. I never could."

Now her mother had her complete attention. "What's that supposed to mean?"

"I just always thought he was wrong for you."

"'Always'? What do you mean you 'always' thought? Alex and I have been together for less than three weeks." And that was being generous. "And you didn't even know we were together until tonight."

"I don't mean now, of course. I mean back when you were in high school."

"Now you've really lost me. There was nothing between Alex and me back then."

"Dear, this is a very small town. You should know as well as anyone how difficult it is to keep a secret. That combined with all those notes he used to write you... Surely you didn't think we didn't know about the two of you."

"Notes?" She thought of the notes they'd sent each other for those few brief weeks in high school. Notes even her best friend Mattie hadn't known about. "How did you know about the notes?"

"Mrs. Nguyen found them in your bedroom and brought them to me."

Shaking her head in confusion and wishing she could shake her mother instead, she said, "And from a handful of notes you and Daddy concluded Alex and I were dating? I barely knew him back in high school. We only spoke a handful of times. We exchanged maybe a dozen notes. That was it."

"So you weren't secretly dating him?"

"No. Why would you even think that?"

This time, her mother looked genuinely surprised. "Well, when he and that Higgins boy fought over you, your father and I just assumed…"

"Alex and Albert Higgins never fought over…" Her voice trailed off as she considered it. "Did they?"

She looked to her mom for answers, even though she knew only Alex could provide them.

Nevertheless her mother nodded. "I'm afraid they did. You didn't know?"

"No, I had no…wait a second, was that why Daddy 'suggested' Alex leave town? Because you two thought Alex and I were secretly dating?"

Her mother fumed and at least had the grace to look ashamed. "Your father believed it would be for the best. For you and for him. The Higginses were prepared to press charges against him and he never could have afforded a decent lawyer. It seemed like the best solution for all involved."

Appalled at her father's questionable ethics, she snapped, "For you and the Higginses maybe, but not—"

"Yes, for Alex, too," her mother interrupted her. "He'd been arrested several times before—he'd been on probation, for goodness' sakes. But he was over eighteen this time, a legal adult. If he'd been charged with assault and battery—"

"So instead, everything was just swept under the carpet and hushed up. Do you have any idea how ethically questionable this is?" Shaking her head, she threw up her hands in exasperation. "Of course you do. You're the wife of a judge. Of a senator."

Her mother stiffened, a hint of indignation creeping into her voice. "Your father did it to protect you—"

"From what? From nothing. There was nothing going on between Alex and me."

"Your father didn't know that."

"Well, he could have asked! I guess that's Daddy at his dictatorial worst." Almost pleading for understanding, she looked to her mother. "Why didn't you ask?"

Staring off into the crowd as if looking into the past, her mother sighed, shaking her head. "I don't know. I guess we thought we were protecting you. You were always such a good girl. So serious. So well behaved. And a boy like Alex Moreno? Always getting into trouble. Well, we could see why you would be drawn to each other."

Of course, Jessica had to admit, they'd been right about that. For her part at least. She had been drawn to Alex even back then.

"Your father thought it would be better if the whole thing just went away. He was worried that if he confronted you about it, you'd do something stupid. Young love can be very stupid, you know."

But she didn't know. She'd never been in love when she was young. The question was, was she in love now?

After a few minutes of awkward silence, her mother excused herself and disappeared, leaving Jessica alone with her thoughts.

Her gaze automatically found Alex in the crowd. He'd ditched her father and appeared to be trying to make his way over to her, a drink in each hand, although he'd been stopped and drawn into yet another conversation.

She hadn't been particularly worried about how he would handle himself tonight, but it was nice to know he was doing just fine without her. Apparently he didn't need her help, after all.

As she turned to make her way back to the table they

shared with Brad and Mattie, she caught a glimpse of the man she'd been secretly looking for all night long: Martin Schaffer, the owner of the Hotel Mimosa. It had taken her several phone calls to convince Martin to drive in for the gala, but since he was the last man Moreno Construction had worked for, she was sure it would be worth it. She'd done some additional poking around online and learned that Martin was active in historical preservation groups across the state.

If anyone could convince the members of the historical society that Alex could do the courthouse remodel, he could.

As she made her way across the crowded room, she renewed her determination to help Alex. His relationship with her may have hurt him in the past, but now she'd finally found a way to really help his career.

Martin greeted her warmly when she approached him, going so far as to pull her into an enthusiastic bear hug. She laughed awkwardly as she pulled away.

"Oh, look, I've embarrassed you." He swatted at her arm. "But I feel like I know you already. Besides anyone who'd go to such great lengths to help out Alex is practically family already."

"So, you know Alex pretty well, then?"

"He's like a brother. But one that knows how to use a hammer. He's hands down the best general contractor I've ever worked with. I'm itching to talk him up to these old biddies you're worried about. But after that long drive, first I'll need a drink. Then I'll want to say hello to the boy himself. He knows I'm coming?"

"It's a surprise," she explained as they made their way across the room to where she'd last seen Alex.

"Excellent." Martin clapped his hands together. "You know, I was surprised when you called."

"Well, I imagine." After all, how could he have antici-pated her calling?

"I mean, I'm just tickled pink he's up for a job like this courthouse of yours, but I certainly didn't see it coming."

"What do you mean, a job like this?" she asked with trepidation. "I thought the job he did renovating the Hotel Mimosa was even bigger than this."

"It was. I just remember how glad he was it was done. He said he couldn't wait to move home and scale things back a bit. Have a personal life for once." He slanted her a suggestive look. "Which I guess he's been doing."

"Hmm," she said noncommittally. Forming an actual response was completely beyond her because she was still trying to sort out exactly what Martin's words meant.

Alex didn't want any more big jobs? Which meant he didn't want the job at the courthouse. So why hadn't he told her?

But here he was, dutifully schmoozing with everyone in town, making the best of a situation he'd never wanted to be in. All so he could get a job he didn't want. All be-cause she'd pushed him into it.

She felt as if Martin had pulled the rug out from under her, and it was just one shock too many. She continued to walk alongside Martin, introducing him to all the right people and saying all the right things, but her thoughts continued to swirl around this problem with Alex.

After tonight, she certainly understood why he'd been so sure a relationship with her would hurt his business. Mere rumors—false rumors, for that matter—about their relationship had already had a huge impact on his life.

No wonder he'd tried to keep her at arms' length. Not that it had done him any good. She'd been so sure of her-self, she'd dismissed all of his concerns. Just ignored them.

And she'd accused her father of being dictatorial. It seemed she was more like him than she wanted to admit.

And unlike him, as well. She still couldn't believe he'd done something so unethical, so questionable. That knowledge skewed everything she knew about herself.

Her mother was right. All her life she had been such a good girl. She'd always assumed it was just part of being the judge's daughter. As though it were a trait she'd inherited or something. Or worse still, something the town had inflicted on her. But now she realized it wasn't just a good-girl image. It was who she was.

Her father's actions horrified her. They offended her. How very good girl-ish of her. How very moral.

It seemed, at the end of the day, she wasn't *Saucy* after all. She was, in fact, exactly what she'd been trying to avoid being all along…a very good girl. Moral, upstanding and—when it came to some things—very proper.

She sighed with resignation. So her mother thought young love could be stupid? Well, adult love wasn't shaping up to be very smart, either. She couldn't change who she was. Not even for Alex. Oh, she'd tried to be saucy, tried to shed that good-girl image, but she couldn't change who she was deep down.

She realized that now. And sooner or later, he would, too.

With that thought sitting heavy in her gut, she once again looked for Alex, only this time, something else caught her attention. Brad and Mattie, dancing together.

Leading her across the dance floor to the old Etta James favorite, "At Last," Brad swung her around and whispered something in her ear that made her giggle and blush before he spun her out the length of his arm. It was a perfect, movie-worthy moment.

And they both looked so happy. So perfectly matched to each other, so completely in love. In that instant, it seemed hard to believe that they hadn't always been in love. That every moment of their lives hadn't been leading up to this one.

But then, maybe they had.

Her breath seemed to catch in her chest as she watched them dance. Suddenly she knew what she wanted.

Yes, she wanted passion. But she didn't want just passionate sex from Alex. She wanted passionate love.

Suddenly she knew what her biggest fear was. It wasn't loving Alex, it was losing him. Not being with him, not living her life with him, was by far the scariest thing she could imagine. Nevertheless, she'd have to give him up.

When she'd started this journey to becoming a *Saucy* woman, she'd promised herself that she'd never again settle for less than she deserved. She deserved to be with a man who loved her, and he didn't. He couldn't love her because he didn't even know her. She'd just spent the past two weeks convincing him she was someone other than who she really was.

18

"DO YOU EVEN WANT the job renovating the courthouse?"

"Sure, but—"

"No, I mean, do you *really* want it? All this time, I've been pushing, thinking it was what you wanted, but now, I'm not so sure."

She sounded so confused and unsure, so unlike herself, that it worried him. "Jess, what's up?"

She stared out the window, not even glancing in his direction as he navigated the winding roads back to her house.

"I just assumed I knew what was best for you. I was so sure I was right. I just kept pushing..." Her voice broke and he heard her clear her throat before continuing. "But tonight when I was talking to Martin, I realized you don't even want the job at the courthouse. After the amazing work you did on the Hotel Mimosa, you had it made, you could have gone anywhere and gotten any job, but instead you came home."

Now she did turn to look at him, and it made him nervous, because he knew what she was about to say and he knew he couldn't lie to her.

"I thought you'd come home so you could show everyone how successful you'd been, but that wasn't it, was it?" She didn't wait for him to answer, but plunged ahead.

"You came home to avoid success, because success made you feel guilty, like you were betraying your parents. That's the real reason why you never worked on a bid for the job at the courthouse. It wasn't just that you thought you wouldn't get it, it's that you didn't want it."

He kept his gaze pinned to the road, trying to think of something to say, but when she asked him point-blank, the words seemed to stick a little in his throat.

"I'm right, aren't I?"

"Maybe." He pulled his hand off the gearshift long enough to run his fingers through his hair. "Yeah, I guess that was part of it. But I don't think even I knew that when I first moved back. I wanted to be closer to my family. And I was tired of running away from my past."

"You should have said something."

"It seemed important to you." He hadn't wanted to disappoint her. And he'd liked the way she stood up for him. No one had ever done that before. Besides, if he'd told her point-blank, she probably wouldn't have hired him to remodel her kitchen. Then he wouldn't have had an excuse to see her every day. To spend time with her.

"Right. It seemed important to me. It *was* important to me. But only because I thought it was what you wanted. I was just so sure I was right, I never stopped to ask you what you wanted."

He didn't like where this was going. When he turned the corner onto her street, relief flooded him. As soon as he set the emergency break in her driveway, he reached for her.

But she flattened herself against the door, just out of his reach.

"Jess, you want to know what's important to me? You are. You're the only thing that matters. I do care about the job at the courthouse. I want it because you want me to have it. I want it for you. I lo—"

She practically lunged across the car, pressing her fingers against his lips, trapping the words in his mouth.

"Don't say that. You don't really mean it. You just think you do."

Huh?

He didn't even get the chance to ask her what the hell she was talking about, because she kept talking.

"You may think you care about me, but you're wrong. You only think that because I've made you believe it."

He grabbed her wrist and pulled her fingers from his mouth. "What are you talking about?"

"I was so sure I could make you want me, that we'd be good together, that I didn't even stop to think about what you would want."

"*You* are what I want."

"No, I'm not. Not really. Don't you remember what you said? You wanted someone light and casual. Someone playful and wild. Someone saucy. I'm none of those things."

"Jessica that was just a random list. That's not what I really want."

But she ignored him completely. "I made you believe I was those things because I wanted to be with you. Just like I pushed you to do the bid for the courthouse because I believe it would make you happy. I was so sure I knew how to fix everything and now I've just mucked everything up."

"But, Jessica—"

"You don't have to worry anymore. I'm through messing up your life. I've decided to go back to Sweden."

"Sweden?" What the hell was she talking about?

"Yes." Her voice hardened with her resolve. "When I was there on business, the company I worked with offered me a job. It's a great position."

All he could do was repeat numbly, "Sweden?"

"This will be for the best. I know it will."

And with that, she threw open the car and ran to her house in a flurry of red silk. For a moment he considered going after her right there and then, but he wasn't sure it would do any good.

She had it all worked out in her head. Boy, talk about mucking things up.

She thought she had it all figured out. But she hadn't counted on one thing. He didn't just think he was in love with the woman she was pretending to be. He knew he was in love with the woman she was.

JESSICA SHUT HER front door behind her, locked the dead bolt and leaned her back against the closed door. She stood in the darkened hall with her head ducked, a heavy lock of her hair hanging in front of her eyes, one hand clenching the beaded purse she'd carried, the other grasping the lone house key she'd kept tucked inside. Holding her breath, she listened for the sound of his truck starting up and pulling away from her house.

Any second now she'd hear it. He'd be mad—furious maybe. The engine would roar to life, he'd slam the truck into gear and tear down the street. The way he used to in his Camaro all those years ago.

She heard the truck start and, when it didn't pull away, she pictured him sitting there. Mulling over her words. Replaying them in his mind, just as she was doing.

Any second now he'd realize the truth of what she'd said, put the truck in gear and drive away. Maybe out of her life forever.

She squeezed her eyes closed, summoning the courage to let him go, when what she really wanted to do was throw the door open and run after him.

This is for the best, she told herself sternly. *For you and him.*

Chanting those words over and over, she dropped her purse and the house key onto the console table by the door and walked down the hall, toward her bedroom. Her boring cream bedroom, which perfectly matched her boring bland house and her boring bland life.

Then she heard the one noise she hadn't expected. The sound of her front door opening behind her. She stilled, held her breath and then spun around.

Alex stood, framed by the open doorway, dangling her car keys from his forefinger.

"Next time you plan a dramatic exit," he said lightly, leaning his shoulder against the doorjamb, "you might want to get your car keys back first."

He tossed the keys in her direction, but she didn't react fast enough and they landed at her feet with a clatter.

She'd just ended their relationship and he was teasing her?

"You brought me back my keys," she said numbly.

"Yep."

His mocking smile wore away at her already frail self-control. "I just broke up with you—I just told you I was moving to Sweden—and you brought me back my keys."

He nodded. "Yeah, that about sums it up."

Shock gave way to stirrings of anger. "I just broke up with you and you're not upset at all. Are you?"

His shoulders shifted beneath the tux jacket as he shrugged indifferently. "No, not really."

"What is wrong with you?" She heard her voice rising toward hysteria, but seemed unable to curb it. "Did our relationship mean nothing to you? Do you feel noth—"

Before she could finish her outburst, he propelled himself away from the door and toed it closed in one quick motion. A second later he pulled her into his arms, molded her body to his and kissed her.

His lips were hot and hard against hers, his mouth demanding, urgent and filled with emotion. Not light and casual emotion, either. Not playful or fun. It was a kiss full of dark possessiveness and layered with complexity.

By the time he pulled away from her, she knew for sure that he definitely felt more than nothing for her.

He stared down at her in the dimly lit hall. A single table lamp in the other room cast a shadow across his face, obscuring his expression. But—despite the intensity of his kiss—his tone was teasing when he said, "You know, it's rude to interrupt someone when they're talking."

"It—it is?"

"Absolutely. I'd have thought you of all people would know that."

"I—I do, but—"

"Then let me finish what I was saying out there in the car. I love you, Jessica."

"But—"

"The woman you are. Stubborn, serious, honest and fair. I love it when you try to be light and playful. I love it when you fail. I love it when you're naughty, but I love it more when you're good."

His gaze darkened as he stared down at her. His fingers

traced the line of her jaw down to her chin where he chucked her lightly. "I love it when you push me harder than I would push myself. Being with you makes me want more than I would want on my own. It was like that even back in high school, when I'd spend hours working on those notes so you'd think I was smart. I even love the way you get all bossy and try to make decisions for everyone else, but I'm not going to let you get away with it this time."

"But don't you see? That's not what I'm doing this time. I'm backing off. I'm letting it go."

That was, after all, the phrase he'd used over and over when she'd pressed him to get his bid completed for the courthouse.

But he shook his head as if chastising her. "No, you're not."

"But—"

"Do you believe I love you?"

"No, you just think you do because—"

"So you didn't believe me when I said I didn't want to put in a bid on the courthouse, and you don't believe me now when I say I love you. It's not different. You're still doing it."

"But—" And damn it, he was right. What she was doing now *wasn't* any different. Except that she *knew* she was right about this…just like she'd been sure before.

With a frustrated sigh, she asked, "So what do we do?"

He pulled her toward his chest, laughing as he comforted her. "You're just going to have to learn to believe me when I say I love you just as you are. Not lighter. Not more playful. Not more wild."

Her breath caught in her chest as relief welled up inside her. "I—I'll try?"

She felt his arm tighten across her back and a tension she hadn't even realized he'd been feeling begin to dissipate from his muscles.

"You know now would be a great time to tell me you love me, too."

She pulled back just enough to look up into his eyes. "I do love you, too. You don't doubt that do you?"

"Good, because you told me over and over again not to settle for less than I deserve. I'm still not convinced I deserve you, but you are what I want. And I want all of you. Your whole heart, your whole mind, forever. And I don't want to settle for anything less than that."

Her happiness blossomed within her. "That works out well. Because I don't want to, either."

She rose up onto her toes as if to kiss him, but he stopped her just shy of it. "I might as well say this now, since I'm on a roll. I don't want to move to Sweden."

Blinking in confusion, she said, "Huh?"

"If you want that job in Sweden, you should take it. I'll even go there with you—hell, people in Sweden need decks or saunas or something—but I'd much rather stay right here."

"I don't want to move to Sweden, either. I just didn't want to be here without you."

He nuzzled her neck with his lips and, at his touch, a shiver of anticipation curled its way through her body. She pressed herself closer to him, leaning up to whisper a suggestion in his ear. This time, she didn't hesitate to use a very dirty word. There were lots of words she'd heard and never used. Lots of things she'd never tried. A lot of them were naughty words, words she'd never said out loud. But some of them were words she'd used all her life but never understood.

Words like commitment, marriage, love and happiness.

Epilogue

JESSICA WENT TRIBAL for her wedding day, too, the backs of her hands painted in a traditional Mendhi wedding design, to signify her transformation from fiancée to wife. On her left hand she wore the antique pearl ring he'd scoured the shops to find. It wasn't the huge diamond some other guy might have been able to afford, but it suited Jessica perfectly. Besides, he'd wanted to replace the pearl necklace she'd given to Miranda.

Jessica's mother sniffed with disapproval when she saw the designs. But then again, she liked almost nothing about Jessica's and Alex's wedding. And the Mendhi was the least of her complaints, given the fact that they weren't even wed in a church, but rather in the just-completed foyer of the courthouse.

Alex had had to push to get the foyer ready in time, but he'd managed it, nevertheless.

Jessica's sole concession to her mother was to have the reception at the country club. And as Alex led her across the dance floor while "At Last" played in the background, she whispered into his ear, "I hate to admit it, but my mother was right. I'm glad we had the reception here."

"We had to," he murmured back. "It was the only place big enough to hold everyone. I told you everyone in Palo Verde loves you."

She smiled into his neck. "They love you, too, you know."

He snorted. "Now that we're married, they do."

But if he was honest, the town had warmed up to him long before their wedding or even their engagement. Sure, there were a few people, like Mrs. Higgins, who still gave him the cold shoulder occasionally, but even she'd begun to warm up once he'd started working on the courthouse.

Dancing with Jessica now, it seemed as if he'd always been as much a part of this town as she had. Surrounded by her family and his, as well as half the town, it was hard to remember why he'd stayed away so long, when clearly, this had always been home.

"Funny," he mused. "It feels like my whole life has been leading up to this moment."

As soon as he heard how cheesy the words sounded, he wished he could take them back.

But then Jessica looked up at him, her head tilted to the side in that way she had, a slightly bemused expression on her face. "That's exactly how I feel."

Her words reminded him all over again why he loved her so much. She was the one person in the world he could say anything to. She always had been.

We hope you found The Passion Collection *to be burning with steamy, seductive excitement.*

*Don't forget, you can experience **brand new** scorching hot sexy reads from Mills & Boon Blaze*

&

passionate, dramatic love stories from Silhouette Desire every month!

Now turn the page for a sneak preview of Turn Me On *by Kristin Hardy, only from Mills & Boon Blaze.*

Available from all good booksellers in January 2006.

Turn Me On
by
Kristin Hardy

Big Drama Behind the Scenes
Kelly Vandervere, staff writer
Daily Californian

When it comes to drama, the play's the thing. It's not just about acting, though. If it weren't for a crew of dedicated behind-the-scenes volunteers, the drama department's spring 1996 production of Shakespeare's *Henry V* would never see the light of day.

Dialogue is key, which is why Trish Dawson and her collaborators from the English deaprtment have spent many hours trimming the script to fit a two-hour college production. It's not all words, though. *Henry V* also includes dramatic battle scenes choreographed by dance major Thea Mitchell.

And the production has to look right. Design major Cilla Danforth supervises wardrobe, coming up with authentic-looking period costumes from the drama department's archives. Paige Wheeler, also from the design department, complements Danforth's work with gorgeous set decoration that evokes the medieval era.

Of course, all that hard work wouldn't mean anything

without the clever marketing campaign of business major Delaney Phillips. And to make sure the production is recorded for posterity, film major Sabrina Pantolini is capturing it in a video documentary.

So when you're in your seats tonight enjoying the premiere of the production, applaud the actors but don't forget to clap a few times for all the other folks who make the magic happen.

1

"WHAT I WANT FROM YOU, honey, is sex." Royce Schuyler, the Home Cinema vice president of programming, stared across the restaurant table to where Sabrina Pantolini sat—poised, sleek and dark like a silky cat. "You give me that, and everything else will follow."

"Royce, honey, I'll give you the best sex you've ever had." Sabrina smiled, her eyes ripe with promise and fun. A golden topaz hung winking from a gold chain around her neck. "This documentary series is going to have people stopping to take cold showers."

"Swingers are old hat. Don't give me swingers."

Sabrina snorted and pushed her short, dark hair back behind her ears. "Forget swingers. That's practically pedestrian. I'm talking about blow job tutors, exhibitionist hotels, you name it. It's perfect for cable—all the stuff that the networks would never have the nerve to touch, and you guys will be putting it right in the late-night living rooms of Middle America."

"With a guarantee like that, I'm looking forward to the pilot."

"Great. Does that mean you're ready to sign on for

it?" Her goat cheese and heirloom tomato salad sat in front of her, forgotten.

Royce shook his head and scanned the restaurant with a practiced eye. "Not yet. I want to see what you've got when you finish the pilot."

"I need working capital, Royce."

"I'm sure you do, but I can't give it to you." He took a drink of his seltzer water. "Right now, you've got no track record and no staff on board."

Sabrina suppressed a surge of annoyance. The money she was asking for was chump change for a cable network like Home Cinema and Schuyler knew it. On the other hand, she was fortunate he was even here talking to her. If she'd been anyone else, she'd have been lucky to meet some mid-level flunky in the city offices. Instead, she was here talking with Home Cinema's vice president of programming in a see-and-be-seen restaurant.

She had no illusions about why she was getting the VIP treatment. Her father, Michael Pantolini, had been the kind of director people talked about in hushed whispers. Even five years after his death in an auto accident, Sabrina was still connected to the Hollywood power structure through her producer uncle, her action-star cousin and her set-designer mother. Sabrina was Hollywood royalty, but if it gave her some small edge, it also made her chafe.

"I can make a better pilot if I have Home Cinema behind me," she said in a slightly bored voice, waving across the room to an actress she knew slightly.

"Find a way to make a hot pilot on your own. That's the mark of a good producer. Bring it to me and we'll talk." Royce took a sip of his drink. "Hey, isn't that your cousin who just came in?"

Sabrina glanced over at the door where Matt Ramsay had just arrived with this month's hot starlet on his arm. Oh yeah, she knew how this worked. Royce expected her to call Matt over and introduce them. It would up Royce's collateral with everyone in the room to be seen talking to the big box-office hero. And maybe the next time Royce was looking to cast an action miniseries, he'd have a better chance of getting Matt. Sabrina stifled a sigh. Sometimes she found the treacly, sycophantic side of Hollywood almost impossible to tolerate.

If she were smart, she'd use Matt to work Royce and get her funding. That was how it was done in Hollywood. Sabrina wasn't always smart that way, though. She had a feisty disposition as classically Italian as the arc of her cheekbones, her vivid coloring and the hollows of her eyelids that somehow lent an extra importance to her every expression. She didn't want to use her family connections to make this happen. She wanted to make *True Sex* fly on its own. If she could have gotten away with it, she'd have used her mother's name. Unfortunately, Sabrina Pantolini was far too well-known from her years in the media spotlight to work incognito.

Matt waved and started over to where she sat.

Sabrina sighed. "All right, Schuyler, I'll get you your pilot in six weeks. You like it, you give me a series contract." She rose. "Thanks for lunch."

"SO ARE YOU AN AUNTIE YET, Laeticia?" Sabrina asked her assistant as she breezed into the office of Pantolini

Productions. Offices, really, if you counted the tiny reception/waiting area as separate from the cramped room behind it. Though her offices were tucked in an old building off Hollywood Boulevard instead of in Westwood, they were hers. Besides, they were big enough in a town where all the important meetings took place in restaurants.

"An auntie? Not so far. My sister's taking her time. Of course, that girl's been late for everything since her own birth, so it doesn't surprise me a bit." Laeticia was long and slender, with gorgeous, mocha-colored skin and doe-soft eyes. When they'd met, Sabrina had wondered how a woman like Laeticia could possibly take on the production coordinator's role of logistics, paperwork and organization, let alone survive the Hollywood meat grinder. To her surprise, the woman was ruthlessly efficient, able to alternately sweet-talk and bully as the situation demanded. Anyone who underestimated Laeticia did so at his peril.

"Patience. You know what they say about watched pots."

"Mmmm. So how did the meeting go with the brass?"

Sabrina moved her shoulders noncommittally. "Well enough, I suppose. They want to see more. Now we just have to deliver."

"That doesn't sound too hard."

Sabrina made a face at her. "Any messages or mail?"

"Your new cell phone is here," Laeticia said, handing her a small box. "I activated it for you. Try not to lose this one, hmmm?"

Sabrina grinned. "You're a lifesaver."

Laeticia picked up a pair of small pink notes. "Gus Stirling called to remind you that the night shoot on the *Hollywood Hauntings* project has moved to the Sunset Boulevard location."

Augustus Stirling, Sabrina's godfather and teacher. The thought of seeing him made her smile, though with the night shoot he had planned, they'd probably go until the sun was coming up. No sleep for her tonight, she thought resignedly. The fact that in her partying days she'd seldom arrived home before breakfast didn't make her any happier about missing her slumber. Back then, she'd crash until three or four in the afternoon if she'd felt like it. Now, she had to rise and shine early in the morning to meet deadlines and get work done.

But Gus had taken her seriously when she'd decided she wanted to work in film and had taught her the job from the ground up. He'd been tough on her, forcing her to prove herself again and again. He wasn't shy about working her hard and she'd be damned if she'd stop a second before he did.

"You also had a call from Kelly Vandervere, reminding you that the Supper Club is at Gilbert's at seven."

Nachos, margaritas and gossip with old friends. Sabrina's mouth curved into an arc of pleasure. That much, at least, would make the rest of the night tolerable. "And?"

"Just remember, don't get too worn out tonight. If Kisha goes into labor later, I might be coming in late tomorrow."

Sabrina winked at her. "Here's hoping I'm on my own and you're an auntie."

"Just what I need—baby-sitting and diaper-changing duties," Laeticia muttered, but her eyes held a smile as she said it.

FIVE HOURS LATER, Sabrina opened the glass door of Gilbert's and stepped into a bar area filled with the sound of blenders. It seemed as if half her time was spent in restaurants, she thought wryly as she passed the hostess stand with a nod. Then she turned the corner and spied the group of women seated at a table, talking animatedly, half hidden by a lattice. The usual faces.

And the usual discussions.

"Forget all this feel-good stuff. Reality is, size matters," said a tawny-haired woman with an angular face.

"Not true." The words were definite, the speaker dressed in a silky floral op-art blouse from the latest Dolce & Gabbana collection. "Bigger might be better, but it's what he does with it that makes the difference."

The first woman snorted. "Oh, come on, Cilla. The guy's twenty-two," she said, taking a swig of her margarita. "He doesn't know enough to do anything with it. With them, it's just in and out, with maybe a few hours sleep in between. At least if it's big, he's got a fighting chance to do some good."

Sabrina ducked around the corner. "On the other hand, there's a limit to size. It has to be big enough for basic purposes, but too much beyond that it just hurts."

Six sets of eyes stared at her blankly.

"Sabrina? Good to see you, sweetie, but what the hell do you mean?" asked the tawny-haired woman, Kelly Vandervere.

Sabrina pulled up a chair at the table and signaled to the waiter for a beer. "Come on, admit it. We've all had to groan through getting pounded by some guy who thinks a monster boner and an ability to recite batting averages in his head is all he needs to send a woman to heaven. Size isn't everything." She speared a pickled jalapeño out of the bowl on the table.

"What are you talking about?" asked Cilla Danforth, an amused frown on her triangular, foxy-looking face.

It was Sabrina's turn to look blank. "Tackle. Aren't you?"

Laughter rose around her. "Apartments," said Kelly, wiping her eyes. "We were talking about my little brother's new apartment. Only someone with your filthy mind would think we were talking about dicks."

"Sorry. It was the thought of all your dirty minds that made me assume you were talking about sex," Sabrina said with dignity, taking her beer from the waiter. "So if you're not talking about it, does that mean that nobody's getting it?"

"Do you guys realize we've talked about sex every single week for the past five years? You're obsessed. Let's do something else for a change." Dark-haired Thea Mitchell, dressed in her perpetual black, scooped up salsa with a chip and crunched it.

Cilla and Kelly looked at each other. "I like talking about sex," Kelly offered.

"Yeah. It's the next best thing to having it," tossed in Delaney Phillips, a corn-silk blonde in a candy-pink lace camisole and a black choker. "I bet you'd change your tune if we just set you up with a man. We could do Trish, too, while we're at it."

"No way." With her curly red hair skinned back from her face and no makeup, Trish almost managed to disguise her gorgeous bone structure. "I'm on dating sabbatical, remember? That's why I hang out with you guys—to live vicariously."

"Well, *somebody's* got to be getting it." Sabrina looked around the table.

"Possibly," Cilla said. "Paige had a date the other night, I know, because she wouldn't go to the gym with me."

Cool and patrician, Paige gave a graceful shrug. "Nothing much to tell. He was just my escort to a fund-raiser."

Five heads around the table perked up. "Spill it," Kelly demanded.

Paige shook her head and the blond layers of her expensive haircut swished and settled perfectly. "His name is Landon, and—"

"That should have sent you running right there," Cilla interjected. "Never date a guy with a trust-fund name. I know these guys, Paige. You're just asking for death by boredom."

"Says the trust-fund kid herself," Trish jabbed lightly.

"I don't have a trust fund."

Trish rolled her eyes. "I'm sorry, a chain of department stores."

"The stores belong to my dad." Cilla twisted her chunky amethyst David Yurman cocktail ring. "I'm just a working stiff like the rest of you, remember? Anyway, we're not talking about me. The guy sounds like a preppster. Where did he grow up, Paige?"

"Greenwich, Connecticut."

"I rest my case," Cilla said smugly.

"He was nice enough. Smart, well-informed." She paused while the waitress set plates of quesadillas in front of them. "Good job in the legal department at Fox."

"Yeah, yeah, yeah." Delaney wrinkled her snub nose. "Get to the good stuff. How did he kiss?"

Paige aimed a chilly look at Delaney, who merely grinned.

"Give it up, Paige. We've seen you cleaning the bathroom in your underwear."

The cool look evaporated and Paige laughed. "I knew I was out of my mind when I moved in with you guys back then."

"Are you kidding? We taught you how to have a good time. Now tell us about the kiss," Kelly ordered.

Paige eyed them. "Too wet. Too much tongue, too quickly."

"Sounds like a first kiss," Thea muttered, taking a sip of her iced tea.

"Was that how your first kiss was?" Cilla asked her. "That's too bad. Mine was pretty good. Jason Stilton, third grade."

"Third grade?" Paige raised an eyebrow.

"He was precocious," Cilla said.

"Or someone was," Delaney said. "I didn't get my first kiss until eighth grade. "Jake Gordon, boyfriend number one." She sighed a little dreamily.

"I don't remember the name of my first kiss, but I bet the location's got you all beat," Kelly wagered.

"I'll bite," Sabrina said. "Where?"

"On the Matterhorn at Disneyland."

"The Matterhorn?" Sabrina reached out for a slice of quesadilla. "You know the make-out ride was the Haunted Mansion."

"Hey, you take what you can get when you can get it."

Delaney snorted. "And when can you get it on the Matterhorn? Try it there, you lose some teeth."

"You know the part where you're getting pulled up the first hill? My girlfriend and I had met him and his buddy in line, so he was sitting behind me in the bobsled. I leaned back to say something to him and wham, full tongue and everything."

"Nothing like jumping in at the deep end," Trish said.

"Shocked the heck out of me. I was thirteen. I thought kissing was about lips. Then we got to the top of the hill and the ride started."

"You didn't keep kissing, did you?"

"God no. We'd have dislocated our necks, or at least lost our tongues."

"Well, I don't know about the first kiss, but my best kiss is still Carl Reynolds, that guy I dated last year," said Cilla, reaching out for a pickled carrot.

"I thought you said he was a waste of a human being," Paige objected.

"Oh, he was. But he was still a great kisser," Cilla said.

"My best kisser was the guy I went out with last week, I think," Kelly threw in. "Of course, that's always subject to change," she said with an appraising glance around the room. "What about you, Sabrina?"

"What, best kiss or first kiss?"

"Best kiss. First kiss is too easy."

Sabrina took a thoughtful drink of her beer and set it down. "Stef Costas, the first time we kissed."

"Definite waste of a human being," Kelly said decisively.

"But a great kisser."

SABRINA OPENED HER PURSE and pulled out a couple of bills to toss on the table. "Okay, that's all for me."

Delaney stared at her. "It's only nine-thirty."

"I've got a night shoot starting in an hour," she explained.

"A night shoot?" Kelly might have worked for *Hot Ticket* magazine for her day job, but as near as Sabrina could tell, she was never off shift.

"For the Hollywood ghost documentary. We're going to the *Château Mirabelle,* where Elaine Chandler overdosed. Supposedly there's a cold spot in her room and guests who've stayed there swear they've seen an apparition."

"Brrr. That's creepy," Trish said with a grimace.

"Don't tell me you believe in ghosts." Kelly gave her an amused glance.

"I'm not so cynical that I don't believe there are things out there we don't understand."

"Hah. You just pretend to be a cynic. Deep inside, you're a mushy romantic," Kelly corrected, pulling her plate forward with relish. "I'm the cynic. Forget about Mr. Right. Me, I'll settle for Mr. Right Now. It's a lot less trouble," she said, eyeing the waiter speculatively. "What I don't believe, Sabrina, is that you, with your multimillion-dollar trust fund, are playing the working schlep. In your shoes, I'd quit in a minute."

Trish broke in. "You are so full of it. You'd report for *Hot Ticket* for free and you know it. Where else would you have official license to poke into things that don't concern you?"

Kelly ran her tongue around her teeth. "Okay, guilty as charged. But seriously, Sabrina, why work so hard if you don't have to?"

"You know why. I want to work for myself."

"So do it. You've got the bankroll," Paige pointed out, patting her mouth with her napkin and setting it on the table.

"That's my family's money, not mine. Plus I don't have the know-how, or at least I didn't. You know the deal I made with Uncle Gus—I work, he teaches."

"But you have worked," Trish protested.

"She's right, Rina," Thea said mildly. "You've been at this for almost five years. Whatever happened to that idea you were talking about for a cable documentary?"

Should she say something or would she jinx herself? "Funny you should ask," Sabrina began, a ridiculously broad grin spreading across her face. "I'm just about ready to start shooting."

A chorus of congratulations erupted around the table.

"What does your family think?" asked Cilla, who knew a thing or two about family legacies, having grown up in her father's retail empire.

Sabrina slanted her a dry look. "You know what my family thinks," she said. "That I'll give it up sooner or later for a party." She permitted herself a mischievous smile. "Or at least that's what they'd think if they didn't know the topic of the documentary. If they did, they might be a little less than thrilled."

"What is the topic?" Paige asked, curious.

Sabrina pursed her lips. "Kinky sex, of course."

Kelly hooted. "Tame, Pantolini. Show me a film that's not about sex."

"Wait till you see this one," Sabrina promised, eyes alight with fun. "Sex clubs, exhibitionists in the act, blow job tutorials. Tonight's my last night working for somebody else. Come tomorrow, I get rolling on *True Sex,* coming soon to a cable station near you."

0206/172/MB014a V2

BEFORE SUNRISE
by Diana Palmer

Enter a world of passion, intrigue
and heartfelt emotion. As two
friends delve deeper into a
murder investigation they find
themselves entangled in a web of
conspiracy, deception...and a love
more powerful than anything
they've ever known.

THE BAY AT
MIDNIGHT
by Diane Chamberlain

Her family's cottage on the
New Jersey shore was a place
of freedom and innocence
for Julie Bauer – until
tragedy struck…

*Don't miss this special collection of original
romance titles by bestselling authors.*

*Available at WH Smith, Tesco, ASDA, Borders, Eason, Sainsbury's
and all good paperback bookshops*

www.millsandboon.co.uk

0206/172/MB014b V2

LAKESIDE COTTAGE
by Susan Wiggs

Each summer Kate Livingston returns to her family's lakeside cottage, a place of simple living and happy times. But her quiet life is shaken up by the arrival of an intriguing new neighbour, JD Harris…

50 HARBOUR STREET
by Debbie Macomber

Welcome to the captivating world of Cedar Cove, the small waterfront town that's home to families, lovers and strangers whose day-to-day lives constantly and poignantly intersect.

Don't miss this special collection of original romance titles by bestselling authors.

Available at WH Smith, Tesco, ASDA, Borders, Eason, Sainsbury's and all good paperback bookshops

www.millsandboon.co.uk

0206/108/MB013 V2

Three fabulous stories from popular authors Anne Mather, Kay Thorpe and Michelle Reid bring you passion, glamour and pulse-raising Latin rhythm and fire.

On sale 3rd February 2006

Available at WH Smith, Tesco, ASDA, Borders, Eason, Sainsbury's and all good paperback bookshops

www.millsandboon.co.uk